The Lies
We Told

Diane
Chamberlain

MIRA

All the characters in this book have no existence outside the imagination of the author,
and have no relation whatsoever to anyone bearing the same name or names. They are
not even distantly inspired by any individual known or unknown to the author, and all
the incidents are pure invention.

MIRA is a registered trademark of Harlequin Enterprises Limited,
used under licence.

Published in Great Britain 2010.
MIRA Books, Eton House, 18-24 Paradise Road,
Richmond, Surrey, TW9 1SR

© Diane Chamberlain 2010

ISBN 978 0 7783 0271 1

58-1210

Printed in the UK
by CPI MacKays, Chatham, ME5 8TD

1950

ACKNOWLEDGEMENTS

As usual, I owe the biggest thank-you to my significant other, John Pagliuca. I don't think John's ever said, "Can we talk about it later?" when I've needed to think out loud about my story. Thank you, John, for all you do to help me write.

While researching *The Lies We Told*, I stumbled across an article by emergency room physician Hemant Vankawala, in which he described his experiences working with evacuees in the New Orleans airport after Hurricane Katrina. Dr Vankawala became my gracious expert on medical relief work, and I don't know how I would have written about the fictional DIDA organisation without him. Other medical advisors were Marti Porter, RN, and paramedic Cass Topinka. Thank you all for being so generous with your time and information, as well as for the work you do.

For helping me learn about my setting, thank you Glen Pierce, Sterling Bryson, Tori Jones, Kim Hennes, Dave and Elizabeth Samuels, Bland Simpson, Dixie Browning and Brooks Preik of Two Sisters' Bookery in Wilmington, NC.

For coming up with the name 'Last Run Shelter', thank you faithful reader and blog commenter, Margo Petrus. Gina Wys helped me understand what life is like after a hurricane. Dave Samuels taught me all I needed to know about helicopters. And Vivian I. Vanove gave me the inside skinny on the Wilmington airport.

For their various contributions, thank you Nellie Mae Batson, Gabe Bowne, Lynnette Jahr, Julie Kibler, Mary Kilchenstein, Ann Longrie, Melinda Smith, Betty Sullivan, Kathy Williamson, and Julia Burney-Witherspoon and her organisation, www.cops-n-kids.org.

For brainstorming help and all-around support and friendship, I'm grateful to the six other members of the "Weymouth Seven": Mary Kay Andrews, Margaret Maron, Katy Munger, Sarah Shaber, Alexandra Sokoloff and Brenda Witchger.

For their invaluable feedback and for always being there for me, my editor, Susan Swinwood and my agent, Susan Ginsburg.

And finally, thank you Denise Gibbs, who helped in too many ways to count. You rock!

To my sister,
Joann Lopresti Scanlon.
We are so lucky to have each other.

Maya

Every family has a story, told and retold so many times it seems firm and irrefutable. Etched in granite. Here are the bare bones of my family's story:

My parents were murdered by a masked stranger, who shot them in our driveway.

My sister, Rebecca, is beautiful, wild, coolheaded and fiercely independent. She needs no one to make her happy. She does, however, need danger.

I am sensitive, quiet, brilliant and fearful, in many ways my sister's opposite. I need safety, protection and a man who loves me.

More often than not, family stories turn out to be etched in sand rather than granite. Even the parts we think are true—even the parts about ourselves—crumble under scrutiny. These are the lies we tell everyone who knows us. These are the lies we tell ourselves.

Prologue

Maya

I KNEW THE EXACT MOMENT DADDY TURNED FROM THE street into the driveway of our house in Annandale, Virginia, even though I was curled up on the backseat of the car with my eyes closed. I was very nearly asleep, a half-fugue state that I wanted to stay in forever to help me forget what I'd done. The rain spiking against the roof of the car was loud, but I still heard the crunch of gravel and felt the familiar rise and fall as the car traveled over the portion of the driveway that covered the drainpipe. We were home. I would have to open my eyes, unfurl my aching fourteen-year-old body and go into the house, pretending nothing was wrong while the truth was, my world had caved in on me. Or so I thought. I had no idea that I was mere seconds away from the true collapse of my world. The moment that would change everything.

Daddy suddenly slammed on the brakes. "What the..."

I sat up, wincing from a sudden bolt of pain in my gut. In the glow of the headlights, I saw my mother running toward the car, her arms flailing in the air. I couldn't remember ever seeing my mother run before. I'd never seen her look wild like this, her wet, dark hair flattened to her head, her dress clinging to her thighs.

My breath caught in my throat and I let out a soft moan. *She knows,* I thought. *She knows where we've been.*

My mother yanked the passenger door open and I braced myself for what she would say. She jumped into the car. "Drive!" she screamed, pulling the door shut. "In reverse! Hurry!" I could smell the rain on her. I could smell *fear.*

"Why?" Daddy stared at her, his profile a perfect silhouette—the wire-rimmed glasses, the slightly Romanesque nose—that would remain in my memory forever.

"Hurry!" my mother said.

"Why are you—"

"Just *go!* Oh my God! There he is!" My mother pointed ahead of us, and the headlights picked up the figure of a man walking toward our car.

"Who's that?" Daddy leaned forward to peer into the half-light. "Does he have on a...is that a ski mask?"

"Dan!" My mother reached for the gearshift. "Go!"

I was wide awake now, fear flooding my body even before the headlights illuminated the man's ice-blue eyes. Even before I saw him raise his arm. Even before I saw the gun. Instinctively, I ducked behind the driver's seat, arms wrapped over my head, but no matter how loudly I screamed, I couldn't block out the *crack* of gunfire. Over and over it came. Later, they said he only had five bullets in the gun, but I could have sworn he had five hundred.

My sharpest memories of that day will always be the blast of that gun, the ice-blue eyes, the silhouette of my father's face, the skirt of my mother's dress sticking to her thighs.

And my sister.

Above all, my sister.

1

Maya

I HAD PASSED THE ENORMOUS LOW-SLUNG BUILDING ON CAPITAL Boulevard innumerable times but had never gone inside. Today, though, I felt free and whimsical and impulsive. All the moms in my neighborhood had told me there were great bargains inside the old warehouse. I needed no bargains. Adam and I could afford whatever we wanted. With the income of two physicians—a pediatric orthopedist and an anesthesiologist—money had never been our problem. It wasn't until I stepped inside the building, the scent of lemon oil enveloping me, that I realized why I was there. I remembered Katie Winston, one of the women in my North Raleigh neighborhood book club, talking about the beautiful nursery furniture she'd found inside. Katie had been pregnant with her first child at the time. Now she was expecting her third. *I'll finally fit in,* I thought, as I walked into the building's foyer, where the concrete floor was layered with old Oriental rugs and the walls were faux painted in poppy and gold.

Every single one of the fifteen women in my book club had children except for me. They were always warm and welcoming, but I felt left out as their conversations turned to colic and day care and the pros and cons of Raleigh's year-round school program. They thought I didn't care. Being a doctor set me apart from most of them to begin with, and I was sure they believed I'd chosen career over motherhood. Every one of them was a stay-at-home mom. Most had had short careers before getting pregnant, and a couple still did some work from home, but I knew they saw me outside their circle. They had no idea how much I longed to be one of them. I kept those feelings to myself. Now, though, I was ready to let them out. I'd tell my neighbors at our next meeting. I hoped I could get the words out without crying.

Today marked sixteen weeks. I rested my hand on the slope of my belly as I walked down the aisle on the far left of the building, past cubicles filled with beautiful old furniture or handcrafted items. I was safe. *We* were safe. Most people waited until the first trimester had passed to tell people the news, but Adam and I had learned that even reaching the twelve-week mark wasn't enough. I'd made it to twelve weeks and two days the last time. We'd wait four months this time, we'd decided. Sixteen weeks. We wouldn't tell anyone before then—except Rebecca, of course—and we wouldn't start fixing up the nursery until we'd passed that sixteen-week milestone.

Smiling to myself, I strolled calmly through the building as though I was looking for nothing in particular. Some of the cubicles were filled with a hodgepodge of goods, crammed so tightly together I couldn't have walked inside if I'd wanted to. Others were a study in minimalism: shelves set up just so, each displaying a single item. Some of the cubicles had shingles in the entryway to give the appearance of a shop on a quaint street corner instead of a small square cubby in a warehouse. Rustler's

Cove. Angie's Odds 'n' Ends. North Carolina Needlepoint. There were few other shoppers, though, and absolutely no one who appeared to be guarding the merchandise. If you wanted to slip a knickknack into your pocket, there was no one to see. No one to stop you. That sort of trust in human nature filled me with sudden joy, and I knew my hormones were acting up in a way that made me giddy.

I ran my fingertips over a smooth polished tabletop in one cubicle, then fingered the edge of a quilt in the next. I passed one tiny cubby that contained only a table with a coffeepot, a plate of wrapped blueberry muffins, a small sign that read *Coffee: Free, Muffins: $1.50 each* and a basket containing six dollar bills. I couldn't resist. I took two of the muffins for tomorrow's breakfast and slipped a five-dollar bill into the basket. I walked on, the irrational joy mounting inside me. People could be trusted to pay for their muffins. What a wonderful world!

I felt like calling Adam just to hear his voice. How long since I'd done that? Called him for no reason? I hadn't seen him before he left for the hospital that morning, and I'd spent the day seeing patients in my office. If all went well with Adam's surgeries today, he'd be home in time to go out to eat. We could celebrate the sixteen-week milestone together. The baby was due New Year's Day. What could be more fitting? The start of a new year. A new life for all three of us. Things would be better with Adam now. Ever since learning I was pregnant, there'd been a tension between us that we hadn't really acknowledged because we didn't know how to get rid of it. If I was being honest with myself, I had to admit the tension had been there much longer than that. Now, though, I was sure it would disappear. We'd talk at dinner that evening, our future finally full and glowing ahead of us. Maybe we'd make lists of names, something we hadn't

dared to do before now. Then we'd go home and make love—
really make love, the way we used to before all our lovemaking
had turned into baby making. Once upon a time, we'd been
good together in bed. I wanted that back.

I saw a sign hanging from a cubicle several yards in front of
me. *BabyCraft,* it read, and I walked straight toward it. This was
the place Katie had mentioned, I was sure of it. The lemony
scent grew strong as I walked inside the rectangular cubicle. It
was filled with furniture, but there was order to the layout.
White cribs and dressers and gliders on one side, espresso-
colored cribs and changing tables and rockers on the other. I
shivered with anticipation, unsure what to look at first. Tags
hung from each piece of furniture, telling me the original
pieces had been refinished to meet twenty-first-century safety
requirements. Lead paint removed. Crib bars moved closer
together. The pieces were exquisite. Although Adam and I had
held back from turning one of the bedrooms into a nursery,
we'd already planned everything to the final detail, lying awake
at night, talking. How many men would take that much
interest? It had been easier to imagine the mural we'd have
painted on the nursery wall than it was to imagine the baby.
That would change now.

I spent nearly an hour in the broad cubicle, typing notes into
my BlackBerry about the furniture. Prices. Contact information for the BabyCraft shop owner. Everything. And finally,
reluctantly, I walked on. I couldn't buy anything. Not yet. I
wasn't ready to tempt fate.

I'd be nearly thirty-five when the baby was born. I would
have preferred to have my first earlier, but I didn't care at this
point. *My first.* There would be more to come, at least one more
baby to use the furniture. Maybe two. *Maybe a houseful,* I
thought, the giddiness returning.

★ ★ ★

Adam called on my cell when I walked into the house.

"Going to be a long night," he said. "Couple of emergency surgeries, and I'm it. You doing okay?"

"I'm great," I said as I slid open the back door to let Chauncey into the yard, spotting the four deer munching our azaleas a second too late. Chauncey tore down the deck steps, barking his crazy head off, and I laughed as the deer raised their indifferent eyes in his direction. They knew he wouldn't take a step past the invisible fence.

"What's with Chaunce?" Adam asked.

"Deer," I said, leaving out the part about the azaleas. Adam thought the deer were funny and beautiful until it came to the yard. "You'll get something to eat at the hospital?" I asked, knowing our celebration would have to wait until the following night.

"Right." He paused for a moment. "I'll be working with Lisa tonight," he said, referring to one of the surgeons who was a good friend of both of ours. "Can I tell her about the Pollywog?"

I smiled. The baby would have his last name—Pollard—and he'd started calling him or her "the Pollywog" a couple of weeks ago. I knew then that he was confident everything would go well this time. I felt the slightest twinge of anxiety over him telling Lisa, but tamped it down. It was time to let the world share our happiness. "Absolutely," I said.

"Great, My." I could hear the grin in his voice. "Let's stay up late tonight and talk until dawn, okay?"

Oh, yes. "I can't wait," I said.

I fed Chauncey and ate a salad, then went upstairs to sit in the room that would become the nursery. The only piece of furniture currently in the room was a rocker. That was one thing we wouldn't need to buy, and if our battered old rocker didn't match the rest of the BabyCraft furniture, I didn't care. It was the rocking chair of my childhood. My mother had nursed and cuddled both Rebecca and myself in that rocker. It was one of the few pieces of furniture I owned that had belonged to my parents. Rebecca had none of it, of course. She lived in an apartment on the second floor of Dorothea Ludlow's Durham Victorian, and her furniture was slapped together from whatever she could find. She was rarely there and couldn't have cared less, but I wished we'd had the foresight to keep more of our parents' belongings. We'd been teenagers then, and furniture had been the last thing on our minds. It was only because the social worker had told us we'd one day appreciate having the rocker that we kept it, too numb to argue with her.

Sitting in the rocker, I imagined the BabyCraft furniture in the room. It would fit perfectly and still leave space for the mural on one wall. I rested my hands on my stomach. "What do you think, little one? Mammals? A Noah's ark kind of thing? Or fish? Birds?" *I'm dreaming,* I thought. How long had it been since I'd let myself dream?

"You're a rarity," Adam had told me early on, when we were still new to each other and everything about our relationship seemed to sparkle. "Part doctor, part dreamer. A scientist and a romantic, all in one endearing package." Oh, how right he'd been, and what an uneasy blend of traits that could be at times. I could see myself as a stay-at-home mom like so many of my neighbors, my life filled easily and completely with the needs of my children. Yet I loved the challenge of my work. I knew I would find a way to do both. My plan for the next five months was to keep working, stopping as close to my delivery as possible as long as everything went well with my pregnancy. *Sixteen weeks.* I was going to be fine.

★ ★ ★

The streets of our neighborhood were deserted as I walked Chauncey before bed. The full moon was veiled by thin gray clouds and a fine mist fell, weaving itself into my hair. It had been a wet August. As we walked beneath a streetlamp, I saw Chauncey's fur glow with tiny damp droplets. The houses were set far apart on the winding, sidewalkless streets, and they were a mix of styles. Brick colonials, like ours, and cedar-sided contemporaries. Woods divided one lot from another, and the trees hugged the road between the houses. Usually Adam was with us for this late-night outing, and walking through the darkness in our perfectly safe neighborhood still sent a shiver through me. Chauncey was a big dog, though. A hundred pounds. Some mix of Swiss Mountain dog and German shepherd, perhaps. He was dark and fierce looking with the personality of a lamb. He was wonderful with kids, and that had been the most important criterion when we found him at the SPCA three years earlier. We hadn't realized then that the wait for those kids would be this long.

The pain was so subtle at first that another woman might not have noticed it. But I'd felt that pain before, the fist closing ever so slowly, sneakily around my uterus.

I stopped in front of a long stretch of fir trees. "Oh, no," I whispered. "No. Go away."

Chauncey looked up at me and I pressed my hand to my mouth, all of my being tuned to that barely perceptible pain.

Was it gone? I focused hard. Maybe I'd imagined it. Maybe just a twinge from the walk? Maybe some stomach thing?

Chauncey leaned against my leg and I rested my hand on top of his broad head. I thought of walking home very slowly, but my feet were glued to the road. There it was again. The sly, sneaky fist.

My fingers shook as I reached for my BlackBerry where it was attached to my waistband. If the surgery was over, Adam would pick up. But when I lifted the phone, it was my sister's number I dialed.

2

Rebecca

"DO YOU EVEN KNOW HOW MANY OF THE MEN AT THIS conference you've slept with?" Dorothea looked around the massive hotel restaurant and Rebecca followed her gaze with annoyance.

"*What?*" she said. "Dot, you're so full of it. I've slept with exactly one. Brent."

She could see Brent, sandy haired and tan, sitting with a group of people at a table not far from where she and Dorothea were eating dinner. He looked like an aging beach bum, though she knew his coppery skin was from the sun in Peru, where he'd been working in a village devastated by a mudslide and not from lazy days on the beach. She'd known him for years. Her stomach didn't exactly flip with desire at the sight of him, but she felt the sort of warmth you'd feel when you caught a glimpse of a good friend.

"I don't mean this week." The end of Dorothea's long gray braid brushed precariously close to her plate. "I mean, of the couple hundred men at this conference, how many have you slept with over the years?"

"Is that a serious question?" Rebecca rubbed her bare arms. She'd worked out for nearly an hour in the hotel's health club that morning and her muscles had the tight achiness she relished. "Why on earth do you care?" She was crazy about Dorothea Ludlow, but the woman could be such a snark.

"I'm just curious. Your libido's always amazed me. You're like a well that's impossible to fill."

The truth was, Rebecca would have to stop and think. She'd have to look at the roster for the Disaster Aid conference, one she'd attended here in San Diego every year for the past ten, and she'd have to struggle to remember who among the attendees she'd slept with. Probably no more than one at each conference. Although there was that one year when she slept with the pediatrician from California as well as that incredibly hot E.R. doc from Guatemala, but that was at least ten years ago, when she was in her late twenties and her moral code had been no match for her sexual appetite. Then there had been at least four or five guys she'd slept with when their paths crossed in the field. The thought was actually a little disgusting to her. Maybe she should reconsider Brent's surprise proposal of the night before.

"Brent asked me to marry him last night," she said. "The man's nuts."

Dorothea raised her eyebrows. "He wants to pin you down," she said.

Brent knew what Rebecca was like. He knew she wasn't the sort of woman you could wrap up in a tidy package and park in a humdrum medical practice and he'd never ask that of her. He shared her need to live on the edge. They'd scuba dived with sharks in Florida. Learned to parachute in jump school. Trained together for a half marathon. Hard to find a guy who could keep up with her like that. But marriage? What was the point?

"I told him no way," she said.

Dorothea toyed with her stir-fried vegetables. "You think you know what you want, babe," she said, "but you only know what you *think* you want."

Rebecca scowled. "What the hell does that mean?"

Dorothea shrugged, and Rebecca knew she'd get no answer from her. She knew Dorothea better than anyone. She knew that when she was snippy, it was the pain of her loneliness coming out. Since Louisa, her partner of thirty years, died last year, Dorothea's usual prickliness had taken on a whole new dimension. But it was her ornery nature that had led Dot to create Doctors International Disaster Aid twenty years ago, when people told her it was too ambitious an idea for one woman to take on. Her stubbornness and passion had made DIDA the respected organization it was today. The work was unglamorous, unprofitable and sometimes unsafe, but it was so very necessary. During the past few years, Rebecca had become one of DIDA's few full-time physicians, Dorothea's right hand in the field. Rebecca had met her at a fund-raiser in Chapel Hill, and Dot had recognized the seedling of passion in her, the fearlessness and the longing to do something truly meaningful with her medical skills. Dot had exploited those qualities with vigor. She became Rebecca's best friend. Mentor. *Mother.* At a small gathering at the home Dorothea shared with Louisa, she introduced Rebecca to her partner, who immediately understood what Dorothea was plotting. Louisa pulled Rebecca into the pantry, out of earshot of the other guests. "Dot's seducing you, Rebecca," she said.

Rebecca's eyes flew open. "What?"

"She's nearly sixty years old," Louisa said. "She's been talking for years about finding someone who'll eventually take over the leadership of DIDA."

"She hardly knows me," Rebecca had said.

"Dot reads people," Louisa said. "She knew just by looking at you that you were the one."

Louisa had been right, of course, and while Rebecca had never come out and said, *Yes, I'll take over DIDA when you're ready to turn over the reins,* it was one of those things that was understood between them without needing to be discussed.

Although Louisa's use of the word "seducing" had at first startled her, Rebecca knew Dorothea had never had any sexual interest in her. Dorothea labeled Rebecca a "one." She believed sexual preference was inborn and fell on a continuum, with complete heterosexuality a "one" and complete homosexuality a "ten" and bisexuality a "five-point-five." When she described people she'd met to Rebecca, she might say "he's a cardiologist, practices in Seattle, a three." A few years ago, Rebecca had been interested in a guy when she was on assignment after an earthquake wiped out a village in Guatemala. When she told Dorothea she was attracted to him, Dot had clucked her tongue. "He's a seven," she'd said. "Can't you see that?"

"Oh, come on," Rebecca had said. "He's totally hetero."

Dot had shrugged. "Just warning you."

He *was* a seven. Maybe even an eight. He'd told Rebecca he wasn't married, but she soon learned that Paul, the man he shared a house with, was doing more than just paying his share of the mortgage. Dorothea had sized the guy up with one quick look. She could be spooky that way.

She had that skill as a physician, too, an ability to diagnose with a glance or the lightest of touches. Rebecca had learned so much from her. Dorothea had made her a better clinician, as well as nurturing her longing to work in disaster areas. "You need a wild streak to do this work, babe," she'd told her during that early seduction period. "And you've got it. But you also need discipline."

"I'm disciplined." Rebecca had been insulted. "How do you think I got through medical school?"

"Different kind of discipline," Dorothea said. "It's a focus. No matter what's going on around you—power out, buildings caving in, mud up to your ankles—you see only the patient. You need blinders."

Rebecca had developed the blinders and the focus and the love of the work. She would never love that there were disasters in the world, but when she'd get a phone call in the middle of the night telling her there'd been a quake in South America and she needed to get to the airport immediately, she felt a current of electricity whip through her body.

"Brent," Dorothea said now, "is a good man."

Rebecca had expected Dot to give her a host of reasons why she shouldn't even consider marrying Brent—or anyone else, for that matter. But Dorothea probably thought of Brent as the best match for her, given their shared commitment to DIDA. Their relationship was built on friendship and mutual respect. That was the best foundation for a marriage, wasn't it?

"Well, yeah." She sipped her wine. "He is. But I don't see the point of marrying him."

"It's probably a bad idea," Dorothea agreed. "But have you thought about what it would be like? The two of you sharing the leadership of DIDA together? Could be amazing, actually. Very fulfilling for both of you."

Rebecca rolled her eyes. "You know, it irritates the hell out of me when you talk like you have one foot in the grave." It also irritated her to think of sharing DIDA's leadership with Brent. With *anyone*.

Dorothea shrugged. "Just being a realist."

"A fatalist is more like it."

Dorothea leaned toward her across the table. "I want you to

be ready to take over the day I can't do it any longer," she said. "It may be twenty years from today or it may be tomorrow."

"Well, I'm pulling for the twenty years," Rebecca said. She added reassuringly, "You know I'm ready, willing and able, Dot. Don't sweat it."

"So back to you and Brent," Dorothea said, and Rebecca realized this was not the first time Dot had considered their sharing DIDA's helm. "You do squabble a lot."

"Squabble?" Rebecca smiled at the word, but she had to admit that Dorothea was right. "True," she said, "but only about the small stuff."

"You both have the fire in your belly for disaster work, that's for sure. He's as wild as you are. Almost, anyway," she said with a wry shrug. "You're positively feral."

Rebecca laughed. She liked the description.

"Neither of you has ever wanted kids or a house in the burbs with a white picket fence," Dorothea continued. "You've got the same values."

Right again, Rebecca thought. She'd never wanted to settle down. She didn't care where she lived, and kids had never been part of her life plan. When she witnessed Maya and Adam's battle to have a baby, the lengths they were willing to go to to get pregnant, she knew she was missing the maternal gene.

"You surprise me, Dot," she said. "I didn't think me getting married would be something you wanted."

"I don't particularly, but it's your choice. Why would I care?"

"Because you like having me living upstairs from you, for starters."

"Get real." Dorothea took a sip from her water glass. "You're pushing forty and—"

"Thirty-eight!"

"And you're not my prisoner. I can't really see you and

Brent as husband and wife. As the leaders of DIDA, though, you'd make a splendid team."

"Well, I'm not interested in getting married. And besides, I don't—" Rebecca glanced across the room at Brent again "—I'm not sure I love him."

"You either do or you don't."

"Well, isn't there something in between? With Louisa, wasn't there a period of time when you weren't sure?"

They never tiptoed around the subject of Louisa, but Rebecca could still see the sadness in Dorothea's eyes at the mention of her name. Rebecca had learned so much about grief working with Dorothea. You didn't hide from it, but you didn't let it rule your life either.

"I met Lou on a Monday." Dorothea looked off into the distance. "I knew I loved her on Tuesday. But it's not always that neat and simple." She returned her gaze to Rebecca. "Don't marry him unless you're sure," she said. "Not fair to him or to yourself. You're an independent woman, with a capital *I*. That's what makes you so perfect for DIDA. Not so perfect for marriage."

Rebecca's cell vibrated in her pocket and she checked the caller ID.

"Maya," she said.

"Ah," Dorothea said. "The princess." She motioned toward the phone. "Go ahead. Take it."

Rebecca leaned back in her chair and flipped the phone open. "Hey, sis," she said.

"It's happening again." There were tears in her sister's voice, and Rebecca sat up straight.

"Oh, no," she said. "Oh, shit. Are you sure? Where are you?"

Dorothea stopped her fork halfway to her mouth and Rebecca felt her eyes on her.

"I'm walking Chauncey and I'm…now I'm just leaning against this damn *tree* because I'm half a mile from home, and I…it's like I think if I just stand here very still I can stop it somehow, but I know I can't. It's over, Becca."

Rebecca stood up, mouthing to Dorothea, *She's losing her baby,* and walked through the restaurant in a blur.

"Bec?"

"I'm right here. Just wanted to get out of the restaurant." She walked into the ladies' room, locked herself in a stall and leaned against the wall. "Where's Adam?"

"At the hospital. I'm sure he's still in surgery."

Rebecca felt helpless. She was three thousand miles away. "Are you bleeding?"

"I'm pretty sure," Maya said. "It feels like it. I'm going to call Katie Winston—one of my neighbors—to come get me. She doesn't even know I'm pregnant. We'd only told you so far. I'm sorry I disturbed you but I just wanted to—"

"Oh, shut up, you goof." Rebecca leaned her head against the tiled wall, eyes closed. "I'm so sorry, Maya. I thought this time it would be okay."

"Me, too."

It was going to be very hard for Maya to tell Adam. This would kill him. Rebecca'd had lunch with him at the hospital the week before, and he'd been unable to keep the smile off his face when he spoke—with cautious joy—about their "Pollywog." His eyes had sparkled, and only then did Rebecca realize how long it had been since she'd seen him look so happy. As much as Maya wanted this baby, Adam wanted it even more. He'd changed in the past couple of years. He was still handsome, of course. Still sexy as hell, even though Maya never seemed to get that about him. But the energy and enthusiasm that had been his hallmark had left him bit by bit as he and Maya failed to create a family. Now Rebecca felt their hope for the future breaking apart like glass. Their relationship, though, was solid. They'd get through this the same way they'd gotten through it the last time. And the time before that.

"Do you want me to come home?" she asked, counting on Maya to say no. "I can catch a plane in the morning."

"Absolutely not," Maya said.

"Look, you call your neighbor and then call me right back and I'll stay on the phone with you till she gets there, okay?"

"I'm all right now. I don't need to—"

"Call me back, Maya. I'm going to worry if you don't."

"Okay."

She hung up her phone but didn't budge from the stall of the restroom. She knew all about life not being fair. She saw it every day with her disaster work. She'd seen it when she and Maya lost their parents. But some things felt less fair than others, and this was one of them.

3

Maya

"ADAM?" MY VOICE CAME OUT IN A WHISPER, ADAM'S NAME on my lips even before I opened my eyes.

"Right here, My," he said. "Sitting next to your bed, holding your hand."

I opened my eyes, squinting against the bright lights in the recovery room. "I'm sorry." I felt crampy from the D and C as I turned my head to look at him.

"You have to stop saying that." Adam moved his chair closer. "It's not your fault."

"I know. I just…what did Elaine say? Boy or girl?"

Adam hesitated. "Boy," he said.

Another boy. Two sons lost. At least two.

"Elaine wants us to come in next week to talk," he said. "To figure out where to go from here."

What did that mean, where to go? Did we dare try again? Could I go through this one more time?

"Okay." I shut my eyes.

"Don't go back to sleep, My," Adam said. "You know how it is. They're going to want you up and out of here soon."

I groaned, forcing my eyes open again. "Why do we do that to patients?" I asked. "It's inhumane."

"I'll take you home and later, if you feel up to it, I'll make you some of my special chicken soup, and I think we have a couple of movies we can watch, and I'll surround you with lots of pillows on the sofa and—"

"Don't do that," I said.

"Do what?"

"Be all…Adamy."

He laughed, though there was no mirth at all in the sound. "All 'Adamy'? What's that mean?"

"All chipper and cheery and energetic and…care-takery." Was I making any sense? I desperately wanted to go back to sleep. I wanted to sleep away the weeks—the *months*—of mourning I knew were ahead of me.

"How would you like me to be?" Adam asked.

I thought about it, though my mind floated in and out of consciousness. Adam could be no other way. His cheeriness was ingrained. It was what I usually loved most about him, what had drawn me to him in the first place.

He smoothed my hair away from my forehead, then let his fingers rest on my cheek. "Want me to be serious?" he asked.

Did I? "Yes," I said. "I know you're sad. Beyond sad." I looked at him again. He'd lost his false smile. His fake cheer.

"Yes, I'm sad," he said. "I'm as brokenhearted as you are. But I want to take care of you today. Today and tomorrow, bare minimum. Let me do that, okay? After that, you can worry about me."

"'Kay," I said. What woman wouldn't kill for my husband?

"I'm going to find out when I can spring you," he said, getting to his feet.

I nodded and once he'd walked away, I closed my eyes again, hoping sleep would return to me quickly.

★ ★ ★

I'd first met Adam in the hospital room of one of my patients. The girl was tiny for eight, dwarfed by the mechanical bed. I could tell she hadn't yet received her presurgical medication, because she was shivering with anxiety when I walked into her room. Sitting at her bedside, her mother held the little girl's hand, and the anxiety was like a ribbon running from mother to daughter and back again.

I had seen them only once before, when I evaluated the girl, Lani, in my office and discussed the surgery I'd perform to lengthen her leg. Lani'd been playful and talkative then. Now, though, reality had set in.

"Good morning, Lani," I said. "Mrs. Roland." I sat down next to the bed. I liked doing that, taking the time to sit, to be at my patient's level. To act as though I had all the time in the world to give them although the truth was, I had three long surgeries that day and really no time at all.

"Will the surgery be at nine, like they said?" Mrs. Roland glanced at her watch. Her hand shook a little.

"I think we're on schedule this morning," I said. "That's a good thing. Waiting around is no fun at all, is it?" I smiled at Lani, who shook her head. Her eyes were riveted to my face as though she were trying to see her future there.

"Do you have any questions?" I asked her.

"Will I feel anything?" she asked.

"Not a thing." I gave her knee a squeeze through the blanket. "That's a promise." I looked up as a man walked into the room.

"Hey." He grinned at Lani, and his entrance into the room was so casual and genial that I assumed he was the girl's father or another relative. "I'm Dr. Pollard, Lani," he said. "I'll be your anesthesiologist during the surgery today."

The new guy, I registered. He'd been working at Duke for

only a week, but I'd heard about him. He was in his late thirties and he wore khakis, a pale blue shirt and a confident air.

"What's an anesthesiologist?" Lani pronounced the word perfectly.

I opened my mouth to respond, but he beat me to it. "I'll make you comfortable during your surgery," he said, one hand resting on the foot of her bed. With the other, he pointed toward the pole holding her saline solution. "I'll give you medication in that IV there that will let you go into a sleep so nice and deep, it'll feel like magic. You'll close your eyes and count backwards from ten. The next thing you know, you'll wake up and the surgery will be over. Then I'll make sure you don't have a lot of pain."

Lani's mother visibly relaxed. I watched it happen, her shoulders softening as she broke into a smile. "I told you, Lani," she said. "You won't know anything's happening, and you won't remember it when you wake up."

"What if I want to remember it?" Lani asked.

"Well then," Dr. Pollard said, "Dr. Ward and I can tell you all about it afterward. We love it when patients want to be informed about their health, don't we?" He looked at me.

"Absolutely." I smiled. I liked the way he made it sound as though we'd been working together for years.

"Good," Lani said. "I can't wait to hear about it."

"I've heard great things about you," Adam said once we'd left Lani's room and were walking down the hall. "Glad I'll be working with you."

What I'd heard about *him* had little to do with his work. Instead, it had to do with his personality, and now I understood why his arrival had started people talking. He was charismatic, filled with a buoyant good cheer. He spoke in incomplete sentences, as though he had so much he wanted to say that he needed to leave out some of the words to save time. That truncated delivery was rare for someone with a North Carolina accent. I remembered, though, that he'd lived most recently in Boston.

"So, you moved here from Massachusetts?" I asked.

"Uh-huh. But I missed North Carolina—I grew up near Greensboro—and I wanted to do some clinical trials, so I'm here now. Glad to be back."

I felt myself smiling as I listened to him. What was that about? He was not particularly attractive. Well, he actually *was,* though not in the conventional sense. He was slender, with brown hair and warm dark eyes, but his features were overpowered by the energy that bubbled out of him. I looked forward to working with him, to seeing him get that energy under control enough to do what needed to be done in the O.R.

"So what exactly did you hear about me?" I sounded flirtatious. Not like myself at all. I was usually all business in the hospital. I was thirty years old and in the last year of a grueling residency, and most of my life had been focused on learning, not on men. Not on dating. I couldn't believe the gooey, girlish feelings I was having. The raw, splayed-open sensation low in my belly. I was not only thinking about how he'd be in the O.R. I was thinking about how he'd be in bed. I'd had exactly two lovers in my adult life and I wondered what it would be like to have him as my third.

"You're well respected," he said. "Very young. How old are you? Never mind. Inappropriate question. Quiet. Calm. Still waters run deep, of course. Unbearably self-confident."

"Unbearably?"

"Well, maybe that's not the exact word I heard. Just…you know, the kind of self-confidence people envy. It comes naturally to you."

"I think you're making this all up," I said. He'd been there less than a week. Surely he hadn't heard all this about me. Yet most of it was true. I was quiet. Calm most of the time—unless something scared me. I wasn't afraid of the usual things. Not anything in the hospital. Not what other people thought of me. My fears were more the primitive variety. A rapist hiding in the backseat of my car. Aggressive dogs. A fire in my condo. *A guy with a gun.* I had nightmares sometimes, though no one I worked with would ever guess.

"I've heard all that and plenty more," he said.

"Well, I'm at home here," I said.

We rode the elevator to the operating suites. The doors opened on the third floor and Adam and I moved to opposite sides of the car to make room for one of the housekeepers and her cart.

"Hey, Charles!" Adam said, as if greeting a long-lost friend.

The woman laughed. "Doc, you crazy!" she said.

"Charles?" I was lost. I looked at the woman's badge. Charlene, her name was. A short, middle-aged woman with streaks of gray in her black hair.

"He calls me Charles." The woman pushed the button for the ground floor and grinned, a blush forming beneath her brown skin. She was under his spell. "Man's crazy."

I had worked in the hospital for several years and had seen this woman nearly every day. I'd never once read her name tag. I'd never greeted her with more than a nod. Adam Pollard had been there less than a week and was already on a teasing basis with her.

"How's the ladies' man doin'?" Adam asked her.

Charlene rolled her eyes. "Goin' be the death of me, Doc," she said.

The doors slid open. "Don't let that happen, Charles." He

touched the woman's shoulder as we walked out of the elevator. "Can't do without you 'round here."

"Do you know…did you know her before you came here?" I asked as we started walking toward the O.R.

"Uh-uh," he said. "Works her butt off. Did you ever notice? She's everywhere at once. She's raising her daughter's kids, too. Daughter's got a monkey on her back."

"Who's the ladies' man?"

"Her ten-year-old grandson. She's worried about him. Can't remember his name, though. I'm crap with names."

"How have you been able to learn all that in a week?"

"I talk to people," he said with a shrug. "How else?"

After Lani Roland's uneventful surgery, Adam caught up with me in the hallway outside the O.R.

"Dinner tonight," he said. It wasn't a question. He said it as if I couldn't possibly have other plans.

"All right," I answered, since that was true.

"Casual or fancy?"

"Casual. Definitely."

"Mama Dip's okay? I've missed that place."

I nodded. "I'll meet you there," I said. "I should be able to get out by six-thirty."

"Cool." He gave my arm a playful punch as if I were a teenage boy. It made me laugh.

He was sitting at a table near the windows when I walked into Mama Dip's a few hours later, and he was already joking with a waitress. He stood as I walked toward them.

"Hey, Maya." He sounded as though we'd known each other for years. He leaned over and bussed my cheek. "Dr. Ward, this is our server tonight, KiKi. KiKi, this is an amazing surgeon,

Maya Ward. She knits together teeny little bones." He pulled out a chair for me, touching my arm as I sank into it.

KiKi smiled at us both. "What can I get you to drink, sweetie?" she asked me.

"Lemonade," I said, unwrapping the napkin from around my silverware.

Adam chuckled to himself as KiKi walked away. "I introduce you as a surgeon, she calls you sweetie," he said. "Gotta love the South. Does that bug you? The sweetie bit?" I loved the way his smile crinkled the corners of his eyes.

"Not at all," I said. I knew plenty of professional women who bristled at the familiarity, but I'd lived in North Carolina long enough that I didn't even notice it.

"I love it," he said. "Boston was great, don't get me wrong, but nobody there ever called me sweetie or darlin' or dear. And you can't get enough kind words. Know what I mean?"

"I do," I said.

KiKi was back with our drinks and I popped a straw into my lemonade.

"You're obviously not a native," he said. "Where are you from?"

"Virginia. Outside D.C."

"How'd you end up here?"

"I followed my sister. She went to medical school at Duke and loved it, so when it was my turn, I followed her lead."

He sat back, eyes wide. "Wow!" he said. "There's *two* Dr. Wards? Where does she practice?"

"She works full-time with Doctors International Disaster Aid, so she's here, there and everywhere."

"DIDA!" he said.

"You know it?"

"I thought of applying to do a stint with them, but never got around to it. Maybe one of these days. It'd be so cool to do that sort of work." He sipped his iced tea. "She's a do-gooder? Your sis?"

"She's…" I hadn't thought of Rebecca that way. *Gutsy* was the word I usually used when describing my sister. But she *was* a do-gooder, and not only with DIDA. Rebecca was my hero. "Yes, she is actually," I said. "I haven't seen her in a couple of months, though we talk all the time when she's someplace with cell coverage. Right now she's working in China at an earthquake site. She's unreachable."

KiKi returned with my bowl of Brunswick stew and Adam's barbecue platter.

"Anything else for y'all?" she asked.

I shook my head.

"We're good," Adam said, though his gaze never left my face. "So, you're really close to your sister," he said once KiKi'd walked back to the kitchen.

I felt like telling him everything. About my life. About Rebecca and the complicated bond we shared. *Everything.* I never felt that way. I kept things locked tight inside me, never wanting to show any dent in my professional demeanor. I knew how to hide my flaws. Rebecca hated my wimpiness, and I'd learned early to erect a brave facade. I needed to work with Adam. Better that he saw me as a competent physician than a woman who could still be unnerved by the past.

"Yes," I said simply. "We are."

"You're so lucky to have a sib."

"You don't?" I finally got around to picking up my spoon, but I was so intent on our conversation that I didn't even consider dipping it into the stew.

He shook his head, swallowing a mouthful of barbecued pork. "No family," he said. "Lost my parents when I was fifteen."

I drew in a breath of surprise. The urge to tell him my own story expanded in my chest, but it was a story I never told. "Both at once?" I asked. "An accident?"

"Exactly. They were coming back from a party. Drunk driver."

"Oh, I'm so sorry," I said. "Did you live with relatives then?"

"Didn't have any of them, either. Just grandparents who were too frail to take me. So I did the foster home thing."

"Was it hard?" I'd been spared foster care. I ate a spoonful of the stew. I loved Mama Dip's Brunswick stew, but now I barely tasted it.

"I got into a good one," he said, blotting his lips with his napkin. "Unusual to be able to stay in one foster home for years, but I did. I'm still in touch with them. Good people."

"You're so—" I smiled "—*upbeat*."

"Just born that way." He shrugged. "Extra serotonin or something. It got me through."

I ate another spoonful of stew, still not tasting it. "I was fourteen," I said.

"Fourteen?"

"When my parents died."

He set his fork down and leaned back in his chair. "You're *kidding*," he said. "You, too? An accident?"

I hesitated. I didn't want to go there, much as I longed to tell him every detail of my life. "Yes," I lied.

"Did you end up in foster care, too?"

"No." I looked down at the stew. "Rebecca —my sister— was eighteen, and she wouldn't let it happen. She took care of me. She made it work."

"You were lucky."

"Incredibly."

"Where does your sis—Rebecca—live when she's not on assignment?"

"Here. Well, in Durham. She lives with Dorothea Ludlow. Do you know who she—"

"The DIDA founder," he said. "Cool lady. Your sister lives with her? She's her—" He raised his eyebrows. Clearly he *did* know about Dorothea.

"No. Dorothea's in a committed relationship with an artist named Louisa Golden. They have this beautiful Victorian, and Rebecca rents the upstairs."

"What's *your* relationship status?"

"You are so blunt." I smiled. "You just…you think of a question and it pops out of your mouth."

"Does that bother you?"

I thought about it. "I like it, actually," I said, "and I'm not in a relationship."

"Amazing," he said. "You're pretty and smart and a catch. You've been working too hard, huh?"

People always said I was pretty, which meant average look- ing, which was good enough. Rebecca was beautiful though, and a force of nature. There were pictures of her on the DIDA Web site working in the field. No makeup, her short brown hair messy and unkempt, a sick child in her arms. The image of her could take your breath away. Even though I was the blonde, blue-eyed, creamy-skinned sister, I seemed to disappear next to her. It had sometimes been hard growing up in her shadow.

"How about you?" I asked.

"Divorced. Two years ago. Super woman, but she changed her mind about wanting kids."

"You mean…changed her mind which way?"

"We went into it—we were married four years—we went into it talking about having a couple of kids. Several, really. Had the names picked out. All that rose-colored kind of fantasiz- ing. I crave family, for obvious reasons."

I nodded. I understood completely.

"Frannie was a reporter for one of the TV stations in Boston. She got caught up in her career and just totally changed her mind. It was bad. Hard when you still love each other and get along well and all, but can't agree on that basic, really important issue. Not something you can really compromise on, you know? Either you want kids or you don't."

"I do," I said, blushing suddenly. It sounded as though I was offering myself to him for something more than dinner. "I mean—" I laughed, embarrassed "—I feel the way you do. I have no family except for my sister. It'll be a challenge balancing kids and work, but it's a priority."

For the first time that evening, he seemed at a loss for words. He chewed his lower lip, gazing at his nearly empty plate, but the silence wasn't uncomfortable. My embarrassment had vanished, and I felt something happening between us in that silence. A shift. A *knowing*. When he looked up again, it was clear he felt it, too.

"You said I'm blunt." He was smiling.

"Well, I didn't mean—"

"I'm going to be even more blunt right now," he said. "I fell in love with you in the O.R. today."

I laughed. He was crazy. "You don't know me," I said.

"So true. So true. I sound like an idiotic kid, huh? But I fell in love with what I *did* know. What I witnessed. Your skill and caring."

"Maybe you're one of those men who can't stand to be without a partner," I said, but I knew where this was going. Where I wanted it to go.

"I've been without a partner for two years," he said. "I've had opportunities. I haven't been interested. Till right now. Today. But I don't want to freak you out, okay? I won't stalk you. Won't call and bug you. I'll leave the ball in your court."

"Maybe you connect to people too quickly," I said, thinking of the housekeeper in the elevator. "You assign them a personality before you get to know what they're really like."

"See?" He grinned. "You're already finding fault with me, just like in a real relationship."

I laughed. Could he be anymore likable? But then I sobered. I looked at him across the table.

"I lied to you earlier," I said.

He raised his eyebrows. "What about?"

"I just…you've been so open. And this is a big part of who I am, so—"

"You don't need to tell me."

"I want to," I said, knowing it was only a half-truth I was about to reveal. "Because I'm not…I'm a complicated person, and you should know that before you sign on."

He laughed. "It's not like I'm buying a house here and you need to disclose all its flaws."

"Don't make this hard," I said, and I must have sounded very serious, because his smile disappeared.

"Sorry. Go ahead."

"My parents didn't die in an accident." I looked down at the table. Pushed the handle of my knife back and forth. "They were murdered."

"Ah, no."

I couldn't look at him. "I don't like to talk about it, okay?" I said. "Just…they were. And it shook me up. Made me afraid of…certain situations where I don't feel safe." If Rebecca had been sitting with us, she'd be kicking me under the table. *Never let them see you sweat.* That was her motto.

"Of course it did." He reached across the table and rested his hand on mine. "Did they catch the guy? I assume it was a guy?"

I nodded. "They caught him and killed him in a shootout."

"What was his motive?"

"He was a disgruntled student of my father's." How often I'd heard those words, *disgruntled student*. I could rarely hear one without adding the other in my mind. "My father taught philosophy at American University." I wrinkled my nose. "Can we not talk about this anymore?"

"We're done." He nodded. "I just want you to know I'm sorry."

"Thanks."

"And you're sweet to want to do the full-disclosure thing." He smiled again, and this time I returned it. "Makes me fall even harder for you, Dr. Ward."

"I'm...a little overwhelmed by tonight," I admitted. "Of how fast this seems to be going. People turn out not to be who you think they are at first."

"Very true," he said. "So we could avoid any pain down the road and not see each other again. Or we can take the risk and go with how really, really good this feels."

I wasn't much of a risk taker. I wished I could talk to Rebecca. I had other friends I could call for advice and commiseration, but it was Rebecca who had my heart, and Rebecca was in China, where her cell phone didn't work. I would, for a change, have to be my own counsel.

"Let's go for it," I said, and I lifted my glass of lemonade for a toast.

4

Rebecca

"WHAT'S WRONG?" BRENT FROWNED AS REBECCA WALKED into his hotel room.

"Maya lost another baby." She flopped onto the edge of his bed. She could usually shrug off bad news. Compartmentalize it and move on. She had to be able to do that in order to work for DIDA and maintain her sanity. But for some reason, this latest miscarriage was really getting to her.

"She was pregnant again?" Brent sat down next to her. "Did you know?"

"I knew, but no one else did. They were afraid to tell anyone after the last miscarriage. She made it sixteen weeks this time."

"Man, that sucks." Brent nuzzled her neck. "Let me make you feel better."

She jerked her head away. "I can't shift gears that fast, Brent," she said. "All I can think about is Maya and Adam. I feel like a crappy sister. Like maybe I should go home and be with her."

"Do I need to remind you you're the speaker at lunch

tomorrow? And the presenter at the…that afternoon seminar, whatever it is?"

"I know."

"It's not like someone died," he said.

She looked at him sharply. "It's *exactly* like someone died."

The night table lamp picked up two sharp lines between his eyebrows. "How can you be pro choice and say that?" he asked.

"Oh, stop it. This is different. This was a sixteen-week-old much wanted baby with a perfectly healthy mother. It's a death to Maya and Adam."

"And apparently to you, too."

"Because of how it hurts Maya." Even as she said the words, she knew it was more than that. She'd *wanted* that niece or nephew. She wanted to be the cool aunt who'd bring gifts from all over the world. The aunt her niece or nephew could confide in, knowing nothing would ever make her blush. She'd wanted to hold Maya's baby in her arms.

Brent sighed and got to his feet, slipping his hands into his pockets. He looked through the sliding glass doors to the small balcony and the view of San Diego harbor. "You infantilize Maya," he said.

She could see his reflection in the sliding glass door. "What do you mean?"

"I mean, you still think of her as your baby sister who needs your protection. She's a grown woman." He turned to face her, the lines still carved into the skin between his eyebrows. "She's a *physician*, for Christ's sake."

"Don't you ever feel protective of Brian or Kristin?" she asked. Brent was the oldest of three.

He laughed. "Hell, no. They were a pain in the ass when we were growing up and they're still a pain in the ass now."

"But you love them."

"Of course. I just don't *dwell* on them. They're adults who can stand on their own two feet."

She wished she could feel as relaxed about Maya as Brent did about his siblings, but Maya was needy and it was Rebecca's fault. As simple as that.

"If I marry you," Brent said, "I'm marrying Maya, too."

"Don't be so dramatic."

"*You're* the one who's being dramatic." Brent walked over to the mini-refrigerator, opened the door and pulled out a beer. "Want one?" he asked.

"Uh-uh."

Brent uncapped the beer. "You want to go over your speech for tomorrow?"

She ran her hand over the fern pattern on the bedspread, smoothing the already smooth fabric. "I could do it in my sleep."

"All right." He took a swallow from the bottle. "I get that you're annoyed with me. Let's just forget about sex tonight and chill. Watch TV. Maybe a movie."

She was too antsy to watch a movie. She thought of going for a run instead, but it was getting late and she didn't feel like changing into her running clothes. She let out a sigh as she kicked off her shoes and drew her feet onto the bed. "Okay," she said.

She let him pick the movie—a Denzel Washington flick—and they leaned back against the headboard of the bed, at least two feet of king-size green-and-white bedspread between them. She couldn't concentrate. She thought of Maya giving Adam the news. Crushing him with it. Had she told him over the phone? Waited till he came home? She tipped her head back, resting it against the headboard, and stared at the dim ceiling. Brent had to know she was still upset, but he was fed up with her and she didn't really blame him.

She didn't know what she wanted from him tonight. It wasn't

that she needed to talk more about Maya and Adam and their lost child. Their lost hope. She just wanted him to comfort her. He wasn't that kind of man, though. One of the things he always said he liked about her was that she never let things get to her.

What if she married Brent and something terrible happened? What if Maya died? *No.* She couldn't go there. What if Dorothea died? Would he tell her to keep her chin up? Change the subject? Drink a beer? Turn on a damn movie? Could the two of them ever run DIDA together without screwing it up because of their bickering? She let out her breath in frustration.

"What?" he asked.

"What do you mean, 'what'?"

"You just huffed."

"Oh. Nothing." She couldn't talk to him about it. He wouldn't understand. Besides, he'd already returned his attention to the movie.

She glanced at the clock on the night table. Ten-thirty. One-thirty in Raleigh. She hoped Maya was able to sleep. She pictured her wrapped in Adam's arms. Now there was a guy who knew how to comfort someone! Thank God he hadn't decided to come to the conference. He was now a DIDA volunteer as well, although he hadn't yet been called to a disaster site. She and Brent had talked him into signing up the year before. He hadn't needed much persuading in spite of the fact that Maya'd been unhappy with his decision. She was worried enough when Rebecca was in the field; she didn't want to have to worry about Adam as well.

"Every time the phone rings," Maya had once told her, "I'm afraid it's going to be Dorothea telling me you were killed by a gang of thugs or an earthquake aftershock or a disease from drinking filthy water." Maya's worry about her was irrational, but not totally over the top. Rebecca had been shot at once in Africa, although she'd never told Maya about that, and she'd had more than a few run-ins with parasites.

Two years ago, she fell down the stairs at Dorothea's and broke her arm. Maya met her in the E.R., and Rebecca was able to make her point: "I've never once been injured on a DIDA mission," she'd said, fighting the pain as the E.R. doc splinted her arm. "It's *home* that's dangerous."

Denzel was running through the darkness with a gun in his hand. Rebecca had no idea who he was after or why, nor did she care.

"You huffed again," Brent said, without shifting his gaze from the screen.

"Excuse me for living."

He grabbed the remote from the bed and hit the mute button. "What is your *problem?*" he asked.

She shifted on the bed so that she was facing him. "What if we got married and something terrible happened?"

"You said you don't want to get married."

"Hypothetically. What if Dot died? Or your sister or brother? Would you shrug it off like this?"

Brent stared at her for at least five long seconds. Then he sighed, rubbing his forehead with his palm, and she knew she'd finally gotten through to him. "Of course not," he said softly. "Whatever happens, we'd be there for each other. We're great together, Bec." He reached for her hand, lifting it to his knee. "We'd do DIDA till we keeled over of old age. The cool thing about you…about both of us…is that we've always been able to roll with the punches, no matter what's happening around us. We're survivors. That's why DIDA suits us." He leaned over to kiss her. "I love you, Rebecca. Don't you get that?"

She nodded, and he wrapped his arms around her. Resting her forehead against his shoulder, she suddenly pictured herself holding Maya's healthy, full-term baby, pressing the infant close to her chest, and she felt a loss so sharp and deep it made her gasp.

She jerked away from Brent.

"What's wrong?" he asked.

She stood up, rubbing her arms. The room was cold, the sound from the TV too loud. "I don't know what's with me tonight," she said. "Sorry I'm being weird. I'm going out on the balcony to smoke."

"Want me to pause the movie?" Brent asked as she slid the glass door open.

She shook her head. "I can't concentrate. Just let it run."

She carried her cigarettes and lighter out to the balcony and sat on the chair overlooking the harbor, trying to shake off the unexpected sensation of losing something precious. Above her, the sky was filled with stars, and below her, lights flickered in the boats lining the piers. She couldn't blame Brent for being irked by her tonight, she thought as she lit a cigarette. She wasn't usually like this. It was as though Maya had crawled under the surface of her skin and she couldn't simply brush her off.

Maybe Maya and Adam would get serious about adoption now. Maya would eagerly adopt, but Adam desperately wanted his own biological child. He'd be such a joyful father, either way. He'd cook for his kids. Make pancakes in the shape of animals, with Maya watching him, smiling, totally in love with her husband and their brood. Adam was equally smitten with Maya. You only needed to be with them for two seconds to know he adored her. Why did Maya get to be loved like that and she didn't? The thought made her feel small and churlish. She'd felt that way ever since they were kids, when Maya'd received their father's attention at every turn. Maya had been so much like him—bookish and studious—while Rebecca had their mother's vitality and spunk. Rebecca'd always been certain of her mother's love, but it was her father's she'd craved, and that seemed out of reach. "I have a scholar and an athlete," he'd say of his two daughters, as though he valued them equally, but everyone knew which daughter he favored. Rebecca was smart, but Maya was smarter. Maya could sit still for hours, with a focus that was uncanny for a child. Their father would read to them in bed, and although Rebecca would try her best to pay attention, she could never make it to the end of a story. "You have ants in your pants?" he'd ask her with a resigned smile, and she'd nod, hopping out of the bed to play with her trucks or run around the house with her arms outstretched, pretending she was an airplane, leaving her younger sister behind to bask in their father's love.

Rebecca blew a stream of pale smoke into the darkness, resting her head against the back of the seat. She hated when she relived the past as though it mattered, nursing an ancient jealousy over her sister's treatment when they were kids. The truth was, they'd both suffered the same loss. If Maya was lucky enough to find a guy like Adam, Rebecca wanted to be happy for her.

That was part of the problem with her and Brent, wasn't it? If she was ever going to get married, she should feel about a man the way Maya felt about Adam. So she and Brent were disaster junkies. Big deal. That didn't feel like enough.

She stubbed out her cigarette on the concrete balcony, then turned to look through the sliding glass door. She could see Brent, the changing colors of the TV screen altering his features second by second. His eyes were wide, absorbed by the movie.

"Rebecca's type triple A," he'd said once, when they were out with friends, and she knew he meant it as a compliment. "You should see her in the field," he'd added. "She never sleeps."

She'd felt his admiration then. His love. He did love her. She had no doubt of that. What the hell more did she want?

5

Maya

THEY KEPT ME OVERNIGHT AFTER THE D AND C BECAUSE Elaine was concerned about the amount of bleeding I was having, but by morning I was doing much better. Physically, anyway. The nurse wheeled me outside to the sidewalk deck where two other women sat in wheelchairs, waiting for their rides home. I was relieved that neither of them had a baby in her arms. I would have lost it.

The woman in the next chair looked vaguely familiar, and I wondered if she was the mother of one of my young patients. I often bumped into them without having a clue who they were, although I would recognize their children anywhere.

Adam pulled up in his silver Volvo and got out. He was pale, his face drawn and tight. The nurse bent over to lock the brakes on the wheelchair, and just as I was about to stand up, the woman who looked familiar spoke up.

"Adam!" she said, and I instantly realized who she was: Adam's ex-wife, Frannie. The one who'd decided she didn't want children. I'd seen pictures of her in Adam's old photo album. She lived in Boston, though, and I couldn't imagine what she was doing next to me on the parking deck. I sank back into the wheelchair.

"Frannie!" Adam exclaimed with his usual effervescence in spite of the circumstances. The tight expression on his face vanished with a smile. He walked to the side of my chair, resting his hand on my back. "Maya, this is Frannie, my ex-wife. Frannie, this is Maya, my—"

"Current wife." Frannie laughed. She had pretty teeth and thick, curly brown hair, but she looked as exhausted and pale as I felt. "Nice to meet you, Maya," she said. "Though I feel like I've been run over, and you probably do, too."

I nodded with a small smile. All I wanted was to get home and into my own bed.

Adam left my wheelchair to open the passenger door of the car. "So…" He looked at Frannie with a puzzled smile. "What are you doing in Raleigh?"

"My husband, Dave, put in for a transfer with IBM," Frannie said, "and we moved here last year. Better weather. Better for the kids."

"Kids?" Adam had been reaching for my arm to help me stand up, but his hand stopped in midair.

Frannie laughed again. "I know, I know." She ran a hand through her curls. "Don't give me a hard time about it. I changed my mind about having them after all. We've got two. Just had my tubes tied, though. Two is plenty. They're a handful."

"*Adam,*" I pleaded, and he reached down again to take my arm. I let him guide me into the car, the muscles in my thighs quivering. He closed the door behind me, shutting out the rest of his conversation with the woman he'd left because she wouldn't have children and who now had two while I—and he—had none.

It was another minute before he got into the car himself. He turned the key in the ignition, then glanced over at me. "Seat belt," he said.

I buckled myself in and he pulled away from the curb.

"How do you feel?" he asked. "Do you want me to stop at the store for anything on the way home?"

I shook my head. The ache in my throat dwarfed the dull pain in my uterus. "If you'd stayed married to her, you'd have children now," I said.

"Maya, don't."

"How can I not?"

"I'm *not* married to her. I don't love her any longer. I love *you*."

"But if you'd stayed married to her—"

"Stop it." He turned the corner with such force that we nearly ran over the curb, and I reached reflexively for the dashboard.

I pounded my fist against the car door. "What's *wrong* with me?" I asked the air. "Why is it so hard for me to have a baby when every other woman on earth can have as many kids as she likes?"

"That's bullshit. You have plenty of company and you know it. Please stop beating yourself up over this."

"Every single one of my friends has kids now," I said. "I'm cut off from all of them. I buy them baby gifts. I try to keep up the friendships and I know they try, too, but it's impossible. They have nothing in common with me anymore. They pity me."

"Right now, you're pitying yourself," he said.

"Well, so what?" I snapped, hurt. "When do I ever pity myself? Let me have five minutes of self-pity, okay?"

We never argued. Never. Yet this felt strangely good and necessary. Cleansing, in a way. But when we came to a stoplight and I glanced over at him, I saw how tired he looked. I saw the lines that creased his forehead. The pink cast to the whites of his eyes. This was not only my loss.

I reached over. Rested my hand on his biceps. "Adam," I said. "I'm sorry."

"It's all right, My," he said with a sigh. "We'll get through it."

Adam tucked me into our king-size bed and handed me an ibuprofen and a glass of water. I swallowed the pill, then sank back into the bed. He leaned over and kissed my forehead. "I know this has been much harder on you than I can even imagine," he whispered. "I know that, and I love you."

"I love you, too," I said. I opened my mouth to say more, although I wasn't sure what words I expected to come out, but he pressed his fingers lightly to my lips.

"Get some sleep," he said.

I was asleep before he had even left the room, and in my dreams, I saw Frannie sitting in her wheelchair, smiling at Adam.

I have eighteen children now, Adam, she said. *Too bad you didn't stay married to me.*

6

Maya

TWO DAYS LATER, ADAM AND I SAT ACROSS THE DESK FROM MY obstetrician, Elaine, in her office. I much preferred being on the other side of that desk, talking to my patients. Educating them. Reassuring them. But my fight for a baby had put me on this uncomfortable side of the desk now more times than I could count.

Elaine thumbed through my chart where it rested on the desk in front of her. She settled on a page, running her finger down it, stopping at the midway point.

"I noticed something during the D and C that made me curious," she said, "and I see that you didn't answer this question on your health sheet when you filled it out a couple of years ago."

"What question?" I asked.

"Did you ever have an abortion?" Elaine looked at me over her reading glasses.

I hesitated. I hadn't been asked that question before, at least not in front of Adam.

"No," Adam answered for me, and for a moment, I let the answer hang in the room between the three of us.

"Why?" I asked Elaine.

"Well, there's some scarring in your uterus that looks like what we might see, on a very rare occasion, from an abortion. Scarring can cause difficulty with conception and especially with holding on to a pregnancy. But since you've never had an abortion, that's clearly not the prob—"

"I have." I cut her off. "I had an abortion."

"*What?*" Adam leaned away from me in his chair as though I'd burned him. "When?"

"When I was a teenager." I looked at Elaine, but could feel Adam's startled gaze resting squarely on my face.

"Were there any complications?" she asked. "An infection?"

I remembered pain that went on and on. Pain I'd ignored. I'd had more pressing things on my mind. "I don't think so," I said. "I had what might have been excessive pain, but I was too young to question any symptoms." I would never tell them *how* young. Fourteen years old. My father had taken me to the clinic, and I remembered the drive home, even though I'd done my best to block all memories of that day from my mind. Daddy had been so quiet in the car. So quiet that I was afraid he no longer loved me. Finally, when we neared our street, our driveway, when we neared the moment that would end his life and tear mine apart, he said, "This is between you and me, Maya, honey. It'll be our secret."

Oh, God. My lost babies. They were my fault. I'd certainly thought about that abortion as I struggled to get pregnant, and I'd never forgotten that first baby, taken from my body only after I'd begun to show.

"Does this mean…" I cleared my throat, unable to ask the question burning in my mind. Next to me, Adam still sat stiffly in his chair, but he reached over to cover my hand with his. I felt so grateful for him, and so undeserving. "Does this mean there's no hope?" I finally managed to say. "That even if I'm able to conceive again, another miscarriage is inevitable?"

"Not necessarily," Elaine said, "but it probably does explain why you've lost three pregnancies. The in vitro took this time, and you'll have to talk to Dr. Gallagher about trying again. I'll send him my report from the D and C and you can talk with him about the pros and cons of giving it another go."

I thought of the months of hormone shots. The always-iffy implantation. The waiting to know if I'd conceived. The hopes raised. Dashed. Raised again. All of that would be nothing compared to the anxiety of once more being pregnant, then waiting for that fist to tighten around my uterus. I didn't know if I could go through it again.

I felt sick to my stomach by the time we got to the car. Neither of us said a word until we'd pulled out of the parking lot into the street.

"I'm sorry," I said then.

He didn't take his eyes from the road. "Why didn't you tell me?" he asked.

I hesitated. "It's something I don't like to remember. And abortion's not supposed to have anything to do with fertility, but…I think I was afraid it…that it *did* have something to do with it. I mean, I got pregnant *then,* and now, as an adult, I have so much trouble conceiving, so I've always had this niggling fear that it was somehow related. Now it looks like it is." My voice broke. I'd already felt responsible for our not having a child, worried that Adam blamed me, subconsciously or not. Now he had a concrete reason to do so. "I'm sorry, Adam," I said again.

"Please stop apologizing, Maya." The muscles in his jaw contracted. "I'm just pissed off you didn't tell me. We've been trying to have a baby for three years—without much luck—

and now I discover that you've kept a pretty damn significant piece of the puzzle from me."

"I know." I started to apologize again, but caught myself. "I wasn't intentionally keeping it from you," I said. "It's something I've tried to forget. I…" My voice trailed off, and I turned my head to look blindly through the window. There was no excuse I could give him that was good enough.

He didn't ask me how old I'd been when I had the abortion or who the baby's father was, and I was relieved. I didn't want to think about it. The damage done back then had harmed far more than my fertility.

Was Adam now wondering if there were other things I'd kept from him? Other secrets? Worse secrets?

If so, he would be right.

7

Rebecca

"YOU WANT TO STAY OVER?" REBECCA ASKED BRENT AS THEY pulled into the driveway of the massive Victorian she shared with Dorothea.

"What do you think?" He'd already put the car in Park and was opening his door. She was fine either way, as long as he gave her some space. Two days after returning from San Diego, Rebecca still hadn't recovered from the conference. Too much food and not enough exercise.

"I swear," she said as they walked toward the outside stairs that zigzagged up the side of the building to her second-story apartment, "four days of meeting and greeting, giving speeches and soaking up gorgeous scenery is more draining than a month in the field."

"You got that right," he said.

The lights on the first floor were burning. Every one of them, it seemed.

"Dot's still up," she said as they started climbing the stairs. "We should say hi."

They stopped at the first landing and Rebecca knocked on the door that led to Dorothea's kitchen. When there was no answer, she opened the door—Dot never locked anything—and poked her head inside.

"You up, Dot?" she called.

"Dining room," Dorothea said.

They walked through the kitchen. The room was turquoise with violet cabinetry, bright yellow hardware, and white appliances. All Louisa's work. Dorothea had given her partner free rein, and although she'd complained about the color combinations while Louisa was alive, she'd done nothing to change them now that Louisa was gone and Rebecca was glad. If she ever cared enough to decorate her own spare apartment, she would use Louisa's energetic palette.

Louisa had been neat almost to the point of being finicky, but her artist's eye craved color, the bolder the better. She would roll over in her grave—had she been buried instead of donating her body to Duke—if she could see her dining room now, Rebecca thought as she and Brent skirted the boxes and stacks of journals and papers that littered the floor.

Dorothea looked up from her seat at the head of the table, where she was typing on one of the two laptop computers in the room. "What time is it?" she asked. Long strands of gray hair were coming loose from her braid, but she looked pretty in the glow from the computer screen. Dorothea was sixty-seven now, and every once in a while Rebecca caught a glimpse of the knockout she must have been when she was younger.

Brent walked to the head of the table and leaned over to kiss Dorothea's cheek, a shock of blond hair falling over his forehead.

"Whatcha up to?" he asked, folding his arms across his chest as he peered down at the screen.

"Watching tropical storms forming," she said.

Rebecca pulled out a chair at the opposite end of the table and drew the second computer toward her. "Anything that looks like trouble?" she asked, getting online.

Dorothea moved the cursor around a bit, gnawing her lower lip as she studied the screen. "Hard to say right now. A few things…maybe. Maybe not."

The dining room had been Louisa's red room. The walls were painted a robust, deep red and one of her paintings—a huge stunning rectangular canvas covered with apricots—brought the room to life. The dining room used to be Rebecca's favorite room in the house, but Dorothea now had so much stuff littered all over the table and the sideboard that the room had lost its charm. It sometimes worried her to see how Dorothea had let things go after Louisa died. Dorothea still had all her faculties. She was as brilliant and committed as ever, but the lack of caring about her surroundings, which served her very well in a disaster zone, didn't work all that well in North Carolina. She never wanted company, with the exception of Rebecca and Brent and a few other DIDA regulars, because cleaning the house was, at this point, impossible. When Rebecca took over directing DIDA, she was going to have a mess on her hands.

"Next thing that comes up, we'll get that brother-in-law of yours in the field," Dorothea said to Rebecca. "I know he's champin' at the bit."

Rebecca clicked the page for the National Hurricane Center. "As long as it's not for more than two weeks," she reminded Dorothea. She doubted Adam could take off more than that. No volunteers were required to donate more than two weeks a year with DIDA, but Dorothea had a tendency to forget that little detail.

"We just came from their house." Brent hovered over Dorothea's shoulder, studying the screen.

"How's Maya doing?" Dorothea asked. "Recovering okay?"

"She seemed pretty good," Brent said, which only went to show how unintuitive he was.

"She's miserable, actually," Rebecca said.

Brent frowned at her. "She seemed okay to me."

"I know her better than you," she said. Maya could wear a smile broad enough to span the Grand Canyon and Rebecca would still be able to see the lie in it. "They're both miserable."

"Well," Brent said, "they're going out to dinner with us Saturday night. We're going to that new Brazilian place. Want to come?"

Dorothea shook her head. "Too much to do here," she said. She was no good at delegating. Rebecca would do a better job of spreading the work around. "Supposed to be a good restaurant, though," Dorothea added.

Rebecca couldn't believe Maya had agreed to the Brazilian restaurant. Maya avoided that part of Durham. A sketchy area, to be sure, but when Brent mentioned it, Adam had lit up.

"Yeah!" he'd said. "I've wanted to try that place!"

Seeing the sudden life in Adam's eyes made Rebecca realize exactly how glum he'd been since their arrival. Maya must have noticed as well, because she nodded her okay. *Trying to please him,* Rebecca thought. *Trying to make it up to him for losing another baby.* Rebecca nearly suggested a different restaurant, but remembered Brent saying that she infantilized Maya and kept her mouth shut. Besides, she wanted to try the restaurant herself.

"So are you two getting married or what?" Dorothea asked with her usual lack of tact. She looked up from the screen, first at Rebecca, then at Brent, and Rebecca could see the hurricane map reflected in her enormous gray eyes.

"I'm waiting for her answer." Brent sounded almost shy. Kind of cute, actually. Rebecca couldn't help but smile at him.

"I've told him I still don't see the point," she said.

Dorothea tipped her head to the side to look at Brent. "How do you stand her?"

Brent laughed. "'Cause I love her," he said.

Rebecca lowered her gaze back to the map. She knew in that moment she did love him. As her friend. As the guy who'd run with her through the streets of Durham in the middle of the night. Who'd bike with her. Jump out of a plane with her. Who wasn't afraid to drop everything at a moment's notice and fly off to a tsunami-wrecked village to do whatever it took to help the injured. But could she love him as her husband? That she didn't know at all.

8

Maya

REBECCA AND I SAT IN THE BACKSEAT OF BRENT'S PRIUS, while the men sat in the front. The three of them were talking about DIDA, Rebecca with her seat belt unbuckled so she could lean between Adam and Brent's seats, monopolizing the conversation, as usual, but I wasn't listening. I wished I'd stayed home. I was still achy and bleeding a bit from the miscarriage and not up to trekking into the bowels of Durham for a meal I would never enjoy. But Adam was excited about it, and Brent was leaving early in the morning for Ecuador, where an earthquake had wiped a couple of villages off the map the day before. How could I say no?

It was still light out, light enough to let me see the neighborhood deteriorate block by block. I glanced at my sister, whose tanned and superhumanly toned arm was stretched across the back of Adam's seat. Her mouth moved with words I barely heard. She was talking about the last time she was with DIDA in South America. Someone had boarded the bus she was riding and stolen money from all the passengers, threatening them with a machete. *Nice, Bec,* I thought. *Nice, reassuring conversation for Brent the night before he leaves.* But Brent was laughing, as was Adam. I was the only one who felt like I was on that bus. The only one who could see the guy coming toward me, the sharp blade of his machete catching daylight as it sliced through the air. I reached for my purse, opened it, poured my money onto the floor of the bus. *Take it. It's yours.*

When Brent suggested this restaurant the other night, I thought for sure Adam would realize its location and offer an alternative. He knew this was hard for me. Either he just wasn't thinking, or he was truly angry with me and didn't care how I felt. But really, I was a grown woman. If I hadn't wanted to come, I should have said so. It wasn't up to them to take care of me. I'd kept my lips sealed, though. Adam was psyched and I was not going to give him one more reason, no matter how trifling, to be disappointed in me. He'd been cool toward me since our appointment with Elaine. I'd apologized over and over for keeping the abortion a secret from him and didn't know what more I could do. One thing I'd learned over the years was that I couldn't change the past, no matter how much I might want to.

"The only time I was in Brazil," Rebecca was saying, "my friends ordered this dish for me in a restaurant and it turned out to be boiled alligator."

Oh, great, I wanted to say. *And why do we want to go to a Brazilian restaurant?*

We drove past a liquor store, where a string of women—clearly prostitutes—posed and preened on the sidewalk.

"There it is." Brent pointed to a tiny glass-fronted building squashed between a pawnshop and a video store.

"That's *it?*" Rebecca sounded both astonished and delighted.

There was no sign above the door. The word *Restaurant* was hand painted on a piece of cardboard taped inside the window.

"Yeah," Brent said. "They're so new, they don't have their sign yet."

"Cool," said Adam.

"Do you see any parking?" I asked, craning my neck. I wanted a spot right in front of the restaurant so we wouldn't have to walk any farther in this neighborhood than was necessary.

"Nothing." Brent looked left and right.

"Is that one?" Rebecca asked. "Up there on the right? Oh. Mini Cooper."

We drove one block. Then another. "Maybe it's not a good night for this," I said.

"There's one!" Brent shouted, and he started to whip the Prius nose first toward the curb, stepping on the brake just in time to avoid creaming the motorcycle that had been hidden from our view in the parking place. "Damn!" he said. "Dude's taking up two spots."

"It's puny," my sister said. "Let's move it!" Before I knew what was happening, she and Adam were out of the car, laughing as they half lifted, half rolled the bike out of our way. I watched the lightness in their movements, the energy, unable to remember the last time I'd seen Adam laugh, and I was glad I'd agreed to come despite my reservations. I wanted to see that smile on my husband's face, even if I wasn't the person to put it there.

Brent managed to squeeze the car into the parking place once the motorcycle was out of the way. We were in front of a wig store. The window was full of mannequin heads, most of them dark skinned, wearing wigs in every shade of the rainbow.

Adam offered me a hand as I got out of the car. "Oh, Maya," he said, sudden sympathy in his voice. "We should have dropped you off out front. Are you up to the walk?"

He meant physically, and physically I was fine. "I'm okay,"
I said, already starting to walk, setting a brisk, *brisk* pace.

"Look out," Brent said as we bustled past the wig shop, "this
woman's hungry!"

The restaurant was long and narrow and packed, but we found
a table in the rear. As we walked toward it, I saw one of the E.R.
docs from Duke sitting against the far wall, and she waved. I
waved back. Seeing her there gave me courage, as if it had not
been a stupid idea to come to this part of Durham for dinner
after all. I began to notice the other patrons. Some dressed up;
most dressed down. White, black, brown. Probably some native
Brazilians, happy to enjoy a meal that reminded them of home.

Rebecca and I took the far side of the table and sat down, facing
the front of the room. By the time Brent and Adam sat down
across from us, I was starting to relax. I liked this place, I decided.
I liked the lively atmosphere. The laughter. The spicy smells.

The menus were handwritten in Portuguese and filled with
bad photographs of the entrées. Sitting across from each other,
Adam and Rebecca leaned over their menus, trying to pro-
nounce the names of the dishes. The table was so small that
their heads nearly touched. Their hair was the exact same shade
of brown, I noticed, and very nearly the same length, Adam's
too long and my sister's too short.

"I want this one." Rebecca pointed to one of the pictures.
"It's the most bizarre-looking thing on the menu." From where
I sat, the entrée looked like a pile of pink flesh covered with
some sort of leafy green vegetable.

"I'm going to pass on that," Adam said with a laugh, and I
was glad he hadn't fallen completely under Rebecca's spell.
When he told me he was joining DIDA, I knew he'd finally
succumbed to her persuasion. I'd always been glad that she and

Adam got along so well, but I wished she'd left him alone about DIDA. I loved my sister, but she could be a steamroller.

We ordered beers while we continued to study the menu, and Adam held up his bottle in a toast to Brent.

"Drink up!" he said. "This'll probably be your last cold brew for a while."

Brent groaned, but he was grinning. "It's going to be so bloody hot down there," he said.

"Next trip is yours, bro-in-law." Rebecca tapped her bottle to Adam's.

"Is that a threat or a promise?" Adam asked.

"Both," she said.

An African-American woman was walking toward the rear of the restaurant, a little girl in her arms. I suspected she was heading for the restroom, but she was looking straight at me, a broad smile on her face.

"Do you know her?" Rebecca whispered.

She wasn't the least bit familiar.

"Dr. Ward!" she said, and for a moment, I thought she meant Rebecca, but her eyes were definitely on mine.

"Hi." I smiled, struggling to place her. Then I noticed the little girl in her arms. "Taniesa!" I said, jumping to my feet. I reached for her, and Taniesa came easily into my arms, as though she'd never connected the pain from her surgery the year before with me. She clutched a small stuffed panda bear in her hand. "You're getting *huge,* baby girl." I planted a kiss on her cheek.

"I seed you and Mama said no, that isn't you, but it is too," Taniesa said.

"And you were right. How are you, honey? How's that arm of yours?"

"Good," she said, and she lowered her head to my shoulder

as if she wanted to go home with me. I could picture the X-ray of Taniesa's left arm, shattered in a tricycle accident, as clearly as if I'd seen it only minutes before. I'd never had a photographic memory when it came to reading, but show me a juicy X-ray or CAT scan or MRI image, and I'd never forget it.

"You mean the world to us, Dr. Ward," Taniesa's mother said. I couldn't remember her name. Taniesa's last name was Flanders, but I knew her mother's surname was different.

"I'm so glad we could fix her up," I said, reluctantly letting go of the little girl and handing her back to her mother. Taniesa had on a sweater against the air-conditioned chill of the restaurant, but I ran my fingers down her arm, picturing the scar beneath the fabric.

Rebecca gave the girl's mother a little wave. "I'm Dr. Ward's sister, Rebecca," she said.

"Oh," I said. "Sorry. This is Brent Greer and my husband Adam Pollard, and this is—"

"Lucy Sharp." Taniesa's mom saved me the embarrassment.

"I like that panda, Taniesa," Adam said. "Is it a girl or a boy?"

Taniesa looked at the stuffed toy as if she was just noticing it. "Girl," she said.

"She have a name?" Adam asked.

"Taniesa."

We all laughed, and Taniesa grinned.

"That was so smart!" Adam's eyes were wide with feigned wonder. "You'll never forget her name, will you?"

God, it was strange watching Adam with other people! I'd forgotten what he was like. How playful he could be. How he used to be playful with me. Our lives had become far too consumed by fertility and pregnancy and worry. We needed to change that, yet I knew he wasn't ready to give up. I knew he wanted a child more than he wanted the sun to rise in the sky.

"Isn't this some place?" Lucy Sharp asked. She glanced down at our plateless table. "You haven't tried anything yet?"

"Not yet," I said.

"What do you recommend?" Brent asked.

"Oh, Lord, anything you get's going to fill you up. Try the Churrasco. It's barbecue, Brazilian style. I never thought I'd like Brazilian food. Who would've guessed? But my sister-in-law got me in here a couple weeks ago and now she can't get me out."

Our waitress came to the table just then, and Lucy Sharp took a step backward. "I'll get out of your hair," she said, "but Taniesa wanted to be sure we said 'hey.'"

"I'm glad you did," I said. "Bye, Taniesa."

The little girl reached for me one more time, and her mom leaned over to let her kiss my cheek.

I have the world's best job, I thought. I watched them walk back to the front of the restaurant, and even before I saw them sit down again, I felt happy and at home and hungry enough to eat alligator meat.

The food was delicious and I was eating coconut flan when I noticed that the crowd was beginning to thin out.

"I'm drunk," Brent admitted happily. He was. Adam was not far behind him. His eyes were glossy and a little unfocused, and the grin he'd been wearing most of the evening was lopsided in a way that made me smile.

"I'll drive," Rebecca said. "Though I'm so stuffed I may not fit behind the wheel."

Adam said something in response, but I didn't hear him. My gaze was on a man who had walked into the restaurant. He was Caucasian, dark haired, wearing a white T-shirt and beige pants and he stood in front of the door, shifting his gaze quickly from table to table. Something about him sent a shiver through me.

He started walking toward us—or at least, I thought he was heading toward our table. His stride was deliberate, his nostrils flared. Then I saw that his eyes—his *ice-blue* eyes—were locked on the two men at the table in front of ours. Adam said something that must have been funny, because Brent and Rebecca laughed, but I'd set down my spoon and was gripping the corner of the table, my heart thudding beneath my breastbone.

I knew better than anyone how quickly these things could happen. The man reached behind his back with his right hand, then whipped his arm out straight, the gun a gray blur as it cut through the air, and I saw the tattoo of a black star on his index finger as he squeezed the trigger.

9

Maya

BEFORE I COULD SCREAM OR DUCK, THE SHOT RANG OUT AND the man at the table in front of ours slumped in his chair. Then I *did* scream, the same way I'd screamed twenty years earlier in my driveway. This time, though, I had plenty of company. The congenial atmosphere of the little restaurant gave way to utter chaos. I bent over in my chair, making myself as small as possible, and I felt Rebecca cover me with her body like a shell. My hands were pressed to my ears, but I still heard footsteps racing toward the restaurant door.

"Get him!" people shouted. "Stop him!" Chairs scraped against the floor, and I heard the *thud* of a table falling on its side.

"Call nine-one-one!" I heard Adam yell.

Rebecca sat up and I straightened slowly from my crouched position, my stomach clenched around the meal I'd eaten. Brent and Adam were already on the floor next to the injured man, who had fallen from his chair in a crumpled heap. Rebecca sprang from her seat to the floor next to the men, while I remained frozen in my chair. The table blocked my view, and I caught only snippets of their conversation. "Press harder," my sister was saying. "Can't get a pulse," Adam said. "Dude's gone," Brent added.

Should I try to help? Could I? This is why the three of them belonged in DIDA and I didn't. I loved my work because it put me in control. "Maya knits teeny little bones back together," Adam always said when introducing me to someone. That's what I loved doing: fixing the fixable.

My gaze sank to my dessert plate, and I saw the splatter of blood across the remnants of my flan. The room spun, and I sprang out of my chair and raced toward the ladies' room in the rear of the restaurant. The tiny restroom was crammed with crying, frightened women who let out a collective scream when I pushed open the door. Just looking at the small sea of hot bodies stole my breath away. I let the door close and sank to the dirty tiled floor of the hallway, my back against the wall.

I couldn't seem to pull enough air into my lungs. *Those cold eyes. The steady aim of the gun.* Gulping air, I lowered my head to my knees and fought the darkness that seeped into my vision. I'd never once fainted. Not the first time I'd worked on a cadaver. Not during my medical training. Not as an intern in the O.R. I'd never even come close. Yet, I could feel the pull of unconsciousness teasing me now. *He's gone,* I told myself. *The danger's over.*

Above the voices and commotion from the restaurant, I heard the distant sound of sirens. The women left the ladies' room en masse, stepping around me, trying not to trip over my feet. I pulled myself into a ball, wrapping my arms tightly around my legs. The sirens grew louder, multiplying in number. I pictured the police cars and ambulances squealing to a stop in front of the building, and I heard new voices adding to the din in the restaurant.

A few minutes passed before Adam walked into the hallway. He squatted down in front of me, his hands on my arms.

"Are you all right?" he asked.

I nodded.

"The guy died," he said.

I nodded again.

"I'm sorry, My," he said. "You didn't need this tonight. I know you still feel like shit." He glanced behind him as if he could see the interior of the restaurant instead of the peeling paint on the wall. Then he sat down on the floor across from me. The hall was narrow enough that, even leaning against the opposite wall, he was able to keep one hand on mine. God, I loved his touch! During the past week, I'd wondered if I'd ever feel him touch me again.

"The cops locked the door, because they want to talk to everyone who was here when it happened," he said. "Especially you and Becca, since you were facing the shooter. But if you're not up to it...I can tell them you're only six days out from a miscarriage and to leave you alone. You could go into the police station instead of—"

"I'm okay," I said. I'd be strong for him. I wanted his admiration, not his pity.

Adam turned his hand to lace our fingers together. "You know," he said, "it was so crazy in there, that when you disappeared, I was afraid you'd been shot. I even looked under the table for you. It scared me." His voice was heavy with emotion, and I knew he still loved me. Only then did I realize how much I'd come to doubt that love.

"I'm okay," I said again, getting to my feet. "I can talk to them now."

The ride home two hours later was quiet and dismal. We were talked out from the interviews with the police, and Brent, now stone-cold sober, drove.

He dropped Adam and me off in front of our house. We started walking up the curved sidewalk to our front door, but I turned as I heard a car door slam and saw Rebecca running toward us.

"Just want to talk to my sis a minute," she said to Adam.

He nodded, pulling his keys from his pocket. "I'll see you inside, My," he said.

We'd left the outside lights on, and I could see the worry in Rebecca's face. "Are you all right?" she asked.

I nodded. "Fine." I looked toward my house, hoping the sight of the light-filled windows and overflowing planters by the front door would erase the image of bloody flan from my mind.

"I was afraid when we picked that restaurant that you wouldn't want to go," she said. "I know you don't like going to that part of town. But it seemed great at first. We were having so much fun. And then *this* had to happen." She shook her head. "It was terrible."

"I'm okay," I said.

Rebecca looked toward Brent's car, then faced me again. "We haven't had a chance to talk about the baby since I got back. I mean, you and me alone. Let's make time before I end up on the road again, okay?"

I wasn't thinking about the baby at that moment. I didn't want thoughts of my baby—my *son*—to be connected in any way to this horrible night, but she was waiting for some response from me. "Okay," I said. "I really…" I looked toward my house once more, thinking of Adam inside. "We have to figure out whether to try again."

"Or adopt."

I shook my head. "I don't think Adam ever will."

"What is his *problem?*" She sounded annoyed. "I want to pound some sense into that man's head."

"No. Don't. He and I have to figure it out. Okay?"

Rebecca ran a hand through her short hair, glancing again toward Brent's car. "This is a terrible send-off for Brent," she said, "but then, you get kind of used to the unexpected when you work for DIDA." It was the wrong thing to say to me now that Adam had signed on as a volunteer, and she caught herself. "But nothing like this has ever happened in all the years I've worked for DIDA," she said. "Really, Maya."

I didn't want to talk about DIDA. What I wanted to say was, *Did tonight remind you of the night Mom and Daddy were killed?* But I would never say those words. Our relationship was so complex. We were close in so many ways. Distant in others. If tonight had reminded her of that other night, I would never know.

"You get some sleep," she said. "Do you have some Xanax lying around?"

"Somewhere," I said.

She touched my cheek with the back of her fingers, the way a mother might touch her child. She was not usually tender, and I was moved by the gesture. Then she pulled me into a hug.

"I love you," she said.

"I love you, too."

We stayed that way, holding on to each other, for close to a minute. No matter how tightly I held her against me though, I felt that long-ago night wedged between us like a solid wall of stone.

10

Rebecca

REBECCA SAT IN HER FAVORITE RED VELVET CHAIR AT Starbucks, shoes off, feet tucked beneath her, a double Americano on the table next to her. She was reading a book written by a guy who'd worked with the Red Cross after the quake in China. Even though she'd worked in China after the quake herself, she couldn't concentrate on the book today. She was impatient and the coffee wasn't helping.

The devastation from the earthquake in Ecuador was much worse than anyone had realized, and she was itching to go down there. Brent had been working thirty miles from the epicenter for a week now, and he'd finally managed to call her on a satellite phone the day before. "Tell Dot we need you here," he'd said. They were extremely shorthanded, but Dorothea didn't want her to go.

"Not until we see what these devils in the Atlantic have on their minds," she said when Rebecca relayed Brent's message.

The tropical storm that had been wallowing a good distance off the coast of Bermuda was now Hurricane Carmen. She barely deserved the name *hurricane,* in Rebecca's opinion. She was nothing more than a puffy white amoeba on the weather map. No one seemed sure where she would make landfall—if she made landfall at all. Possibly South Carolina. Possibly farther north, along the Outer Banks. But the storm was so pathetic that evacuation was voluntary, and Rebecca knew that most people would stay to watch the waves swell and the wind howl and enjoy being as close as they could get to danger while remaining perfectly safe. Durham and the rest of the state were promised buckets of rain and a little wind, but so far, nothing more than that, and Rebecca couldn't believe she was stuck in North Carolina because of potential rain. She had to admit, though, that Dot had a sixth sense about storms. Rebecca sometimes thought she had missed her calling and should have been a meteorologist. She wondered if, when it was her turn as DIDA's director, she'd be able to determine who was needed when and where with Dorothea's precision.

"It's not just Carmen I'm concerned about," Dorothea had said to her in her dining room–slash–office that morning. She'd pointed to the weather map on her computer. "See these two guys north of Haiti?" She ran her finger over two other amoebas. "I don't trust them one bit."

"Okay." Rebecca had given in. "Whatever." So now she was biding her time—working out at the gym, running, catching up on e-mail and helping Dorothea with DIDA's mind-numbing administrative tasks.

She'd finally had a couple of hours alone with Maya the evening before. Over their Frapuccinos at this same Starbucks, they'd talked about the baby. They'd sat in the courtyard outside so Rebecca could smoke, and she'd loaded Maya up with advice: It was too soon to make a decision about trying again, she'd said. Maya needed to put the whole baby thing out of her mind for

a while. She had to give Adam time to grieve before reintro-
ducing the topic of adoption. Maybe by then he'd be ready.

Maya listened in that patient way she had, looking more at
her mug of coffee than at Rebecca. And when Rebecca had
offered every last bit of sisterly advice she could come up with,
Maya leaned toward her.

"I know you have my best interest at heart, Bec," she said,
"but you can't really understand how this feels."

Rebecca didn't know why the words hurt her so much, but
they did. Maybe because they were the truth. She *couldn't*
understand. She was out of her league, and that was a feeling
she loathed. She thought of telling Maya about that weird
fantasy she'd had in Brent's hotel room of holding the baby, that
powerful sense of loss, but caught herself in time. Maya's loss
was real; hers was imagined.

"Well," she'd said, "I *want* to understand."

"It's creating issues between Adam and me," Maya said.

Rebecca frowned. What did she mean by "it"? Maya could
be so vague. She had a way of talking around a subject instead
of coming out and saying what she meant. "What do you
mean?" she asked. "Because he won't adopt or what?"

"Partly," Maya said. "I haven't told you a lot of this because
I didn't want you to worry, but ever since the first miscarriage,
things haven't been the same between us."

She remembered that lunch she'd had with Adam a few
weeks earlier when he talked about the Pollywog. How happy
he'd looked. How she'd realized then that some of the joy had
gone out of him in the last year or so.

She stubbed out her cigarette and leaned forward. "You two
are solid, Maya," she said. "All couples have their ups and
downs." She held her breath, waiting for Maya to tell her once
again that she couldn't understand since she'd never been
married, but Maya only shrugged.

"I know," she said. "But this just...this feels bad."

Adam and Maya. Maya and Adam. Their personalities were entirely different—extroverted versus introverted, jocular versus serious—but together the two of them formed one whole, balanced human being. Rebecca couldn't imagine Maya without Adam. She couldn't imagine her *own* life without Adam in it as her brother-in-law.

"This is a phase," she said. "You'll get through it, honey. You can't rush it. You can't do anything about it. But—" she leaned forward again "—the thing you *can* do something about is work, and I think you're working way too hard right now." Work was a topic she *could* understand and she felt herself on safer ground. Maya was covering for one of her partners who was on vacation. Someone else could have covered for him—someone who hadn't miscarried a couple of weeks ago.

"I need to stay busy," Maya said. "You know how I am."

She did know. Work had always been Maya's way of coping. Even after their parents' deaths, when their lives had been turned completely upside down, Maya threw herself into her schoolwork. Her teachers and the school counselor had been astounded. Maya had always been a good student, the type who didn't have to study all that hard to do well, something Rebecca had envied since she'd had to cram to get the same grades. But after their parents' deaths, Maya lost herself completely in her studies, graduating from high school in three years instead of four. Everyone talked about how amazing she was. No one paid much attention to the fact that Rebecca had sacrificed her own first year of college to play mother and father to her sister, or that she'd fought the system to keep Maya out of foster care or that she'd cooked and cleaned and done the laundry while Maya rose to the top of her class.

The thing that really changed about Maya after the murders,

though, was her transformation from a happy-go-lucky kid into a girl afraid of her own shadow. Totally understandable. She'd been right in the line of fire. Who could go through something like that and remain unchanged?

Rebecca closed the book on the Chinese earthquake, giving up. She hadn't absorbed a single word in the past fifteen minutes. Swallowing the last of her Americano, she got to her feet. She'd go for a run. Lose the negative memories.

She left the store and headed for her car, walking quickly as though she could leave the memories behind, but it wasn't so easy. The whole time she and Maya had been talking the night before, Rebecca had been thinking about the shooting in the restaurant. She hated guns, hated treating gunshot victims, although she did it, wanting to save their lives with a desperation that went beyond the simple practice of medicine. Two decades had passed, yet she still saw her parents' bloodied bodies in every shooting victim she treated.

The incident in the Brazilian restaurant had to remind Maya of that night. Rebecca had seen the panic in her eyes. She'd still been trembling later, when Rebecca hugged her good-night. They never talked about their parents' murder. It was an agreed-upon, unspoken rule between them. Yet she knew that Maya had to blame her for that night.

Maybe even more than she blamed herself.

11

Maya

"HOLY SHIT, MAYA," ADAM CALLED FROM THE SOFA IN THE family room. "Come look at this."

I closed the dishwasher and walked into the family room. Outside the windows, the rain created a dark, undulating curtain so thick I couldn't see the woods behind the house. It was eight o'clock, so I wasn't sure how much of the darkness was encroaching nightfall and how much of it was the storm. Either way, it was the sort of weather that made me glad to be inside. Chauncey sat at the sliding glass door, looking discouraged.

Adam pointed toward the TV. "They're in Wilmington," he said. "They're saying now it's a category four."

I sat down on the sofa next to him. On the screen, a newscaster dressed in a slicker and hood held on to a lamppost to keep from flying away. He was trying to shield his eyes against the wind and rain, shouting to be heard above the din. I squinted at the TV. "Is he…where is he?" I asked. Wilmington was less than three hours from us, and I loved the charm of the city on the Cape Fear River. "Is that the Riverwalk?"

"Right," Adam said. "He's near the Pilot House. Listen."

"...not moving," the reporter said. "Just sitting at the mouth of the Cape Fear. There's no one out here on the downtown streets, but most people didn't evacuate. Some were starting to, because the next storm, Erin, is expected to make a direct hit. And that's a problem—" He slapped his hand on his hood to keep it on his head. "A *big* problem," he said. "We've got people who were trying to leave and are now stuck on the roads because of flooding and downed trees. They tried to...you know...get out, but it's just too late." The reporter was getting blown all over the place. His knuckles were white where he clung to the pole. "You know the next named storm was Donald, but that one sort of just...fizzled, but the big...but Carmen...no one expected this. This...strength. And of course, no one expected her to make landfall here." He fiddled with his earpiece. "Some people are trying to leave the area, like I said, but there's already flooding on some of the major roads and many, if not most, of the minor roads. And I tell you...if this next storm, Erin, packs this kind of punch while people are here...unable to evacuate..." Something blew past his head and he ducked, then recovered. "If it packs this kind of punch," he repeated, "we're going to have a major catastrophe on our hands."

Chauncey had moved to my side. He rested his big head on my knees and I massaged my fingertips into the short fur on his neck. "I hope there's enough of a break between the storms that people can leave." I glanced out the window, but now it truly *was* dark outside and I couldn't see a thing. I'd been worried about the rain and wind in our own yard. I could still remember Hurricane Fran, which hit North Carolina shortly after I moved to the state. I was in medical school and sharing an apartment with Rebecca at the time, and I remembered trees lying helter-skelter everywhere. "How bad is it supposed to get here?" I asked Adam. "Did they say?"

He shook his head, putting his arm around my shoulders, and I felt relief well up inside me. Except for that moment in the hallway of the restaurant after the shooting, he'd shown me little affection since the miscarriage. I was trying not to read too much into it, trying not to be neurotic and insecure. I snuggled close to him. I wanted our intimacy back. I wanted to be able to *talk* to him. We used to talk so easily to one another. Now, though, the things that were on my mind didn't feel safe to bring up, because they would make me sound small and pathetic and I knew he wanted me strong. Worse, I was angry with him for the way he was shutting me out. I'd rarely felt anger toward Adam before, and I didn't know what to do with it. My hormones were still toying with me, and the things that were on my mind, the things I couldn't get *out* of my mind were: my lost child, Adam's ex-wife, laughing about having children after all, and the abortion I'd never told him about. Sometimes I thought to myself: just sit him down and say, *Adam, please, I need to get all this out. Please just let me talk without telling me everything's fine, not to worry. Please.* But I didn't. I was afraid, and I wasn't even sure what it was that I feared.

The guy on the TV screen was growing repetitive, but he was still riveting to watch. "Dorothea was right," I said.

"What do you mean?"

"This is why she told Rebecca not to go to Ecuador. She had a feeling about these storms. So I guess Rebecca will be going to Wilmington or wherever the damage is the worst once they let up."

"…didn't really have a chance to board up along the coast," the reporter was saying.

"I may go, too," Adam said.

I lifted my head from his shoulder. "Really?"

He nodded. "If it turns out they need DIDA down there, this would be a good first assignment. You know...in our backyard. Better than Ecuador."

"Definitely," I said, but I didn't want him to go. I didn't want him to be in DIDA, period. But he was right. I would be far more comfortable having him in North Carolina than South America.

"...has the meteorologists scratching their heads, because this storm—this *cat four* hurricane—just wasn't supposed to go down like this."

The TV showed a satellite image. The hurricane was a stunner, huge and round with a perfect blue eye. It sat at the mouth of the Cape Fear and the projected path drove it straight up the river. A meteorologist with long, glossy red hair moved onto the screen and was about to open her mouth when the TV went dark, along with every light in our house.

"Knew that was going to happen." Adam stood up. "I'll get the flashlights."

"I already did," I said, getting to my own feet. As soon as the rain had started that afternoon, I'd taken them from the cupboard where we kept the emergency supplies. "The weather radio's there, too," I said, feeling my way toward the kitchen. "And the candles. They're all on the island."

I heard the ominous cracking sound of a limb being torn from a tree and stopped in the doorway of the kitchen, waiting for the *thud* I knew was coming, hoping the limb didn't hit the house. I heard the snapping of other branches as the limb fell and held my breath until it finally hit the earth. The whole house shook, and Chauncey began barking furiously, running around my legs, his tail thwacking against my thighs. It was going to be a long, long night.

★ ★ ★

I heard the sound of chain saws even before I opened my eyes in the morning. Adam was already up, and I stood at our bedroom window to survey the yard below. It didn't look bad. Tree limbs and branches littered the lawn, but they were small and I knew we could drag them back into the woods without much trouble. I hoped the front yard had suffered no more damage than the back. The odd thing was, the world outside was still gray. Almost dark, as though the storm was not quite finished with us.

Adam poked his head in the bedroom. "No coffee," he said, wrinkling his nose.

"Oh." I wrinkled mine back at him. "Power's still out?"

He nodded. "The yard's good, though. The Scotts have a big one down across their driveway. I'm going to take my chain saw over there."

"Okay." I smiled. As long as no one had suffered any major damage from the storm, I knew the men in the neighborhood would enjoy the chance to play with their saws that morning. "I'll start picking up the yard," I said.

I dressed and went downstairs, dialing Rebecca on my cell as I walked.

"Hey," she answered. "Any damage at your house?"

"Power's out, but we're good," I said. "How about there?" The trees around Dorothea's house were far smaller than ours.

"Nothing," she said. "Couple of shingles off the roof. Have you turned on the TV?"

"Can't," I said.

"Oh, that's right. Well, Wrightsville Beach is practically under water. And wait till you see Wilmington. The river's flooding a bunch of the buildings on Front Street."

"Oh, you're kidding. We saw on the news that people couldn't evacuate in time. Are there injuries? Will you be going?" Would *Adam* be going?

"Tons of people stranded," she said. "It's hard to say what's going on because nobody can get in or out. But Erin is right behind. They expect her to hit tomorrow morning."

"Already? Hit where? I thought Erin wasn't due until..." I tried to remember what the predictions had been for the second storm.

"They thought Tuesday, but it suddenly started moving," Rebecca said. I heard the excitement in her voice. My sister loved a great disaster. "It's not as big because it's not spending enough time over the water to gain strength, but it's still a four, and the area just can't handle another drop of rain."

"I hope..." I pictured images from Katrina. "I just hope all the people are safe."

"Me, too," Rebecca said. "Is Adam there? Dot's probably going to want both of us to go down there after Erin, unless she turns out to be nothing."

"He's somewhere in the neighborhood with his chain saw."

Rebecca laughed. "The air's buzzing here, too," she said. "Okay, have him call me when he gets in. How are you doing?"

"I'd kill for a cup of coffee, but that's not much to complain about."

"Hey, sis? You know what they're calling these two hurricanes?"

"What?"

"The sister storms," she said.

I thought about that. "Maybe they'll be like us, then," I said. "Carmen was the wild and crazy one, and Erin will be tame and mild."

"Let's hope you're right," Rebecca said.

12

Rebecca

ALTHOUGH THE DAY WAS CLEAR, REBECCA COULDN'T remember a more nauseating helicopter flight. She and Adam were strapped into the fold-down seats of a military helicopter, along with a disaster medical team from Asheville. On the floor between them were stacks of supplies and equipment, poorly anchored. They tilted and shifted from side to side, and Rebecca finally shut her eyes to stop the vertigo, disappointed with herself over her queasiness.

"Check it out!" Adam shouted over the sound of the rotor.

She loosened her seat belt so that she could turn toward the window behind their heads, and the sight made her gasp. Below them, the flooding Cape Fear River covered the earth nearly as far as she could see, and the sunlight reflecting off the still water was blinding. Treetops and the roofs of houses looked like litter strewn across the water's surface. On one of the roofs, she saw two figures. A man and a child.

"Do you see that?" She pointed in the direction of the twosome on the roof. "We need to get them!"

She leaned across Adam to tug at the uniformed arm of the guy sitting next to him. She'd spoken to the man before takeoff, and he seemed to know quite a bit about the evacuation efforts. He was an older guy, gray haired with deep frown lines across his forehead, but clearly in fantastic shape. He looked as though he could lean out the door of the chopper and scoop people from their rooftops with his bare hands.

"There are people on a roof down there!" she shouted to him. "Can we get them?"

He shook his head. "We're not equipped," he said. "One of the rescue choppers'll see them."

There certainly were plenty of other helicopters. She watched them zip through the air, buzzing precariously close to one another. Some were huge and olive-drab, like the one she and Adam were in. Others were tiny and colorful, most likely donated to the cause by private companies. Rebecca could no longer see the roof where she'd spotted the man and child, and she hoped one of the choppers had already managed to pick them up.

She leaned toward Adam, her lips close to his ear. "The worst part of DIDA work is when you feel helpless," she said, and he nodded.

It was rare that she felt helpless, though. She was a problem solver and the more chaotic the setting, the better she performed. Dot had once gone so far as to call her a magician. "The only woman I know who can manage two dozen patients at one time, make a jetload of supplies appear overnight and still find time to sleep with the best-looking dude on the site," she'd said, annoying the hell out of Rebecca. Dot was one of the few people who knew how to yank her chain.

The gray-haired man abruptly unbuckled his seat belt and walked to the front of the helicopter, leaning into the cockpit to talk to the pilot. Rebecca watched him, wondering if he would mention the people she'd seen on the roof. He spoke with the pilot for several minutes. Like the other DMAT team members flying with them, his battalion dress uniform was blue, while her DIDA uniform was dark gray. His multiple pockets, though, bulged just as hers did. In hers, she carried two water bottles, batteries, an MRE, a protein bar and her cell phone, which Dorothea told her she might as well leave behind. The cell towers near the Wilmington airport, where the evacuees were being taken, were down. Rebecca brought it along anyway, and she knew Adam had his as well.

The man returned to his seat. He leaned toward Adam and Rebecca. "I was wondering why we went past the airport," he said.

"We did?" Rebecca had been so mesmerized by the helicopters that she hadn't even noticed the airport.

"Right," the guy said. "The pilot got word that someone on the ground was shooting at the choppers."

"You're kidding," Adam said. He looked a little green.

"They think it was a rumor, so now we're going down."

Rebecca gave Adam a "whatever" shrug of her shoulders. She faced the swaying tower of supplies again, tightening her seat belt, and psyched herself up to face whatever they'd find on the ground.

She sensed Adam's disorientation as they climbed out of the helicopter, and remembered feeling the same confusion the first time she'd landed in a disaster area. The tarmac was brutally hot, the sun so bright and the smell of jet fuel so strong that her head instantly began to pound. There was no time to waste, though, and they joined the DMAT team in unloading the supplies from the helicopter. Adam was quick to get a grip on his confusion.

She saw the energy she'd always admired in him as he climbed back into the cabin and began handing boxes and crates down to the volunteers on the tarmac. *He's going to be good at this,* she thought. She remembered her conversation with Maya at the Starbucks a few nights earlier. A little separation was probably the best thing for the two of them right now. Time apart would give them a new perspective on their problems.

On the runway in front of them, she could see the string of helicopters landing and taking off. The choppers remained on the ground only long enough to dump their human cargo of evacuees before lifting into the sky again. *Just like Katrina,* she thought, as she watched so many people pour from one chopper that she knew they must have been piled on top of one another inside the cabin. Most of them were empty-handed, although a few clutched overstuffed plastic garbage bags. Mothers grabbed the hands of their children. One man carried an elderly woman in his arms. Rebecca turned back to the task of unloading the supplies. She would see plenty of these people in the days to come. There was no time to worry about them now.

"You two!"

Rebecca recognized Dorothea's booming voice over the din from the helicopters. She turned to see the older woman standing near the bottom of the steps leading up to the concourse, her gray uniform a few shades darker than her braid and her hands forming a megaphone around her mouth. "Get your gear and come inside!" she called.

They finished unloading the chopper, then rummaged through the cargo until they found their duffel bags and ran together into the terminal.

Inside the glass walls of the concourse, the din changed from the roar of the helicopters to the buzz of human beings

confined in too small a space to hold them. The gates looked
as they might during a freak snowstorm on Christmas Eve,
when all the flights had been grounded. People were everywhere. They slumped in the chairs. They sat on the floor,
leaning against one another to stay upright as they tried to sleep.
Long lines snaked to the restrooms, as well as to the few bottled
water stations Rebecca could see.

She and Adam followed Dorothea through the corridor to
the lobby, and Rebecca felt Adam's hand light against the small
of her back. He was so physical, and she liked that about him.
He was always touching Maya—an arm around her shoulders,
holding her hand, smoothing her hair. Brent touched Rebecca
when he wanted sex; he was so damn predictable. They'd be
walking home from a restaurant, and if he took her hand, she
knew what he was after. The only good thing was that she
nearly always wanted it, too.

In the lobby, Dot ushered them into a small office and closed
the door. Two desks took up nearly all the space in the room,
and there were no chairs. "Okay," Dorothea said. "Have a seat."

Rebecca boosted herself onto the edge of one of the desks,
but Adam dropped his bag at his side and remained standing,
hands in his pockets. He rocked on his heels as though raring
to get to work.

"Is there any organization to what's going on out there?"
he asked. Clearly he thought there was none, and Rebecca
guessed he was close to being correct, but it wasn't the sort
of question you asked Dorothea Ludlow. He didn't know
Dorothea well, so he couldn't really have known. She tried
to keep a smile off her face.

"Damn straight, there's organization!" Dorothea said, gray
eyes flashing. "We've accomplished more here in two days
than you could in a month."

Adam held up his hands in surrender. "I believe you," he said with an uncertain laugh.

Rebecca grinned. "Don't beat up on my brother-in-law," she said to Dorothea.

"I can already see I'm going to have to separate the two of you." Dorothea shook her head in mock disgust.

"We'll behave," Rebecca said.

Dorothea folded her arms across her chest and leaned against the second desk. "Well, listen up, and I'll tell you the setup," she said. "The concourse is where the majority of evacuees will hang out for now. Here in the lobby, on either end, is where the medical teams are setting up the tent walls. I'll let one of the DMAT workers give you the full rundown. Look for Steve. He's in the baggage-claim area." She looked at Rebecca. "We've got the four zones going, like we did with Katrina," she said, and Rebecca nodded. She would explain what that meant to Adam later. "No one expected this many people, and the teams are over-whelmed—" Dot looked at Adam "—which is *not* the same as disorganized. We're trying to get some more teams in here. Like I told you, the cell towers are down, but I have a sat phone. Here's your two-way radios and some extra batteries." She pointed to the radios on the cluttered desk behind her. "No power, needless to say. The medical areas'll have some AC from generators, but the rest of the terminal's a damn steam bath." She turned her attention to Adam again. "We need the princess here," she said.

Rebecca laughed. Dorothea said that nearly every time they landed in a disaster area. She knew Rebecca would shrug off the idea, but Dot probably saw Adam as fresh meat. Adam, though, had no idea what she was talking about.

"Who's the princess?" he asked. His face was open and boyish, and Rebecca was getting a kick out of seeing him so out of his element.

"She's talking about Maya," she said. "Dot thinks anyone who doesn't work for DIDA is soft."

"Maya's not soft," Adam said. Rebecca liked hearing him come to Maya's defense, even though they both knew that Maya was as soft as mashed potatoes.

"We need her here." Dorothea patted the pockets of her uniform jacket, as if checking her supplies. "We've got a mountain of kids with mountains of problems, and we have no pediatrician. Not one. And as you can see—" she motioned in the general direction of the tarmac, although they couldn't possibly see it from the office "—the people keep pouring in."

"Maya can't do it," Adam said.

"She knows that," Rebecca said. "She's just being a pain in the butt."

"There's a difference between *can't* and *won't.*" Dorothea suddenly clapped her hands together. "Okay!" she said. "Let's get to work." She opened the office door and marched out, and Rebecca watched Adam stare after her, openmouthed.

"Wow," he said. "I had no idea what a bitch she is."

"Really?" Rebecca stood up from the desk. "I thought that was common knowledge." They left the office and made their way through the sea of tired, anxious people, following the signs leading toward the baggage-claim area. She felt uncomfortable that she'd put Dorothea down.

"Dot's not really a bitch, Adam," she said as they crossed the central lobby, where broad green beams formed a crisscross pattern beneath the high open ceiling. "It's hard for her to believe that not everyone feels as passionately about disaster work as she does. She can make people do what they don't want to do. That's why DIDA is a success. Why it works."

"Right," he said. "I get it."

They passed beneath a replica of the Wright brothers' plane.

Beyond that, Rebecca saw the canvas tent walls. An extremely young guy in a gold DMAT uniform rushed toward them as they neared the tent.

"Adam and Rebecca?" he asked.

They nodded and Rebecca thought he was going to hug them, he looked so pleased.

"Fantastic!" he said. "I'm Steve."

"Hey, Steve." Adam reached out to shake his hand. "How're you holdin' up?"

"Haven't slit my wrists yet," Steve said, "though I've considered it. Let me get you oriented real quick because there's no time to waste." He started walking toward the tent walls, and they fell into step on either side of him. "We're basically out of control, but we're improving," he said. "We've got nurses and PAs doing triage out on the tarmac as soon as people get off the choppers. And here's the scoop on the tents. Tent One there." He pointed to the tent farthest from them. "That's for the walking wounded. Sprains, cuts, minor respiratory problems." He nodded toward the tent in front of them. "Tent Two is urgent care. We've had a couple of women in early labor. Compound fractures." He shook his head. "Saw three of them already this morning. People don't belong on roofs."

"I thought this was the baggage-claim area." Adam turned in a circle, searching for the carousels.

"Inside the tents," Rebecca said.

"Right," Steve said. "They don't design airports to house evacuees." He led them to the other end of the lobby, pointing to the door leading to a stairwell. "Do *not* go down to the basement," he warned. "The addicts took it over with the first wave of evacuees and things aren't pretty down there."

And will only get worse as they run out of drugs, Rebecca thought.

"Where are the pharmaceuticals being kept?" Adam asked, clearly thinking the same thing.

"What little we have is in one of the rental car offices," Steve said. They'd reached the area by the ticket counters, where two more tents had been set up. "Here's the third tent," he said. "The E.R. of the operation. Cardiac arrest. Seizures. Active labor. That sort of thing. We have *no* supplies, by the way. You'll figure that out soon enough, though."

"And the fourth tent?" Adam asked.

Rebecca knew what the fourth tent was for, but she let Steve tell him.

"The expectants," he said. "The ones who would die no matter what. Palliative care in that one. Letting the families be with them, if there are any family members around."

Adam nodded. "Mostly elderly," he said.

"Right," Steve said. "A lot of them are from one of the small hospitals that had to be evacuated. Then we've been getting a lot…way too many…from nursing homes. Sadder than hell." He looked from Adam to Rebecca and back again. "You brother and sister?" he asked.

"What?" Adam laughed.

"You look alike," Steve said.

Rebecca and Adam exchanged a glance. Rebecca took in Adam's dark eyes. Brown hair. She supposed they *did* look alike, especially in their DIDA uniforms. She tossed an arm around Adam's shoulders, breathing in the scent of soap and aftershave, knowing it would be her last whiff of a well-groomed man for quite a while. "He's my darlin' brother-in-*law*," she said to Steve, "but thanks for the compliment."

"Hey!" Adam grinned. "That's *my* line."

"Well, whatever," Steve said, and she could tell he had no time to joke around. He pointed toward the ticket counters.

"You can put your gear over there. I've got to get back to the concourse."

Steve took off down the hallway, and Rebecca and Adam dumped their duffel bags behind the ticket counters. Rebecca watched Adam fill his lungs as if he knew he wouldn't have another chance to catch his breath for the next two weeks.

"Welcome to DIDA, bro," she said, and they headed for the tents.

Rebecca spent most of the day with the patients needing urgent care, while Adam worked in the emergency tent. Dorothea had been right about the children. They were everywhere. Asthma attacks were rampant. Broken bones. Fevers. Wounds that were already oozing and infected. Rebecca didn't know how Maya worked with kids all day. It was the one area where Maya was tougher than she was. "I'm just used to it," Maya would say, as if it was no big deal.

As Rebecca's fifth patient was brought to her, she already felt her frustration rising. The screaming five-year-old boy had broken at least a dozen bones in a fall from a tree onto the roof of a car. He should have been airlifted directly to a hospital, not stuffed into a helicopter with dozens of other people. Yet she knew there'd been no time to triage the evacuees as they were scooped up by the choppers. It was up to them to separate the sickest, the most gravely injured, from the others who could be treated here in the terminal. Those in the worst shape, like this little boy, would be airlifted inland. Yet as he screamed during Rebecca's examination, she couldn't help but wonder if Maya would be handling him differently. In her head, she heard one of her sister's favorite refrains: *Children are not simply miniature adults when it comes to medicine.*

She saw Adam from time to time during the day when he'd

transport one of his emergency patients to her tent. They weren't able to exchange more than a few rushed words with each other, always about a patient's condition and treatment, yet she felt connected to him. She was so glad he was there. She hoped the work hooked him and that he'd want to do his two weeks next year as well.

Around dusk, she finally took a break. She jogged down the long hallway to the concourse, dodging evacuees, relieved to be out of the tent and moving her muscles. In the concourse, she headed for the water station and spotted Adam standing near the windows. Grabbing a bottle of water from one of the pallets, she went to stand next to him. He glanced at her without speaking, and in his face, she saw the toll the day was taking on him. She'd never before noticed the fine lines around his eyes or seen the tight, unsmiling set of his lips.

"Are you okay?" she asked.

"Yeah," he said with a sigh. His gaze was fixed on the never-ending line of helicopters as they landed, dumped their passengers and took off again. "It's different than I expected, though," he said. "Rougher and—I don't care *what* Dorothea says—disorganized as hell."

"You get used to it." She didn't want him to lose heart.

He took a swallow from his water bottle. "I decided after the first few crazy hours to stop fighting it," he said. "To see it as a challenge." He glanced at her again. "I was thinking of you," he said. "I figured, if Bec can do this year-round, I can handle it for two measly weeks."

"No doubt about it," she said.

"I admire you, kiddo." He put his arm around her shoulders.

"Don't make me blush," she jested, but his words meant something to her.

"Look at that." He pointed to one of the choppers, and they

watched as the doors opened and a river of people—mostly children—literally poured from the cabin onto the tarmac. Adam quickly lowered his arm from her shoulders, pressing his hand to the glass as though he could stop them from falling. They watched as the kids landed on top of one another. Rebecca had seen worse. Much worse. She rested her hand on Adam's back, and he shook his head. "This is a horror show," he said.

They watched volunteers on the tarmac help the kids get to their feet, trying to create order out of chaos. One of the volunteers, a woman, waved to a group of men standing at the side of the tarmac. She held up four fingers, and the men rushed toward the helicopter, carrying four litters between them.

Rebecca heard Adam groan, probably picturing four more patients swelling the ranks inside the tents.

"That's it," he said. "I'm calling Maya."

"*What?*" Rebecca asked, stunned. "You're not serious."

"I am."

"She won't come," Rebecca said. "She *shouldn't* come. I don't think she's recovered from the miscarriage yet, Adam. Emotionally, I mean. I talked with her the other night, and she's still a mess. And that incident in the restaurant was really—"

"She needs a project," he said. "She needs to get outside of herself."

Rebecca felt a small spark of panic she couldn't quite get a handle on. An ages-old need to protect her sister, maybe? Maya didn't belong in the airport. She needed things neat and orderly. She'd be a wreck.

But she knew there was something else behind her panic besides wanting to protect Maya: she'd liked sharing this day with Adam. Sharing the experience. They were two high-octane doctors who could throw themselves into the fray. Maya, on the other hand, would hold everyone back. She'd be high maintenance, sapping some of Adam's energy from his work and getting in the way.

Was that it? Was that really the source of her trepidation?

It was true that Maya would be high maintenance. She'd need some hand-holding. Yet there was still something more, and if Rebecca was being honest with herself, she knew what it was: DIDA was her world. It was where she shined. She didn't want to have to share that world with her sister. Ever.

"It's a bad idea, Adam," she said. "Can you imagine how she would have reacted if she'd been on our helicopter when that guy said we were being shot at?"

Adam gnawed his lip, and she knew she'd hit him with a dose of reality.

He finished his bottle of water, leaning his head back to get every last drop. "You're probably right," he said, his attention again on the injured kids who were now being carried across the tarmac. He rubbed his neck, then gave her a smile, the crow's feet like tender wounds at the corners of his eyes.

"Back to the tents," he said.

13

Maya

"YOU MUST BE A VERY POPULAR GIRL, HALEY," I SAID AS I walked into the examining room, where my fourth patient of the afternoon sat with her mother.

Haley, whose pixyish haircut and delicate Asian features made her look younger than her ten years, seemed mystified.

"How did you know?" She sat on the examining table, her arm in a cast.

"Well, not every patient I see has about—" I pretended to count the names scribbled on the cast "—a hundred signatures on her cast."

Haley laughed.

"It's made it bearable," her mother said. She wore her own cast on her lower leg, and her crutches rested against the counter. They'd been in a car accident in the spring and were both lucky to be in my office at all.

"Mom didn't want anybody to write on *her* cast," Haley said. "Not even me."

I had a memory of my own broken arm. It was actually

Rebecca's memory, not mine, because I'd only been two at the time and couldn't recall exactly what happened. I'd fallen off a swing and broken my humerus. My arm was in a cast, and Daddy took to carrying me everywhere. Finally Rebecca, who was six at the time, yelled at him over dinner one night, "She broke her *arm*, not her leg!" It was a memory I couldn't recall, and yet I treasured it. I loved picturing my father carrying me around. Loving me that much.

I made small talk with Haley and her mom as I checked the girl's hand for swelling and numbness. "Are you still having much pain?" I asked.

"Hardly any," she said. She was a stoic kid. She hadn't even complained the first time I saw her in the hospital, despite the fact that her radial head had snapped from the bone. She was also adorable. Her mom was a big-boned woman, blond and fiftyish, obviously unrelated by blood to her daughter. Every time I saw them, I felt hope. Adam and I could adopt a child like Haley, I thought, or like any of the other adopted kids I saw in my practice. Adam didn't get it. He didn't witness the parent-child bonds I saw every single day, bonds that had nothing to do with blood and biology.

There was a knock on the door and my receptionist, Rose, poked her head into the examining room. "Dr. Pollard for you on one," she said.

Adam! "Thanks, Rose." I turned to Haley's mother. "Excuse me," I said, "but I need to take this call."

I rushed to my office. He'd been gone two and a half days, and I hadn't expected to be able to hear from him yet. I was used to long periods without contact during Rebecca's absences, but it felt different to be so out of touch with Adam. When I wasn't at work, I was glued to CNN, horrified by the news of missing and stranded people and the images of boats moving from house to house in a desperate search for survivors. *Disaster team personnel are treating hundreds of patients in the airport,* CNN reported, and I assumed that's where Adam was calling from.

I sat down at my desk and picked up the phone. "Adam!" I said.

"Hey, My." He sounded exhausted, but I thought there was a smile in his voice.

"I didn't think you'd be able to call!"

"The cell towers are still down, but I'm using Dorothea's satellite phone. How are things there?"

"Oh, things are fine here," I said. "I'm more concerned with how things are where *you* are. It looks horrendous on TV."

"Understatement," he said. "Are you in the middle of something?"

"I have a patient, but I can take a minute. Are you anywhere near Rebecca?"

"Uh-huh. They have a bunch of medical tents set up in the airport lobby, and the whole terminal, every part of it, is wall-to-wall people. It's really sad, My. Most of them have lost everything."

"I can't even imagine it," I said. "Is there food?"

"MREs."

"Ugh. Where do you sleep?"

He laughed, but there was no mirth in the sound. "I think I've gotten two hours since I arrived, but it's not too bad. There's a big carpeted conference room on the second floor and the volunteers sleep on the floor."

Ouch. He wasn't the best sleeper even in our king-size bed.

"You know…" His voice trailed off. "There aren't enough of us here," he said. "We're trying to do the impossible, really, and…there are no pediatricians…" He stopped talking altogether.

"Are you okay?" I asked.

I heard him sigh. "I thought I could guilt-trip you into this," he said. "Into coming."

I hesitated. "Coming? *There?* I'd be more of a liability than a help, Adam."

He didn't respond, and I continued. "I heard one of the helicopters carrying doctors was shot at. I was worried it might be yours and Rebecca's."

He made a sound of annoyance. "That was just a rumor. The only thing to worry about here are all the sick and injured people who need help."

He couldn't really be asking me to come. "Adam, I can't."

He let out a long breath. "I know," he said. "It's all right."

"What would I do with Chauncey?" I asked, although I knew the answer. Our neighborhood teemed with teenage pet-sitters.

"I said it's all right," he repeated.

I ran my fingers over the keyboard on my desk. "What are you seeing?" I asked.

"You name it. Heart attacks. Women in labor. Broken bones. Infections. Lots of chronically ill folks who just need maintenance meds. Loads of respiratory problems. And…there are so many kids here."

Kids. And no pediatrician. That was why he thought I could help.

I rubbed my temple. "God, I am such a baby," I said.

"It's okay."

"But you called to try to talk me into it."

"I just got…it was an emotional reaction to what's happening here. All around me. I knew you could help, so I felt like I should try to persuade you. That wasn't fair."

"You're still trying, but I'd be useless there."

"Look, someone else needs to use this phone," Adam said.

"I don't know when I'll be able to call again." He was disappointed in me. I heard it in his voice.

"Okay," I said, unhappy with the abrupt end to our conversation. "I love you. And tell Rebecca I love her, too."

"Will do."

I hung up the phone and looked down at my orderly, uncluttered desk. Patient files were neatly stacked on the left. My prescription pad and two pens were lined up next to my mouse on the right. "You coward," I said out loud as I stood up. I left my office and walked down the sterile hallway to the sterile examining room where my well-cared-for patient waited for me. I thought of Adam and Rebecca, the people I loved most in the world, doing what they believed in less than two hundred miles from my office, and wondered why I was in Raleigh and not with them.

14

Rebecca

BY THE THIRD DAY, REBECCA WAS DIZZY WITH EXHAUSTION. Her vision blurred as she administered some of their dwindling supply of oxygen to a man with emphysema, and her voice echoed in her head as she tried to calm a woman going into premature labor. She'd managed to brush her teeth in one of the stifling, fetid restrooms, but that was her only concession to hygiene, and she knew the unshowered smell of her own body was mixing with that of the people around her. It was only going to get worse, but she'd been in DIDA long enough to know that a force inside her would soon take over. The force that no longer craved sleep, and that could see clearly through the blurred vision and hear every word a patient spoke despite the echoes. That force had never failed her, but it took time to get there.

She hadn't seen Adam all day and wondered how he was doing. Some people never did learn how to handle the unrelenting human tragedies and the chaos of a disaster site. Adam was used to the controlled environment of the O.R. He'd looked as though he'd been sideswiped by a train, hollow eyed and soaked with sweat, when she last saw him. Yet his focus had been tight on the shoulder wound he was treating at the time, and she'd felt encouraged. She had faith in him and wished she'd had a moment to tell him it would get better. That force—the ferocious energy he didn't know he had inside him—would kick in, and he would be fine.

Around two in the afternoon, when the dizziness became so intense she thought she might keel over in the middle of examining a patient, she left the tent and went upstairs to the conference room for an MRE and a bottle of water. She lowered herself to the floor near the glass wall overlooking the tarmac. Slipping the MRE pouch into the heater sleeve, she rested it against the window and drank water while she waited for the beef stew to warm up. From where she sat, she had a perfect view of the string of helicopters landing, unloading evacuees, then taking off again. She had to figure out where they would put all these people. They might need to set up tents in the parking lot. The airport simply wasn't big enough for the number of evacuees. In a few days' time, it had become a small impoverished city with too little food, too few restrooms, too few medical personnel to treat the burgeoning population of patients, and thick, hot, putrid air that was difficult to breathe. The two shops in the lobby had been thoroughly looted, and there were rumors of worse crimes, especially in the basement. Yet she witnessed, as she always did, bonds forming between evacuees who'd met on one of the choppers or in the waiting areas at the gates, the seedlings of friendships that would last a lifetime. She saw strangers helping strangers, women taking turns watching one another's kids, men helping to carry the wounded into the terminal. It was always this way. Ninety-nine parts human kindness for every one part depravity.

She was eating the stew when she noticed a man on the tarmac. He was dressed in a pale blue polo shirt, gray pants and leather work gloves as he helped unload a woman and her wheelchair from a helicopter. His back was to her, and she could see the cut of his triceps as he reached up for the chair. She felt that familiar pull low in her belly that had dogged her since she was a teenager. Lord. How could she even think of marrying Brent—marrying *anyone*—when her body was so quick to respond to the nearest hunk of male flesh? Was she *normal?* She was thirty-eight. At some point, wasn't her libido supposed to settle down?

The man leaned over to say something in the woman's ear, and even from where she sat, Rebecca could see the elderly woman's hand shake as she reached up to touch his cheek. Tears sprang to Rebecca's eyes. She'd worked for three days in a sea of suffering people without her eyes so much as burning, but witnessing two seconds of humanity between the aid worker and the old woman was doing her in.

A younger female volunteer pushed the wheelchair toward the terminal, and the man straightened up, stepping back from the chopper. He opened a bottle of water and rather than drinking it, poured it over his head. Rebecca smiled, thinking of how wonderful that small shower must feel.

The man turned to start walking toward the terminal, and she let out a gasp. *Adam.* She cringed. She'd been sitting there seriously lusting over her sister's husband.

She'd gotten to her feet and was grabbing another bottle of water from the broad conference table when Adam walked into the conference room.

"Hey," he said when he spotted her. He was drenched, his arms covered with grime as he pulled off the leather gloves and reached for a bottle of water. His chin and cheeks were shadowed with stubble.

"How are you holding up?" It was hard to look at him, as though her attraction to him from moments earlier might be visible on her face.

"Doin' okay." He took a long pull on the bottle, then surprised her with a grin. "I thought DIDA doctors would be practicing medicine, not offloading helicopters." She could tell he didn't mind, though. Not one bit. He was all right. No, not just all right. He was loving it.

He looked past her shoulder toward the door. "Here comes the boss," he said, and Rebecca turned to see Dorothea approaching them.

"Just got word that a camp flooded twenty or so miles from here," Dorothea said. "Two hundred kids. They're flying them in now."

"Just what this place needs," Rebecca said. "Two hundred more bodies." But she was already thinking of where they could put them and how they could change their triage system to cope.

"You." Dorothea poked Adam's damp chest.

"What about me?" he asked.

"I've been watching you," she said. "You take to this stuff like a pig to mud."

"Good to feel needed," he said with a shrug, as though Dorothea's backhanded compliment meant nothing to him.

"And here's a mindblower for the two of you," she said. "Got a call about an hour ago, and guess what? The other Dr. Ward is coming."

"The...*Maya?*" Rebecca asked.

"She's at RDU, getting ready to board a helicopter."

They stared at her, stunned into silence. *Oh, no,* Rebecca thought.

"You're shittin' me," Adam said.

"Spoke to her myself," Dorothea said.

Rebecca tried to picture Maya boarding the helicopter, and she could almost *feel* her sister's apprehension. This was a phenomenally bad idea in too many ways to count.

"Well, what d'ya know." Adam grinned. "That's my girl."

"I can't believe it," Rebecca said, as though sharing his admiration. Inside, her heart sank like a stone.

"Believe it." Dorothea picked up a water bottle and gave the cap a twist. "I've got to get back downstairs but just wanted to give you the heads-up." She headed for the door, calling back to them over her shoulder, "I need to find a new nickname for that one," she said.

Rebecca watched her walk away for a moment, then she and Adam looked at each other. Adam smiled, holding up his water bottle in a toast.

"To Maya," he said.

Rebecca tapped her bottle to his. "To my awesome sister," she said, and turned away quickly to hide her dismay.

15

Maya

I WAS TWO DIFFERENT PEOPLE. I THOUGHT ABOUT MY SPLIT personality as the helicopter rose into the air. We banked to the east, and below us, I watched the terminal of Raleigh-Durham Airport disappear. Definitely two different people. In my office and in the O.R., I was so strong I sometimes amazed myself. Decisive. Skillful. And above all, unafraid. I was proud of who I was. Who I'd become.

Then there was the woman who'd cowered in the hallway of the Brazilian restaurant. The woman who was flying to the coast, not thinking of how she could help the victims of the sister storms, but rather how she could please her husband by being there. How she could pull him back to her when she felt him slipping away. And there was the woman who was not afraid of flying, not even in this tiny four-seater helicopter, but who was afraid of landing at the airport CNN said had turned into a "third world country."

"I *hate* flying," said the woman sitting next to me, "and this is the worst, flying in this teeny little thing." She was a twenty-something nurse named Janette. I'd met her and the two other DIDA volunteer nurses only moments before we boarded. I felt sympathy for her. The skin over her knuckles was taut and white as she clutched a paperback book in her lap.

"This is actually pretty luxurious," I tried to reassure her. The use of the bright-red four-seater helicopter and its pilot had been donated by a business in Raleigh, and the four of us—three women and one man—sat facing each other on buttery soft beige leather seats. It was noisy, though. So noisy we had to yell to be heard. Other helicopters—huge ones, unlike our petite luxury craft—lumbered through the air above and below us. "This will be the last time we're comfortable for a while."

"Even if we crashed," the man sitting across from me said, "we'd probably be fine. It's not like we're all that high."

Well, that's bullshit, I thought to myself as I looked out the window at the trees and buildings far below, but I knew he was only trying to comfort Janette.

"Let's not talk about crashing," the third nurse said.

"I heard they're running out of supplies," the man said.

"And I heard there's a lot of violence at the terminal," Janette said.

I did *not* want to hear about violence.

The male nurse scoffed at Janette. "Any time you put a few thousand desperate people together, there's going to be some dustups," he said.

"It's a lot more than dustups," the other woman said. "My father wanted me to take his *gun* with me."

Janette laughed. "You're joking."

"No, I am not. It's not like when you go to the airport for a flight. There's no security checkpoint you have to go through. People can bring any weapons they want. If you had minutes to leave your house and you're some redneck fool and you know you're going to head into God only knows what kind of situation, you'd grab your gun and—"

"Wow, look at that!" I said, pointing out the window, not even certain what I was pointing to. I needed them to shut up so I could hold on to my fragile calm. "Look at all the downed trees," I added. There *were* plenty of downed trees. Loblolly pines crisscrossed the land below us like toothpicks topped with green cellophane frills.

Everyone peered out their windows and began talking about the storms, and I was relieved I'd managed to change the subject. As the terrain below us changed from solid ground to a huge glittering lake, we all grew quiet. I'd seen the images on TV, but still felt unprepared for the devastation below. Streets disappeared beneath the brown water, and in some areas, the only evidence of a road was a green highway sign jutting from the floodwater. The roofs of houses and commercial buildings looked as though they were floating. A blue boat rested on one of the roofs, a car on another. I saw small boats sailing between the houses, rescuers wearing helmets and life vests. It reminded me of images from Katrina. People died here. No doubt about it.

I clutched my backpack as I got off the helicopter at the Wilmington airport, helped by a skinny young woman in uniform. I was wearing scrubs, although Dorothea had said not to worry about what I wore—she had a DIDA uniform waiting for me. I had another set of scrubs and a few changes of underwear in my backpack, along with toothpaste, toothbrush, a small container of shampoo and a comb. "Just bring the bare essentials," Dorothea had warned me. I'd brought my BlackBerry, though. If service was restored, I wanted to be able to get in touch with my office. I'd left my partners in the lurch, although I'd covered for one of them recently so they could hardly complain.

The woman guiding me toward the terminal shouted something to me, but I couldn't hear over the deafening roar of the helicopters. Next to us, someone drove a long string of baggage carts toward the building, and at first I thought the carts were carrying blankets or clothing, possibly donated for the evacuees, until I realized they were carrying *people*. Men and women lay stacked against one another, feet bobbing off the sides of the carts as they rode toward the building. Were they dead or alive? It was a horrifying sight. I grabbed the arm of my escort, pointing toward the baggage carts.

"Those people!" I shouted above the noise. "Who are—"

She glanced at the carts. "Nursing home, most likely," she shouted back. I could tell by the cavalier shrug of her shoulders that this was not the first time she'd seen evacuees transported like cattle in the last few days.

Inside the airport, the concourse was crammed wall-to-wall with people, sleeping and talking and shouting. I was prepared for the air to be hot, but heat was not all that greeted me. The smell—a combination of sewage and locker room and death—sucked the air from my lungs.

"Help me!" a woman called from somewhere. "I'm dying!"

I tried to see where the voice was coming from, but more people were pushing into the concourse behind me, and the woman escorting me drew me forward.

"Just follow the signs to baggage claim!" she said, her mouth close to my ear so I could hear her, and I realized she was going to leave me there in the midst of the chaos. She pointed to the overhead sign that read Baggage Claim. "Okay?" she asked, and I nodded.

"Bobby!" a man next to me shouted. "Where are you? Bobby!"

My escort disappeared into the crowd. Momentarily overwhelmed, I stood aside as a couple of people in DMAT T-shirts

tried to cope with the new arrivals. If there was any organization here, I couldn't see it. I watched an elderly man and woman
get knocked down by the throng of newcomers. I stepped
forward to pull the couple out of harm's way, but another fresh
wave of people suddenly poured through the concourse door
and I lost sight of them.

"Maya!"

I turned to see Adam jogging toward me. He had dirty hair
and three days' worth of stubble, but he looked wonderful to
me. He gave me a quick hug, just long enough for me to breathe
in the scent of his sweat. "Let's get out of this mess!" he shouted,
pulling my backpack from my shoulder onto his. "Come on."

I walked with him down a long corridor lined with people,
some sleeping, some talking, some crying, and I realized what
seemed so different here from the situation with Katrina. So
many of Katrina's victims had been poor—people with no
means to escape the area before the storm hit. Here, *everyone*
had been trapped because of Carmen's sudden change of
course. The sister storms were equal-opportunity destroyers,
and the people lining the corridor were of every race and, I
guessed, every economic stratum.

Adam and I didn't speak until we reached the lobby, where
the medical tents had been set up. I'd been in the Wilmington
airport once before, but except for the green beams high above
our heads and the replica of the Wright brothers' plane, I
wouldn't have recognized it. Adam turned to face me, hands
on my arms, and smiled.

"I can't believe you came," he said. "You're incredible. And
gorgeous." He wound a strand of my hair around his finger and
smiled. "You're also the only clean person I've seen in days."

I laughed. I didn't feel incredible or gorgeous, but I loved
that he saw me that way. I wanted to ask him about the rumors

of violence, but bit my tongue. If he thought I was incredible for being there, I didn't want to give him a reason to change his mind.

Someone called his name. He looked over his shoulder toward a woman standing at the entrance to one of the tents and waved. "Be there in a sec," he called, then turned back to me. "Do you need some time to settle in? You okay from the chopper? Or do you want to get to work?"

"To work," I said.

He caught my hand, pulling it to his lips for a quick kiss. I felt bizarrely happy despite the chaos and heat and stench that surrounded me. Adam seemed alive in a way he hadn't for so long. He was happy and he loved me, and for the first time in weeks, I thought, *We're going to be all right. We're going to make it.*

The reality of the critical situation in the airport hit me anew as we walked past the tents and he explained the difference between them. "Dorothea wants you in Tent Three," he said. "Urgent care. Rebecca's in there, too."

We passed the second tent, and I was shocked by what I saw to our right. Between the second and third tents was a broad sea of people, all of them lying on litters on the ground. The litters nearly touched, side to side, end to end.

"Are these…are these just evacuees sleeping?" I asked. "Or are they all patients?"

"Patients," he said grimly. "See why we need you?"

"Oh my God." I couldn't wrap my mind around the sheer number of bodies lying on the floor. Nurses and other volunteers moved among them, squatting next to one, trying to calm another with a few words spoken as they passed by.

"We're not able to do much in the way of medicine here, My," Adam warned, as though he wanted to keep my expectations in check. "We just need to stabilize people and get the most critical patients out of here as fast as we can. We can only do what we can do," he added, and I knew he had become, in a few days' time, seasoned to this work. To Rebecca's work. I doubted I ever would be.

We reached Tent Three, but before walking inside, Adam pointed toward a corner of the lobby. "MREs and water are over there," he said.

MREs. Well, that would be another first for me.

Inside the tent, the air felt ten degrees cooler than in the terminal itself, and there appeared to be some organization. To my right, nurses were triaging patients. Ahead of me, on either side, were cots where people waited to be examined and around which family members or friends anxiously wrung their hands. Some areas were set apart by portable canvas walls. In the distance, I spotted Rebecca. She was palpating the abdomen of a woman who screamed, trying to push my sister's hands away.

"So," I said to Adam, "what happens if someone needs more care than you can give them here?"

"We airlift them to one of the hospitals." He ran his hand up and down my arm. "Just this afternoon we sent out a couple of acute abdomens, two women in active labor, two MIs that I know of and a bunch of injuries in need of immediate surgery."

A woman rushed toward me, a notepad in her hands. She wore a gray T-shirt with DIDA emblazoned on it in white letters. Her hair was pulled back in a sloppy ponytail.

"You're the other Dr. Ward?" she asked.

"Yes."

"Dot wants you down at the end," she said. "Come on."

I glanced at Adam. "See you later," I said with barely a twinge of apprehension.

He winked at me. "Break a leg," he said.

The woman in the DIDA T-shirt practically ran through the

tent, her ponytail bobbing, and I had to scramble to keep up with her. We passed Rebecca, who looked up from her patient and called out, "You rock, sis!"

"I'm a nurse," the woman said. "Susan. I'll be splitting my time between you and another doc." She led me into a small, canvas-walled cubicle where my first patient already waited for me, screaming her platinum-blond four-year-old head off. I could tell from the way she clutched her swollen, misshapen wrist to her chest what the problem was. I began examining her as she wailed on her mother's lap. I listened to her lungs and heart, before Susan leaned over and whispered, "No time for a thorough exam."

I nodded. Of course. No time, and no X-ray machine either. And no anesthesia, for that matter.

"What's your name?" I asked the girl, who only continued screaming in pain.

"Vanessa," her mother said.

"We should just splint her and get her in line to be airlifted out," Susan whispered to me.

"She needs to go to a hospital!" her mother said. "She needs X-rays, doesn't she? Surgery?"

"Do your fingers tingle at all?" I asked the little girl. "Do they feel like this?" I tapped my fingers rapidly on her good hand. She just screamed louder. "How did you do this, Vanessa?" I asked. "Did you fall off of an elephant?"

Momentarily startled by my question, the little girl halted her screaming and nearly smiled before starting up again.

"She tripped on the wet deck stairs while we were trying to get in the rescue boat," her mother said.

"How long's the wait for a plane, or a helicopter or whatever, out?" I asked Susan.

"For a fracture, days," Susan said quietly.

"She can't wait days!" The woman hugged her baby girl to her. People were dying here. Having heart attacks and ruptured appendixes and all sorts of medical emergencies, but if this had been my little four-year-old, I would have felt the same way.

"I can set this," I said, "but we have no way of anesthetizing her."

"Oh, God," the mother said.

"It'll be fine," I said, in the strongest voice I could muster, trying to alleviate the woman's anxiety. "Then we'll splint it and give her some medication to make her more comfortable and then get you out when we can." I glanced at Susan, hoping I hadn't misspoken. "What do we have?"

"Acetaminophen," she said.

"Ah, good," I said, as if that would have been my first choice.

"We'll do this quickly," I said to the girl's mother. "You hold her right here." I guided her hands to the child's upper arm. "Vanessa, I don't want you to think about penguins," I said. "Whatever you do, don't think about penguins! Okay?"

Vanessa stopped screaming, staring at me wide-eyed.

"Susan, you pull on her hand."

Susan gave me a look that said *you've got to be kidding me,* but she grasped the little girl's hand and I quickly slipped the bones back into position. Vanessa let out a scream that made my ears ring.

"Done," I said, standing up straight.

Vanessa screwed up her face in anger and kicked my thigh, and we all laughed.

"I deserved that," I said. I felt nearly euphoric, full of relief and a sense of accomplishment. I had no way of knowing this would be the easiest thing I'd be called on to do for many days to come.

16

Rebecca

THERE WAS ONLY A GENERATOR-POWERED LAMP BURNING IN the conference room, and the soft light was a relief after a long, long day in the medical tents. Rebecca found a stretch of empty floor near the windows and lay down, bunching her jacket beneath her head as a pillow. She stretched out, unkinking her aching muscles one by one. The carpet felt like concrete beneath her bones.

She'd lost track of Adam and Maya sometime during the last thirty-six hours, but Dorothea'd told her that Maya was holding up "just fine."

She wondered if Maya had heard the rumors of mounting violence in the terminal. The rumors were flying so rapidly from person to person now that Rebecca figured there must be some truth to them. In the basement, the addicts who'd managed to escape their homes with their stashes of drugs were beginning to run out, and it was getting ugly down there. A teenage girl supposedly had been raped and beaten. A man—again in the basement—supposedly had his throat slit ear to ear.

They were seeing plenty of folks with withdrawal symptoms in the tents, that was for sure, and now a few DMAT workers kept an eye on the dwindling pharmaceuticals, more precious than gold, in one of the car rental offices. With every whisper of, "Did you hear…?" or "Be careful in the stairwell!" Rebecca thought of Maya. She didn't want her sister to feel afraid. She truly didn't. They needed her, and if she was actually holding up well, as Dorothea said, that could only be a good thing.

Her jacket made a terrible pillow. She adjusted it so that the pocket containing the radio was not right under her cheek. She was about to close her eyes, when she spotted Adam and Maya beneath the long, boat-shaped conference table. The dim light made it difficult to see them, but she could tell that Adam was propped against one of the broad wooden legs, and Maya lay with her head on his lap. Rebecca suddenly remembered their wedding day. She hadn't known Adam well then; she'd been out of the country while their relationship was moving full speed ahead. She remembered taking him aside to tell him, "If you hurt her, I'll kill you." He'd laughed, having no idea how serious she was, and she'd had no idea then how little she had to worry about. She couldn't know then what joy he would bring to them both. They'd been two sisters grappling with a painful past, each in her own way. They hadn't known how much they needed Adam's light heart until he walked into their lives and filled them up.

She watched them now, and she couldn't help but be touched as Adam bent low to kiss Maya's forehead.

God, Rebecca thought, *let them have a child. Please.*

She felt that phantom baby in her arms again, the same baby she'd imagined holding in Brent's hotel room. A sudden thought came to her, bizarre and out of nowhere: Maybe she could be their surrogate. Maya couldn't seem to carry a baby to term, so what if Rebecca could do it for her? For both of them? She rested her hand on her flat stomach. What would it be like, to feel a baby growing inside her?

What the hell are you thinking?

She'd never wanted to be pregnant. Pregnancy would get in the way of her work. Her life.

"You'll be missing something." How many of her annoying friends with children had said those words to her, like a hushed, sacred warning, when she told them she never planned to have kids? She'd always scoffed at the sentiment.

The baby in her arms. The sensation was creeping her out.

She looked over at her sister again. She and Adam seemed to be talking. Maya moved a hand through the air, slowly, as though illustrating a point. Adam caught her hand. Held it to his lips.

Rebecca closed her eyes and something coiled inside her chest like a snake. It wasn't until she felt the hard, flat carpet beneath her hand instead of the flesh of another human being that she recognized the feeling: envy. She didn't care if they needed Maya here. She wanted her to go home.

17
_____

Maya

IT ALL HAPPENED SO FAST.

Two volunteers carried a boy, a tiny dark-skinned little guy who couldn't have been more than five, into my canvas-walled safe haven. The men shouted at me to move the teenage girl I was treating for a cut on her forehead. I grabbed the girl and pulled her out of the way just as the men dumped the unconscious boy onto the cot.

Susan took the shocked girl by the hand. "Come with me," she said, quickly guiding her out of the cubicle, and I leaned over the little boy to make sure he was breathing. His eyelashes were so long, they lay like dragonfly wings against his cheeks.

"What's wrong with him?" I pulled off my gloves and reached for a fresh pair from the flimsy table next to my chair.

"Shot," one of the men said. "Bullet went clean through him."

I stopped the glove halfway onto my hand. I saw that the front of the boy's black T-shirt was wet with blood. In all my years as a physician, I'd never treated a gunshot wound, not even during my miserable rotation in the E.R., and that had taken some tricky, guilt-inducing maneuvering on my part. I was stuck now, though.

I quickly slipped the gloves on my hands. "Help me get his shirt off," I said to one of the men, and I reached for the hem of the small T-shirt, bracing myself for what I would see on the body of that skinny little child. We gently eased the shirt over the boy's arms and head, and with one glance at his chest, I felt certain he was going to die.

Ten minutes later, I'd hooked the boy up to an IV and was racing next to the bobbing litter as a couple of volunteers— high school kids—carried him through the terminal. I was winded and sweating by the time we ran outside and onto the tarmac, where the helicopter stood silhouetted against the dusky sky. Two other litters were already inside, along with Janette, the nurse who'd flown with me to the terminal a couple of days earlier. *A couple of days?* I felt as though I'd been there at least a week. I helped Janette and the teenagers load the little boy's litter into the cabin, then I leaned inside to speak to Janette.

"He was shot through the chest," I shouted as the rotor blades began to turn. "The bullet exited between the eighth and ninth rib."

Janette looked confused. "You're coming, too!" she said.

"No!" I shouted back. "I'm staying here."

"Dot said you're coming with me. I can't manage three critical patients alone!"

I shook my head. "She didn't say anything to me about—"

"Get in!" The voice came from the tarmac behind me, and I turned to see Dorothea running toward me, gray braid flapping against her shoulder. She was carrying a backpack that looked a lot like mine. "Go on!" she said, pressing the pack into my arms. "I put some extra supplies in here for you. The pilot'll bring you right back."

This was all happening too fast. I glanced behind her toward the terminal, longing to go back inside with Adam and Rebecca.

"I can't go," I said. "I—"

"Grow up, Princess!" she snapped. "Get in!"

There was no arguing with her, especially not with that little boy in desperate straits inside the chopper. Janette was right; she couldn't manage three patients alone. Before I could think about what I was doing, I scrambled into the helicopter. I caught a glimpse of the pilot, a woman who looked no older than the high school kids who'd carried the boy's litter.

"Everyone in?" she shouted to me.

Someone shut the cabin door, giving her the answer.

There were no seats, and the litters had been tossed haphazardly on the floor leaving barely enough room for Janette and me to sit between them.

Within seconds, we were in the air. The litters slid against my legs as we ascended at an angle into the darkening sky. Janette and I clung to whatever protrusion we could find on the walls. For me that was a metal ring close to the floor. I felt stunned to suddenly find myself high above the terminal. I thought I might throw up, my body rebelling against the chaos of the past few minutes.

"This one's seizing!" Janette let go of the post she'd been clutching and knelt next to one of the patients, a shirtless young man who jerked so violently he popped one of the straps on his litter. I swallowed the bile rising in my throat and scooted over to help her.

"How long is the flight?" I shouted to the pilot. I wasn't even sure what hospital we were aiming for.

"Forty-five!" she shouted back.

I looked at the three patients—the guy with seizures, an elderly woman who was groaning in her sleep, her hands clutched tight across her chest, and the tiny gunshot victim. Would any of them survive another forty-five minutes? At least this flight gave them a chance. The terminal could offer them nothing.

The little boy moaned and I turned to look down at him, glad I'd given him a little morphine in his IV in case he regained consciousness. I leaned low, my lips against his ear so he might be able to hear me. "You're safe," I said. "It's going to be all right."

Once the man's seizure had run its course, I hung on to the metal ring again and looked out the window. We flew over floodwaters and dark swamps. Soon, treetops spread out in all directions below us, a black carpet in the fading light. The drone of the rotors was deafening but steady, so that when it suddenly shifted to a chunking, grinding sound, it startled me. I glanced at Janette, recalling what she'd said on our earlier flight together about hating to fly. Her eyes met mine, and I saw her mouth the words, *What's going on?* I thought of the variety of perfectly normal sounds you'd hear on a plane, how they'd change depending on whether you were ascending or descending. Could we already be starting our descent?

The pilot suddenly shouted to us, but I couldn't make out what she said. Janette, closer to the cockpit, understood though, and she turned to me with a wild look in her eyes.

"She said to brace for a crash!" she shouted.

"What?" My heart rocketed in my chest.

"Brace!" Janette shouted again, as she grabbed the post on the cabin wall.

I tightened my grip on the metal ring as the helicopter suddenly bucked, then rolled to one side. Losing my grasp, I slid across the floor, the litters pinning me to the wall. I ran my hands over the wall, searching in vain for something to hang on to. Drawing up my legs, I wrapped my arms around them, and saw the dark carpet of trees zooming toward us. I buried my head against my knees as we broke through the treetops, finally letting go of the scream I'd been holding inside.

18

Rebecca

REBECCA WAS STITCHING THE PAPER-THIN SKIN OF AN ELDERLY man's forearm when she spotted Dorothea striding toward her in the tent.

"Come see me when you're through with this patient," Dorothea said.

Rebecca glanced at the string of patients sitting and standing along the wall of the tent. It was nearly midnight and she was far behind. "Can it wait?" she asked from behind her mask as she knotted the final stitch.

"No." Dorothea was already walking away. "I'm in my office."

Rebecca looked at the man whose arm she was stitching. "She'd better have a good reason, huh?" she asked him as she snipped the thread.

He looked over at the line of patients. "A damn good one," he agreed.

She found Dorothea talking on the sat phone in the office behind the ticket counter, which she'd claimed for DIDA use in the last couple of days.

"Gotta go," Dorothea said, hanging up and sliding the antenna back into the phone. She motioned toward one of the three chairs in the room, although she herself stood leaning against the desk. "Sit," she said.

"What's up?" Rebecca stayed on her feet. If she sat down, she was afraid she'd fall asleep.

"The chopper Maya was on had some sort of problem," Dorothea said. "The pilot sent a Mayday message and said she needed to make an emergency landing."

Rebecca frowned, searching for a different meaning behind the words than the one Dorothea was implying. "Where are they?" she asked. "Can another chopper get to them?" She looked up to see Adam in the doorway.

"Come in, Adam," Dorothea said.

Adam glanced at Rebecca as he walked into the room. "What's going on?"

"Maya's helicopter had to make an emergency landing," Rebecca said.

"No." He looked from her to Dorothea. "Where?"

"They don't know where," Dorothea said. "The chopper has an ELT on it—you know, like a GPS system? But they haven't been able to pick up a location for it."

Rebecca leaned forward. "You mean, they get a signal from the ELT but can't pin down the—"

"No," Dorothea interrupted her. "They're not *getting* a signal. It's not functioning."

"What would cause it to malfunction?" Adam ran his hand over the stubble on his cheeks, and Rebecca noticed that his fingers were shaking. He looked as exhausted as she felt.

"I have no idea," Dorothea said. "You know, maybe it was the sort of mechanical problem that causes—" she shrugged her shoulders "—a massive shutdown of everything. I just don't know."

Rebecca remembered their helicopter flight to the terminal. Water everywhere below them. Where would the pilot find a dry spot to land? If they were farther inland, though, they'd be okay.

"How long were they into the flight before he called in the emergency?" she asked.

"It's a she," Dorothea said, "and I don't know that either." She sighed, and for the first time since her arrival at the airport, Rebecca saw a weariness in her mentor's eyes. "Lots of questions and no answers right now," Dorothea added.

"Are they searching for the chopper?" Adam asked.

"It's too dark," Dorothea said. "They'll start flying over the route it was on first thing in the morning."

"They should be looking *now*," Rebecca said.

"Too dark," Dorothea repeated.

"Maya will be so afraid," Rebecca said to Adam.

"I just hope she's *alive* enough to be afraid," Adam said.

"Oh, don't say that, Adam!" She remembered envying Maya the night before. Wanting her to go home. The memory turned her stomach.

"Let's not get dramatic about this," Dorothea said. "She and everyone aboard are probably fine—or in the case of the critical patients, as fine as they can be. Most likely, the pilot found a safe place to put down and for whatever reason, the ELT just isn't functioning. And of course, the cell towers are still down, so they have no phones."

"Maybe they're all trying to walk out," Rebecca said.

"No, they'd stay with the patients," Adam said. "Maya wouldn't leave them."

"You're right." Rebecca could picture Maya making that decision to stay. That was Maya's strength: caring for her patients. She decided right then that she would hold tight to that strong, safe image of her sister. But even as she tried to keep the thought in her mind, it faded away. Maya would be afraid. She'd be immobilized by fear.

There was no way she could sleep, so Rebecca went for a long run around the exterior of the airport, through the parking lots, across the tarmac and back to the parking lots again. Then she worked through the rest of the night. She splinted legs, stitched cuts, medicated children suffering from the nausea and diarrhea running rampant through the terminal, and calmed worried parents, all the while a mantra playing in her head. *She's okay, she's okay, she's okay.* At the other end of the tent, she watched Adam going through the same motions. They were the only doctors up all night. The only two people in the entire terminal, she thought, who had no desire at all for sleep.

As soon as the sky began to lighten in the morning, she and Adam hurried out to the tarmac to talk to the pilots who'd be searching for Maya's helicopter.

"I'm going with you," Rebecca said to one of them. She was already climbing into the cabin when he grabbed her arm.

"Better if you stay here, Doc," he said. "We'll need the room to pick up evacuees along the route, and we'll be calling Ms. Ludlow with regular updates."

"I am *going*," Rebecca insisted, but this time Adam took her arm and drew her away from the cabin.

"Let them do their job." His face was pale beneath the dark stubble. "And we'll do ours here. It's not going to make a difference if you're in one of the choppers or not."

She thought of fighting them, but knew they were right. Besides, what if she was in one chopper and Maya was picked up by another and brought back to the airport? Rebecca wanted to be there the moment Maya stepped onto the tarmac.

As the morning wore on, though, with the calls to Dorothea from the pilots few and far between, she began to regret her decision. She tried to concentrate on her patients, constantly checking her two-way radio to make sure it was turned on.

By noon, there had been no sighting of the downed helicopter. Everyone's best guess was that it had flown off course to find a clear spot to land.

"I'm going out on the next chopper," Adam told her when Dorothea radioed them with the news—or lack of it. They were in the concourse, standing together in a sort of invisible bubble that blocked out the chaos surrounding them.

"I'm going, too," she said. "I should have gone earlier."

"It wouldn't have made any difference," Adam said. "And you should stay here in case she shows up. Get some sleep. There's another DMAT team arriving from Texas this afternoon, so Dorothea said for us to do what we need to do. That's go on the chopper for me and sleep for you."

"I can't possibly sleep, Adam."

"You need to, Bec," he said. "You're wiped out. When I get back, it'll be my turn, okay?"

Rebecca stared hard at his worried face. "When you get back, I want Maya to be with you."

He looked through the terminal windows toward the tarmac, shoving his hands into his pockets. His shoulders sagged. "This is my fault," he said. "She came here to please me."

"She was handling it so well," Rebecca said.

"I know." He shut his eyes. "She was great."

Rebecca slapped his arm. "She *is* great!" she said. "Don't talk about her in the past tense."

He gave her a tired smile, then drew her into a hug. "I didn't mean it that way," he said. She felt his bristly cheek brush her temple. "Go to sleep, okay?"

★ ★ ★

She didn't sleep. Didn't even bother trying. She treated patient after patient in the urgent-care tent, taking a break every once in a while to run to Dorothea's office to see if she'd heard anything.

"I'll let you know the moment I do," Dorothea said, looking up from the desk she'd taken over as her own.

"It's getting too late." Rebecca looked at her watch. It was after six. Adam had left on the chopper around one. If he disappeared, too, she didn't know what she'd do. "I need someone to take me up," she said. "I can't stand this sitting around."

"Adam's chopper refueled in Fayetteville," Dorothea said. "That much I know. They're going to keep looking until it's too dark to see."

Rebecca swiped both hands through her hair. She was no good at waiting. She never had been.

"Get some sleep, babe," Dorothea said. "The Texas DMAT team is getting oriented and they'll be up and running any minute."

"Like I'm not needed," Rebecca scoffed. "You're already missing Adam and Maya."

"I'd rather have you wide awake tomorrow than screwing up tonight." Dorothea stood, giving her a shove toward the door. "Up to the conference room," she said. "Seriously. I don't want you back in the tent until morning."

She didn't go to the conference room. Instead, she carried her cigarettes and a bottle of water out to the tarmac and sat on the edge of an empty baggage cart to smoke. The air was hot and sticky from an earlier rain. A few helicopters were still doing their dance of bringing evacuees in and airlifting the most critical patients out. They had their lights on now as the sky grew dusky. She squinted into the distance at each incoming chopper, trying to determine if it might be the blue-and-yellow bird that had carried Adam away that afternoon.

Where the hell was he? By the time she had lit her third cigarette, the string of incoming helicopters had nearly stopped for the night. Maybe his chopper had landed someplace inland. But then why hadn't Adam contacted Dot?

She was about to stub out her cigarette when she saw a light in the distance, the chopper a dark smudge against the evening sky. She knew, before even seeing the color of the helicopter, that it was the one carrying Adam. She jumped to her feet. In her mind, she saw him climbing out of the chopper, holding his hand out to help Maya deplane. She saw it so clearly that by the time the helicopter set down on the tarmac, she was smiling.

"Rebecca!" She turned to see Dorothea walking toward her from the terminal, sat phone in her hand. Even in the dusky light, Rebecca was able to read the grim look on Dorothea's face, and she lost her smile. She turned back to the helicopter, where Adam jumped from the cabin. He didn't reach up to help Maya deplane. Instead, he started walking toward her.

"*What?*" Rebecca shouted, looking from him to Dorothea and back again.

Adam reached her. He put his hands on her arms. The flesh beneath his eyes looked dark and raw.

"It crashed," he said.

"*What* crashed?" She shook her head rapidly, as if she could stop the words from coming out of his mouth.

"We saw it, but we couldn't get to it."

She tried to hit him, to shut him up, but he caught her hand, surprise in his eyes. Rebecca felt Dorothea put an arm around her waist as if she was afraid she might fall over.

"Oh, God." Rebecca pressed her hands to her mouth. "What...could you see *anything? Anyone?* What do you mean, you couldn't get to it?"

"Listen," he said. He motioned toward the baggage cart. Its metal sides glinted in the light from the chopper. "Let's sit, okay?"

"No!" She pulled free of Dorothea's arm. "Tell me!"

"I *will*." He nearly barked the words, then closed his eyes. "I will," he said more calmly. "I just need to sit."

The three of them sat down on the baggage cart, Adam between the two women. Rebecca felt the length of his body against hers, and she couldn't tell if the tremor coursing through her limbs was coming from him or from herself.

"There wasn't much light," he said, "so we couldn't see well at all."

"Do you know if—"

"I don't know." He interrupted her. "I don't know if anyone...survived or what. We were nearly out of fuel by the time we saw it. It was in a densely wooded area. A lot of trees and brush. And the chopper was caught in some branches above a river or a stream. It was hard to tell exactly what we were looking at."

She opened her mouth to ask him the thousand questions running through her mind, but he held up a hand to stop her.

"Let me finish," he said. "Our pilot called another chopper with a search and rescue team aboard to get out there, since we had to come back for fuel. They were going to find the closest place to the...to the crash site where they could land. There weren't many possible landing sites close by. Then first thing in the morning, as soon as it's light, they'll hike into the—"

"Why not *now?*" Rebecca jumped to her feet. "Don't they have any fucking *flashlights?*"

"The terrain's too difficult to negotiate in the dark," Dorothea said.

"How do *you* know?" Rebecca snapped.

"Because I just spoke to the search and rescue guys." Dorothea looked at Adam. "They *did* find a place to land, but it's about a half mile from the crash site."

"Well, someone take *me* out there tonight, then!" Rebecca said. "I'll look for her."

"This chopper—" Adam nodded toward the helicopter he'd just left "—will take us out early in the morning, and we can meet up with the S and R team then."

"*Adam,*" she pleaded. He seemed so dense. "What if she's...if they're injured! Time matters! It's ridiculous to wait. We—"

"You didn't see it out there, Rebecca." He glared at her. "No one can search out there at night. Trust me."

She pulled a cigarette from her pack and lit it, her hands shaking wildly. She pulled the smoke deep into her lungs.

"What did you see, Adam?" Dorothea's voice was calm. In the growing darkness, it seemed to come from miles away. "Did it look like the sort of crash that...do you think anyone *could* have survived it?"

"I don't know. The chopper was on its side, and like I said...it looked like it was suspended above a river...or rushing water, anyway, and it was getting dark, so I'm not sure exactly what the situation is."

What if it falls overnight? Rebecca thought, but by now, she knew better than to give voice to her fears. What good would it do?

"Is the other DMAT team here?" Adam asked Dorothea. "Can you spare us in the morning?"

"Yes, they're here, and absolutely."

A lie, Rebecca knew. No one could be spared. But Dorothea had to know they were going, whether they were needed in the terminal or not.

★ ★ ★

They slept—or tried to sleep—on the conference room floor, Adam beneath the table where he and Maya had taken to sleeping, Rebecca by the windows. She stared at the ceiling, silent tears running down the sides of her face. She didn't save Maya when she was fourteen only to lose her now.

Getting to her bare feet, she walked across the floor to the table. She squatted beneath it, then sat on the floor cross-legged next to Adam. He started when she put her hand on his shoulder. In the darkness, she could barely tell when he opened his eyes.

"She's alive," she said. "I swear, Adam, I would feel it if she weren't. But I think she's hurt, and with every hour that passes…every *minute* that passes… It's just too long. What if she dies overnight while we're here twiddling our thumbs because it's too damn dark to search for her?" Her voice cracked and she bit the inside of her cheek to keep from crying again.

"Shh." He sat up and pulled her toward him, his arms around her and his stubbly chin against her forehead. "We'll go as soon as we can, Bec," he said. "We'll find her."

She clutched the fabric of his T-shirt in her fist, breathing in the rank scent of him. Of herself. "I can't lose her, Adam," she said.

"I know. I know." He rocked her like a child. "Neither can I."

19

Rebecca

THERE'D BEEN MOMENTS, TOO MANY TO COUNT, WHEN Rebecca had resented Maya. Moments she'd envied her. A million moments when she'd been irritated by her timidity. But in her most honest moments, Rebecca knew that Maya was a better person than she was. Rebecca had that "good Samaritan, noble physician" reputation, but it was Maya who did her work quietly and without fanfare. Maya who lived a calm, clean life while Rebecca was, she thought truthfully, a hedonist, out for herself more often than not.

Yet Rebecca would lay down her life for her sister. That was also the truth, and on that long-ago night in their childhood driveway, she very nearly did. She would do it again if she had to. As she and Adam climbed out of the helicopter in the small clearing a half mile from the accident site, all Rebecca could think about was finding her sister. Finding her *alive,* because losing her suddenly felt like losing her arm or her leg. Losing her would be like losing part of her heart. Maybe even the best part.

They'd landed next to the search and rescue helicopter that

had arrived the night before and were greeted by the S and R team: two women, two men and one golden retriever named Rocky. It was barely daylight, and a gray pall hung over the clearing. As the chopper's rotors stopped spinning, an eerie silence filled the woods, broken only by the echoing, early-morning calls of the birds.

They exchanged introductions with the S and R team. The pilot who had flown them in also had search and rescue training, and he seemed to know the team. The conversation swam around Rebecca's head in a haze. She'd slept little the night before as she lay next to her wakeful brother-in-law, so aware of his presence and grateful for it. Now her thinking was muddy, as though her mind had room for only one thought and that was *find Maya*.

"Okay," said one of the men. "Let's head out."

She knew he'd given them instructions, orienting them to how they would proceed in the search, but she hadn't heard a word. She hoped Adam had.

They began walking at an almost leisurely pace into the dense woods and Rebecca thought they were acting more like a bunch of hikers than a search and rescue team. She started to plow ahead of the group, her gaze darting into the woods.

"Ma'am!" one of the men called to her when she'd passed them all. "Get behind us!"

"You're too damn slow," she said over her shoulder.

Adam caught up to her, taking her arm. "They know what they're doing, Bec," he said quietly.

"I can go five times faster by myself."

"It's not about speed," one of the women said.

Adam nodded his head behind him. "Come on."

Reluctantly, she gave in, and Adam drew her to the side to let the searchers pass them. She hated being at their mercy. She was used to leading, not following.

The two men and the pilot carried a small pontoon boat, and they once again took the lead. The search team members all wore orange T-shirts, baseball caps and backpacks from which helmets and inflatable life vests dangled. Rocky sniffed indifferently through the brush. The terrain was just plain weird, full of spindly pines, twisted live oaks hung with Spanish moss, and spongy ground that gave beneath their feet. Branches smacked Rebecca in the face and invisible cobwebs clung to her cheeks and hands as she tripped over the roots of trees. The woods were dark and claustrophobic, and she understood now why a search would have been impossible during the night.

She tried peering through the undergrowth as they walked, looking for Maya, as though her sister might simply be wandering among the trees. They walked for what felt like a long time, Rebecca and Adam obediently bringing up the rear of the party. Rebecca was beginning to feel disoriented.

"I swear," she said to Adam. "How do they know this is the right way?" She looked back over her shoulder. There was no trail at all and the view in every direction looked the same.

"I'm sure they know what they're doing," Adam said again.

Rebecca called ahead to the team. "We should look for them along the way in case any of them were able to walk away from the crash site," she said.

One of the women spoke over her shoulder. "We'll go to the site first and assess what we find," she said. "If there are survivors, we'll most likely find them there."

One of the men pointed ahead of them, a little to the left of the way they were headed. She followed the direction of his arm, and through the thick, leafy branches, saw what had drawn his attention. A broad, horizontal chunk of army-green metal was visible through the trees. Rebecca drew in a breath and started to rush forward, past the women, the men, the dog.

"Maya!" she shouted.

"Careful!" one of the guys called after her. "There's a drop-off ahead of us."

Rebecca fought her way through the brush, even though she'd lost sight of the green metal. "Maya! Anyone!"

"Stop!" one of the women called.

She heard the sound of rushing water ahead of her and stopped abruptly. Her eyes searched the woods for the green metal. She turned to the others, breathless. "Where did the helicopter go?"

The men carrying the boat rested it carefully against the trunk of a fallen oak. "It's that way," one of them said, pointing. "But let *us* walk in front."

She stepped aside, the bubbling sound of the invisible water unnerving her. Adam caught up to her and she sensed the tension in his body as they stepped aside to let the others pass.

"There she is," one of the women said, and Rebecca felt as though someone had thumped her heart with a mallet.

"Maya?" she asked. "Where?"

One of the men turned to her. "She means the chopper," he said, and it was now light enough for her to see the sympathy in his eyes.

With a few more cautious steps over rocks and roots, she was able to take in the scene herself, all in one horrible, hope-stealing moment. She stopped walking and simply stared.

"*Shit,*" Adam said. She felt both his hands circle her arm as though he was trying to keep himself upright. She knew exactly how he felt.

The helicopter lay on its side, suspended precariously in the squat, stubby brush above a river of rushing water. It was perched high enough in the trees for Rebecca to see that the side of the craft—the side parallel to the water—had been peeled back like the lid of a sardine can. She pressed her hands to her eyes as if she could make the scene disappear. She'd witnessed the worst that life had to offer: men burned beyond recognition, children crushed by pillars of concrete. Yet the mangled helicopter was the most horrific thing she'd ever seen.

"Don't rush forward," someone warned her. "It's hanging by a thread."

"I've been here before." One of the men looked around him. "Near here, anyway. This was a creek." He pointed to the water below. "Now it's a damn river."

One of the S and R guys was scrambling down the bank of the creek, and Rebecca guessed he was trying to get into a position to see inside the chopper's cabin. The dog started to run after him.

"Rocky, come!" one of the women called. Rocky nearly squeaked to a stop before turning around neatly and trotting back to the woman's side.

The man on the bank balanced himself against a splintered tree trunk, holding a pair of binoculars to his eyes as he studied the helicopter.

"Can you see inside?" Rebecca started to run down the bank, but one of the women caught her shoulder and held her back.

"Looks empty," the man called. "I'm guessing no one was strapped in."

Rebecca studied the rough bank and frothy water below them, trying to remember what Maya had been wearing. The damn gray DIDA uniform, no doubt. She'd blend right into the water and terrain.

"Maya!" she shouted again, unable to stop the word from coming out of her mouth.

"I think the pilot is still in there." The man with the binoculars was bending low, trying to get a better look into the cabin.

"Alive?" one of the women asked.

"Can't tell," the man said. He looked up at the helicopter, then below him at the creek that was now a river and shook his head. "This ain't gonna be easy," he said.

They divided into teams. Two of the men stayed behind to find a way to get to the pilot. One of the women, the pilot, Adam and Rocky began searching the woods close to the crash site, and Rebecca and the other woman—she still didn't know any of their names—took the pontoon boat into the rushing water to search the bank.

The current was swift, but the water near the bank was so littered with rocks, fallen trees and debris, that it slowed their progress. They'd been exploring the overhanging brush for twenty minutes when, a distance away, Rocky started barking. Rebecca looked up to see the dog high on the bank behind them, staring down at the water.

"There must be something there!" Rebecca said, although all she could see was more scrubby undergrowth and tree limbs.

The woman from the search team turned the tiller so that they headed upstream again. She pointed to the area that was still drawing Rocky's noisy attention.

"Is something there?" Rebecca could see nothing other than a tangle of brush at the side of the frothing stream. Then she began to make out what had drawn the dog's attention. "It's a litter!" She started to stand.

"Sit down!" the woman commanded, and she sank again to the bottom of the boat, leaning forward hungrily to see who was attached to the litter. Certainly it wouldn't be Maya, yet she felt irrational hope that it could be—and that somehow, she would be alive.

The woman held on to the limb of a downed tree to hold

the boat steady, while Rebecca reached toward the litter, trying to flip it over. She struggled, leaning far beyond the side of the boat, the water streaming over her arm as she grasped the aluminum tubing.

"Be careful it doesn't get caught in the current!" the woman shouted.

Rebecca strained against the rushing water to turn the litter. It flipped over all at once, and she drew away in horror. The man's gray skin was so scraped and tortured it was hard to tell that he *was* a man. Worse, his legs had been sliced off above the knees.

"Oh my God." Rebecca sank back into the boat. "That must have happened when he fell out of the chopper." Could Maya have suffered a similar fate? "The metal cut off his legs."

"Uh-uh." The woman studied the man's injury with a dispassionate eye, as though she saw things like this every day. "Alligator," she said. "An alligator did this."

Oh, no. Rebecca thought of Maya suffering a similar injury, maybe clinging to a downed tree nearby, too exhausted to call out. She hoped the woman was wrong.

They made sure the litter was secured to a tree limb so it wouldn't wash away. Then they continued exploring the stream and the bank, following the current. Rebecca's eyes hurt from trying to pierce the veil of vines and branches. They found shards of metal from the chopper, someone's jacket, a bicycle, several tires. The creek gradually widened as it neared the river, and Rebecca's feeling of helplessness mounted. She watched a short, leafy branch of a tree, little more than a twig, as it was buffeted by the swollen waters. It rose and fell in the frothy stream, slipping ever nearer to the river. She watched it rise over one last bubbling wave before it was propelled into the wide, wild Cape Fear, where it quickly disappeared underwater. The sight made her queasy.

"We need to go back," she said suddenly. "We need to look closer to the crash."

"Look at this river." The woman drew her arm through the air to take in the expanse of water in front of them. "And look how fast this creek is running. Unless it got stuck on something, like that one guy we found, everything from the crash has moved in this direction."

"That 'it' you're talking about is my sister," Rebecca said, but she knew what the woman was saying. She knew it was the terrible truth. Unless Maya had been able to survive the crash, and unless she'd somehow managed to fall from the cabin of the helicopter in a way that didn't kill her, and unless she'd managed to free herself from the racing water, she was out there now. Out in the Cape Fear River.

She lowered her head to her knees, wrapping her arms around her legs. She was so, so tired, and she expected to cry. To *sob*. She was ready for the tears, but they didn't come. Instead, a numbness settled over her, a cold, dead sensation so completely devoid of emotion that it would have frightened her if she could have brought herself to care. She welcomed the numbness. Embraced it. She no longer wanted to feel a thing.

20

Maya

WHAT WAS THAT NOISE? IT RUMBLED INSIDE MY HEAD, SO loud that it made my teeth ache as I typed chart notes at the nurses' station.

"It's cannons!" someone shouted. "They're rolling cannons toward us!"

I peered down the hospital corridor and caught my breath. Yes! Someone was pushing a huge black cannon toward me across the long, rough wooden floor. I tried rolling my chair away from the computer, ready to flee. Where should I go? Where was everyone? I stood up, but wasn't sure I'd be able to run. To *move* at all. My side hurt. My head. Oh my God, my *head!* My chest was on fire and I could barely draw in a breath. And what was wrong with my leg? It felt as though a shark was tearing my shin apart.

The cannon suddenly rammed into the nurses' station, the barrel smacking my temple, and I screamed.

My eyelids snapped open and I knew in a heartbeat I was not in the hospital at all. A dream. A *nightmare*. Light flickered around me. Golden light. Moving away, then coming close enough to make me wince. Above me, I saw the angled wooden beams of a ceiling, and the slant of them made me dizzy. Was I in an attic? Where *was* I?

My body shook uncontrollably, although I was definitely not cold. I was *suffocating*. The shifting golden light sucked all the oxygen from the air, and the hatchet that had split my head in two lodged itself deeper into my skull. The cannon rumbled again, but now I understood. *Thunder.* It was loud, and I pressed my hands to my ears.

I heard a woman's excited voice, the words unintelligible.

"Help," I pleaded, my throat so dry I wasn't certain I'd made a sound. "Help," I said again. I didn't know what sort of help I needed. I wanted only to be freed from the pain. From the suffocating heat.

"I'm right here, ma'am," the woman said. She leaned forward so I could see her in the shimmery light. *The Virgin Mary,* I thought, even though I knew that was irrational. I remembered a picture my parents had in our home when I was very little, back before Daddy talked my mother out of her Catholicism with his intellectual, philosophy professor's arguments. Like Mary in that old picture, this woman had a halo of spun gold around her head.

"Mary." I reached a hand toward her face. I wanted to touch her perfect cheek, gold in the flickering light. Everything, everything was gold, even my hand where I lifted it toward her.

"Is that your name, ma'am?" She was holding a wet cloth to my forehead, where the pain was the worst.

"Thank you," I whispered.

"I bet you're right thirsty," the woman said. "I got a pitcher of water over here, just waitin' for when you waked up." She started to move away and I panicked.

"No," I pleaded. "Don't leave me."

She leaned over me, a look of concern on her face. There was a small scar dissecting her pale left eyebrow. The halo, I saw now, was hair coming loose from a clip or a ponytail. She was young, barely a woman at all. Her eyes, when the flickery light caught them just so, were the color of leaf buds.

"Beautiful eyes." My words were so quiet that even I couldn't hear them. The woman did, though, and she laughed.

"I can't wait t' tell Tully you finally waked up," she said.

Tully? I searched my memory. "Who's Tully?" I rasped.

"Tully brung you here," she said. "He saved your life, ma'am. Miss Mary. We was scared you wasn't going t' come to, but you did. And you're gonna be fine now Lady Alice got that leg stitched up. I know that must've hurt like a bitch, but you was so out of it you hardly griped at all."

The words were coming fast, and they made no sense. "Where am I?" I asked.

"Last Run Shelter," the woman—the girl? Yes, she couldn't have been more than eighteen—said. "Bet you never heard of it."

A crack of thunder split the air in the room, making me jump. There was another noise, too. Drumming. Rain? I stared at the angled rafters above me and knew rain was coming down hard, spiking against the roof a few feet above my head. "I'm not in the airport?" I asked.

"You need another blanket, ma'am? Miss Mary? You're burnin' up, but you're makin' the whole house rock with that shakin' of yours."

"The airport?" I repeated. Where was Adam?

"That chopper you was in," she said. "It crashed over to Billings Creek."

I shut my eyes. *Brace for a crash!* My body jerked with the memory. I looked up at the girl. "The others," I said. "Where are they? There's a nurse. A little boy. And—"

"Hush," the girl said. She turned away, and I wanted to grab her. Keep her close. The gold light flickered in the room, and I saw that it came from a lantern she was carrying.

"Come back," I managed to say.

"I'm right here, ma'am," she said. "Just gettin' you some water. You ain't had none since Tully brung you here."

She helped me raise my head to sip from the glass she was holding, and the hatchet cut more deeply across my temple. Water dribbled down my cheek and the girl brushed it away with warm fingers. I wanted to hold her hand, turn my cheek to press against it.

She drew away a bit to set the glass down.

"You're a doctor?" she asked.

"Yes," I said.

"We figured right, then."

"The others," I said again.

"Hush, now," the girl said. "I'm goin' to git Tully. Let him know you come to. I'll leave the lantern with you. We ain't had no electric since them storms come through." She glanced toward the dark window. "Just what we need, right?" she said. "More rain."

"Don't go," I whispered, but she was already gone. I shut my eyes and slipped into sleep again, as the drumming of the rain and the rumbling of the cannon faded into the distance.

It hit me in the middle of the night—the cramping in my gut that put every other pain in my body into perspective. I struggled to sit up in the pitch-black darkness, one hand grasping the edge of the narrow bed, but I fell back onto the pillow, my head spinning. Even if I could get up, how would I find a bathroom in the dark? I felt my bowels loosen and there wasn't a thing I could do about it besides hope I was in the midst of another bad dream, one I would soon wake up from.

★ ★ ★

Someone was moving my body, turning me first one way, then another. The smell was nearly overwhelming and I tasted bile rising in my throat. I felt a warm rag on the back of my thighs. My bottom. Between my legs. I opened my eyes. The light in the room was entirely different now, lemony and thick. The girl was there, cleaning me as if I were a baby.

"Sorry," I whispered.

"What, ma'am?" the girl asked.

"Sorry," I said again.

I thought I heard her laugh. "It's all right, Miss Mary," she said. "I got you cleaned up good as new, now."

I blinked and absorbed what I could of the room without turning my head, afraid the dizziness would overwhelm me if I did. It was a small cube. A narrow door—a closet?—was on the wall opposite me. One window, the glass cracked on an angle in the lower pane, let in the sun. The walls were covered with faded, ancient-looking wallpaper. Gold diamonds on a cream-colored background. Aside from my cot, the only other furniture was an old dresser, the walnut veneer peeling off the front of the drawers, and what looked like a bassinet made of dingy white wicker, cracked and broken in places. The bassinet was pushed into a corner, as though it had been used many years ago and no longer served a purpose.

I looked back at the girl who was drying my legs with a towel and realized I was nude from the waist down. I didn't care. Nudity was the least of my worries.

"What's your name?" I asked.

"I'm Simmee," the girl said. "And you're Mary."

"No," I said, realizing only then that she'd been calling me by that name. "Not Mary. *Maya*."

"Oh, I thought you said Mary." She smiled. "Well, now, we each got ourselves a funny name, ain't we?" She leaned out of my line of sight for a moment, then stood next to me again. "Lady Alice says I should get you walking," she said. "Ain't good to being layin' down so long, she says. And I need to show you where the bathroom is in case this happens again. I'm puttin' some of my pants on you now, okay, ma'am?"

I felt her lift my left leg, then my right and she slipped soft fabric up to my hips. "You ain't got no shoes, but I think you'll fit in some of mine."

"No shoes?" I said. Where were my shoes?

"I got to wash your pants and things with the sheet," she said. "We ain't got another sheet, so I had to put towels on the bed for you for time bein'."

"Thank you for doing this," I whispered.

"Happy to do it, Miss Maya."

"Simmee," I said, "I need to go back to the airport."

"Can't go nowhere, ma'am." Simmee stood next to the bed, the bundle of foul laundry in her arms. "Floodwaters got us wrapped up tight," she said. "Last Run Shelter's turned into Last Run Island for a spell. I'm afraid you're good and trapped here, just like the rest of us."

21

Rebecca

THEY FLEW BACK TO THE AIRPORT LATE THAT EVENING. Rebecca stared blankly out the window at the darkening sky, the numbness now in every cell of her body. Even when Adam turned to her to ask, "Should we have stayed with the searchers?" she didn't bother to answer him. More searchers were flying in. There was only room in the clearing for two helicopters, and the search and rescue team members who were already there nearly pushed them aboard the blue-and-yellow chopper. The searchers found euphemistic ways of saying that she and Adam would only be in the way; it was time for the professionals to take over. They needed equipment to reach the pilot, they said. They needed another boat. They needed...Rebecca couldn't remember what else they'd said. They pushed her, and she'd allowed it, walking toward the helicopter, unable to feel her feet. Her legs.

"Rebecca?" Adam nudged her, asking again, "Should we have stayed?"

She didn't respond. Just stared out the window, holding tight to the numbness.

The searchers had somehow determined that the pilot was dead. "Most likely killed instantly," one of them had said. So, in fourteen hours of searching, they'd found the pilot, the poor guy who'd been defiled by an alligator and many, many scraps of metal. That meant that four people were still missing. And there was this: thousands of *other* people were still missing. Who knew how many were trapped in their homes? Who knew how many lay underwater on their streets and in their yards? Rebecca didn't want to hear anyone say, "Why spend all these resources on four missing people when thousands are still unaccounted for?" She didn't want to hear it. She didn't want to think about that delicate leafy branch as it dipped and danced in the rushing water of the stream on its way to the river, where it had been instantly, irrevocably, lost. And so she didn't think. She didn't think about anything at all.

When they reached the airport, she went directly to the urgent-care tent, leaving Adam to update Dorothea on their day. She dug into her work, glad to be with patients who didn't know or care who she was and what had happened. They cared only about themselves and, in many cases, about one another, because there was a contagious kindness among these people now. The more trapped they felt, the more their injuries festered, and the more frightened they became, the more they seemed to sense they were in this together. She witnessed the kindness as a woman offered the last half of her bottle of water to an elderly man. As a young man held a stranger's feverish child on his lap. She wanted to be with these hurting people. She was one of them now. Maybe she could help them even if she couldn't help herself.

Sometime in the middle of the night, Rebecca spotted Dorothea walking through the tent toward her, and a moment of sheer terror broke through the numbness at the sight of her.

"No news," Dorothea said quickly. Then she drew Rebecca away from her patient, despite her protests. "I've sent Adam to bed," she said. "And I want you to go up now, too."

"I'm fine here." Rebecca couldn't meet Dorothea's gaze. Instead she looked at the line of exhausted, sweating, sick and injured patients.

"No, you're not," Dorothea said. "I insist you get some sleep. I'll get one of the fresh DMAT docs to take over here."

Rebecca looked at her then. "Don't make me go," she said. Her voice sounded wounded to her own ears, but she steadied herself, clinging hard to the numbness.

Dorothea looked defeated. "I'm worried about you," she said.

"Don't be."

"Two more hours." Dorothea looked at her watch. "That's it. Then you're going to sleep."

Rebecca nodded noncommittally, then headed back to her canvas-walled cubicle.

Hours later, she was examining the tender belly of a teenage girl when everything changed. Early-morning light turned the canvas tent walls a pale yellow, and all at once, the numbness left her with such suddenness that she gasped. Everything around her snapped into focus: The moaning African-American girl on the cot. The worn green flip-flops on the girl's feet. Her own pale fingers where she pressed them against the girl's dark skin. The tray of instruments at her side. *Snap, snap!* She lifted her hands from the girl as if she'd been burned. Rushing from the cubicle, she grabbed a nurse by the arm.

"Gotta get out!" she said. "Girl with lower right quad-rant—" She couldn't finish the sentence. She ran through the tent, then through the sea of evacuees waiting for their turn inside. She ran through the lobby and the long corridor and the concourse crowded with people who had nowhere to go. Pushing open one of the gate doors, she raced down the stairs and out onto the tarmac, where the roar of the choppers coming and going filled her head. At the wall of the building, she bent forward and screamed and screamed and screamed, letting the choppers steal the sound of her voice, until she had no voice left to steal.

22

Maya

I KNEW I HAD A FEVER EVEN BEFORE I OPENED MY EYES. MY mind was logy, thick with the heat, and I was soaked with perspiration. The room was filled with rosy light, and I guessed it must be close to dusk. I must have slept for hours. I remembered waking up long enough to check the wound on my leg. There it was—a gash nearly the length of my shin that someone named Duchess Alice or Queen Alice had stitched closed with thick thread. The skin around it was hot and red, and I knew I was in trouble. Deep trouble, in too many ways to count. At least one of my ribs was broken. It ached when I took in a breath and made me yelp when I changed position on the bed. My head had a throbbing lump near my right temple and the hair above my ear felt stiff to the touch. *Blood.*

I'd awakened one other time to use the small bathroom with its cracked blue wall tile and rust-stained tub. My intestines still grumbled, but the worst was over. *The water,* I thought, remembering the glass of water the girl—Simmee?—had given me. *I can't drink any more of that water.*

I got out of the bed, straightening the ragged old towels I'd been lying on. Opening the door of the room, I walked into the dark, narrow hallway. So far, I'd seen only that hallway and the bathroom across from the room where I was staying. Where was I? What had Simmee called it? A shelter? I only remembered bits and pieces of my brief conversation with her.

The dizziness teased me, and I had to brace myself against the walls as I walked down the short hallway. I was barefoot. Where were my shoes? The hallway opened into a small kitchen. I had the feeling everything about the house was small. I leaned against the doorjamb in the kitchen, keeping my breathing as shallow as I possibly could to avoid the pain in my rib cage.

The kitchen was a pale pink, the sort of soft pink someone might use in the room of a baby girl. The appliances—a short, round-shouldered refrigerator and an electric stove—looked ancient. A small rectangular table surrounded by four chairs sat in the corner near the screen door.

A second open doorway stood to my left, and I headed for it. I found myself in a living room full of mismatched furniture far too big for the space. The sofa was a broad brown-and-cream plaid, its cushions sagging. A green floral chair, overstuffed and missing one ball leg, tilted in the corner behind an ottoman. A dark brown prefab wall unit held a small TV that I doubted still worked now that TVs had gone digital. The wood-plank floor was covered by an oval rag rug. Despite the shoddy furnishings, the room was neat and uncluttered. I walked across the room—it took me only four steps—to peer through the two curtainless, shadeless windows. Outside, I could see only the deep green of shrubs that blocked all but a few rays of pink sunlight from entering the room.

I turned around to head back to the kitchen, and that's when I saw the guns. I caught my breath, grabbing the edge of the tilted chair to steady myself. The two guns were propped against the wall near the living room door. Were they rifles? Shotguns? I didn't know the difference. The only type of gun that would be forever branded in my brain was the Colt automatic that had killed my parents.

I wanted to get out of that house. I needed to get back to the airport and Rebecca and Adam.

"Simmee?" I called as I walked into the kitchen again, but my voice sounded as though I hadn't used it in months. I pulled open the screen door, nearly falling down the two concrete steps that led into...not a yard, exactly. More of a jungle. The world outside the house was so green that it made me woozy, and I had to hang on to the rusted iron railing that jutted from the steps. The brush and woods were wildly overgrown, and the trees seemed to cradle the house with their branches. I was in a suffocating green cage. Ahead of me and to the right, though, I could see a path through the undergrowth. It was narrow and uneven, carpeted with sandy white soil and criss-crossed with tree roots. It entered the tangle of green at a vertigo-inducing angle, inclined a little, then veered to the left out of my line of sight. My stomach heaved just looking at it. I lowered myself to the top step and closed my eyes.

"Well, hey, Miss Maya."

It was a man's voice. I forced my eyes open, and saw Simmee and a young guy walking toward me from the path.

I gripped the railing and tried to stand, but the muscles in my legs wouldn't cooperate. It was like trying to stand on limp spaghetti.

The guy rushed forward. "Easy, now," he said, offering me his hand. I leaned hard against him as I rose to my bare feet. "Let's get you back inside," he said. "Sim, you get the door. That's a girl."

Simmee opened the screen door for us, and the man helped me into the kitchen. He pulled out one of the chairs from the table, and I sank into it, letting out my breath. I tried to smile at them. "I'm a mess," I said.

"Oh, no, Miss Maya," Simmee said. She opened one of the cabinets and pulled down a plastic glass. "You're just beat up somethin' fierce."

The man grinned at me, his arms folded across his chest as he leaned against the side of the old refrigerator. "Well, all I can say is it's good to see you among the living." He studied me with a curious smile. "You don't remember meeting me this mornin'," he said. "Do I got that right?"

I shut my eyes, trying to sort memory from dream. He didn't look familiar, but I did vaguely remember seeing a man in the doorway of the room where I'd slept. "Begins with a T," I said, looking at him again. He was staggeringly handsome. Mid-twenties, maybe, and very fair. Blue eyes. Blond hair. He had a strong, square chin and a broad chest beneath a black T-shirt. Gold hair shimmered like sunlight on his forearms.

The guns, I thought. *The guns are his.*

Simmee filled a glass with water from the faucet. "This here's my husband, Tully," she said. "He's the one that saved you."

I had so many questions for him. Where did he find me? Where were the other people from the helicopter? But all I could seem to manage was, "I need to get to the airport."

"Here you go, now, Miss Maya," Simmee said, handing me the glass. "You need to drink. You're all dried out inside."

My hand shook so violently as I tried to take the glass that Simmee had to hold it to my lips. I suddenly remembered my bout of diarrhea and pushed her hand away. "The water," I said. "Where is it from?"

Simmee looked surprised. "The tap, of course." She pointed to the sink.

I shook my head. "I think maybe that's what made me sick during the night."

"You sayin' our water's no good?" Tully smiled, and I was relieved that his voice was teasing.

"I...maybe because of the storm?" I guessed. "Or maybe you all are just used to it and my system's not. Do you have any bottled water?" I looked around the kitchen as though I might spot a bottle of Dasani or Aquafina, and knew the quest was ludicrous.

Simmee and Tully both laughed. "Water's perfectly fine here, ma'am," Tully said. "But hey, Sim. Check them bags I found with her. I saw some bottles of water in one of 'em." He pointed beneath the table. I leaned over, wincing at the pain in my rib, and saw my backpack along with a couple of duffel bags on the floor. I felt as though I'd bumped into a friend in a foreign country. In an instant, though, the real-life nightmare came back to me.

Brace for a crash!

I remembered dropping like a stone, my hands pressed against the window of the helicopter, the treetops coming closer, closer, the litters pressing hard against my legs.

"Oh," I said weakly, as I sat up straight again, rubbing my temple in confusion. "Where *is* everyone?" I searched Tully's face as Simmee bent over for the baggage. "The people who own these other bags? Where are they?"

"Let me get them, honey," Tully said to Simmee, gently moving her aside. "Down too low for you." He scooted the other chair out of the way, drew the bags from beneath the table and slid them in front of the stove. They stank of fetid water.

I hated the way he avoided my question, but right then, I was hungry for what I had in my backpack. I pointed toward it. "I have pills in there to sterilize water," I said, glancing from Tully to Simmee. "And antibiotics. I have a fever. I think…" I stopped myself from saying the wound on my leg was infected, which it most certainly was. I didn't want to insult them again.

Simmee handed me the backpack, and for the first time, I realized she was pregnant. *Quite* pregnant. She wore a loose, sleeveless dress, but still. How had I missed that round belly?

The pack was wet and smelly beneath my fingers as I struggled to open the clasp. My hands trembled from hours— days?—without food or water, except for that one glassful that had gone straight through me. I finally managed to flip open the top of the bag and reach inside.

"You're a doctor, right?" Tully asked from the doorway as I pulled a bottle of water from the backpack, uncapped it and drank. My stomach balked, and I forced myself to pause in my drinking.

"Yes," I said, remembering that Simmee had asked the same question. "How did you know?"

"All the stuff that was with you on the chopper. I looked through some of them bags for identification. Saw all the first-aid stuff."

"Where are the others?" I asked as I unzipped the plastic bag that held the antibiotics. I shook two capsules from one of the bottles and swallowed them with the rest of my water. "Where are the people who were with me on the helicopter?"

Tully scooted the second chair closer to me, turned it around and straddled it. "Ma'am," he said, "I'm sorry to tell you this, but I believe you was the only one that made it out of that bird alive."

"Oh, no." I remembered my patient, the little boy, as clearly as if I'd seen him only moments earlier. I remembered Janette, the nurse. "Are you sure?" I asked. "Did you find me…where did you find me?"

"Ma'am—Miss Maya—we had some serious floodin' from these sister storms. I was out in my johnboat on Billings Creek checking out the damage and I saw the chopper. It was stuck in some trees. Not real high up. Looked like it broke a bunch of branches and come to rest maybe fifteen, twenty feet from the ground. The side was tore off and y'all fell out. Like you wasn't strapped in."

"We weren't," I whispered.

"I climbed up and could see a lady… Was the pilot a girl?"

I'd forgotten that. I nodded. The motion sent my head spinning again.

"Well, she was still in her seat, but she was…" Tully shook his head. "She passed," he said quietly. "Everything from the plane was on the ground, half in the water, like."

"She don't need to know everythin'," Simmee said quietly.

"I want to know," I said. "There were three patients and a nurse besides the pilot and me. You didn't see any of them?"

"No, ma'am. The water was right swift. You wouldn't believe it. Usually just a trickle through there. Only thing that saved you was you got caught in the branches and whatnot on the bank. You and these here bags. It's a miracle you landed where you did or you wouldn't be here. And a miracle I got to you when I did, 'cause that water was still rising."

Why me? I thought, starting to tremble again. *Why did I live and not the others?*

Simmee leaned close to me, resting her arm around my shoulders. "You was meant to live," she said softly, as if privy to my thoughts. She smelled of powder or laundry soap or something clean and beautiful. How she could stand being so close to me and my stench, I didn't know.

"Thank you for rescuing me," I said to Tully, my voice thick. I clutched my rancid backpack to my chest. "I'm with DIDA," I said. "That's a doctors' relief organization and we're working out of the airport in Wilmington. I need to get back there."

He shook his head. "The water...it's been crazy. It was already way higher than normal, but it come up even higher overnight and washed my johnboat away. Snapped the rope where it was tied to the dock. Ain't never happened before. We was already cut off from the mainland. We can't go nowhere till the water goes down or we get our hands on another boat."

Trapped. I remembered the word Simmee had used to describe our predicament.

"Is this an island?" I asked.

"Not usually," Simmee said. "But it is right now."

"This here is Last Run Shelter," Tully said. "It's connected to the mainland by a skinny ol' strip of land. When it floods, we're usually stranded for a few days. Maybe a week at most. But I ain't never seen it flood like this."

"Me, neither," Simmee said, "and I lived here all my life."

"How far is it to the Wilmington airport?" I asked.

"As the crow flies, about fifty miles," Tully said, "but there ain't no crows that can carry you."

"Well..." I looked around the kitchen. "Can I use your phone?"

Simmee laughed. "We ain't got a phone."

"I had a BlackBerry—a cell phone—with me." I started digging through my backpack again. "The cell towers were down, but maybe they're back up by now." I pulled medical supplies, a flashlight, batteries and two MREs out of my bag, setting them on the table. "My phone's not here," I said.

"Maybe it fell out?" Tully suggested.

I remembered Dorothea running toward me with the pack

as I was loading the little boy on the chopper. Maybe it had fallen out then.

I looked at Tully in frustration. "Is it possible…I know you've already done a lot for me, but could you go back to where the helicopter went down and wait there for help to come? Or at least leave a note saying where I am?"

"Not without a boat," Simmee said.

"People will be looking for me," I said. "My sister's a doctor with DIDA. My husband, too. They'll be looking for me." My voice broke. "How will they find me?"

"You're alive, ma'am," Simmee reminded me, and I knew she was telling me I should feel grateful for that fact. "Everything else'll sort itself out in good time."

"I know," I conceded, but only momentarily. "Maybe one of your neighbors has a boat? Or at least a phone?"

"Us and Lady Alice are the only ones stubborn enough to live out here," Simmee said. "And Lady Alice ain't got no boat. No phone, neither."

"Who's Lady Alice?" I asked. *The one who screwed up my shin,* I remembered.

"Just our neighbor." Tully stood up and stretched.

"She lives through the woods that way." Simmee pointed out the window. "I fetched her when Tully brung you here 'cause she knows some things about doctorin'."

"She's not a real doctor like you," Tully said. "But she stitched you up good, right?"

I nodded. My shin was on fire and I hoped the antibiotics would kick in quickly. I drained the rest of my water, then rooted through the Baggies looking for the water purification tablets. "If you'll give me a pitcher," I said, "I'll use these tablets to make some water that'll be safe for me to drink."

"Sure." Simmee reached into one of the cupboards and

pulled out a plastic pitcher. I started to get to my feet. "No," she said, her hand briefly on my shoulder. "You set." She filled the pitcher with water and handed it to me. I wasn't sure how many tablets to add to it. I'd never used them before and never thought I'd actually need to. I dropped one into the pitcher and hoped for the best.

"Thanks," I said.

Simmee moved to her husband's side, and Tully put his arm around her.

"She's gonna be a good mama, ain't she?" he asked, but he wasn't really talking to me and I knew it. He was talking to the air. To the heavens. To whatever force had put him together with the beautiful, kind and ethereal creature at his side.

I thought of how she'd cared for me. Cleaned me up. Dressed me. "She will be," I agreed.

I watched as Tully leaned over as though he might kiss Simmee's cheek. Instead, he breathed in the spun gold of her halo, and for a moment, I forgot about being afraid. Instead I felt touched. Touched and, finally, truly, grateful.

23
Rebecca

THEY SAT ON LOST LUGGAGE IN A SMALL ROOM NEAR THE tents in the baggage-claim area. Adam leaned forward from his perch on a huge chestlike suitcase, elbows on his knees, and looked at her without speaking. His eyes were red. At some point, he'd found the time and privacy to cry. Rebecca hadn't seen him give into it, but then she'd been asleep for four hours, thanks to the Valium Dorothea had forced on her. She'd taken the pill without a fuss, knowing it offered her the only chance at sleep, and without a few hours downtime, she'd be of no value to anyone. And she wanted to be of value. It was the only cure for the unaccustomed helplessness she felt and the only way she could keep her mind off Maya's fate.

Had it happened quickly, so quickly Maya'd felt no fear? She vacillated between hoping her sister was still alive in the woods, and hoping she'd been killed on impact, the way the searchers had assumed the pilot had died.

Now, she sat across the small room from Adam on a network of soft-sided suitcases she'd arranged so that they formed a sort of recliner. This was a fitting room for the two of them, she thought. Lost luggage. Lost people.

The upper portion of one wall of the room was made of glass, and Adam abruptly sat up straight, peering through it. "Here comes Dot," he said, getting to his feet.

Rebecca rose awkwardly to find that her legs were asleep. She sat down again with a thud as Adam opened the door.

"No news," Dorothea said before either of them could ask.

"Give me the phone again," Rebecca whispered, reaching toward Dorothea. She'd lost her voice since her screaming episode early that morning. Dorothea pulled the satellite phone from its holster and handed it to her.

Rebecca yanked the antenna to its full length and dialed Maya's number, while Adam and Dorothea waited patiently for her to act out the charade.

You've reached Dr. Maya Ward.

Rebecca pressed her lips together at the sound of Maya's voice. She wanted to dial the number over and over again, as if hearing Maya *sound* so alive could somehow make her *be* alive. She felt Dot and Adam's eyes on her, though, and handed the phone back to Dorothea. "When's the last time you heard from the S and R team?" she asked.

"Half an hour ago." Dorothea lowered herself to the one chair in the room. "They've been good about staying in touch, but they have zilch to report. They airlifted the pilot and the other body out of—"

"They're searching the woods, too, right?" Rebecca interrupted. It hurt to talk and she rubbed her throat. "I mean, not just the water."

Dorothea nodded. "They have searchers and dogs in the woods," she said. "I'm confident they're doing a good job, babe." She slapped her hands on her knees, straightening her back. "Now," she said, shifting to her don't-give-me-any-crap voice, "I want the two of you to go home."

"No," they answered together. They'd talked about it when Rebecca woke up from her Valium-laced sleep. They were not going anywhere. It was the one good thing—the *only* good thing about this whole mess: she and Adam were on the same page.

"We're not leaving," Adam said, and he sat down on the chest again as if planting himself in the room. "I feel closer to her here. I can't go back to our house right now. I'd go crazy." He shook his head. "I want to be where I'm needed."

"Same here," whispered Rebecca.

"Why am I not surprised?" Dorothea said. "Will you at least take the rest of today off? Just…chill. Talk. Do whatever you need to—"

"We're working," Rebecca said, and she knew she was speaking for both of them.

"Either we're working here or we're going back to the crash site," Adam said to Dorothea. "Pick your poison."

Dorothea sighed. "Okay," she said. "You win. But pay attention to yourselves and each other. If either of you feels like you're going down, come to me. Tell me. You don't have to be superheroes." She got to her feet. "We're going to make some major changes here in the next couple of days," she said.

"How so?" Adam asked.

"They've got one of the roads cleared. Had to lift a couple of huge boats off it, if you can believe that. So they're opening one of the Wilmington high schools as the new evacuation center, and we'll be setting up a clinic there. FEMA and the Red Cross'll bring in cots and supplies. The roads leading to Wilmington are still iffy, but they're bringing in buses from somewhere and tomorrow they'll start moving the evacuees over. We'll gradually shut down operations here and move over there."

"Do they have power?" Rebecca asked.

Dorothea shook her head. "No. They're bringing in extra generators and they'll take these over. There's a cafeteria there, of course, but it'll still be MREs unless the power comes back on."

Rebecca pictured a high school. There'd be a gym. An auditorium. Classrooms. She could see the possibilities. "How will it be set up?" she asked. "Will we use—"

"Babe, forget the administrative stuff, okay?" Dorothea said. "We have other folks who can take care of that. Focus on the medical."

"So we'll actually get cots?" Adam smiled, and Rebecca wondered how he managed to raise the corners of his lips. "I'm going to miss the conference-room floor."

"Well, here's even better news," Dorothea said. "They're moving trailers into the high school parking lot for the volunteers. We're cramming four people to a trailer, but if you don't mind sharing, you can have one to yourselves."

Rebecca looked at Adam and gave him a nod.

"Fine," Adam said.

"No problem," Rebecca agreed. She wanted Adam close by. The only thing that made this nightmare bearable was knowing she was not in it alone.

24

Maya

WHEN I WOKE UP THE FOLLOWING MORNING, I WAS FILLED WITH panic even before I opened my eyes. I was trapped on an island with strangers, surrounded by water that, for all I knew, might still be rising, and I felt horribly, dizzily nauseous and disoriented. I'd slept most of the day before, turning down the canned peaches Simmee had offered me sometime during the evening, but I'd had plenty of the chemical-tasting water. I wasn't sure if that was the cause of my roiling stomach or if fear was the culprit. It was far better to wake up here, with two caring people, than alone on the creek bank, I told myself. The thought that I might have regained consciousness in the wilderness with floodwaters cresting over my face did nothing to decrease my sense of panic. I hoped the others had been dead before the water reached them.

Sheets were once again beneath me on the bed, and I couldn't remember how they got there. Dappled sunlight shimmered across the gold-and-cream wallpaper, and dust motes danced in the air near the windows. Carefully, I sat up, my body like a dry old board that cracked and splintered as it bent. I put my feet on the floor and waited for the dizziness to pass before standing up. On the old dresser, my DIDA uniform pants and T-shirt were neatly folded, along with a pair of panties that did not belong to me. I guessed that mine had been beyond saving. Next to the clothing was a pair of old tennis shoes. I needed to wash. No way would I put on these clean clothes while I still stank of swamp and sweat. I left the room and crossed the hall to the bathroom.

There was a small curtained shower stall in the corner of the bathroom, but I didn't dare risk using it. Between my light-headedness and the long wound on my shin, a shower could only do me harm. I did my best to wash in the sink, then dressed in my clean clothes. Simmee's shoes were an excellent fit, although if I had to do any walking, I'd miss my orthotics. They were pretty low on my list of things to worry about.

In the corner of the shower, I found a big bottle of shampoo and I carried it and a threadbare towel into the kitchen where I leaned over the rust-scarred sink, turned on the water and squirted shampoo onto my hair. I gingerly rubbed the blood-caked area above my ear, not wanting it to start bleeding again. Bending over was excruciating. My broken rib felt as though it was slicing into my lung, and lifting my arms over my head only made it worse. I thought of giving up, but I already had the shampoo in my hair. As I let the water flow over my scalp, I thought of how Adam and Rebecca must have felt when they realized I was missing. Did they think I was dead? *Oh, God.* I couldn't bear the thought of what they were going through. If only I could get word to them that I was all right!

"Let me."

I started at the sound of Simmee's voice, the back of my head knocking into the faucet.

"Easy," she said, as she ran her fingers through my hair. "Go on now. Put your arms down."

I lowered my soapy hands to the edge of the sink and closed my eyes.

Simmee turned off the water as she worked the lather into my hair. "We need to watch how much water we use," she said. "We got a big ol' holdin' tank under the house, but who knows how long the electric'll be out, and we can't get water out of the well without it."

"I'm sorry," I said, realizing I'd used up some of their limited water supply.

"Oh, no matter," she said. "This has got to be killin' your back, leanin' over like this. And you got this big ol' goose egg on the side of your head, don't you? Didn't even know you had that. Does it hurt?"

"A little," I said.

"I'll make short work of this," Simmee said, and I felt the firm orb of her belly pressing against my side as she rinsed the shampoo from my hair. She turned off the water and wrapped the towel around my head. "There you go," she said. "Watch your head on this here faucet when you stand up."

"Thank you." I straightened up slowly, leaning against the sink for support. I tried smiling at her as I blotted my hair with the towel. "I couldn't stand the way I…how filthy I felt."

"I bet." Simmee dried her hands on a kitchen towel, then studied me hard. "You're shakin' all over," she said. "You need to eat somethin'. We had t' eat all the icebox food days ago so it didn't rot, but I got them canned peaches I told you about. I got all kinds of canned food, actually. And eggs." She pointed to the table, and I saw a small basket of eggs in the center.

"Where did you get them?" I asked.

"Our chickens," she said, then grinned. "Get 'em every morning, whether we want 'em or not. Let me cook you up some."

I glanced at the old electric stove. "How?" I asked.

"We got a grill in the yard," she said. "Got a smoker out there, too." She pulled one of the chairs from beneath the table. "You sit," she said. "You're rattlin' the walls with that shakin'."

I was so weak from the little I'd done that morning that I nearly fell into the chair. I wasn't hungry, but knew I needed to eat. "All right," I said. "Eggs'll be great."

She brought breakfast to me in the living room, so I could sit on the three-legged overstuffed chair and elevate my leg on the ottoman. She'd made three perfect eggs, sunny-side up, and I managed to get two of them down before my stomach balked. I even drank half a cup of the coffee that Tully'd brewed on the grill.

"I don't like coffee, myself," Simmee said. She sat on the plaid sofa, and I had the feeling she enjoyed watching me eat, the way a mother might take pleasure in nursing her child back to health. "Tully, now," Simmee continued, "that boy can drink a bucket of coffee three times a day."

"Where *is* Tully," I asked. I hadn't seen him since the night before.

"Huntin'," she said. "He'll git us somethin' for supper."

I glanced toward the door where I remembered seeing the guns. Only one was propped against the wall now.

"What does he hunt?" I asked. I didn't have a single friend who hunted, and it had always struck me as barbaric. Right now, though, I could see how useful his hunting skills could be.

"Oh, everythin'," she said with a shrug. "Rabbit. Turkey. Sometimes deer. He fishes a lot, too, but he don't like it as much without the boat." She laughed. "Tully loves it when the power goes out, though," she said. "He plays like he's on that survivor show."

"You're lucky to have him, then," I said.

"Yes, ma'am, I am."

I set my plate with its one remaining egg on the wobbly table next to my wobbly chair. "Simmee," I said, "I need to figure out how to get back to the airport." I looked at her almost apologetically. She was so nice and I felt as though I was insulting her hospitality with my need to escape. "That skinny strip of land Tully was talking about…could someone wade across it to the mainland?"

Simmee's eyes widened. "Oh, no, ma'am," she said. "It's way too deep, and even if it wasn't, there's a bad current. It'd sweep you off your feet in no time. You ain't got no idea how bad the crick is right now."

I looked at her helplessly. "What am I going to *do?*" I asked.

She shrugged. "Patience is golden," she said, not unkindly.

"Right." I sighed. My shin burned and I leaned forward to pull up my pant leg. The wound was still red and swollen around the black stitches, but I thought it looked a little better.

"Lady Alice been sewing us up a long time," Simmee said. "Sewed up Tully's foot one time. He screamed bloody bejeezus while she was doin' it, too. He ain't as tough as he looks, sometime."

"And your eyebrow?" I touched my own eyebrow in the exact spot where Simmee's was split in two.

"Yes." She shivered, at the memory I supposed. "We had ice last winter, and I slipped gettin' firewood. Tully was out and I was bleedin' to death, practically, and had to slip and slide over to Lady Alice's tryin' to hold a rag to my head the whole time." She touched her scar with her fingertips. "Lady Alice, she boils the thread and needle and cleans her hands with this special soap she saves just for sewin' people up."

"Is she...royalty?" I asked.

"What's that mean, 'royalty'?"

"Well, why do you call her Lady Alice?"

Simmee shrugged again. "That's her name. Lady Alice Harnett. The name she was born with. Lady Alice, I mean. Harnett's what she married into. Don't know what her other name was."

"Where does she live?"

"Right close," Simmee said. "We'll visit her when you're good enough to walk."

Oh, no we won't, I thought. I planned to be home in Raleigh long before my leg was healed.

"Lady Alice and my gran was friends when they was comin' up," Simmee said. "They didn't have no schools for black kids here back then, but my gran would teach Lady Alice things. Even though Gran only made it to fifth grade herself."

Lady Alice was black. I realized I'd been picturing a woman who resembled Queen Elizabeth.

"So..." I tried to puzzle out how Simmee and Tully came to live in this remote area. "You grew up here?"

"Sure did. So did my mama and my gran. And Gran's kin, too. They was moonshiners, which is how Last Run got its name. Gran brung me up after my mama died. Then a couple years ago, Gran died, too." Simmee looked past me, as though she could see her grandmother standing behind me. I nearly turned to look. "You're stayin' in her room," she said, returning her gaze to mine. "She was sick a while. Bad lungs. Hope that don't spook you, sleepin' where she died."

"No, of course not," I said. "I'm grateful to have anyplace at all. I'm sorry you lost her, though."

"Yeah," she said. "I miss her."

"Did you go to school?" I asked.

She looked, I thought, a little insulted by my question. "Of course," she said. "I got through ninth grade, but that's when Gran took sick and she needed me to stay home."

"Did Tully grow up here, too?"

"Oh, no. He showed up about a year before Gran died. He lived in a tent."

"Really!"

"He's just one of them outdoorsman types. Amazin' I can even get him to sleep in the house."

"How long have you two been married?" I asked.

"Oh, we're not married the church way or nothin'." She picked at the fabric on the sofa cushion. "Someday maybe, but it don't matter to me. We're like common law. We been together a couple years. Practically since he come to Last Run."

"How old are you?" I asked.

"Seventeen."

And they'd been together nearly a couple of years? The words *statutory rape* slipped into my mind. I knew more than I wanted to about statutory rape. Maybe out here, people didn't worry about that sort of thing. Besides, it was clear Tully loved her. I remembered the way he'd inhaled the scent of her hair the night before. *She's gonna be a good mama, ain't she?*

"How long *you* been married?" Simmee asked.

"Three years." I wanted to be with Adam right that second. I thought of how warmly he'd treated me in the airport. It had given me hope, even though we'd carefully tiptoed around any loaded topics. No talk of babies. Definitely no talk of adoption. "His name's Adam," I said.

"You got kids?"

"Unfortunately, no."

"Maybe that's good, though." Simmee smoothed her hand

over her belly. She was wearing the same dress she'd had on the day before, and the fabric was stretched taut across her middle. "They'd be right scared now, with you missing."

Simmee was the sort of pregnant woman artists painted, all light and airy and golden. She was the sort of pregnant woman I used to look at with envy, longing for that gravid belly, for the baby inside. But I felt no longing, looking at Simmee. I felt only sadness, because I no longer trusted my own body to carry a baby to term.

"When is your baby due?" I asked.

"I don't know exactly." Simmee smiled down at her belly as if she could see her future son or daughter there.

"Didn't the doctor give you a due date?" I asked.

Simmee drew little curlicues across her belly with her fingertips. "I ain't seen one." She studied the invisible design she was making instead of looking at me, as though she knew I wouldn't approve of her answer.

"Not even...not at all?" I asked.

"No, ma'am," she said. "Lady Alice says I'm healthy and the baby's healthy. Kicks like a trapped possum, I swear. Lady Alice had eight kids, so she knows all about it." She looked directly at me again. "All I care about is that it's healthy," she said. "That's the only thing."

"Will you go to the hospital to have it?"

"We ain't got money for no hospital," Simmee said.

"Well, there are ways to have the birth and your care covered."

She drew more invisible curlicues on the fabric of her dress. "Lady Alice'll take care of it," she said. "Deliverin' it, I mean."

"Is she...is Lady Alice a midwife?"

"What's that?"

"A midwife. Someone trained and licensed to deliver babies."

Simmee gave me a patient look. "Well, I guess after eight

babies of her own and deliverin' plenty more, she's trained good enough," she said with a smile. But there was something behind the smile, I thought. Something that made the hair on the back of my neck stand on end.

Something a little like fear.

25

Rebecca

THE HELICOPTER LANDED ON THE ATHLETIC FIELD OF A ONE-story-high school that looked as though it might have been built in the late fifties or early sixties. Climbing out of the chopper with Adam, ducking low as they moved quickly onto the open field, Rebecca felt as though she'd been born around that same time. She'd aged a good ten years in the past few days. She looked at the track that circled the field, hoping she'd have time to run later. She *had* to run. Had to keep herself centered. They had so much to do. They had to make sure things were set up properly in the school, treat the incoming evacuees, and most critically, stay on top of the search efforts. They needed to make sure Maya's case didn't get lost in the sea of missing persons.

"Where are the trailers?" Adam asked as the chopper rose into the sky above them.

Rebecca lit a cigarette, then pointed toward the school. "Probably on the other side," she said.

"Hey!" A teenage girl wearing an orange Day-Glo vest called to them from the side of the field. "Are you Adam and Rebecca?"

"Yes!" Adam shouted.

The girl approached them at a trot. Her brown hair was in a little flip that bounced with each step. "I'm one of the volunteers," she said as she neared them. "I'm going to take you to your trailer." She did an about-face and set out a few yards ahead of them, and Rebecca and Adam followed wordlessly behind her, lugging their duffel bags. It was blistering hot on the field, and Rebecca was drenched with sweat by the time they'd walked around the far corner of the concession stand and the parking lot came into view. A white brick wall bordering the lot proclaimed Welcome—Viking Territory! Five trailers were already parked close to the building, and two trucks were in the process of towing in a couple more.

"What's the chance of air-conditioning?" Adam asked Rebecca.

"Good chance." She pointed to the generator sitting behind the trailers. "Our own little source of power. Hallelujah." She'd stayed in trailers before, ones nearly identical to the simple white tin cans in front of them. The trailers were cramped and Spartan, but there would be electricity they'd have to be careful not to abuse, and there would be actual beds, a luxury after the floor of the airport. Not that she expected to be able to sleep.

The girl turned to smile brightly at them, pointing to the trailer closest to the school. "There's pizza inside for you," she said.

Adam hiked his bag higher on his shoulder. "You're kidding." The stubble on his cheeks and chin could almost be called a beard now, and Rebecca thought it looked good on him.

"Donated by a local place that wasn't damaged," the girl said. "They sent some over for you two and for the rest of us who are setting up stuff in the school. It's been there a while, so it'll be a little cold, but still—"

"That's great," Rebecca said. The volunteer was too perky

for her to deal with. She wanted to get inside the trailer and dump her duffel bag. She needed to get her bearings and figure out what to do next. "Do you have a key?" she asked.

"It's in the door. Two of them on a chain. And I don't think you're supposed to smoke in there." She pointed to Rebecca's cigarette.

Rebecca considered blowing a smoke ring in her face, but thought better of it. "Where I smoke is none of your business," she said.

"Smoke's going to come out of her *ears* if you don't watch it," Adam warned the girl, though his voice was light and kind.

"I'm just *saying*," the girl said. "And I'm supposed to give you a message from Dorothea Ludlow."

Rebecca stopped walking, her muscles suddenly tight. "What?"

"She said to tell you that you're just supposed to get settled into the trailer this afternoon and not go over to the school."

Rebecca let out her breath and exchanged a look with Adam. Beneath the beard, his face was the same white as the trailer, and she knew that the last two seconds had stolen the color from her face as well.

"Okay, fine." Rebecca started walking again.

They reached the trailer and she turned the key in the lock, then looked over her shoulder at the volunteer. "Thanks," she said. "We're good."

"Miss Ludlow said she'll be pissed off if she finds out you went over to the school."

Rebecca stared daggers at the little twit.

Adam took the girl's arm and walked a distance away from the trailer with her. "We know Dorothea," Rebecca heard him tell her, "and we're not afraid of her being p.o.'d, but thanks for letting us know."

The girl hesitated, but finally seemed to realize her job was finished. "Okay." She sounded chipper, then added as she walked toward the school, "Thanks for volunteering!"

Rebecca crushed her cigarette beneath her shoe before climbing into the trailer. She took two steps to one of the narrow settees on either side of the small, built-in table and flopped down. "Thanks for preventing me from killing her," she said as Adam followed her inside.

He smiled. "No prob." He raked a hand through her short hair as if she were his kid sister. "Bet she's a cheerleader," he said. "I thought all that bubbliness was kind of cute." He pulled a couple of bottles of water from his duffel bag and tossed one to her.

"I thought it was kind of insufferable." She watched as Adam looked to the right, where the double bed was tucked into one end of the trailer, and to the left, toward the long built-in couch that would serve as the second bed.

"Has a little cottage charm," he lied as he sat down across from her. He was sweet, and she regretted her bitchiness.

"Better than the conference room," she said.

A pizza box and two paper plates rested on the table between them, and Adam lifted the lid to peer inside. "I think this is the first time in my life that the smell of pizza is turning my stomach."

"Mine, too." She raised the lid higher and frowned at the cheese pizza. She lifted a slice, so cold that it came away cleanly from its neighbors, and took a bite. It may as well have been cardboard. "I can't taste a thing," she said. She had a jarring realization. She'd worked in dozens of disaster zones and had never lost her appetite or her sense of taste. As a matter of fact, she'd usually been ravenous. You *had* to be ravenous to enjoy MREs. But for weeks after her parents died, she couldn't taste or smell. She'd lost twenty pounds in a month. She took another bite of the pizza, moving it around in her mouth with her tongue, determined to taste it. Nothing.

She set the slice of pizza on one of the paper plates. "We'll go over to the school after we're done eating." She needed to get busy. Keep herself from thinking.

"Absolutely," Adam said. "We'd go out of our minds hanging out here at the Ritz." He took a bite of pizza, and his eyes slid closed and stayed closed while he chewed. He was falling asleep, and Rebecca felt a smile cross her face.

"Do I look as tired as you do?" she asked.

His eyes popped open and he looked surprised at finding himself in the trailer with a mouthful of pizza. "Whoa," he said. "I was in another universe for a minute."

She sighed. "Another universe sounds great right now, doesn't it?" She poked at the congealed cheese on her pizza with her fingertip. "I need to be sure they're setting up the clinic the right way," she said. "Sometimes the volunteers don't know what makes the most sense, from a medical standpoint."

Adam leaned back on the settee, his sleepy eyes studying her. "You have so much...I don't know...*inner strength*," he said.

"Ha," she said. "Then why do I feel like I'm falling apart?"

"Maya always says you can get things done no matter what's going on around you, but I never saw it firsthand before."

Rebecca looked down quickly at the almost casual mention of Maya's name, and whatever was left of her so-called inner strength seemed to slip away. "I didn't want to leave the airport." She gave her head a small shake. "I know it's irrational, but I feel like...what if she comes back there looking for us and she doesn't know where we are?"

"Hey." Adam set down his pizza and reached across the narrow table to cover her hand with his. "If she returns to the airport, she'll find us, kiddo," he said. "She's more capable than you give her credit for."

"She's fragile, Adam."

"You need to get over that," he said. "I think I know her better than you do, as an adult. You still think of her like a kid."

She remembered Brent saying that she infantilized Maya. Maybe she did.

"That's your family story," Adam said. "Rebecca's the tough, brave, wild one who raised her little sister single-handedly. Maya's the brainy mouse who needs to be taken care of. She might not be as tough as you are, but she's tougher than you think. And you're probably more of a wuss than you let on."

"Am not." She made a face at him. She was embarrassed at letting him see her vulnerability when he'd just applauded her strength. "Anyway, I *said* it was irrational." She got to her feet and picked up her duffel bag from where she'd dropped it on the floor. Setting it on the counter, she began unpacking. When she pulled out her cell phone, she flipped it open out of habit and let out a gasp.

"My cell's working!" she said.

Adam jumped to his feet, digging through his own bag for his phone.

"Mine, too," he said, "though the battery's just about had it."

Rebecca speed dialed Maya's cell number.

You've reached Dr. Maya Ward.

She stomped her foot in frustration. "Damn it, Maya, where *are* you?"

Adam leaned against the counter. "You were out there, Bec," he said soberly. "You saw even more than I did. Do you honestly think she's still alive?"

She felt like throwing her phone at him, and if she hadn't needed it so badly, she would have. "Don't *you* give up hope," she said. "We both have to stay positive." She sat down on the settee again. "I've worked in so many disaster sites where bodies were never recovered, at least not while I was there," she said. "And I never got it. Not really. I never completely understood what those families were going through. I just focused on my work."

"That's what you were *supposed* to do," he said. "That's what I do in the O.R. What your sister does."

"And will do again," she said, as if daring him to challenge her words.

He hesitated, then nodded solemnly. "I hope she'll be able to do it again," he said. Then he dropped his gaze to his phone and began scrolling. "I have hundreds of messages."

Rebecca checked her own messages, hunting for Maya's familiar phone number. She scrolled through the numbers once. Then again. Many of her friends had called, some of them repeatedly. She looked for unfamiliar numbers—numbers of people who might have found Maya and were calling to let her know. There were a few she didn't recognize and she wondered if she should try calling them.

"Check your voice mail," Adam said. He lifted his phone to his ear, then impatiently lowered it, pushed a button, lifted it again. In another moment, she was doing the same. She clicked through calls from friends, her automobile insurance carrier, more friends, a reminder of a doctor's appointment she'd missed, and finally, Brent telling her to call him on his sat phone.

She gave up listening to her messages and called Dorothea.

"Ludlow," Dorothea answered.

"We have cell coverage here," Rebecca said.

"Super!"

"Give me the number for the guy heading the S and R team," Rebecca asked.

"I just spoke with him not two minutes ago, babe. Nothing's changed."

"I want the number anyway." Rebecca blindly hunted in her duffel bag for a pen, but Adam handed her one before she could find it. Dorothea gave her the number and she jotted it on the top of the pizza box.

"And look, Rebecca," Dorothea said, "Brent just called. He's been without a phone himself until this morning. He's got a sat. Wants you to call him."

"I will," she said. "Call me the second you hear anything, okay?"

"Of course."

She hung up and felt uncertain what to do next. Adam sat across the table from her, still scrolling through his calls. He glanced up. "It must be all over the news about Maya," he said. "Everybody's calling. I'm going to check in with one or two friends and have them call everyone else for me."

"Good idea," she said, but she made no move to dial her own phone. She didn't want to talk to anyone. She didn't feel like explaining what was going on or answer questions or hear—premature—condolences.

She was staring woodenly at the phone when it rang. The number on the caller ID was unfamiliar, which filled her with both hope and apprehension as she flipped the phone open.

"Hello?"

"Rebecca!" Brent's voice boomed in her ear as if he was sitting next to her instead of thousands of miles away in Ecuador.

"Hi," she said, barely able to mask her disappointment. She'd wanted it to be one of the searchers with good news. She'd wanted a miracle.

"Oh, no," he said, picking up on her flat tone. "Is there news? I spoke with Dot just a little while ago and she said—"

"No. No news."

"I just can't believe it," he said. "Poor Maya. She finally gets the gumption to do something outside her comfort range, and now this."

Adam started talking to someone on his phone, and Rebecca walked to the end of the trailer with the double bed. "I know," she said as she sat down.

"Dot said you went out to the accident site."

"I did. It's a…" She didn't want to relive the scene. She didn't want to think about the pilot hanging from her seat belt or the guy whose legs had been chewed off by an alligator. "This whole thing is a nightmare," she said.

"Look, Rebecca." He sounded so cool and calm. So together. He was always that way in a crisis, which is what made him such a good DIDA doc. She was usually that way herself. "It's still really bad here," he said. "I have things I have to wrap up tonight, but I'm going to come home tomorrow. I want to come down there and be with you."

"No, don't." She didn't want him here. He knew Maya. He *cared* about Maya, but he didn't love her the way she and Adam did. She felt the way she had when Dorothea had told her Maya was on her way to the airport—that intense aversion to having her come. If only…if *only* she could turn back time and insist that Maya stay home.

"Don't come," she said to Brent. "You just said it's still bad there, so stay. I'm going to focus on my work here. There's so much to do."

He hesitated. "I think I should be with you," he said.

"I'm okay. Adam's here. They just moved us into a trailer."

"How's he doing?"

She saw Adam a few yards away from her at the table. He held the phone to his ear with one hand and rubbed his forehead with the other. His mouth moved, but she couldn't hear what he was saying. She knew he felt the same pain and fear and love that she felt. It was a bond Brent would never be able to share.

"He's hanging in there," she said.

Brent was slow to respond again. "You sound…I don't know. Not like yourself."

"I don't *feel* like myself." She didn't. For the first time in her adult life, she felt impotent. Even after her parents died, she'd been able to take control despite the terror and the guilt. She'd had to.

"What can I do?" Brent asked.

"Keep thinking she's okay," she said.

Once more, he hesitated. "Rebecca…do you really think—"

"Yes!" she said sharply.

"I wish I was there with you right now," he said. "I wish I could hold you."

It wasn't like Brent to speak so lovingly, and she knew what most women would say. What she *should* say: *I wish you could, too.* That would be a lie, though. She was many things, but a liar was not one of them.

"I know," she said. "Thank you."

"I love you," he said.

"You, too," she said, because she did. Not the way he wanted. Not the way she wished she could. But she did love him.

Closing her phone, she sat on the bed a while longer, watching Adam. He still rested his head wearily on one hand. She could hear his voice now, flat and tired. Listening to him, she felt her body sink into the thin mattress. Grief could absolutely paralyze you, she thought, and she refused to be paralyzed.

She needed a run. Just a quick one before she checked out the school. Getting to her feet, she could hardly wait for the oblivion the track would offer her. She changed into her shorts in the coffinlike bathroom, then jotted the word *track* on the pizza box in front of Adam. He nodded without moving the phone from his ear.

★ ★ ★

She had the track to herself. At the north end, she stretched for a long time, loosening her muscles, clearing her head. She wouldn't let in a single thought, nothing more than the mantra of her footfalls on the surface of the track. She began running, her pace steady and soothing. *Left, right, left, right.* She listened to the soft padding of her feet against the ground, and soon her breathing settled into an easy rhythm.

She circled the south end of the track and saw the bleachers to her right. Three people sat in the midsection, and she blinked, because she was certain no one had been there a moment earlier. Yet there they were, as familiar as if she'd seen them the day before. Husband. Wife. Daughter. She wouldn't look at them. She kept her eyes straight ahead. *Left, right, left, right.* She wouldn't look.

Run, Becca, run! the woman shouted.

Always her mother cheering her on, while Daddy and Maya sat with their noses buried in books, rarely—if ever—glancing in her direction.

At least they come to your meets, her mother'd said when she complained. *Not everyone's whole family comes.*

Daddy'd sit with his arm around Maya, reading over her shoulder, pointing to something on the page. Helping her with her homework, maybe. Rebecca didn't know. All she knew was that he never looked up. No matter how fast she ran. No matter if she *won*. Rebecca could win a thousand trophies and they couldn't compete with a single one of Maya's A's.

She was at the north end of the track now and she looked over her shoulder at the bleachers. Empty.

"No one was there to begin with, you idiot," she said out loud. She slowed her pace, the muscles in her legs quivering, her stomach tight around the one bite of pizza she'd eaten. She thought of the ghosts on the bleachers. *My whole family may be gone now,* she thought suddenly. *I have no one.*

A shudder of grief coursed through her. She stopped running altogether, bending over to catch her breath, her hands on her knees, knowing that she'd spent too much time resenting Maya and not enough time loving her, and wishing for a second chance.

26

Maya

I OPENED MY EYES TO SEE A TINY AFRICAN-AMERICAN WOMAN standing in the doorway of the living room. I must have fallen asleep sitting in the cockeyed chair, and now I felt as if I were dreaming. Squinting my eyes, I lifted my head from the back of the chair.

"Well, lookit you!" the woman said. "You're alive. I was afeared for a second you done met the reaper, way you was sittin' there, dead to the world."

I sat up straighter, wincing at the pain in my rib cage and the stiffness in my lower leg. "I was pretty out of it," I said. Through the window screen, I could hear the chickens in their coop, clucking and scratching the dirt. "Are you looking for Simmee?"

"No, sweetness, I'm lookin' for *you*." She limped across the room toward me. "I wanted to check that leg of your'n. Though if Simmee's around—" she glanced toward the kitchen "—I want to git her to do them tarrit cards for me."

Lady Alice. Nothing like I'd been picturing her. She was a teeny speck of a woman; she couldn't have been more than

four-foot-ten. Her short gray hair was thick, and she was
dressed in black pants, a black shirt with seed pearl buttons,
black boots and a black shawl. It was an incongruous outfit
anytime, but particularly in the warm early days of September.

"You're Lady Alice?" I asked.

"Sure am." The woman sat next to my legs on the ottoman, then drew my right leg onto her lap, handling it like a
piece of delicate china. "Gettin' tiresome without the
electric, ain't it?" she said, rolling my pant leg carefully up
to my knee. "I brung a flashlight so I can git a good look
here." It wasn't yet dark in the room, but she ran the beam
of the flashlight up and down the long wound. The glow
from the light played on her cheeks. She had to be at least
sixty, but except for the deep laugh lines around her eyes, her
skin was as smooth as a girl's.

"Looks good, don't it?" she said, more to herself than to me.
"Them pretty little stitches?"

I looked down at my leg. It was still red, but definitely improving. "Yes," I said. I wouldn't tell her about the infection
or the antibiotics. "Thank you for treating it."

"I used to sew all the time back when my hands was good,"
she said. "Made quilts for everone of my babies, and their
babies, too."

I saw that her fingers were gnarled, the knuckles inflamed.
It must have hurt to run that row of delicate stitches up my
shin, and I saw her handiwork in a tender new light.

"Tully told me they was other folks on that plane with you,"
she said. "Sad about that girl pilot. He said it was a right mess
out there."

"I was lucky he came along when he did." I meant it and
yet I wanted even more from him. I wanted him to come up
with a way to get me back to Adam and Rebecca.

"Yes, ma'am," Lady Alice said. "That Tully, he's a good 'un." She rolled the pant leg down again. "Where's he at? Out huntin'?"

"I think so." I had no idea how long I'd slept. I looked toward the wall by the door again. One gun was still missing.

"I need to get back to the airport," I said, as though Lady Alice might have some magical way of transporting me there that Simmee and Tully hadn't thought of. "Tully said his boat washed away. You don't know where I can get a boat, do you?" I nearly whispered the question in case Simmee was close by. I was remembering her "patience is a virtue" statement.

"I had one myself." Lady Alice stood up and looked out the window, hands on her hips. "Belonged to Jackson, but once he was gone, didn't see the point no more. Give it to my son Larry in Ruskin. Simmee always gets me what I need when she goes to town."

"Jackson was your husband?" I asked.

The woman turned to me, a look of surprise on her face. "No, darlin'," she said. "My *son*. My baby. They didn't tell you 'bout him? Lost him two months ago. Tully's the one found him, just like he found you. Only he was too late for Jackson."

"Oh, I'm sorry." I wasn't sure what else to say, but a silence stretched between us and I felt the need to fill it. "How old was he?"

"Twenty-two. Him and Tully was like this." She held up two twisted fingers, as close together as she could get them. "Like brothers. Tully showed up about the same time Larry left home, and Jackson was talking 'bout leavin' hisself. Couldn't take bein' cooped up with a old lady. Then Tully come and Jackson had himself a new huntin' and fishin' buddy. I know Tully's takin' it bad. Hurt him almost as bad as it hurt me," she said.

"What happened?" I asked.

Lady Alice sighed, a huge sound coming from that tiny

body. She walked over to the plaid sofa and sat down, leaning forward with her hands on her knees. "He went fishin', like he done nine-million-trillion times before," she said, "and the boat got stuck in the muck over to Billings Creek. He got out to—" she made a jostling motion with her arms "—wiggle it free, an' I reckon he slipped. Hit his head on a tree stump or rock or…don't really matter what. Tully went lookin' for him when he didn't come home, but by the time he found him, it was too late. He brung him home to me over his shoulders. Cryin'. Ain't never seen Tully cry before. More'n the sight of my own son with that big ol' split across his forehead, I see Tully's face when I remember that night. See them tears smudging down his cheeks."

"I'm so sorry," I said again.

The screen door squeaked open, and we both looked toward the kitchen.

"Do I hear Lady Alice?" Simmee smiled as she walked into the living room. God, she was a beautiful girl. The falling orange sun sent shards of light into the room, and Simmee's hair and skin glowed so brightly that it nearly hurt my eyes to look at her.

Lady Alice stood up. "Nothin' wrong with your ears, child." She did her best to wrap her arms around Simmee and her belly, but her fingertips barely reached the girl's back. "I brung this one into the world," Lady Alice proudly announced to me, "and right soon I'll be doing the same for her own little one."

"Hope not too soon," Simmee said, and the anxiety I thought I'd detected earlier was there again in her face.

"Oh, you'll be fine, Simmee," Lady Alice said. She looked at me. "Child worries too much. Thinks she can't take care of a little one."

"She's taken very good care of me," I said.

"See that?" Lady Alice said to Simmee. "You're worryin' on no account. Now, where your tarrit cards at?"

"You want another readin' already?" Simmee asked. "Done one just last week, Lady Alice. What d'you think's changed?"

"Don't sass," Lady Alice said.

"All right. You wait here while I get 'em. You mind Miss Maya bein' here while I do the readin'?"

"'Course not." Lady Alice smiled at me as she sat down again. "Maybe Miss Maya wants her tarrit read, too."

No way, I thought.

The screen door squeaked again as Simmee walked into the kitchen, and I knew Tully must be home. I felt a rush of hope. Maybe he'd come up with a plan to get me out of there.

"You git us some supper?" I heard Simmee ask him. I couldn't hear his response, but a moment later, he walked into the living room, the gun slung over his shoulder, and suddenly the shards of light that had so enchanted me in Simmee's face turned Tully's eyes an icy blue. I looked away quickly, even though I knew I was imagining the ice in his eyes. The day after the shooting in the Brazilian restaurant, I'd been shocked to learn that the killer's eyes had been *brown,* not the blue I could have sworn I'd seen when he raised the gun.

"How's our patient doin'?" Tully asked. He moved out of the light and I could look at him again—at his perfectly normal, pretty blue eyes. He was grinning. "How d'you like rabbit, Miss Maya?" He seemed to take up more of the space and air in the room than the three of us women put together.

"I've never had it," I admitted.

"Oh, girl, you in for a treat!" Lady Alice slapped her knee.

Tully walked across the room, slipped the gun from his shoulder and leaned it against the wall next to the other one. There was a smear of something dark on his cheek. *Blood,* I thought.

"She's right," he said to me, then turned to Lady Alice. "And I got plenty, Lady Alice, so don't think you're gettin' out of here without havin' supper with us."

"I'm fine at home." Lady Alice dismissed him with a wave of her hand.

"You're a stubborn ol' woman," Tully said, but his voice was filled with affection.

Lady Alice looked at me across the room. "This boy's so good to me," she said.

I was frustrated with the banter. They were treating me like a houseguest instead of someone desperate to go home.

"Tully?" I examined his face for a sign that he'd given my plight even the tiniest bit of thought. "I still need to figure out how to get back to the Wilmington airport," I said. "Have you thought of any options? I asked Simmee if it was possible to wade across to the mainland, but—"

"Only if you want to drown yourself." Lady Alice cut me off with a laugh.

Tully sat down on the sofa and leaned toward me, elbows resting on his knees. "I think that strip of land connectin' us to the mainland might be gone for good this time, Miss Maya," he said. "Happens, you know. Look at them barrier islands along the coast, how new inlets slice straight through 'em after a good storm. I think Last Run might be a permanent island itself, now." He sat back. "Ain't no big deal, though. Larry'll come check on Lady Alice here eventually, and she'll tell him 'bout you and next thing you know, you'll be back with your kin."

"When do you think he'll come, Lady Alice?" I asked.

"Oh, he'll come when the spirit moves him," she said. "No tellin' when that'll be."

So would he come in a week? A month? I seemed to be the only person concerned that we were cut off from the rest of the world without power. "What will you do if Last Run *has* turned into an island?" I asked Tully.

He looked at me as though he didn't understand my question. "Just keep on like we are now," he said. "No difference, really. We ain't got no car to begin with. We just need to get us another boat." He smiled at me, that perfectly symmetrical, handsome-as-all-get-out smile, as he got to his feet. "You don't understand us 'cause you ain't like us," he said. "You like your luxuries, but we ain't never had any so we don't miss 'em. They just tie you down, anyway."

"You're probably right," I agreed because I didn't know what else to say. I remembered Simmee saying that Tully loved it when the power went out. He was definitely eating up the survivalist routine.

"I'm gonna go clean that rabbit," he said as Simmee returned to the room. He pecked her on the cheek. "Y'all work up an appetite with them tarrit cards now, hear?"

"Oh, we will." Simmee was carrying a small rectangular, maroon velvet bundle. The tarot cards, no doubt. She sat next to Lady Alice on the sofa, and I sank lower in the lopsided chair. I felt a bit chastened by the conversation with Tully, as if I was expecting too much from him. From all of them. Maybe I was. I was an intruder in their lives, after all.

Simmee placed the velvet bundle on the table with great care. Unwrapping the fabric, she removed the deck and rested it on the corner of the table. Then she spread out the velvet, smoothing it with her hands, and began shuffling the cards.

"You thinkin' of your question, Lady Alice?" she asked.

"'Course," Lady Alice said.

Simmee apparently had a little ritual worked out, steps she took with the deck to make it look like something sacred. She cut the cards with exquisite care. She held her hands flat above

Lady Alice's as the older woman cut the deck again. Then she began laying the cards on the velvet. "Now, you keep thinkin' of your question while I make the septic cross," she said.

I frowned. Septic cross? I'd observed enough tarot card readings back in my college dorm days to know that the pattern in which the cards were laid out was called a Celtic cross. I didn't know why, but hearing Simmee mangle the term, knowing she had probably mangled it for years and maybe even learned it that way, both touched and hurt me. I wanted to laugh and cry at the same time.

From where I sat, the cards looked old and worn, almost flimsy. Simmee glanced at me. "Want to come join us here, Miss Maya?" she asked.

"No, thanks." I'd never been one for the occult. I didn't believe in any of it on a rational plane, but I supposed I *did* believe on some gut level, which is why, although I'd watched my friends have their cards read, I'd never wanted a reading myself. I was afraid of hearing something I didn't want to hear, and that was especially true right now, when my future felt so uncertain.

"Some people don't like to know the future." Simmee read my mind, as she flipped one more card off the top of the deck.

"Me, I like to be prepared," Lady Alice said with a firm nod of her head. She was staring at the cards as if they'd disappear if she took her eyes off them.

I rested my aching head against the back of the chair and watched the two women, one very young, the other slipping into her senior years. One fair as wheat, the other dark as molasses. Lady Alice giggled at something Simmee said, and I smiled at the warmth between them.

I'd nearly dozed off again by the time they were finished. "You stay and eat with us, Lady Alice," Simmee said. "Tully'll walk you home later in case the moanin' starts."

The moaning?

"Ain't all that hungry." Lady Alice got stiffly to her feet. "You just watch our patient, here, 'right?" She waved to me. "Bye, now, sweetness," she said.

"Goodbye, Lady Alice," I said. "And thank you."

Simmee remained seated on the sofa, straightening the deck of cards with her hands before wrapping them again in the velvet cloth. We heard the screen door squeak open, then shut with a bang. Simmee lifted her gaze to me and I saw that her eyes glistened.

"She keeps hopin' I'll say somethin' about Jackson," she said. "That's her son that died."

I nodded. "She told me."

"What'd she say about him?"

"How Tully found him."

Simmee flinched, and I understood. I knew how a memory could make you flinch. "It was awful," she said. Then she sighed, leaning back in the sofa. "She didn't used to wear them black clothes all the time. She don't take 'em off now 'cept to wash 'em." She looked at the velvet-covered deck of cards. "Don't know what she wants to hear, exactly, but I know that's what she's hopin' for. That I'll say somehow he ain't dead. That it wasn't his body Tully brung to her house."

I felt the burden Simmee was carrying.

"What did you mean about the moaning?" I asked.

"Oh, nothin' really. Lady Alice believes the woods are haunted."

"By Jackson?"

Simmee looked surprised. "Jackson? Oh, no, no. By the *slaves*. In the olden days, the slaves was dropped off in Wilmington and was forced to walk all the way to Fayetteville, right past Last Run, though I guess it wasn't called Last Run back then.

Anyway, a bunch of 'em died on the way and she thinks they haunt the woods, so she don't like to walk through them alone at night. She also says—I don't know if this part's true—that some of the slaves escaped and started livin' here at Last Run, and they're her kin."

"Wow," I said.

"I hear the moanin' myself sometimes. Gran said it was the slaves, just like Lady Alice, but Tully says it's the trees rubbin' against each other."

I nodded at the deck of cards on the table. "Do you believe in them?" I asked. "The tarot cards?"

She shrugged. "Gran done 'em all my life," she said. "She believed in 'em. I don't tell people if I see bad things comin'. What's the point? Lady Alice, I just see good things, but she don't want to hear about all the good things happenin' with her seven live kids. She just wants to fill up that hole Jackson left."

"Her youngest," I said.

"An' her best. The onliest one that took care of his mama. The others is worthless."

"You know her others?"

"Oh, yeah." Simmee rolled her eyes. "I knew all her kids. They was older than me and they'd torture me, but it was just kids havin' fun. All the others moved away down to Georgia… can you imagine? All your kids leavin' you? 'Cept Larry, I guess. He helps out. He don't like me, but when I take the boat over to Ruskin, I walk to his house and he takes me to the store. I get groceries for Lady Alice on top of for ourselves and he gives me money for hers."

"Why doesn't Larry like you?"

She shrugged. "Don't rightly know. Probly 'cause I was always taggin' along after him and his brothers. Bein' a nuisance."

"Doesn't Tully go with you to Ruskin?" I asked.

She rolled her eyes again. "Tully hates leaving Last Run," she said. "Don't matter. I'm used to it. He gets the meat and fish, I get the other things." She stood up, one hand against her back as if it ached, then opened the drawer of one of the end tables. She reached inside and pulled out a photograph, which she brought over to me.

I took it from her and held it toward the light from the window. The image was striking. Tully, his fair hair a little longer than it was now, grinned widely, flanked on either side by his two dark-skinned friends. Each man held a bottle of beer in his hand and they could have been any three, good-looking college-aged guys at a party. Simmee leaned toward me and I held the picture so she could see it. She ran one fingertip down the side of the image.

"That's Larry on the left," she pointed, "Jackson on the right and Tully in the middle, of course. They was goin' on a fishing trip. Larry's wife took the picture."

I remembered how it had felt a short time earlier when Tully came home from hunting, how he'd instantly filled the room—the *house*—with male energy. Now he was alone at Last Run Shelter with only women for company. I wondered what it had been like for him to lose his friend.

"It's got to be hard for Tully to be out here with just you and Lady Alice after having a guy friend to hang around with," I said.

"I s'pose so." Simmee took the photograph from me, looking at it one last time before returning it to the drawer again.

"Won't Larry come again soon to check on his mother?" I asked, hoping Simmee would have a better answer than Lady Alice had offered.

Simmee sat down again. "He come out the first day after the storm," she said. "Said he almost didn't make it, there was so much…*mess* on the creek and the water was so fast. He brung Lady Alice—and us, too—food and batteries and charcoal and such, and tried to talk his mama into goin' back to Ruskin with him, but she wasn't havin' none of it."

"Why not?"

"Would you leave your home, Miss Maya?"

I thought of my house. My beautiful neighborhood with its tree-lined streets. I let in the thought that hurt more than I could bear—Adam and Rebecca's reaction to my disappearance. I needed to be with them *right that minute*. I needed to go home. My chest ached with the need.

"No, I guess not," I said.

"Larry don't know our boat's gone," Simmee said, "so he don't know we're stuck out here now."

"So…what's your best guess as to when he'll be back?" I pushed. My hopes were pinned on the guy in the photograph.

Simmee gave me a mischievous smile, then leaned forward to tap on the deck of tarot cards. "We could try to find out," she teased.

I smiled back at her. "I'll pass," I said, although if I thought the cards could truly tell me, I would beg her for that septic cross.

27

Rebecca

"Do you mean the tango?"

Rebecca was cleaning one of the gurneys with an antiseptic wipe, but she looked up at the sound of Adam's voice. He was sitting on the other side of the classroom-turned-clinic with his patient, a woman well into her eighties, and he suddenly rose to his feet, holding his arms out to her.

"I've never done it," he said. "Can you teach me?"

With a chuckle, the woman stood up and stepped into his arms. She began humming a tune, leading Adam as best she could around the cramped quarters of the room, dodging chairs and tables, the crash cart, a gurney, a wheelchair. Dressed in a purple jersey and beige pants, she took long, sultry steps, her slender, graceful body pressed close to Adam's. Adam was awkward but game, and their smiles quickly spread throughout the room to the nurses, the volunteers, the patients. The man with the sprained ankle started to clap. The three-year-old girl with the black eye jumped up and down. Watching Adam, Rebecca felt close to smiling herself. *He makes people feel good about themselves,* Maya had once told her.

Yes, Rebecca thought. *He does.*

"Good God."

Rebecca turned to see Dorothea standing behind her, an amused expression on her face.

"He is so outrageously inappropriate," Dorothea said. "I love it."

"I know." Rebecca held her breath as Adam lowered his partner in a careful dip. "Me, too."

Adam and the woman took their bows, and everyone applauded. The dance had lasted all of twenty seconds, and each second had taken a year off the old woman's face. Rebecca didn't know what had brought her to the clinic in the first place, but she was going to leave cured.

"So, aside from 'dancing with the docs,' how are things going in here?" Dorothea looked around the room. It was divided roughly into six examining areas staffed with physicians, physician assistants and nurses, with a couple of nurses doing triage near the doorway. "Looks like controlled chaos," she said.

"Exactly." Rebecca organized her tray of equipment as she spoke. "We're waiting for some partition walls. Then we're golden."

It amazed her how much they'd accomplished in two days' time. Practically overnight, the school had been transformed into a sort of refugee camp. Only part of the building was being utilized, because the generators couldn't provide enough power for the entire school, but the environment was far more civilized than it had been in the airport. More generators were expected, and in a few days, the kitchen would be able to produce at least one meal a day.

Three of the classrooms had been transformed into clinics, one of them staffed entirely with volunteer mental health workers who were at least as busy as the medical staff. A smaller classroom housed a makeshift pharmacy, and a few more rooms were devoted to helping people find housing and cope with insurance headaches. It was hardly a happy atmosphere. Many of the evacuees had lost all they owned, and many others lived with the uncertainty of still not knowing *what* they'd lost. Which is why those rare moments like the one Adam had offered the elderly woman—and by extension, everyone else in the clinic—were pure magic.

"Take a break," Dorothea said to her now.

"Soon," she agreed as she wheeled the clean gurney against the wall and peeled off her gloves.

She was working long hours, and she was so glad to be busy. Every minute of every day, she was reminded that she was not alone in her heartbreak. The patients she treated didn't know what she was going through, but she found strength in their strength, and the sympathy she showed them seemed to wend its way back to her somehow. There was a fine line, though, between giving her all to her work and being overwhelmed by it, and she knew she was treading that line on unsteady feet.

So did Dorothea.

"I'm serious, Rebecca," Dorothea said. "Break." She called to one of the triage nurses working near the classroom door. "Next patient is mine!" she said, shooing Rebecca out of her workspace. "You haven't stopped moving in two days. Get a nap."

With her treatment area snatched out from under her, Rebecca had little choice. "Okay," she said, heading for the door. She looked at Adam, wishing he could take a break with her, but he was busy with another patient and she left the room.

She and Adam had been glued at the hip since they arrived at the school. They'd pitched in with the grunt work before the arrival of the evacuees. They'd helped set up long, neat rows of green cots in the gymnasium. They'd organized the cafeteria, with its pallets of bottled water, hand sanitizers, snack food and MREs. Always together, and whether that was Adam's doing or hers, she couldn't have said. All she knew was that she wanted to be near him—near someone who understood what was going on inside her. Adam got it, because he shared it.

She walked through the school's hallway, which was crammed with people sitting and sleeping on the floor as they waited for their turns inside the clinic, and headed for the exit. She passed the room that had been set up to aid family members find other family members. She found herself glancing into that room with longing. She wished she could step inside to discover a new method of finding Maya, a way that no one had yet thought of, because it still struck her as impossible that her sister had vanished from the face of the earth when she fell from that helicopter. So much had been accomplished in two days, and yet the search for Maya and the other passengers on the chopper had made no progress at all.

Inside the trailer, she didn't even consider sleeping. Instead she spent her break as she and Adam had been spending all their free moments: on the phone, calling hospitals throughout the eastern part of the state, describing Maya to overburdened social workers. She sat on the bed, her back against the trailer wall, the list of phone numbers she and Adam were working from next to her.

She supposed if Brent were there, she'd be sharing this bed with him. In the trailer as well as in the clinic, he'd be like a wall between her and Adam. He'd get in the way of the growing intimacy she felt with her brother-in-law when they were working, talking or simply lost in their own fears for Maya. Cut off from Adam, she would feel ten times more alone.

On their second night in the trailer, Rebecca was so exhausted that she fell asleep on top of the thin bedspread covering the double bed. It seemed like only moments later that Adam was shaking her shoulder.

"Wake up, Bec," he said. "Dot's here."

She sat up quickly, her head instantly clear despite the darkness.

"It's not about Maya." Dorothea's voice came from the middle of the trailer, and Rebecca saw the bright disc of a flashlight bobbing in the darkness. There was a second flashlight, and the cones of light bounced off each other over the little table in the kitchenette.

Rebecca got to her feet as Adam turned on the dim kitchen light, and she saw that Dorothea had a man with her. The two of them turned off their flashlights as Rebecca padded into the kitchen. The man was about fifty years old. He was bearded and bespectacled, and his bare arms were muscular and heavily tattooed.

"What's going on?" Rebecca glanced at Adam, but he only shrugged. They both wore the same clothes they'd had on all that day and the day before. She knew she looked as disheveled as he did. They had a shower now in their tiny bathroom. What they didn't have was the time to use it.

"This is Cody Ryan," Dorothea said. "He's head of the search team at the site of the chopper crash."

Rebecca sucked in her breath. "Why are you here?" she asked.

"Tell us something good, man." Adam made it sound like a dare.

The guy—Cody—shook his head. "Nothing good, I'm afraid," he said.

Rebecca turned to Dorothea. "You said this wasn't about Maya!" she said.

Dot put her hand on Rebecca's arm. "It's not. Not...directly." She physically moved Rebecca to the long built-in couch that Adam was using as his bed. Adam had already sunk down on it, and when Rebecca sat next to him, he put his arm around her. Tugged her closer.

"We found one of the bodies this evening," Cody said. "A girl. Woman. Not your sister, though."

"Janette Delk," Dorothea said. "New DIDA nurse. You hadn't met her yet. I spoke to her parents tonight." She shook her head. "First volunteer I've lost."

Rebecca stood up to hug the older woman. She knew Dorothea would take the loss personally, no matter how well or how little she had known the nurse. "I'm sorry, Dot," she said, but Dorothea was already extracting herself from Rebecca's hug, easing her onto the couch again. There was something more. Something they were not saying.

"Where?" Adam asked. "Where'd you find her?"

"On the banks of the Cape Fear," Cody said. "A few miles from the crash site."

"*Fuck.*" Adam leaned forward, rubbing his head in his hands, and Rebecca knew what he was thinking.

"Maya could be anywhere, then," she said.

"Well, now, that's not completely true," Cody said. "But finding Miss Delk gives us an idea of what the current was doing that day."

Adam looked at him. "If Maya's *dead,* you mean," he said. "You mean, you now know what the current would do with a *body.*"

Rebecca knotted her hands together in her lap. "Don't give up looking in the woods," she pleaded. "If she got out alive, that's where she'd be."

"We're in the woods, miss," he said with an expression that told her he was not a quitter. "Trust me," he added with a half smile. "We don't give up easy."

"There were litters on that chopper," Adam said. "Wouldn't they have shown up by now?"

"We've only seen the one," Cody said. "Now today, though, we did find some articles of clothing."

For the first time, Rebecca noticed the plastic grocery bag he was carrying. "I showed them to Dr. Ludlow, and she ruled them all out as possibly belonging to Miss…to Dr. Ward, except this shoe, so we wanted y'all to take a look at it."

He lifted the bag toward Rebecca and Adam and neither one of them reached for it. On the man's forearm, Rebecca read the words *So Others Might Live* angled in blue ink. She wanted to run her fingers over the tattoo. Wrap her hand around it. She didn't want to touch the bag he held, though. After a moment, Adam took the bag from the man and rested it on his lap.

Don't open it, Rebecca thought. *Don't. Don't.* If they didn't open it, didn't see what was inside, Maya could still be safely traveling through the woods.

But Adam opened the bag to reveal a Nike tennis shoe. Once white, now gray and battered.

"Nearly everyone wears Nikes," Rebecca said, but Adam was reaching inside the shoe, digging a little with his fingertips, and she knew what he was after. He pulled out the orthotic.

"It's hers." His voice was almost too soft to hear.

Rebecca drew in a ragged breath. "Where did you find it?" She raised her gaze to Cody's. There was such sympathy in his eyes.

"On the bank of that creek. Billings Creek, they call it."

Adam reached for her hand. He held it on his thigh as he

stared like a wounded puppy at the shoe and orthotic in his lap. Rebecca didn't shift her gaze from Cody's.

"I'm going out there with you," she said to him. "I can't stand this waiting."

"Not a good idea, miss," he said. "Excuse me for saying so, but you'd be in the way."

"Let them do their job, Bec," Adam said quietly.

She blew out a frustrated breath. "All right," she said. "But...just don't give up."

"We're doing everything we can," Cody said, "and like I told you, we're nowhere near ready to give up."

But did he think he was looking for a person or a body? she wondered. She clutched Adam's hand hard and didn't bother to ask.

28

Maya

THE PATH BETWEEN SIMMEE'S HOUSE AND LADY ALICE'S WAS barely a path at all, although I was certain it had existed for decades. It was so narrow that vines grabbed our arms as Simmee and I walked along it single file, and we had to duck beneath thick branches and step carefully over roots and rocks that jutted from the sandy soil. The light was dappled in places, nonexistent in others, and I walked gingerly, protective of my bad leg. Simmee was ahead of me, and I quickly lost count of all the times she said, "Watch out now," as we dodged one obstacle or another, just as I'd lost track of how long I'd been trapped at Last Run Shelter. I'd spent many hours asleep, many more hours worrying, and still many more hours fighting my physical pain and sense of disorientation. Four days was my best guess. Maybe five or six, if I counted the days I'd spent in and out of consciousness when I first arrived. I didn't know. All I knew now, as I followed Simmee through the claustrophobia-inducing undergrowth, was that I had turned a corner in my recovery. The dizziness had completely disappeared. The wound on my scalp was still tender to the touch, but my head had finally stopped aching, and either the pain in my rib cage was improving or I'd simply grown accustomed to it. Lady Alice's stitches on my shin were no longer infected, although I was still careful about taking the antibiotics. I was certain I'd screwed up the dosage, given my inability to tell one day from the next, but it didn't matter. All in all, I felt better. Physically, at least. Emotionally, though, I was a bigger wreck with each passing day. I cried in bed each night, thinking about Adam and Rebecca and how worried they would be, and I spent my waking hours trying to come up with ways to get back to them.

I was more familiar with Simmee and Tully's property now, and walking out the kitchen door no longer felt like walking into a green cage, but Last Run still seemed like another planet to me. I was a city girl—or at least a suburbanite—through and through. Behind their house was the large chicken coop Tully had built. Twelve hens laid eggs and scratched at the ground and ate feed that Tully made himself out of who-knew-what. On the other side of the house stood an ancient charcoal grill, a weathered picnic table and a charcoal smoker, which reminded me of a giant version of one of my antibiotic capsules. Although I hadn't yet seen it, apparently there was a concrete fire pit a short distance from the house, which is where they burned their garbage. "We bury it after it's burned," Simmee told me matter-of-factly, "but critters get into it anyhow."

My shin and ribs protested this trek through the woods, but I had two reasons for wanting to go to Lady Alice's with Simmee. First, I needed to remind Lady Alice to tell her son, Larry, about me when he showed up. Lady Alice was sweet, but a little flaky, and I worried it might slip her mind. Second, I didn't want to be at the house alone when Tully returned from hunting. We'd had a minor clash over supper the night before that had left me uneasy. Up till then, Tully had been nothing but kind to me. Sensing my distaste for the game he'd been feeding me, he'd tried fishing the day before from the bank. He came home empty-handed and cranky, cursing the creek for stealing his boat. He grabbed one of the guns and a few hours later brought home an opossum.

I couldn't bring myself to eat the greasy opossum at dinner, though, settling instead for a can of chicken and rice soup cooked next to it on the grill, and maybe my rejection of his food set the tone for our conversation.

"I'd like to see the creek," I said as we ate in the pink kitchen. "Especially the part where Last Run Shelter is connected to the mainland."

"What for?" Tully asked.

"In case it's lower by now," I said. I hadn't seen *any* water in my time at Last Run. I could have been in the middle of West Virginia, for all I knew. "Have you seen it in the last couple of days?" I felt as though we weren't exploring all possible means of getting me back to the airport. Simmee had said that *I* wouldn't be able to wade across the creek, but maybe Tully could. Maybe he could even *swim* across. "There *must* be a way for me to get out of here."

Tully's eyes darkened, though, the blue nearly the color of a night sky. He set down his fork, and tension suddenly filled the room. I had the feeling I'd insulted his integrity as well as tested his patience.

"Listen, Miss Maya." He bit off the words. "I'm sorry you're stuck here where you don't want to be, and I'm sorry your ol' man's probly worried sick about you, but *you'll* be able to get out of Last Shelter when we can *all* get out of Last Shelter."

I shifted my gaze from his eyes to my soup and felt the color rising in my cheeks. For the first time, I thought of what my presence must be like for him. He had a very pregnant wife, no electricity, and no way to get supplies. I was another mouth to feed and an intrusion on their private life, and now I was badgering him to fix something he had no way of fixing. I wouldn't bug him about leaving again.

"I'm sorry," I said. "I'm just…I'm worried about what this is like for my husband and sister."

"You know," Simmee said abruptly, "I didn't eat no 'possum till Tully come here."

Her awkward attempt at changing the subject touched me, and I hurt for her. I felt her discomfort at the tension in the kitchen. The discomfort I'd caused.

"Really?" I said, and I was relieved to see, from the corner of my eye, Tully pick up his fork again.

Ahead of me now, Simmee carried a basket of smoked rabbit and flatbread she'd made from water and weevily flour and baked over the coals. When we were getting ready to leave for Lady Alice's, she'd called me into her bedroom. Like the rest of the house, the bedroom was uncluttered. Two mismatched dressers stood against one wall. The double bed was covered in a hand-stitched quilt, and an old bentwood rocker sat in the corner. Simmee stood in front of the full-length mirror attached to the closet door. She was holding her dress, this one a pink-and-white stripe with cap sleeves, up to just below her breasts, and between the scrunched-up dress and her panties was her beautiful big beach ball of a belly.

"Lookit this little fella pitchin' a fit," she said, grinning at her reflection.

I moved closer to her, reaching my hand tentatively toward the taut skin. Simmee took my hand and placed it on one side of her belly. I felt the movement beneath my palm, the pointy knob of a knee or elbow rolling against my own skin. The tangible proof of life relieved me. I don't know what else I had expected. Women carried babies and gave birth to them long before obstetricians and hospitals and prenatal vitamins came into existence. I could already picture this infant. He'd probably pop out with an Apgar score of ten, a robust baby with a lusty cry that would rock the little house. Fair skin, like Simmee's. A smattering of pale hair on his head. Soft blue eyes like Tully's.

I met Simmee's gaze in the mirror. "I think your baby will be perfect," I said.

Simmee nodded. "Don't need no doctor to tell me that." She looked in the mirror again, turning a little to the side. "I already love him—or maybe her—so much." She nibbled her thumbnail. "Feels like *too* much."

"Impossible to love him too much," I said. I understood, though. Oh, how I understood. Loving too much could only set you up for hurt.

Simmee dropped her dress over her belly, then sat down on the bed to tie on her sneakers. "How come you ain't got no kids, Miss Maya?" she asked as she worked at the laces.

I watched her tying her shoes, wondering how to answer. Did I give her the simple answer I offered to strangers? *Not ready yet. Maybe someday.* Or did I give her the answer I saved for intimates. The people who deserved the truth.

"Tully says it's on account of you're a doctor," Simmee said. "You ain't got no time for them."

I sat down on the beat-up bentwood rocker. "We've tried to have children," I said. "It's hard for me to get pregnant, and when I do, I miscarry."

Simmee looked at me, her mouth in a little O. "Is that when the baby comes too early to live?" she asked.

"Exactly," I said. "They came very early, and I lost them."

Simmee toyed with the laces on her shoe. "And you want them bad," she said. "I can tell by your voice."

"My husband and I both do," I said. "That's one of the things that drew us together. We both wanted a family." And what, I wondered, would keep us together if that family was never to exist?

"I'm so sorry I made you touch my baby," Simmee said.

"Oh, no, honey," I said. "I'm very happy for you."

"Maybe you can adopt some kids." She looked hopeful, and I wondered how to respond. All at once, I realized the truth I'd been hiding from myself: I did not want another pregnancy. I couldn't go through it all again. I *couldn't*. And I didn't have to. The thought filled me with unexpected relief, mixed with a sudden, disconcerting anger at Adam for his unwillingness to consider adoption. I would take any child—older, special needs, foreign—*any*. I would fill his or her life with love, and I'd fill my own life at the same time.

I realized I was gripping the arms of the rocker, and Simmee was watching me intently. I wouldn't malign Adam. Not to Simmee or to myself.

"Yes, we could," I said simply.

Simmee leaned back on her elbows. "What's your husband like?" she asked.

It felt like months instead of days since I'd seen Adam. "He's handsome, like your Tully," I said, picturing him. "I mean, he looks completely different, but they're both good-looking. He has brown hair and big brown eyes."

"I bet he's real smart."

"He is. He's the kind of person who lights up a room when he walks into it," I reminded myself, shaking off my unsettling feelings about him from a moment earlier. "He's the kind of person everyone loves."

"He's good to you?" Simmee asked. "Treats you right?"

I pushed away the memory of his coolness toward me after he learned about the abortion and thought of the old Adam. The sweet guy I'd married. "He's wonderful to me," I said. "He puts up with all my quirks and neuroses."

"What's neuroses?"

"Oh." I shrugged. "Just…anxiety. Worries."

"I got them, too," Simmee said soberly.

"Everyone does," I reassured her.

"This baby is my neuroses."

I was surprised. "Why do you say that?" I asked.

"Just—" she rubbed her hand over her belly "—I worry a lot about him. Or her."

"That's a totally normal mommy neurosis," I assured her with a smile. "Every mother feels the same way."

Simmee looked down at her stomach again. "Can you tell by looking how soon this baby's gonna be born?" she asked.

I shook my head. "I'm not an obstetrician—a doctor for pregnant women—and it's hard to tell," I said. "But you look like you've got about another month to me."

"That's what I thought," Simmee said. "Even though I can't imagine gettin' bigger. Lady Alice says you count weeks instead of months. That the baby comes at forty weeks. I pretty much know when it happened, and I was countin' the weeks, but I lost track." She suddenly got to her feet. "We should go," she said. "You sure you're up to walkin'? It's not far, but I know your leg ain't 'xactly in the best shape."

I told her I wanted to go with her and that I felt fine, even though now that we were on the path, I thought my decision had been shortsighted. Still the thought of being alone in the house when Tully came home made me queasy after our tense conversation from the night before. Talk about neuroses.

★ ★ ★

Lady Alice's house was a shack. There was no other word to describe it. It was a single story with a pitched roof made half of tin, half of some other material I couldn't identify. The narrow boards that sided the building had once been white, but the paint had worn away to reveal the weathered wood beneath. Two small windows trimmed with fading red paint were on the side of the building, and a stubby brick chimney jutted from the roof. Most startling to me, though, was the small front porch. It was doorless, though some of the windows still held screens, and it had a shingled roof with a hole in one side, as though a giant had punched his fist through the rafters. Growing from the doorway were thick green vines. They spilled from the unscreened windows and climbed the front walls.

I grabbed Simmee's arm from behind. "This is where Lady Alice *lives?*" I whispered.

"Yes, ma'am," she said. "And it looks like she got some damage from the storm she didn't tell us about."

I wondered what part of the sorry mess in front of us constituted storm damage. Surely this monstrosity had been many years in the making. I felt at once sad and angry. Sad that this old woman who'd raised eight children had been all but deserted by them and was left to live in a run-down hovel, and angry that she had a son, this Larry-in-Ruskin, who wasn't doing much to help her fix the place up.

We stepped onto the porch, kicking vines out of our way.

"Oh, Lordy," Simmee said, and I realized what she'd meant about the storm damage. A huge tree limb jutted from the wooden floor. We looked up at the hole in the porch roof, and could see that the limb had served as a missile. What a bone-jarring sound that must have made, I thought. "Glad it came through the porch and not the house," Simmee said with a shudder. "I need to git Tully over here to fix this and cut these damn vines back. He does it every once in a while, but this time of year, it ain't enough."

I wasn't listening to her. On the porch floor next to the door, beneath the leaves and detritus, stood an iron boot cleaner and I stared at it, stunned. It was identical to the one we'd had when I was a child, and the unusual filigree pattern in the metal transported me back to a house I had no desire to revisit. I'd never seen another boot cleaner like it, and could happily go the rest of my life without seeing one like it again.

Simmee knocked on the door that hung askew on its hinges. "Lady Alice?" she called.

I tore my gaze from the boot cleaner as the door squeaked open. "Well, hello there!" Lady Alice said, her eyes bright at the sight of Simmee. Maybe at the sight of me, as well. She was wearing her black outfit again.

"Why didn't you tell us about this, Lady Alice?" Simmee scolded, pointing behind her at the limb that nearly filled the tiny porch.

"Oh, it's just the porch," Lady Alice said. "Who cares about the porch?"

Clearly no one, I thought.

"I'll tell Tully about it," Simmee said. "He'll get this mess outta here and patch the roof."

"No rush on that," Lady Alice said. "Larry'll do it next time he—"

The unmistakable blast of gunfire exploded somewhere in the distance, swallowing Lady Alice's words, and I gasped, startled.

"What's the matter?" Simmee asked me, as though she hadn't even heard the sound. The boot cleaner had gotten to me even worse than I'd realized.

"Sweetness looks like she done been shot herself." Lady Alice laughed, definitely more *at* me than *with* me. "Tully just kilt your dinner," she said. "You can bet on it."

I forced a smile. "Speaking of dinner," I said, motioning to the basket Simmee carried. "We brought you some rabbit Tully smoked." My voice shook, and neither of them missed it.

"Don't mind her," Simmee said to Lady Alice. "She got neuroses."

Lady Alice widened her eyes. "You got nerve pain, child?" she asked, and I was impressed that she recognized the root word *neuro*.

"No, I'm fine," I said. "Simmee's teasing me."

"Oh, she'll do that," Lady Alice said. "Once this girl gets to like you, she'll tease the daylights outta you." She drew Simmee across the threshold with a hand on her arm. "Y'all come in," she said. "It's a might better inside than out here."

It was. The living room was tiny and dim, the only light coming from two small windows, but it reminded me of every grandmotherly room I'd ever been in: neat and clean, and filled with treasures. Framed photographs covered the simple wooden mantel and the end tables, though it was too dark for me to see the people in the pictures. The top of every table was covered by a doily, and quilts, folded with precision, blanketed the backs of the sofas and chairs.

"I'd offer you somethin', but ain't nothin' worth offerin' without the damn stove or Frigidaire," Lady Alice said.

"We don't need nothin'." Simmee sat down on the sofa with a heaviness I hadn't seen in her before. I'd thought about myself on the walk. My leg. My ribs. I hadn't thought about what it was like for her to lug that baby through the woods. I wondered if her due date might be closer than I'd thought.

"You sit, too, Miss Maya." Lady Alice motioned to the chair

next to me, and I lowered myself into it. She remained standing herself, peering into the basket Simmee had set on her coffee table. "Smells right delicious," she said.

"Lady Alice," I said, "your son—Larry—hasn't been by, has he?"

Lady Alice broke off a small corner of the flatbread Simmee had made and nibbled it. "No, darlin'. Haven't seen hide nor hair of him."

"If he comes, please be sure to send him over to Simmee and Tully's," I said. "I need to get home. People are so worried about me." I was beginning to sound like a broken record.

"Oh, I bet they are!" Her sympathy encouraged me. "I'll be sure to tell him. Don't you worry."

"He probly won't be 'round for a while," Simmee said, and I wondered if she, too, was getting fed up with my prodding.

"What keeps you out here?" I asked Lady Alice, hoping the question didn't sound rude. "Wouldn't you rather live near your children?"

"Oh, I'd like to be near my children 'n' grandchildren, sure 'nough." She folded her arms and sat down on the edge of a chair. She looked spryer than I'd noticed the other day. Right then, she looked as though she was in better shape than either Simmee or myself. "I even have a couple of great-grands in Georgia." She smiled. Her teeth were small and white, but one canine was missing. "But I don't belong in no Georgia," she said. "Don't belong in no Ruskin, neither. This is home. Prolly you can't understand that." She narrowed her eyes at me. "You bein' a worldly woman and all. But I was born here," she continued. "Not in this house exactly. House I was born in fell apart in seventy-three. Then Dee—that was my husband—he built this one. More folks lived out here then. Not a lot, but more 'n just me and Jackson and Tully and Simmee." She mentioned Jackson's name as though he still lived with her. "I'll never leave here," she said firmly. "Never. This is my house and my trees and my crick. I love this here shelter and crick, even when the damn thing's got a mind of its own, like it do right now."

I was stuck on the word *crick*. A crick sounded like something you could simply hop over.

Lady Alice stood up and limped toward Simmee, leaning down to kiss the top of the girl's blond head. "And right soon there'll be a little one joinin' us here," she said. "The cycle'll start all over again. There's beauty in belongin' somewhere, Miss Maya. Can you see that? Beauty in belongin' to a place. To callin' that place home."

"I know," I said wistfully. "I know exactly what you mean."

I felt more than neurotic on the way back to Simmee and Tully's. Hearing the gunshot had spooked me. I knew Tully wouldn't shoot either of us on purpose, but what if he saw us moving through the woods and mistook us for an animal? What then? I wanted to hurry, but Simmee was taking her time.

"Look through there." She pointed to our right.

I glanced through the tangle of brush and trees and saw the glint of sunlight on water. I caught my breath.

"Is that the creek?" I asked.

"Sure is," she said.

Finally!

"More of a river right now," Simmee said. "Come on." She turned off the path and I followed her, struggling to keep my balance as branches and leaves smacked me in the face. I couldn't wait to see the water, though. To see a way *out*.

In a moment, it was in front of us, and it was not a creek at all. Not by any stretch of the imagination. It *was* as broad as a river, and a raging one at that. Bushy shrubs poked through the surface here and there, and the water tore around the branches. I shaded my eyes against the sunlight and looked across the water to the green, swampy-looking forest in the distance. The view was a weight in my heart. Even if I could somehow get to the other side of this body of water, what then? It looked just as desolate on that side as it did where Simmee and I were standing. It looked *worse*, in fact.

"The part of the creek that covers the strip of land linking Last Run Shelter to the mainland...where is that?" I asked. "Is the creek narrower there?"

"This is it, Miss Maya," Simmee said. "See them treetops?" She pointed toward the center of the raging creek, and I realized that the shrubs jutting from the frothy water were indeed the tops of trees. "Them trees are on the side of the dirt road that runs between us and the mainland."

The weight in my heart grew even heavier. I let out a long breath, then suddenly had an idea. The fact that I was only now coming up with it made me realize exactly how out of it I'd been for the past few days. "Maybe I could make a big sign and put it on the bank here," I said, "so if a boat goes by, the people would see it. I could say...I don't know, I could write my name on it. Tell whoever it is to stop here and go to your house. I could add a little map and—"

I stopped talking when I realized that Simmee was looking at me as if I'd grown a second head.

"Ain't no boats comin' 'round here, Miss Maya," she said. "You need to get past it. It's like Tully said. You ain't goin' nowhere till this creek goes down."

I looked at the boiling, swift expanse of water again. It was pretty, in a way. The trees in the distance were a thousand shades of green velvet. I thought of Lady Alice. There was beauty in belonging to a place, she'd said. This was home to her. Home to Simmee. Home to Tully. But it wasn't home to me, and it never would be.

29

Rebecca

REBECCA HAD GOTTEN LITTLE SLEEP THE NIGHT AFTER Dorothea and Cody Ryan brought Maya's shoe to the trailer. She hadn't been able to still her mind. She'd tried counting backward from one hundred. She tried picturing herself at Machu Picchu, one of her favorite places on earth. She tried reliving jump school, remembering the thrill of the free fall before she pulled the cord. But her mind kept drifting back to the peeled-open helicopter, the raging stream and to what she now imagined had been Maya's final frightening moments. It was so unlike her not to be able to sleep. No matter what was going on, she was usually out the second her head hit the pillow. She wanted to wake Adam up so she wouldn't be alone with her thoughts, but he was snoring softly on the couch, and it wouldn't be fair.

In the clinic the following morning, she was trying to keep her eyes open when a woman rushed into her cubicle with her son, a boy of about eleven in the throes of an asthma attack.

"It's never been this bad!" the woman said as Rebecca helped her lift the boy onto the gurney they were using as an exam-

THE LIES WE TOLD

ining table. The dark-haired boy was wheezing with such intensity that he couldn't answer Rebecca when she asked him his name. His green eyes looked straight through her as if he didn't hear the question. He was very still, all of his energy going into his breathing.

"Tristan," the woman answered for him.

The boy's eyes were wide with terror, and Rebecca didn't blame him. He was, quite literally, suffocating.

"Stay sitting up, Tristan," Rebecca said as he tried to lie down. "Lean forward a little. Lean on your mom. It'll help you breathe," she added, although she was afraid not much she could do for him in the clinic was going to help. She and Adam had arrived that morning to discover that their makeshift pharmacy had been ransacked overnight. Entire cabinets of medications and supplies had been carried out of the building. She'd stared at the empty room in a stunned fury.

"Does he have an inhaler?" she asked as she listened to the boy's lungs. They sounded even worse than she'd feared.

"We ran out last night. They told me he could get another here." The woman tried to whisper so her son wouldn't hear. She had the boy's green eyes and was probably a beauty in her pre-evacuation world. Now her blond hair was lank, glued to her forehead with sweat. "I've never seen him this bad before," she said. "Does he need to go to the hospital?"

Rebecca was a step ahead of her. She'd already waved over one of the volunteers—the girl who'd led her and Adam to their trailer a couple of days earlier. Her name was Patty, and she had lost every shred of her perkiness since the evacuees started pouring into the school.

"Call EMS for status asthmaticus," Rebecca said when the girl was close enough.

Patty opened her mouth, and Rebecca held up a hand to

stop her. She knew what she was going to say, and didn't want
Tristan or his mother to hear it: both ambulances dedicated to
the school were gone. Adam had sent a man suffering a heart
attack and a woman in labor to the hospital in the last forty-
five minutes. "Just call for the next available," she said. "And
tell Dr. Pollard I need him. Then wait outside for the ambulance and lead them right here. And close my cubicle," she
added. The fewer distractions Tristan had, the better.

Patty flipped open her cell phone, wheeling the partition
into place as she stepped out of Rebecca's cubicle.

"Can you speak, Tristan?" Rebecca asked.

He let out a few gasps, then said, *"Mom."* The word came
out of his mouth in a raspy, guttural wheeze, followed by more
gasps for air, and his mother started to sob.

"Oh, baby!" she said, pressing her hands flat against her
cheeks. She looked at Rebecca. "Why aren't you giving him
anything?" she asked. "Do something for him! Please!"

"You need to breathe slowly and calmly, Tristan," Rebecca
said, as she stepped intentionally between mother and son.
Tristan's lips were beginning to turn blue, and his mother's agi-
tation was only making things worse.

"Calm down, honey!" his mother said. "Breathe slowly,
like she says!"

Rebecca needed to get this woman out of her cubicle.
Tristan stared straight ahead of him, his eyelids beginning to
droop. He was tiring quickly, Rebecca thought. Soon, he'd be
too tired to breathe.

She was relieved when Adam stepped in front of the partition. In one second, he took in the situation—the wheezing
boy with the cyanotic lips, the terrified mother, the overburdened doctor—and reached for the woman's arm.

"I'm Dr. Pollard," he said quickly. "Ma'am, you come with

me into the hallway, so Dr. Ward and I have room to treat your son."

"I can't leave him!" she cried, grabbing Tristan's arm.

Adam pried her hand from her son. "Come with me, ma'am," he repeated, "and I'll explain what we're going to do." He glanced at Rebecca. "You called EMS?" he asked, and Rebecca nodded.

Tristan's breathing worsened momentarily as his mother disappeared from the cubicle. "It's all right, Tristan." Rebecca kept her voice far calmer than she felt. "Your mom will be right outside the room, and we're going to wait here together for the ambulance to come. They'll have everything you need to feel better."

She watched him struggle to exhale. Nearly a decade ago, she'd lost a little boy to an asthma attack in a dusty collapsed house in Chile. She didn't want to lose this one, yet she felt as powerless now as she'd felt then.

Adam reappeared in her cubicle.

"Do we have any O2?" she asked.

He shook his head. "Sent the last canister with the MI."

Anger mixed with her apprehension. If this had happened the night before, she would have had everything she needed at her fingertips. Epinephrine. Oxygen. Albuterol. IVs. Terbutaline, if necessary, and she had the feeling with Tristan that it *would* be necessary. Now she had nothing.

She looked at Adam. "I'll do manual exhalations," she said.

"Good." Adam took her place in front of Tristan, and Rebecca hopped onto the gurney and sat behind the struggling boy.

"Look at me, son," Adam said. "Just concentrate on my eyes." His voice was quiet and calm, almost serene.

"I'm going to help you breathe, Tristan," Rebecca said into the boy's ear. She let her own voice mirror the calm in Adam's, although she felt anything but serene herself. Slipping her hands beneath Tristan's T-shirt, she spread her fingers over his ribs. "It's going to feel strange at first, but I promise it will help you breathe better." She waited to hear his next wheezing intake of breath, then squeezed his slender rib cage to help him expel the air. Tristan grabbed Adam's arms in a panic.

"It's all right," Adam said. "I know that felt weird, but she's doing just what she should be doing to help you breathe better, and she's the best doctor in all of North Carolina, so you just keep looking at me. Right at my eyes."

Tristan let out a brutal, wheezy cough. He panicked the next time she squeezed his ribs as well, this time with a heartbreaking whimper.

Oh, honey, she thought, her cheek against his musky-smelling hair. She knew she was hurting him, but it couldn't be helped. She blocked the little Chilean boy from her mind.

"Listen to me, Tristan," Adam said. "We don't have any medicine to give you, so until the ambulance comes, you have to be your *own* medicine, and you're doing a great job. You can do it. You can slow down your breathing and get very, very, very calm."

The third time she squeezed his lungs, Tristan stopped fighting her, and she knew he was beginning to feel some relief. She began to feel it herself.

Although she couldn't see Tristan's face, she knew the boy's gaze was locked on Adam's brown eyes, as was hers. She could see the overhead lights reflected in the dark irises, the lashes thick and black. She remembered Maya telling her about him after their first date. She'd sounded smitten, so rare for Maya. "He has these *eyes,* Bec. They're so amazing. *He's* so amazing." She knew now what had drawn Maya to him. She knew what her sister had fallen in love with.

Tristan's mother and Patty rushed back into the room with paramedics and a stretcher. Someone pushed the partition out of the way, and in moments Rebecca, Adam and the paramedics had Tristan on the stretcher, an oxygen mask on his face, an injection of epinephrine under his skin. "Thank God, thank God!" his mother wept. "You'll be okay now, Tristan." She took her son's hand in her own.

The boy turned his head on the stretcher until he spotted Rebecca and Adam standing above him. He looked from one of them to the other.

"Y'all...saved...my life," he wheezed.

Adam leaned over him, brushing a lock of dark hair from Tristan's forehead. "You saved it *yourself*, kiddo," he said. "Don't ever forget that."

He stepped back as the stretcher was wheeled into the hallway. He looked at Rebecca and they exchanged a smile. She would have liked to talk to him. To tell him about the boy in Chile. To tell him what it meant to her to save *this* boy's life. To tell him what a terrific dad he would be someday, because one way or another, he had to be a father.

She pictured Adam and Maya up late at night with a sick child, holding him, comforting him, the little boy cradled between their bodies, sure of their love. And sometime during that fantasy, the woman changed from Maya to herself, and she was awash in tenderness for the boy and for Adam, her heart so full it hurt, and she realized the metamorphosis only after the image had taken root so firmly in her mind that she couldn't shake it.

She wasn't sure she wanted to.

30

Maya

"WHAT FISH CAN YOU CATCH AROUND HERE?" I WAS TRYING TO make conversation with Tully as I sat on the concrete stoop, waiting for Simmee. She and I were going to pick berries. I'd been trapped at Last Run Shelter for nearly a week, and the one thing I'd learned was that neither of my hosts was lazy. Right now, Tully was lighting the charcoal in the smoker. If he wasn't hunting or fishing or cleaning and cooking his catch, he was cutting brush back from the house, repairing the chicken coop, burning and burying garbage, or hammering shingles on the roof. I had the feeling Simmee did her fair share of home maintenance when she wasn't as big as the house itself. I could have sworn she'd doubled in size since I'd been there, and every day she seemed a little more tired, a little more winded. But she kept on going. "Lady Alice says better to keep movin'," she told me. And so she did.

"Well," Tully said as he added some wood to the smoker, "depends on the season and where you're fishin'. If I had my boat, I could get to the river and I could get us some bigger fish. But there's plenty of good fishin' here. Catfish, shad, striped bass. Herring, though Simmee don't like it." He smiled to himself. "She ain't fussy about much, but herring ain't her cup of tea. The black crappie you can get fishin' off the bank. They're dumb as twigs. They'll latch on to your hook even if you ain't got nothin' on it."

We'd eaten crappie the other night, and I'd been relieved the fish tasted better than its name suggested.

I watched him work with the smoker, wondering how to bring up my latest idea for getting off Last Run Shelter without riling him. He'd made it clear at supper the other night that he didn't want to talk about it, but I'd thought of a new plan and it was burning inside me.

Leaving Last Run wasn't the only thing I thought about, though. While I spent much of my time worrying about myself—was anyone still looking for me or had they given me up for dead?—I found myself increasingly thinking about Simmee. I thought of what it would be like to raise a child out here in stifling isolation. I'd long known that I would be an overprotective mother, never letting my children out of my sight, and with good reason. I knew how rebellious kids could be. How gullible, vulnerable and downright stupid. I knew the things Rebecca had done. The things *I* had done. I knew only too well how quickly normal teenage rebellion could slip way out of control. I pictured Simmee's son or daughter going to the mainland, craving the taste of freedom. Going wild with it. I shuddered at the thought.

Not only did I worry about Simmee's future and how she would raise a child at Last Run, I worried about things that *hadn't* happened to her. What if Tully'd never come along when he did? What would have happened to her after her grandmother died? Would she have moved in with Lady Alice? Then I started thinking about Lady Alice's son, Jackson. If

Tully hadn't found his body, would Lady Alice ever have known what happened to him? Would she still be wandering these woods looking for him? The thought of the two women struggling without Tully was painful, and I knew that in a very short time, I'd come to care about them. I was so different from them. My upbringing. My education. My life experiences. But a woman could know another woman's heart without having one other single thing in common.

Tully, though, was pure male. As male as a male could be, and he was a challenge for me to talk to.

This is ridiculous, I thought, as I sat on the stoop watching him fiddle with the smoker. I had to tell him what I was thinking or I would burst.

"I'm really grateful to you, Tully," I began.

"Oh, yeah?" He glanced up. "Why's that?"

"For bringing me here and feeding me and giving me a roof over my head," I said. "I don't want you to think I'm not grateful, but I can't help trying to think of ways to go home." I was no longer picturing myself returning to the airport. It was *home* that drew me now. Raleigh. Adam. My house. My bed. My garden. My dog. My *life.* "I was thinking about…this is not something *you* would have to do…but if you could just tell me how *I* could do it, then—"

"Do what?" He fiddled with the knob on the front of the smoker.

"Build a raft." I blurted it out.

He looked at me incredulously, mouth open, eyes wide, before bursting into laughter. I felt relieved. I hadn't been sure how he'd react, and derisive laughter was better than anger.

"What are you now," he asked. "Huck Finn?" He put one foot up on the picnic table bench and leaned forward, arms on his knee. "Listen to me, Miss Maya, we might be able to build a raft, but even *I* wouldn't take a raft out on that ol' creek the way it's acting right now. You ain't got no idea what you're talkin' about."

I shut my eyes, pressing my hand to my forehead in frustration. "What about a sign?" I looked at him again. "A sign I could put on the bank somewhere where a boat might see it. Simmee said boats wouldn't go by that area between Last Run and the mainland, but—"

"And she's right. You should listen to her." He sounded annoyed with me now. He lowered his foot from the bench and peered inside the smoker again.

"I'm just trying to think outside the box," I said.

He wiped the sweat from his grimy forehead with the rag he wore tucked into his waistband. "You know," he said, looking at me, "I like you. I'm glad I found you before the river got to you, 'cause you're a good lady, and I bet you're a real fine doctor. I know you're smart and all, but you don't know nothin' about living here." He folded his arms across his chest, the rag dangling from his fingers. "Don't you think I'd get you outta here if I could?" he asked. "Think about it. You're eatin' our food, using up our coal and kerosene and water, an' makin' more work for Simmee at a time when she don't need no more work. If there was a way to get you outta here, I'd do it. Believe me."

I leaned away from him on the stoop, suddenly very uncomfortable. He'd said he liked me, but the tone of his words told me something entirely different. I *did* believe him, though. I was in their way, and he wanted me gone. I was mortified by the thought that I might be making more work for Simmee. Was I? I thought of how I lolled around the house with my leg up most of the day, as if I were on vacation at a bed-and-breakfast.

"I'm so sorry," I said. "I know it must be hard having an extra person around, especially with the power being out."

He brushed away the comment. "We're all stuck here together," he said, turning back to the smoker again. "You just gotta tough it out like the rest of us."

Behind me, the screen door opened and Simmee walked onto the stoop, a plastic bucket in her hand. I stood up, a little shaky from the conversation with Tully.

"I swear, I got to pee every two seconds," Simmee said.

"Normal," I said. "Are you sure you're up to this?"

"Berry pickin'?" She made a face that said *you are such a wimp*. "Not exactly climbin' Mount Everest, now, is it?"

"No." I smiled. *Mount Everest*. Every once in a while, she said something that reminded me she had gone to school. She had learned things. Retained things. What more could she have learned if she'd been given the chance?

We picked blackberries and blueberries. Simmee found the bushes with the ease of someone who knew the woods the way I knew my kitchen in Raleigh. We had the bucket filled in no time at all, our fingers stained purple. Then Simmee led me along a narrow path that seemed to go on forever. Finally, I saw the glimmer of water through the brush and soon we'd come to the bank itself. In front of us were two splintery steps leading down to a floating wooden dock. In spite of her girth, Simmee trotted down the steps and onto the dock, then turned to look up at me.

"C'mon," she said. "Let's put our feet in the water."

I held my arms out at my sides for balance as I stepped onto the dock. It rocked beneath my feet, and I stepped gingerly to the edge, where Simmee was already taking off her shoes. My mind was suddenly racing. Couldn't this dock serve as a raft? It was huge and would probably be cumbersome, but if the creek ever calmed down…I looked at the trees on the mainland. I imagined getting to them and then, somehow, finding my way to civilization.

"Could this dock…could someone use a pole to move the dock across the creek to the mainland?" I pointed to the opposite side of the water.

Simmee laughed. "Well, first of all, you'd get halfway across and get stuck on treetops or rocks or whatnot. And second of all, I hate to tell you this, Miss Maya, but that ain't the mainland. It's just another island."

"It is?" I stared at the thicket of trees and brush across the water from us.

"Yes, ma'am."

I slumped down on the dock.

"You need to just accept it," Simmee said.

"You're right," I said with a sigh. I took off my borrowed shoes and examined the stitches on my shin. Carefully, I lowered my feet over the edge of the dock, relaxing when I saw that the water wouldn't reach the healing wound on my leg. "You are absolutely right."

Simmee wiggled her feet in the water. "Heaven," she said. "Ain't it?" She popped a blackberry into her mouth, then pushed the bucket an inch in my direction. I ate one. It was the sweetest blackberry I'd ever tasted.

"And here's another thing." Simmee pointed behind us. "Them two steps we just come down?" she said. "Well, there's actually twenty of 'em."

I turned to look behind us and suddenly understood what she was saying. The water had risen so high that it had covered eighteen of those twenty steps. The dock we sat on was usually many feet—many yards—lower than it was now.

"Unreal," I said. I looked across the water at the thick wall of trees. "Is this where Larry will come?"

"Probly not." She ate another berry. "There's another dock closer to Lady Alice's house."

Maybe I could find that dock and camp out on it, waiting for Larry. I brushed the thought from my mind. *Just accept it.*

"But this here dock is closest to our house," Simmee said. "This is where we kept our johnboat. You know what a johnboat is?"

I shook my head. "Just a little boat?" I guessed. That's what I'd pictured when Tully had mentioned his boat.

"It has a flat bottom and motor at the back, and you got to pull the rope to get it started and steer with the tiller."

"Oh." I nodded. I'd never heard the term *johnboat* until Tully'd mentioned it the other day, but I'd actually piloted just such a boat as a teenager during a two-week stay at a camp in the mountains. At the time, I'd thought of the camp as a *pity camp,* since it was for kids in foster care. Even though I lived with Rebecca, someone, maybe one of my teachers, had enrolled me in the camp. It wasn't long after my parents' murder, and I'd been too emotionally wounded to connect with the other kids, but now I remembered the boat. I'd loved it. I'd take it out alone on the lake. I couldn't yet drive and had no way of escaping the world I'd come to hate and fear. The boat had given me respite. "I know exactly what you mean," I said. "I went to this camp on a lake once, and they had boats just like that. I'd go all over the place in that boat."

"Really?" Simmee sounded downright shocked that I knew how to do anything other than be a doctor. "You could start it and steer it and everythin'?"

"Really." I shrugged. "It was a long time ago, but I remember how much fun it was."

"Well, we don't…*didn't* use our boat much for fun," she said. "Tully used it for fishin', of course, and I'd use it to go to Ruskin. That's the nearest town. Here's how I go." She pointed directly ahead of us, where the water disappeared around a bend in the trees. "I just keep going that way for a while. Then I come to this kind of fork place. Not sure how it looks right now, with the water so high, but you can probly still tell it's a fork. There's a bunch of old pine trees without no tops. They just stick up straight there, so you can't miss it really. Then I take the left fork. You always want to just keep goin' left, even when you come to this…sort of shed you can see on the right. It looks like you should go right there, but you don't. Probly now you can only see the top of the shed, 'cause sometimes the water come up close to it even after a little storm, but—" She stopped speaking abruptly. "Are you listenin' to me?" she asked. "It's rude not to listen."

I wasn't listening. I was still back at that camp. God, I'd been an unhappy kid. Grieving, lonely and filled with unbearable regret. I'd destroyed my mother's life. My father's. My sister's.

"So, were you listenin'?" Simmee asked again.

"Sort of," I said, pulling myself back to the present. "You were telling me how you go to Ruskin."

"Mostly you just keep stayin' left. If you kept on goin' that way, you'd end up in Fayetteville, eventually." She lifted her feet from the water, then slowly eased herself down until she was lying flat on the dock.

"Are you all right?" I asked.

"Lie down and look up," she said.

I checked the dock for bugs, then lay down. Above us, the trees formed a lacy canopy.

"Pretty, ain't it?" Simmee asked.

"It is," I agreed.

Neither of us spoke for a moment. Then Simmee drew in a breath.

"I like having you around, Miss Maya," she said.

Guilt nipped at me. I so desperately wanted to leave. To

return to my own life. My real life. But Simmee's words gave
me some comfort. Maybe Tully was wrong. Yes, I'd made
more work for Simmee, but I was giving her something in
return. Friendship.

"I'm glad I've gotten to know you," I said honestly. "You're
a wonderful young woman."

Simmee held out her hand. "Give me your hand," she said.

I felt a sudden awkwardness. Were we going to lie there on
the dock holding hands? But I offered her my hand anyway. If
that's what she wanted, I would do it.

She took my hand in both of hers, shifting a little on the
dock until a circle of sunlight pooled on my fingers. Then she
turned my hand so she could see my palm.

"I can read palms," she said. "Gran taught me."

I laughed, half relieved, half disconcerted. "I don't believe
in palm reading," I said.

"It's not like tarrit." She sounded reassuring.

I considered pulling my hand away, but thought better of it.
"Don't tell me anything bad that can happen," I said. "Don't
tell me how long I'll live or anything like that."

"I thought you don't believe in palm reading," she teased,
and I laughed again.

"I just…that predicting the future kind of thing gives me
the creeps."

"Palm readin' don't have nothin' to do with predictin',"
Simmee said. "It's about what's already happened." She traced
a line on my palm. "See here? This says you been in a helicopter crash."

I smiled. "Charlatan," I said.

"What?"

"Fake, it means. I called you a fake." I turned my head
toward her and caught her smile.

"You got a double lifeline," she said.

"What's that mean?"

"It's good. They call it a sister line. It means you got someone in your life watchin' out for you. Like a guardian angel."

"My sister." My eyes instantly filled. Surely by now, Rebecca thought I was dead.

"She's a doctor, like you. Right?"

"Yes." My voice was thick.

"Rebecca," she said.

"Yes."

"She older? Like somebody who looked out for you?"

"Exactly." Rebecca had put her own life on hold for me. I would never have survived my adolescence without her.

Simmee studied my palm, but I had the feeling it was no longer the network of lines she was seeing. Her mind seemed far away.

"I lost everybody," she said sadly.

"Your mother and your grandmother," I said. "I'm so sorry."

"My mama died havin' me," she said.

"Simmee!" I sat up abruptly, pulling my hand away. "I didn't know that!" I suddenly understood the bits and pieces of anxiety I'd picked up from her surrounding the birth of her baby: Lady Alice had delivered Simmee, and Simmee's mother had died during that birth. In a few weeks, Lady Alice would deliver her own child. No wonder she was afraid.

Simmee tried to sit up, and I had to help her. Her body seemed too cumbersome for her to manage. She took my hand back, holding it palm side up in her lap, not reacting in the slightest to my words. "That's why my gran brung me up my whole life," she said. "She was sick a while before she passed, but Tully was here by then, livin' in the tent between our house and Lady Alice's. Gran loved him. She said he was my guardian angel, even though I ain't got no double lifeline. Gran said she felt like it was okay for her to pass then, knowin' I had Tully with me." She fell silent for a moment as though lost in a memory, then looked down at my palm again. Squinting, she moved my hand a little away from her until it rested beneath another puddle of sunlight. She touched a spot on my lifeline, then shook her head.

"What?" I asked, in spite of myself.

"Just this little square," she said. "Don't fit. I'm probly lookin' at it wrong." She touched another line. "Anyway, I can see where you miscarried them babies." She touched the line, counting. "Four of them, right?"

I pulled my hand away. "No," I said, shaken. "Three."

"I must've mistook one of them little lines, then," Simmee said, but she looked hard into my eyes and I wondered if she saw them there, the four children I had lost.

31

Rebecca

THE WALK BETWEEN THE SCHOOL AND THE TRAILER WAS SHORT, but very, very dark. Rebecca and Adam aimed the beams of their flashlights on the sidewalk ahead of them, not wanting to miss the steps to the parking lot.

She was not herself today. She was not herself lately at all, and she wasn't crazy about the brittle, addle-brained, lily-livered woman she felt herself turning into. It didn't matter that she had a good excuse—a missing sister. Even her patients were getting to her, and she'd nearly always been able to keep the personal Rebecca and the professional Rebecca separate. Today, though, she'd had to work hard to prevent one from tainting the other. First, there was the asthmatic boy, Tristan. Then two little kids with broken arms. A frightened old man whose wife had disappeared in the move from the airport. And worst of all, a woman who delivered a stillborn infant on the floor of one of the abandoned classrooms. She hadn't let Adam take care of that poor woman; she'd done her best to keep him from even learning about her. He didn't talk about the recent loss of his own baby, but she knew it had to be tearing at him, so as soon as one of the volunteers gave her the news about the woman and her baby, Rebecca swept into that classroom and did what needed to be done. It had taken a toll on her, though. The woman. The beautiful, still infant. Afterward, she went out to the track to clear her mind. She'd considered running through the parking lot and the streets instead of the track, not tempting the threesome on the bleachers again, but she pulled herself together. She wasn't going to let the ghosts of the past get to her in that way, and she was relieved that, this time, they left her alone.

Now, Adam pointed his flashlight in the direction of the stairs. "When I signed on with DIDA, I never expected I'd have to be a pharmacist as well as a physician," he said. They'd been restocking the pharmacy with replenished supplies all evening.

"I warned you," Rebecca said. "You just didn't believe me when I told you we had to do a little bit of everything." The conversation was insipid, a good camouflage for her jumbled thoughts. On top of everything else, that weird fantasy of her and Adam comforting a child together kept slipping into her mind. It had returned to her unexpectedly throughout the day, doing nothing to ease her disorientation. *I need a shrink,* she thought each time she imagined herself holding a child between them. Sometimes they were in the child's bedroom. Sometimes in a bathroom, their son or daughter—it *was* their son or daughter—battling a stomach virus. Sometimes the child was a boy. Other times a girl. Sometimes he or she was ten years old. Other times two.

What was the same every time was the deep sense of contentment, of love, between them. Mother, father, child. She'd never fantasized about being a mother before. Maybe when she was very young, before her parents' deaths. But playing mother to her teenage sister had wiped away that fantasy with a massive dose of reality. Now, it was as if her falling-apart mind was pouring a lifetime's worth of maternal fantasy into this one day. It was overwhelming.

More bizarre had been her need to see Adam during the day. Not to talk to him. Just to catch a glimpse of him. She saw him with new eyes. She'd always thought of him as slender, but now she saw that his shoulders were actually broad—as broad as a swimmer's. How could she never have noticed them before? His eyelashes seemed to have grown thick and dark overnight. She watched him bandage a cut on a man's leg, mesmerized by the movement of bone and tendon beneath the skin of his hands, by the angular shape of his fingers, the dusting of dark hair on his forearms.

Your sister's husband, she warned herself.

"There's nothing wrong with fantasizing," Dot had told her years ago, "but do you have to act on every whim?"

This was one whim she wouldn't act on. Ever.

Her cell phone rang, the jangling sound shaking her from her thoughts, and she pulled it from her uniform pocket. She recognized the number for Brent's sat phone and slipped the phone back into her pocket without answering.

"Brent," she said to Adam. She was interested only in calls from Dorothea, the S and R team, or any unfamiliar number that might belong to someone who had found Maya.

"What's with you and him?" Adam asked.

The beam of her flashlight caught the top step and she reached for the railing. "I don't want to get married and he wants to," she said. "I try to feel what he wants me to feel, but it's not there." *Was* she trying? Did she care anymore? The past couple of weeks had altered everything.

"You're good together," Adam said.

"Are we?"

"Well, yeah. Except that ever since we got here, I can tell you'd just as soon not talk to him."

At the bottom of the steps, Rebecca shined her flashlight toward the trailer and they headed in that direction. "I have other things on my mind," she said.

"I don't think you have to marry the guy, but it *is* cool how you both love DIDA," Adam said. "You don't want a family, so together you—"

"I think that may be changing all of a sudden." She cringed. She couldn't believe she'd said it out loud.

"What do you mean? He wants kids?"

She hesitated. "Me," she said. "I mean, I might."

He stopped walking. "Since *when?*" He shined his flashlight directly into her face and she pushed his arm away.

"I know it's crazy," she said. "Probably just a…I don't know. A phase. It started with—" she hesitated again, unsure if she should bring up the loss of his child "—Maya's miscarriage."

"How so?"

"I started having these…it's not conscious. It's not like I'm thinking, 'Oh, I want a baby' or anything like that. But I keep thinking about how good it would feel to hold a baby. And I get this weird…this *longing.*"

"Whoa." Even in the faint light, she could see Adam smile. "Rebecca Ward wants to be a mom. Will wonders never cease?"

"I don't think that's it," she said, backpedaling. "What I really wanted was for you and Maya to have a baby for me."

He nearly laughed. "I beg your pardon?"

"A niece or nephew. I didn't used to care, but I knew I'd have none of my own and I loved the idea that I'd still get to hang out with a cool little niece or nephew."

He lost his smile, and Rebecca could have kicked herself. She touched his arm. "I'm sorry. My fantasy nephew was your real baby. I'm really sorry."

"No sweat," he said, and he started walking again. Silence enveloped them, and she wished she could rewind their entire conversation and start it over again.

After a minute, he put his arm around her shoulders in what felt like a show of forgiveness. "Maybe it's time to have a little chat with Brent," he said. They had nearly reached the trailer. "See if he might be harboring the same secret interest in having kids."

"You know," she said, "I shouldn't have said anything." She was acutely aware of the pressure of every one of his finger-tips, and wished the skin on her shoulder was bare. "I don't really want kids. You have kids, then you die and leave them to fend for themselves."

Adam had let go of her shoulders to reach for the trailer door, but he stopped to stare at her. "Hey, drama queen," he said. "Did you get any therapy after your parents died?" His voice was half teasing, half serious.

"Oh, leave me alone," she said. "Just open the door."

Inside the trailer, she sat down at the table. "I can't have kids," she said.

He had opened the refrigerator, but he turned to look at her. "You *can't?*" he asked in surprise.

"Oh, I suppose I could physically, but DIDA's my life, Adam. I'm totally committed to it. And DIDA and kids don't mix. Plus, I know Brent doesn't want them. And anyway, I don't love Brent. Not the way I should. Not the way Maya loved you," she added. The past tense hung in the air between them. She didn't correct it and neither did he. "From the start, it was right with you two," she said. "I constantly measure what Brent and I have against what you and Maya had, and Brent and I come up short."

"You can't do that." Adam took a bottle of iced tea from the refrigerator and sat down across the table from her. "You can't compare one relationship with another. That commitment to DIDA you and Brent have? That's worth a lot." He pulled a protein bar from his pocket and began unwrapping it. "I *like* this work. It's challenging and different and I'd like to do a lot more of it. Maya, though? The only reason she came here was to try to please me."

Rebecca thought of the protein bar she had in her own pocket, but felt too tired to eat. "Maya told me…" She hesitated, unsure whether she should reveal a sisterly confidence. "She was worried about the toll the miscarriages were taking on your relationship."

"She said that?"

"Uh-huh."

Adam looked out the window toward the dark parking lot, and she watched the muscles in his forearm flex as he took a swallow from his tea. "It's true," he said. "Things weren't great with us. It was the whole…not-being-able-to-get-pregnant thing. Then the miscarriages."

"You seemed really good together at the airport," she said, remembering the night she'd watched them beneath the conference room table. The closeness between them. The envy she'd felt.

He shook his head. "I was trying," he said. "I was proud of her for coming. But…" The dim kitchenette light carved deep lines around his eyes as he played with the wrapper of his protein bar. "There was something else," he said. "I still don't quite understand it, and I figured we'd have time to deal with it later. I didn't want to talk to her about it until she was more together emotionally from this last miscarriage." He shook his head, and Rebecca caught a glimpse of his sadness. "Sixteen damn weeks," he said. "This was a hard one."

"I know. I know it was hard for you both," she said. "But what else was bothering you?"

"Maya never told me about the abortion she had," he said.

"Maya? An *abortion?*" Rebecca laughed. "She probably never told you about it because she never had one. What made you think she did?"

"Oh, she had one. She told me, but only when her doctor asked her about it in front of me."

It was as if someone had told Rebecca that the color red was actually green. "I don't believe it," she said. "While she was married to you?"

"No, when she was a teenager."

"I...Adam, that's *insane.*" She leaned toward him across the table. "I would have known. She would have told me. She never even *dated* when she was a teenager, at least not in high school. When she was in middle school, boys were always calling her because she was so pretty. But after our parents died, she became this total introvert. So it doesn't make sense. And she would have turned to me with something like that. She knew I wouldn't be judgmental. Who did she say it was? The father?"

"She didn't. We never got a chance to talk about it. Her obstetrician said she had some scarring in her uterus and asked if she'd ever had an abortion, and Maya said yes, when she was a teenager."

Rebecca stared at him, her mouth open.

"She was so upset about it that I didn't want to press her. I figured we'd talk about it later." He raised his hands in frustration. "It's in the past anyway. Nothing can be done about it. The thing that bothered me isn't that it happened, but that she never told me. Don't you think that's the kind of thing a wife would tell a husband, especially if you're trying to have a baby? If you have a decent relationship with your husband, don't you think you'd want to talk about the baby you aborted? How you felt about it? *Something?* It just seemed so crazy that she never said anything about it to me."

"I feel like you're making this up."

He frowned. "Why the hell would I make this up?"

Rebecca pressed her hands to her temples, trying to make sense of what he was saying. "She didn't date," she repeated. "She was a bookworm. But…" She remembered back to those years. After their parents died, she and Maya moved to an apartment. Rebecca had been accepted to George Washington University in D.C., but she'd had to put those plans on hold to prevent Protective Services from sticking Maya in foster care. Instead, she worked as a nurse's aide to bring in money. She tried to time her work schedule so she'd be there when Maya got home from school, but it had not always been possible. Could Maya have had a secret boyfriend?

"Oh, Adam," she said. "Why didn't she tell me? I thought she knew she could trust me with anything." She wondered if Maya had been afraid to burden Rebecca with yet another complication in their lives. "She must have gone through whatever it was all alone. Why didn't she come to me?"

"Maybe it happened when she was in college," Adam said. "Maybe when she was eighteen or nineteen. She was in the dorm, then, right? So you wouldn't have known."

The thought gave her some comfort. Maya had the abortion when she was older, surrounded by friends at school. Yet it still bothered her that Maya had felt, for whatever reason, unable to confide in her about something so life altering.

"There was this one guy she dated when she first went to college," Rebecca recalled. "She would have been seventeen then. I know they were lovers because she told me about it. Not in any great detail, but she said they were sleeping together and she was going to go on the pill. Maybe she got pregnant before she went on birth control. I could see her having an abortion then. Just starting school. Knowing she was way too young to be a mother. But I still don't know why she wouldn't tell me."

"Or me."

Rebecca heard the edge to his voice. "You're angry with her," she said.

Adam stood and tossed his wrapper in the trash can near the sink. "You know I don't want to be." He started straightening the sheet on the built-in couch where he'd been sleeping. "I'm not angry now. I love her and I want her to be miraculously safe and for us to have a chance to work things out. But I *was* angry when I realized she'd had an abortion and never told me about it. I hated that she kept something so important a secret from me."

"She was afraid. She knew how much having a baby meant to you."

"And to her."

"Yes, to her…but she would have been willing to adopt. She would have *loved* to adopt."

He ignored her comment. Instead, he picked up the pillow from the couch and tried to plump it between his palms. She knew that nothing he did could fluff the pillows they'd been given.

"Maya said you wouldn't consider it." She heard the accusation in her voice.

"I was…" He sat down on the couch. "It's hard for me to give up the hope of having my own child."

"An adopted child *is* your own child."

"You know what I mean. I have no family. No blood relatives. I just wanted my own biological child." He shook his head. "Was that so wrong?"

Rebecca got to her feet and ran her hands through her hair. "No," she said. "It wasn't so wrong. Maya was a big girl. She could have said 'I quit' whenever she wanted. But you were meant to be a father, Adam. I can see it when I watch you with your kid patients. What does it matter if a child's related to you by blood or not?"

Adam didn't seem to hear her. There was sadness in his eyes that she wished she could erase. "I put her through too much, Bec," he said. "I was upset after I found out about the abortion, but I didn't talk to her about it. She knew I was upset, but she wasn't talking to me either, and...*damn*." He leaned back against the wall and closed his eyes. "Now it's too late," he said. "It's too damn late."

Rebecca lay in the double bed, listening to the cicadas. The evening was cool, and she and Adam had opened the windows before turning in. As tired as she was, she knew she'd once again have a hard time falling asleep. The conversation with Adam had her tied in knots. An abortion. *When, Maya? Why didn't you tell me?*

Had Maya known something Rebecca had tried so hard to hide? That tangled web of love and hate she felt for her? The admiration tainted by resentment? Her mind and heart could barely hold the contradictions. Lying there, she felt as though she might explode with them.

She thought of the hurt look in Adam's eyes as he realized he'd probably never have a chance to talk with Maya again. So much regret in his face. Such yearning for a second chance. She knew that feeling, although she hadn't recognized it in herself until tonight. She'd been carrying the feeling around with her for days, and now it was keeping her awake. She had her own set of regrets. Her own yearning for a second chance with her sister. She knew exactly how it felt when you realized that too much had been left unsaid.

32

Maya

I WOKE UP IN THE ROOM THAT WAS BEGINNING TO FEEL HALF like home, half like a prison. How long had I been there now? Definitely more than a week. Two weeks? I should have made marks on the wall to keep track, the way a prisoner might in his cell. I doubted there was a calendar in the house. Tully and Simmee knew it was September or January or April by the slant of the sun through the trees.

I turned on my side and my eyes fell on the old bassinet in the corner. This room was to be the nursery, although I knew it would never meet my personal definition of the word. I thought of the mural Adam and I had fantasized about for the nursery in our house.

No. I wouldn't go there. Wouldn't think about our babies. Our house. I wouldn't think about *Adam.* Especially not about Adam. In the past few days, as I realized I didn't want to endure any more fertility treatments or another pregnancy, my love for him had become tainted by a resentment I didn't want to feel. I didn't want to think about my life at all.

I would think instead about Simmee.

I looked at the bassinet again. The baby would be here in a few weeks. I sat up, an idea taking shape in my mind. If I was stuck here, it was time I made myself useful. I wouldn't let Tully accuse me of making more work for either of them.

I dressed quickly, then found Simmee in the kitchen where she sat next to the window, mending a tear on a pair of Tully's pants.

"Good morning," I said. I filled a glass with water from the tap and took a sip. I'd stopped sterilizing the water a few days earlier and had not gotten sick. Most likely, my illness that first night had been due to the floodwaters that had come close to drowning me.

"Morning," Simmee said, without looking up.

I sat down across the table from her, the glass between my hands. "I have an idea for something we can do today," I said.

"What's that?" She glanced up at me then, and I saw that her eyes were rimmed with pink.

I set the glass down on the table. "Are you all right?" I asked.

"Fine," she said, her attention again on her stitching. "What's your idea?"

I hesitated, deciding not to press her. "Let's fix up the baby's room."

She frowned at me. "What do you mean, fix it up?"

"Get it ready. Do you have any paint? You or maybe Lady Alice?"

She shrugged. "Maybe some old paint under the house. Probly not still good."

"Well, maybe good enough," I said, although I was wondering: exactly how old? Could there be lead in it? "I thought maybe we could...I don't know. Freshen the room up with some paint over the wallpaper. Or if you had a couple of different colors, we could paint designs on the walls. We can make a mattress cover for the bassinet." I realized I hadn't looked inside the bassinet to see if she'd already thought of bedding. "Does the bassinet have a mattress, or—"

"Do you ever feel trapped?" she interrupted me.

I sat lower in my chair, nearly sinking into it. Hell, *yes,* I felt trapped. But this wasn't about me. "Do you feel trapped, Simmee?" I asked.

She set the pants and her needle down on the table and looked me in the eye. "I love this baby, Miss Maya." She seemed so different this morning. I'd come to think of her as other-worldly. Today she looked all too human.

"Yes," I said. "I know you do."

"I love it with my complete heart, but I'm so scared." She wrapped her arms around herself as if she were cold.

"Oh, Simmee." I leaned forward, my forearms stretched toward her on the table. Of course she was scared. "I under-stand," I said. "But everything's going to be fine, honey. What happened with your mother was an aberration...an unusual circumstance."

She looked down at the pants again but didn't release her arms from across her chest.

"Listen to me," I said. "I don't think for an instant that you'll have a problem, but I really wish you'd have the baby at a hospital. Wouldn't that ease your mind?"

"Tully won't go along with that," she said.

"Why don't I talk to him about it." I sat up straight again. "I'll insist." What gave me the right to insist on anything? "Once Larry comes and you can get a new boat, then you'll be able to get to the mainland and have your baby there. If there's a problem...and there is *not* going to be a problem...but if there is one, you'll feel more confident that you'll be safe."

"I keep feelin' like the baby's gonna come soon." She glanced at me almost shyly. "Maybe before Larry comes. If that happens, at least you'll be here. You can birth it for me, can't you?"

I was taken aback. One way or another, I planned to be long gone by the time Simmee's baby arrived. "Of course," I said. "Most likely, Larry will have shown up by then and he'll help you get a new boat and you can have the baby at the hospital, because I *am* going to talk to Tully about this. But if the baby comes sooner, of course I'll help you."

For the first time since I'd walked into the kitchen, Simmee smiled. "You bein' here's a blessin', Miss Maya." Then she glanced through the window screen, and I knew without her saying a word that she was looking to see if Tully was nearby. I knew before she opened her mouth that what she was going to say next was something she didn't want him to hear.

"I need to tell you somethin'," she said quietly. "It's real important."

"Okay." I kept my voice as low as hers.

Simmee licked her lips. "I want you to have my baby," she said.

I didn't know what I'd expected her to say, but that wasn't it. "Why would you say that?" I asked.

Simmee looked down at Tully's pants and ran her fingers over the fabric. Her chin trembled. I wanted to hug her. Make that trembling stop.

"You can give him a better life than me," she said without looking up.

"Simmee." I reached across the table for her hand. I had to tug it a little to get her to look at me. "Material things are not what matter most," I said, although I was thinking, *God, yes. I could do so much more for this child!* I erased that thought from my mind before I dared to feed it. "You love your baby. You've said so, and it's so clear to me that you do. I know you can't wait to hold it in your arms, and you're going to be such a good mother. Look at how you took care of me. You're a caretaker, Simmee. You're meant to be a mom."

Simmee pulled her hand from mine and hugged herself again. "You don't understand," she whispered. "You can't know. You can't understand how it is."

"Do you mean what it was like growing up out here? So isolated?"

She shrugged with a half nod, not looking at me.

"I know it must have been hard for you." I pictured her as a child, taking the boat across the water to go to school, having to leave her classmates behind as she returned to Last Run Shelter each day. At least she'd had Lady Alice's children to play with. Simmee's baby would have no one. "Maybe you and Tully can move to the mainland," I said.

"He won't."

"Maybe for the sake of the baby, he would," I said. "He loves you, Simmee, and he's excited about this baby. You know that."

"I know." She shut her eyes. I could see the slender blue veins in her eyelids. She looked so fragile.

"So maybe for the good of your baby, he'd be willing to move someplace where his son or daughter would have better chances," I continued, but I thought of how stubborn Tully could be and how he relished his backwoods lifestyle. It would kill something in him to give that up. Still, people made all sorts of sacrifices for the sake of their children.

"Why won't you take it?" Simmee asked me. "You want a baby, and I want you to have him." Her eyes glistened. "Is it 'cause it ain't your blood kin?"

I shook my head. "It's because he's *yours* and I know you'll fill him up with loads of love." My arms began to ache with the thought of cradling her baby. Simmee was only seventeen.

Seventeen! "There are social services to help you," I said. "You have so much to give, Simmee."

"Please."

"The way you're feeling right now is normal," I said. "It's normal to be overwhelmed. You'll feel differently when the baby comes and he looks up at you for the first time. You won't want to let him go then. I promise."

She stood up abruptly, picked up the pants and her scissors from the table, and walked past me toward the hall. In the doorway, she stopped and turned to look at me. Her eyes were flat and empty and she suddenly looked closer to thirty-seven than seventeen.

"You're wrong," she said. "You ain't never been so wrong."

33

Rebecca

SHE WAS AVOIDING ADAM.

They'd been on different work schedules since their conversation a few nights earlier, Rebecca dragging herself into the
trailer just as he was leaving, and she was responsible for the
change in their shifts. She couldn't handle another long conversation with him. She was not a "long, heavy, deep conversation" type of woman. Maybe that was why Maya had kept
things from her. Rebecca could talk about DIDA all day, but
cross the line into emotional territory and she was ready to bolt.
That was one reason she was putting off calling Brent, although
Brent was worse than she was when it came to that sort of
intimacy. Adam, though…Adam was a champ at it, and that
felt both dangerous and seductive, because she found herself
craving a closeness she'd never known she needed. She couldn't
believe she'd gotten into the whole baby hunger thing with him
when she didn't yet understand it herself. Now she felt both
exposed *and* attracted to him and totally confused about her
feelings, and she didn't handle confusion well. It seemed she

couldn't talk to Adam without revealing things she didn't want to reveal. She couldn't look at him without noticing how damn gorgeous he was. And when he'd fling a brotherly arm across her shoulders, the same way he had for years, every molecule in her body now suddenly stood on high alert.

So she was avoiding him—as much as she could avoid someone she was sharing a trailer with. She resolved to think only about her work, and only once did that resolve slip—when the volunteer, Patty, mentioned that she now wanted to be a doctor herself. "It was so awesome watching you and Adam save the life of that asthmatic boy," she said, and Rebecca remembered the reflection of the overhead light in Adam's eyes, the gentleness of his voice. The memory sent a shock wave of heat through her before she could put up a wall to keep it out.

Most of the time, though, the work inside the school provided a welcome distraction as the hours turned into days. A few things had improved: some of the evacuees, especially those with the money to move into hotels, had left the school, and housing was slowly being found for others. Although the power was still out, there were more generators now and chicken-and-rice casserole had been baked in the kitchen and served to a thousand or so people the night before. After more than two weeks of MREs, the casserole tasted like manna from heaven. Best of all, in Rebecca's opinion, the medical supplies had been well replenished and National Guard members now stood outside the makeshift pharmacy's door twenty-four hours a day.

In spite of the improvements, the medical staff was still extremely busy in the clinic. People whose chronic illnesses had been neglected during the first week of the crisis were now paying the consequences. Wounds that had seemed inconsequential days ago now festered with infection, and viruses spread like wildfire throughout the school, particularly among the children.

The doctors and nurses who'd been working in the airport and the school for the past couple of weeks had, for the most part, left Wilmington for their homes and jobs around the country. Dorothea no longer bothered to ask Rebecca and Adam if they wanted to leave, though. Instead, she simply sent the replacement medical staff to them for orientation and training. In a way, it was like starting all over again as she and Adam helped the stunned new volunteers cope with the human casualties of the sister storms.

Rebecca finished her shift in the clinic around sunrise one morning, but instead of returning to the trailer, she sat on the ground in front of the Welcome—Viking Territory! sign and lit a cigarette. Leaning her head against the wall, she shut her eyes. She was so tired that when she felt the unmistakable bite of a mosquito on her forearm, she ignored it.

"Hey, Bec."

She opened her eyes to see Adam walking toward her, ready to start his day shift, a thermos of coffee in his hand.

"Coffee?" She couldn't mask the hope in her voice.

He smiled, handing her the thermos. She took a long swallow and gave it back to him.

He lowered himself to the ground next to her. "Trade you another sip for one of those." He pointed to her cigarette.

"You're kidding."

"Uh-uh."

She pulled the pack from her pocket, handed it to him and watched as he shook a cigarette onto his palm. He lit it from the end of hers and drew the smoke into his lungs as though he always had a cigarette with his morning coffee.

She frowned at him. "Since when?" she asked.

"Well, not since I was twenty, actually." He blew a stream of smoke into the pink morning air. "It just looked so..."

delicious, watching you inhale." He laughed. "I thought, why the hell not?"

She understood. It felt like there wasn't much left to lose.

"I think you've been avoiding me," he said after they'd smoked a moment or two in silence.

"How can I avoid you?" she countered. "We share a trailer."

"Exactly my point. We share a few square feet of space and haven't spoken to each other in days."

She rested her head against the wall. Here we go again, she thought, wondering what to reveal, what not to reveal. She sighed. "Talking to you the other night made me realize…" She felt too tired to have this conversation now, yet it was better that they have it by the light of day. What *was* it about him that made her want to talk in spite of herself? "I was so upset that Maya had an abortion and never told me about it." She'd always said—always *believed*—that she and Maya were as close as two sisters could be. Yet that was a sham, wasn't it? A lie they were both careful to tend and nurture. Learning about the abortion only drove that fact home to her. She tipped her head against the wall to look at him. "There was a lot of unfinished business between her and me, too," she said.

"Like what?"

"Like, we never, ever talked about our parents' murders." The words came out in a rush, as though she knew if she didn't say them quickly, she wouldn't say them at all.

"What do you mean, 'never, ever'?"

"We never really got it all out in the open," she said. "I'm sure she blamed me, and I…we just moved on with our lives after it happened. We let it become this gigantic elephant in the room." She stubbed out her cigarette in the grass and immediately pulled another from the pack.

"Why would she blame you?" Adam took the matches from her and lit her cigarette, cupping his hands around it, although there was no breeze. She smelled the soap on his fingers, the scent an aphrodisiac, and she turned her head away as she inhaled.

"Because I brought Zed into our lives," she said, blowing the smoke from her lungs.

"Who's Zed?"

She looked at him quizzically. He sounded as though he'd never heard of Zed before. Maybe Maya had never told him his name. "The guy who killed our parents," she said.

He frowned. "I thought the killer was a student of your father's. Some kid who was pissed off about his grade."

Rebecca was dumbfounded. "I can't believe she didn't tell you," she said.

"Tell me *what?*"

In the parking lot, Rebecca saw Dorothea leaving her trailer. This was not the time for an interruption. "Let's walk," she said, getting to her feet. She nodded toward the lot. "Dot's coming."

Behind the school, they turned left and began walking along the border of the woods.

Rebecca helped herself to another swallow of his coffee. She could think of only one reason that Maya had kept Adam in the dark about Zed's identity.

"Maya must have been trying to protect me, Adam," she said. "She didn't want you to look down on me. Zed *was* one of our father's students. But he was also my boyfriend. My ex-boyfriend."

"Back up," Adam said. "You've lost me."

She let out a breath. "I was eighteen."

"And Maya was fourteen. That much I know. It sounds like that's *all* I know, though."

"I fell for Zed. He was twenty. I met him at a party, and he was sexy and hot looking, but he was also a total asshole. I just couldn't see that part of him.

"I was obsessed with him. He dealt drugs, and I thought that was cool. My father hated him, which made him even more appealing to me, of course. My parents forbade me to see him, which infuriated him. I started sneaking out to see him. Maya knew what I was doing, though she would never have told on me. My parents figured it out, though, and really clamped down, and I stopped seeing him. That's when Zed started acting crazy. He kept trying to see me, following me home from school. That sort of thing." She took a long drag on her cigarette. "He once told me he'd kill my parents for breaking us up, but I thought… I just blew him off," she said. "Kids said things like that all the time."

"Wow," Adam said. "How much of this did Maya know?"

"Well, I sure never told her he said he'd kill our parents. And she didn't know that I…" She stopped, unsure how—or why— she would tell him the rest.

"That you what?"

"I was so stupid," she said. "I went back to seeing him. He was seductive and I was…I've thought about it so many times, Adam. My motivation. He was hot, my father hated him, I wasn't allowed to see him, and I was a wild child. A bad combination. So that's the other thing Maya didn't know. I never told her I started seeing him again." She glanced at Adam. His gaze was on the ground as they walked, his brow furrowed. "I never told *anyone* that," she added.

He put his arm around her shoulders, and the scent of soap, of shampoo, filled her head. "You've been carrying a lot of crap around inside you, haven't you?" he asked.

She could only manage a nod.

"And I can't believe that Maya never told *me* any of this," he said.

"Well, now you know," she said. "And of course you know the rest of the story."

"I don't know *what* I know, anymore, Bec," he said testily, dropping his arm to his side. "I'm beginning to wonder if she's told me half-truths throughout our whole relationship."

"Oh, no, Adam," Rebecca said, but how did she know that? She no longer felt as though she knew her sister.

"She told me a masked stranger—who turned out to be your father's student—killed your parents in your driveway. And she was in the backseat. Is that true?"

She nodded. "I was upstairs," she said. "I heard the doorbell. My father was picking Maya up from a class or something. He was always taking her someplace or picking her up. She was Daddy's little girl." She was appalled at hearing the bitterness in her voice and hoped Adam hadn't noticed it. "My mother was home and I figured she'd answer it. Then I heard our car pull in the driveway and the squeal of brakes, which was weird, because my father would usually just pull into the garage. My mother started screaming." She stopped walking, pressing her hands to her eyes, and she felt Adam take the cigarette from between her fingers. "I looked out my bedroom window," she said, lowering her hands. "It was March, so it was dark out even though it wasn't that late." She looked into the woods behind the school, but what she saw was not the trees in front of her. She was back in her childhood bedroom, staring out the window. "In the headlights, I saw a guy standing in front of the car. I knew right away it was Zed. I couldn't see him well, but I knew by his build and the way he was standing who he was."

She plucked the cigarette back from Adam's hand, took a shaky drag, then crushed the butt into the grass beneath her shoe. "My mother was…" She was afraid she was going to cry. "Oh God, Adam, I can't stand to remember this!"

He put his hand on the back of her neck. "Don't then," he said. "You don't have to."

But she *did* have to. She wanted to finish what she'd started, to say it all out loud to someone, for once. "My mother got in the car," she said, sitting down in the grass, as though her legs couldn't hold her up any longer. "I guess she was trying to…I don't know *what* she was trying to do, exactly. Zed started shooting through the windshield. I ran downstairs and outside, screaming for him to stop."

Adam sat down facing her. "Weren't you afraid?"

"I should have been, but I wasn't. Not for myself, I mean. I guess I didn't believe he'd hurt me at first. But I was *terrified* for my family. He didn't even turn around when I shouted at him. Just kept shooting. We had a boot cleaner by the front door and I picked it up. It was incredibly heavy, but it felt like a feather to me. I had superhero strength, all of a sudden. I ran toward him and when I got a few yards away, I threw it at him."

She plucked a blade of grass from the ground and tied it into a knot. Adam watched her without speaking. Without pushing.

"It hit him in the shoulder, and he dropped the gun," she said. "Then he turned on me. He grabbed me and I thought he was going to kill me. I was kicking him and screaming for my parents and Maya, and he clamped his hand over my mouth. He said, 'You tell the cops it was me, and I'll be back to kill Maya, too.' Then he got down on the ground. I couldn't figure out what he was doing, but later I realized he was getting the gun he dropped. He ran away and I opened the car door. My parents were…" She tossed away the knotted blade of grass and ran a trembling hand through her hair. "It was a bloodbath," she said. "Maya was curled into this little ball behind the driver's seat. She was covered in blood, and at first I thought she'd been hit. She wouldn't move. She wasn't even crying. Just in shock. I heard sirens, because some neighbors had called the police. Everything is kind of a blur to me after that. Neighbors came over. The police came. Ambulances. It was the most horrible night of my life. I wouldn't let go of Maya. Literally. I would *not* let go. They took her to the hospital and I insisted on riding with her. I just kept holding her." Rebecca raised her eyes to meet Adam's. "I want to hold her now, Adam."

"I know." He touched her knee. "Me, too."

"The police questioned us, and I was afraid and completely irrational. I told them I thought the guy was one of my father's students and gave them the address where I knew Zed lived with a bunch of druggies. Maya heard me, and she just parroted what I'd said, and there we were, in the lie together. The police went to the house where Zed was staying, and he shot at them and they killed him. I was so relieved he was dead. If I could have killed him myself, I would have."

"Maya told me you wouldn't let social services put her in foster care."

"How could I? It was all my fault. I had to take care of her. I was going to keep us together no matter what. We had some life-insurance money and we'd inherited the house. I sold the house, and Maya and I moved into an apartment. We had some emotional support from family friends, but no therapy. We both should have been in therapy, but it was the last thing on my mind." Rebecca'd been so frightened and wounded during that time. No one seemed to pick up on her weight loss. Her exhaustion from too many nights without sleep. She'd cut herself off from her social life to focus on her penance: Maya and work. She didn't sleep with another guy until medical school, when, with Maya safely in college, she began making up for lost time.

sorry -
beetroot!

"It's unbelievable how well you and Maya did in school after going through all of that. I mean, I know you took a year off to work, but she…from what she told me, anyway, it sounds like she didn't miss a beat."

"It was our way of handling the grief," she said. "Just like now. The way you and I are working such long hours here. It keeps us from thinking."

"Right." He sighed.

"I was always afraid that, deep down, Maya knew I was still seeing Zed." She lit another cigarette. "That I was still sneaking out with him. I told her once right after it happened that I hadn't been, but she said she didn't want to talk about it. I've always wondered if she thought I was lying to her and she was angry. I never brought it up again." She peered into his eyes. "So do you see what I mean?" she asked. "About unfinished business? There was so much left unsaid between us."

Adam leaned back on his hands. "I never got the impression that she blamed you for anything," he said. "I think she was grateful that you kept her out of foster care."

"I know. But I feel as though…" She shrugged. "It *was* my fault, really. Zed was only angry with my parents because of me."

"Give yourself some credit, Bec," he said. "Don't you see how remarkable you were? You were eighteen. You made the kind of mistake every eighteen-year-old makes—falling for the wrong person. You ran a household, raised your sister, became a doctor and helped her become a doctor, too."

She smiled, grateful to him for trying to ease some of the burden she carried. Quickly, though, she sobered. "There's an elephant right here, right now," she said.

"What do you mean?"

"What we're both thinking about Maya, but aren't saying."

He was quiet, and she knew he understood what she was talking about.

"It's hard to let her go," he said.

"Unbearable," she agreed. Leaning forward, she did what she'd wanted to do for days. She wrapped her arms around him, and he embraced her with his own, and they sat that way for a long, long time.

34

Maya

I SAT IN THE KITCHEN FOR A GOOD THIRTY MINUTES AFTER MY conversation with Simmee. I wasn't sure whether to follow her to her bedroom or not. She'd walked away from me, and I thought I should give her privacy if that was what she wanted. My mind was reeling from our talk, and I didn't like my thoughts one bit.

I was being offered a baby and I believed that, at that moment at least, Simmee sincerely wanted me to accept her offer. Adam was so against our adopting, though. Maybe it was the hassle factor that was at the root of his objection. Maybe if we could adopt a baby freely given to us, he'd feel differently. I knew in my heart of hearts, though, that was not the case. We'd talked about it enough. He wanted that blood tie. That damned blood tie I was unable to give him.

Besides, Simmee's baby had a father, and I was sure Tully would never agree to relinquish his child for adoption. Simmee was making the offer under duress. She was frightened of having this baby. The whole idea of giving birth had to conjure up the loss of her mother for her. All the problems and deprivations of her own childhood at Last Run Shelter, most of which I couldn't begin to relate to, were coming to the fore as she prepared to bring a new and utterly dependent life into the world.

She was only seventeen—in many ways, a child herself—and living in poverty. Would social services even allow her to keep the baby if they knew about it? Was that why she thought Tully would be so resistant to her giving birth in a hospital? Was he afraid the baby would be taken from them?

I left the house, determined to talk to him. I would make him understand. He didn't know what it was like to be a woman about to give birth, especially a woman whose mother had died as Simmee's had. I needed to make him see.

I found him behind the house, where he was sitting with his back to me on a long flat rock. In front of him, a fire roared in the concrete pit where they burned their trash, and dark, acrid smoke rose into the treetops.

My steps slowed when I spotted him, remembering how uncomfortable I'd felt during our last conversation in the yard. "Hey, Tully," I said as I neared him.

He started a bit in surprise, turning toward me. "Hey," he said. "What's up?"

"Can I talk to you for a minute?"

"As long as it's not about buildin' a raft," he said with a hint of a smile. "Set yourself down." He nodded toward another rock near the fire pit. I started walking toward it but froze when I saw the rifle in his hands.

"Don't freak out," he said. "I'm just cleanin' it." He leaned over to lay the rifle on the far end of the long rock, as if showing me he had no plans to use it in my presence. "I know you're not too keen on firearms," he said, tucking the end of the rag he'd been using into his pocket.

"How do you know that?" For some reason, I felt paranoid.

"You look at 'em like they got a life of their own." He laughed. "Like they can go off all by themselves."

"They…" I lowered myself to the rock. It was hot beneath my thighs from the heat of the fire as well as from the mounting heat of the day. "I'm just not used to being around them," I said.

"Me, I've been around 'em all my life." He stood up and poked at the fire with a long stick. Sparks flew into the air and I could see the wrapper from a package of ramen noodles curl into the flames. Watching him work with the fire, I thought of how he was always on the go. He had the energy of two men. He could get a good job if they lived on the mainland.

"My father took me huntin' from the time I could walk," he said. "And livin' out here, we'd get pretty sick of fish if we didn't hunt." He'd said "we" as though Jackson, his hunting buddy, was still alive. I remembered Lady Alice telling me that Tully'd cried when he brought Jackson home to her. It was hard to imagine the tough guy in front of me shedding tears. I knew from the fathers of my young patients, though, that looks could be deceiving.

"Well, I'm glad you're good at it or we'd be starving," I said lamely. I hated how awkward I was coming to feel around him.

He tipped his head to one side, appraising me. "So what's on your mind?" he asked.

I drew in a breath, glancing at the rifle, as though I *did* expect it to go off all by itself. "I wanted to talk to you about Simmee," I said. "About your baby."

He stopped poking the fire, and I saw the worry in his eyes. "You think somethin's wrong?" he asked.

"Oh, no," I said. "Not at all. Simmee seems very healthy, and she's going to be an excellent mother, just like I think you'll be an excellent father." I tried to smile, hoping he didn't think

I was patronizing him, which, of course, I was. "You'll have your own child to take hunting in a few years."

"Yes, ma'am," he said. "I'm looking forward to that, for sure." He folded his arms across his chest, the stick hanging from his fingers as he waited for me to continue. He could probably tell that I had plenty more to say.

"What if it's a girl?" I stalled.

"Ain't no law says a girl can't hunt, is there?"

"Not that I know of." I shifted on the hard rock and wiped my perspiring forehead with my hand. "But here's why I wanted to talk to you," I said. "Simmee's nervous about having the baby here. I mean, giving *birth* here." I wouldn't get into Simmee's concerns about raising a child at Last Run Shelter. One thing at a time.

"She is?" Tully frowned. "She ain't said nothin' about that to me."

"Well, I think she's trying to be brave," I said. "Plus, she probably doesn't want Lady Alice to know she has reservations. But think about it, Tully. Her mother died giving birth to her, and Lady Alice was attending her then. So naturally she's a little nervous that something like that could happen to her."

"But it won't." He sat down on the rock again, and it shifted a little beneath his weight. "You said yourself, she's healthy."

"I think everything will be fine," I said. "But sometimes the unexpected happens and things can go wrong very quickly. It would be so much safer for her to have the baby in the hospital. And it would ease her mind so much."

He frowned again like he didn't quite get what I was saying. "I wouldn't want to move her when she's, you know, ready to have the baby," he said. "We could be out on the water and anything could happen."

His argument made no sense to me at all. "It's only, what?

Five or ten minutes across? You'll have another boat by then, I'm sure." I was counting on it.

"And then we'd need to get to Larry's." He looked toward the waning fire, as if thinking the idea through. "We usually walk from where we dock to his house, but it's a couple miles and she wouldn't be able to walk all that well. And then it's still a ways to the hospital."

I opened my mouth to offer a rebuttal I hadn't yet formulated, but he kept going.

"And we ain't got no money," he said with a shrug. "What if they kick us out? Plus, there's those diseases in hospitals. That's how my grandfather passed. My ma insisted he go to the hospital this one time for his sugar, and he got sick while he was there from some bug and was dead before you know it." He leaned over to pick up a twig and tossed it on the fire. "Just seems a lot safer to let Lady Alice do it," he said.

"Maybe if you talked to Simmee," I suggested. "See which risk she's willing to take, having the baby here or in the hospital." I hadn't thought about how they would get from the dock to Larry's house, though. It never occurred to me that it would be that difficult.

He stood up and gave another poke to the base of the fire, and when he turned to look at me, his face had gone hard. "Look," he said, "you need to watch steppin' in where you don't belong. Outsiders think they know what's best 'cause that's the way *they* do it, but they don't understand about our lives." The dying flames altered his features and I looked down at my hands before his eyes could turn to ice. My heart was pounding all out of proportion to what he was saying. I glanced at his rifle or shotgun or whatever it was. I could almost hear how it would sound going off out there in the middle of nowhere, the way it would echo through the woods and across the water.

I stood up, brushing ashes and sand from the back of my pants. "I understand," I said, but I knew I was just plain wimping out.

"Right," he said, and he leaned over to pick up his rifle.

"I'll see you later." I turned and it was all I could do not to run back to the house. My body tensed as I walked away from him, waiting for the bullet to crack open my skull. I turned the corner, pulled open the screen door and then sank into one of the kitchen chairs. My hands shook so hard I had to lock them between my thighs to keep them still. I should have tried harder, I thought. Should have apologized for overstepping my bounds, but told him I'd help them figure out how to get from the dock to the hospital, and that there would be financial help for Simmee and the baby. I could help them financially *myself* if they needed it. But I'd chickened out because he'd raised his voice two decibels and the blue of his eyes threatened to turn to ice and he was within a few feet of a gun, and now it would be impossible for me to bring up the topic with him again. I felt as though I'd failed Simmee in the way I'd handled the conversation.

I only hoped I hadn't made things worse.

35

Rebecca

SHE WAS CATCHING THE SORE THROAT AND STUFFY NOSE THAT was running rampant through the school. She'd felt fine during her shift in the clinic until around three in the morning, when she noticed it hurt to swallow and her sinuses felt swollen and achy. By the time she climbed into the trailer at sunrise, with acetaminophen, decongestant and cough lozenges crammed in her pockets, she was certain she was sick.

Adam was pouring coffee into his thermos. "Uh-oh," he said, "you look like crap."

"Don't touch anything I've touched," she said. "Don't even *breathe* in here or you're doomed."

"Poor Bec." He screwed the lid on his thermos. "What can I do for you before I take off?"

She headed for the double bed, but he stopped her with a hand on her forehead.

"Fever, kiddo," he said.

"I refuse to be sick." It hurt to talk.

"Have you taken anything?"

She pulled the acetaminophen from her pocket and shook a couple of the pills onto her palm. He handed her a bottle of water and she winced as the pills scratched her throat on the way down.

She felt even closer to Adam since she'd told him about her parents' murder. Closer, and a hundred times lighter. Maybe she hadn't needed to talk to *Maya* about that night as much as she'd needed to talk to *someone* about it.

She was sitting on the edge of the bed taking off her shoes, when Adam peered through the window to the parking lot.

"Dot's here," he said. He opened the door and Dorothea climbed into the trailer.

"Morning, you two," she said. Rebecca no longer panicked at an unexpected visit from Dorothea, but something in the tone of the older woman's voice caused her hands to freeze above her laces.

"What is it?" she asked.

Dorothea leaned back against the kitchen counter, arms folded. "They're calling off the search for the crash victims," she said.

Rebecca shut her eyes. *"No."* The word came out as a small, strangled sound. The end of the search wasn't really a surprise; nearly two weeks had passed, and the search and rescue teams were stretched thin, with hundreds of other people still missing from the storms. Yet the complete loss of hope, the loss of *answers,* that Dorothea's announcement carried with it was hard to bear.

Adam sat down next to her on the edge of the bed and pressed her hand between his.

"I'm sorry," Dorothea said. "I know this has been hideous for both of you, and that you have no—" she hunted for a word "—closure. I also know that you must hold me responsible, since I asked you to talk her into coming."

"No, Dot," Rebecca said.

"This wasn't anyone's fault," Adam said.

Dorothea stared at the floor. "Well," she said, "I guess I'm not as forgiving of myself as you two are. I insisted she get on that chopper." She looked at them. "She was a good worker," she said. "Definitely *not* the wimp I thought she'd be."

"I told you." Adam tightened his grip on Rebecca's hand.

"You were right." Dorothea sounded so tired. "One of the churches is having a memorial service tomorrow night for the storm victims," she said, rubbing the back of her neck. "I think Maya and the nurse and pilot need special mention. I'll do it, if you like."

"No, I'll do it," Adam said. "Unless you want to, Bec."

She should be the one to do it, but she would need months, maybe years, to sort through her feelings and come up with what to say about her sister. She shook her head. "I don't think I can." Her voice was barely a whisper.

"You'd be fine," he said. "But I'd like to do it. You can tell me if there's something you'd like me to say. It can be a statement from both of us."

"I'll leave you two to work this out." Dorothea shoved her hands into her pockets. "The service is at seven, and a van'll pick us up by my trailer." She glanced at Rebecca. "You get some sleep, babe," she said. "You sound like you've got the crud that's going around. And, Adam, take the day off."

"I'll be in later." Adam got to his feet and walked Dorothea to the door. Rebecca didn't move from her perch on the edge of the bed, one shoe off, the other unlaced. She heard Adam whisper "…not going to leave her alone," and she was glad. She didn't think she could handle being alone just then. She'd lost more than her sister in these two weeks. She'd lost her fire. Her steel. At times, when she imagined babies in her arms or her parents on the bleachers, she wondered if she was also losing her sanity.

She took off her other shoe and lay down on the bed, but instantly sat up again. "I can't breathe when I lie down," she said to Adam. "My nose is too stuffy."

Adam took his own pillow from the couch and propped it up on top of hers at the head of the bed. "Try sleeping sitting up partway."

"I'm going to get your pillow all germy," she said.

"Like I care." He went into the bathroom, and she heard the water running. When he came out, he had one of their thin white washcloths in his hands. He'd wet it and folded it into a rectangle, and he rested it on her forehead. He was so gentle. She was glad now that Maya had had his caring as long as she did.

He sat on the edge of her bed as she tried to get comfortable. She could breathe if she lay on her right side, propped up by the pillows, though she had to hold the washcloth against her forehead so it didn't fall. Her back was to Adam, and for a long time, neither of them spoke.

"Are you okay?" she asked softly.

He didn't answer right away. "It's not like this was unexpected," he said.

"That's not what I asked."

"I'm okay."

"You can go to the clinic," she said, although she didn't want him to leave. "I'm just going to sleep."

"I don't want to go," he said. "Not yet."

Her eyes were closed, and Maya's face was on the inside of her eyelids. She blinked but couldn't get rid of the image. Maya was smiling. She didn't look like a woman who'd suffered many losses, but she *had* and it wasn't fair.

"It's never enough," she said, her voice breaking.

"What is?"

"You can never get enough of somebody you love," she said.

"It's like…I wish I had been with her every single day. Every minute of every day."

"I know." He rubbed her shoulder.

"She's on the inside of my eyelids."

He laughed. "Mine, too."

"Really? She's smiling. Is she smiling on the inside of your eyelids?"

He hesitated. "Yes," he said, in a way that made Rebecca doubt his honesty.

"I wish I'd talked to her every day, the way some sisters do. We should have. But I was always away someplace without cell coverage." She hadn't been the best sister. "If I could have her back, I'd do that. Talk to her every day."

"There's something I want, Rebecca," he said abruptly.

She thought he meant something tangible. Did she have something of Maya's he wanted? A keepsake. "What?" she asked.

"I want you to always be my family." His voice was husky. "We might not technically be in-laws any longer, but I want us to stay family forever. Okay?"

She rolled onto her back, her head pounding and stuffed with cotton, and said, "Maya wouldn't want it any other way."

He nodded, leaning forward to turn the damp washcloth over on her forehead, and when she shut her eyes again, she could have sworn Maya's smile grew wider.

36

Maya

I'D BEEN AT LAST RUN SHELTER AT LEAST TEN DAYS. PROBABLY longer. I could tell from the way the skin itched and drew tight around the stitches on my shin. It was time—*past* time—for those stitches to come out.

"Do you have any little scissors or a razor blade?" I asked Simmee. We were washing the inside of the living room windows. Simmee'd noticed a smudge on one of them an hour earlier, and she was off on a tear, mixing vinegar and water and starting to scrub, her belly so big she could barely get close enough to the windows to clean them. "My stitches are ready to come out," I said.

"Lady Alice'll do it." She worked her rag into a corner of one of the panes. The sharp smell of vinegar filled the room. "I ain't got nothing little enough you can use."

I sighed quietly, not wanting her to hear. "Okay," I said. "I'll go over there when we're done." I thought of walking through the woods alone and looked at the wall by the front door. One of the guns was gone. Tully was out there, ready to mistake me for a deer. "You want to come with me?" I asked.

"You okay goin' by yourself?" She glanced at me. "My back's givin' me fits today."

"Sure, I'll be fine," I lied. Maybe I should put it off. Maybe Simmee would be up to it tomorrow. It wasn't that far to Lady Alice's, though, and I was being ridiculous. "Why don't you sit down and let me finish the windows?" I said.

For a minute, I thought she'd agree, but she shook her head. "I like doin' this," she said. "I like doin' a task you can see the outcome quick, like this. That's why I like cleanin'. I think about what I'm doin'. I think about this here glass, how it was made and everything." She stood back and studied the window she was cleaning, moving her head from side to side, checking for streaks. "I do that every single time I clean a window. Keeps me from thinkin' about other things."

She had a better attitude than I did about housework, that was for certain. My mind was anyplace but on the window I was cleaning. My mind was on *her*. She'd been so light and sunny when I'd arrived at Last Run, and now seemed dark and weighed down. I wanted to lift that darkness, but was coming to think it would have to lift on its own. It would disappear when the baby came, I was sure. This was a frightening time for her—waiting for labor and delivery, her mother's fate hanging over her head.

For hours after I turned down the offer of her baby, Simmee wouldn't speak to me. I finally sat her down, my hands firmly on her shoulders, and told her I would help her any way I could, short of taking her baby. I told her how honored I was that she trusted me to raise her child, but that it was her hormones talking and that she shouldn't make any irrevocable decisions now. I would make sure a visiting nurse came out to check on her and the baby. I would send her money, if that's what she needed.

She listened to me, and I thought she truly understood what I was saying because she finally nodded and said, "You're probably right." Yet for another day, there was a new tension between us that saddened me. Only now did it seem to be lifting.

Things seemed to have settled down between Tully and me as well, after our rocky conversation by the fire pit and my ridiculous rush to get into the house and away from his rifle. At supper that night, he acted as though nothing had passed between us, telling off-color jokes and leaning over to nuzzle Simmee's neck, and I joined him in the pretense. I felt confused about my role. He was certainly right that I was an outsider, better educated, with values honed in a world where money was of little concern and where what was best for people seemed perfectly clear. Who was I to push my values on people who didn't live in my world? Yet Simmee's anxiety gnawed at me. *She* wanted something from me, something I couldn't give her.

When we finished the windows, I set out for Lady Alice's. I was a wreck walking through the gloomy woods, with their tangled vines that caught at my feet and arms and neck. The woods had seemed spooky enough to me when I'd walked through them with Simmee. Alone, I found them utterly unnerving. Every sound—squirrels rustling in the leaves, the snap of a twig—made me jump, and I nearly ran the last half of the path to Lady Alice's. I was overjoyed to see her small run-down shack come into view. A clothesline hung between the corner of the house and a nearby tree, and Lady Alice's black outfit was pinned to the line. I wondered what she'd be wearing. I couldn't picture her in anything other than black.

A bright blue tarp now covered the hole in the porch roof, and the branch that had nearly filled the porch now lay on the ground nearby. *Tully,* I thought, touched as I imagined him struggling to get that branch out of Lady Alice's porch.

Lady Alice must have seen me approaching the house, because she already had the screen door open for me when I stepped onto the porch.

"Hello!" she said. She wore a long-sleeved cotton dress, tiny pink and green daisies dotting a purple background.

"You look *lovely*." I smiled, intentionally ignoring the filigreed boot cleaner by the door. It was easy to smile now that I was out of the woods. I was already dreading the walk back.

"Oh, just don't look at me." She brushed away the compliment with a wave of her hand. "I don't feel right in this dress with Jackson gone, but today's washin' day."

"Well, I was hoping it could also be 'take Maya's stitches out' day," I said. "Do you have time?"

"Sure 'nuff," she said. "Can always make time for you, Miss Maya."

I followed her through her house toward the kitchen. The living room was dark as we passed through it, and I could barely see all the quilts and doilies as my eyes tried to adjust to the lack of light. In the kitchen, Lady Alice picked up a worn leather bag, exactly like those old bags doctors used in the days of house calls. She smiled at me as she lifted it from the counter. "My medical kit," she said with some pride. I suddenly pictured her trying to save Jackson when Tully brought him to her after his accident. Had he already been dead then, or had he died in her arms despite her ministrations? I didn't want to think about it.

Lady Alice opened the bag and, with a reverential air, took out a lidded plastic container. She lifted the lid to reveal a green bar of soap, and I remembered Simmee telling me something about the "special soap" Lady Alice used when she treated her patients.

I watched as she scrubbed her hands carefully in the sink.

The soap gave off a strong, piney scent. *Irish Spring,* I thought to myself with a smile. Her special soap.

"We'll go out to the back stoop," she said, turning off the faucet with her scrubbed fingertips. "Light'll be best out there."

I followed her out the back door, and we arranged ourselves on the wooden steps. I leaned against the house, rolled up the leg of my uniform pants and let Lady Alice lift my leg on her lap. I suddenly remembered a day long ago when Daddy had held my leg in his lap to pluck gravel from my skinned knee. It had hurt like the devil, but I didn't cry. "You're my brave girl," he'd said. I *had* been brave once upon a time. Could you recapture something like that? Could I walk through the woods without jumping at every sound?

I looked down at my leg stretched across Lady Alice's thighs. A couple of weeks' growth of leg hair caught the dappled sunlight. The hair was very blond, but still a revolting sight. I hadn't seen hair on my legs since I'd started shaving when I was twelve.

Lady Alice opened her bag again and pulled out tweezers and a pair of genuine suture scissors.

"Where did you get your medical supplies?" I asked.

"My uncle Jimmy was a doctor," she said. "He'd come 'round from time to time. When he died, he left me this here bag in his will. I reckon he saw the most promise in me, his own children bein'—" she gave me a conspiratorial glance "—soft in the head."

I laughed. Her clean hands had now touched everything: the bag, my leg, the wooden step, her dress, the scissors. I thought of asking her to at least boil the scissors first, but then let the question drift out of my mind. *What the hell,* I thought. The wound was closed and clean. I'd survive.

She used the tweezers and scissors expertly and, despite my initial misgivings, I was impressed. "You're good at this," I said.

"Oh, nothin' to it." She snipped and tugged. Snipped and

tugged. Cleaned a bit of dried blood from my skin with gauze and alcohol. "Been doin' it so long, I can't remember when I didn't know how."

"I was glad to see that Tully's working on your porch," I said.

"Oh, Larry done the most of it."

"Larry?" Her head was lowered over my leg, her voice muffled, and I thought I'd heard her wrong.

"Yes'm. He come yesterday mornin'. Brung me groceries and tried to git me to go back with him, but I told him ain't no way I'm leavin'." She chuckled. "Which is what I always tell him. He'd fall out if I said I was comin'. Maybe one of these days that's what I'll say jest to see what—"

"Larry?" Every muscle in my body tensed. "Your *son*, Larry? He was here *yesterday?*"

"Yes'm, he sure was."

"But…did you tell him about me? I thought you knew I need to go home! I thought you knew—"

"What you gettin' all fired up about?" she asked. "Hold this here leg still, now, or I'll end up snippin' somethin' we don't want snipped."

"Lady Alice!" I removed my leg from her lap with half the stitches still intact. Leaning forward, I grabbed her arm. "Why didn't you say anything to him about me needing to get home?"

"Why you so upset?" She backed away from me a little, confusion in her eyes. "Tully was here helpin' him with the roof, 'n' he didn't say nothin', so I figgered you musta changed—"

"*Tully* was here? At the same time as Larry?"

"That's what I'm tryin' to tell you, child." She smoothed a hand over my cheek. "Tully didn't say nothin' 'bout you, and I figgered you made up your mind to stay and help me birth Simmee's baby, you bein' so close to her now and all."

I filled with rage. "How *dare* he!" I shouted. "He's keeping me a prisoner!" I stood up, running my hands through my snarled hair. "I need to go *home*, Lady Alice!" I said. "I have a husband and sister who probably think I'm dead. They don't know what happened to me!"

Lady Alice got to her feet and pulled me into a hug. I felt her coarse hair beneath my chin, and the scent of Irish Spring filled my nostrils. "It's gonna be all right, child," she said. "You safe here. Larry'll come 'round again and we'll straighten it out next time. Tully just mistook what you said, that's all."

"I never said *anything* to make him think I wanted to stay!" I'd started to cry. My body convulsed with my tears, and she tried to hold me even tighter, but I pulled away, far too upset to be consoled. I struggled to replay my conversation with Tully over in my mind. *Had* I said something that would lead him to believe I wanted to stay for the birth of the baby? Absolutely not. No way.

Suddenly I remembered the boat and nearly laughed with relief. "He must have told Larry about the boat washing away!" I said. "He probably told him to bring us—Tully and Simmee—another boat, and then they'll take me out of here." Even as I spoke, I knew my reasoning didn't make sense. Why didn't he simply ask Larry to take me? And why didn't Tully *tell* me if that was his plan? "Did Tully at least ask Larry to call my family, or—" I stopped myself. Of course not. Tully would have no idea how to get in touch with Adam or Rebecca. "This is…this is *unbelievable!*"

"Sit down, Miss Maya." Lady Alice's voice was suddenly strident, so much so that I took my seat again on the step.

I looked up at her. "I can't believe he didn't say anything to Larry," I said. "I just can't believe it."

She sat next to me again. "Now why do you think he'd keep it to hisself?" she asked.

"I don't really care. All I care about is—"

"You think 'bout it. Think why that man want to keep you here."

Ransom? I wondered. *Have I been kidnapped? Would he try to get money from Adam?* But even as that thought spun through my mind, I knew it was ridiculous.

"He wants *you* to birth Simmee's baby." Lady Alice spoke slowly, as though I was one of her soft-in-the-head cousins. "You. A real doctor. I'm a old woman, 'n' it's prolly got him tied up in worry." She waved her hands through the air. "I'm no fool, Miss Maya. I know that girl's scared silly same thing's gonna happen to her what happened to her mama. Tully's jest as scared. So it's good you here. Everbody wants you here."

"But *I* don't want to be here," I snapped. "I want to go home."

"I know you do, child. I'm sorry I didn't say somethin' to Larry myself. I was…" She looked into the woods, gnawing at her lip, and I thought I saw genuine regret in the set of her features. "I feel right bad," she said. "I was jest thinkin' 'bout myself and how glad I was t' see Larry and get some food in the house." She took my hand in her tiny one and held it on her knee. "Truth is, Miss Maya, I don't know why Tully didn't say nothin'," she admitted. "If it got to do with Simmee and the baby, then you ain't got long to worry. That girl ready to pop."

I let go of her hand. "I need to talk to Tully," I said, getting to my feet again, but she caught my arm.

"Maybe you don't want to bother him with this," she said. It sounded like a warning.

"Yes, I do."

"Well, let me finish them stitches." She reached toward my leg. "Then you free to go tear into that man, if you like. But think about Simmee. Think about how good it'll be for her to have you here when that baby come."

★ ★ ★

He was skinning a rabbit on the old picnic table by the smoker, and I started yelling at him as soon as I spotted him from the path.

"You didn't tell Larry I was here!" I shouted. I came to stand across the table from him, not looking at the bloody mess between us. Not looking at the sharp blade in his hand. I put my hands on the table and leaned toward him, staring hard into his eyes. "Why didn't you tell him? You *know* I need to get out of here. You *know* that!"

He looked unmoved, almost bored, by my outburst. "You been to see Lady Alice?" he asked.

"She told me you didn't say anything to Larry." I straightened up. "How could you do that to me?"

"Did too tell Larry," he said. "And Lady Alice knows it. She was right there, tellin' us where to move that big ol' branch that wrecked her porch."

"Then why am I still here? Why am I not on my way home?" My voice cracked with rage. "What the hell is going *on?*"

"Lady Alice said you changed your mind about goin'."

"*What?*"

"Said you decided to stay till Simmee had the baby."

I was speechless. I didn't know who or what to believe. "She said *you* wanted me to stay till Simmee had the baby!"

"Oh, yeah?" He let out a short bark of a laugh. "Well sometimes people put their own ideas in other people's mouths, now don't they? Lady Alice…she's a nice ol' gal and all, but she don't always tell the truth."

"Tully, *you* knew I need to get out of here. I don't care what Lady Alice said. *You* knew and you didn't do a damn thing about it!"

He worked on the rabbit, his expression impassive. "Well, you bein' so close to her and Simmee now…" He shrugged, glancing up at me. "I figured you had some girl talk and they knew more what you wanted than I did."

I glared at him. "What about your boat?" I asked. "You said when Larry came by you'd ask him to find a replacement for your boat."

"An' I did." He worked at the rabbit on the table while I kept my eyes locked on his face. "He's gonna look around, he said. Get me a good price."

"When?"

"He'll find one when he finds one. Not like you can snap your fingers and make a boat appear." He lifted his hand as if to snap his fingers, but his hand held the knife, and the blade caught a sliver of sunlight that made me blink.

He looked down at his messy work on the picnic table and I surveyed him in silence. So which one of them was telling the truth? Which one wanted me there to help deliver Simmee's baby? I lowered myself to the end of the bench, confused and defeated, and I knew there was no way I could get that answer. What did it matter, anyway? I was stuck here regardless. I wanted to believe Lady Alice. I trusted her. Felt affection for her. Tully was keeping me here because he was afraid Lady Alice couldn't manage Simmee's birth alone. Maybe he *was* scared and just couldn't admit it to me, so he had to blame Lady Alice. Tully wasn't the sort of man to admit to his fear. I watched his face as he worked on the rabbit. His eyelashes were long and blond and fell in soft crescents on his cheeks—an almost feminine feature on a body that was otherwise one hundred percent male. They made him look suddenly vulnerable. *He's afraid,* I thought. *Afraid of losing Simmee.* A tiny bit of my fury slipped away.

He looked up suddenly. "You still here?" he asked.

"The least you could have done was made sure Larry got in touch with my family."

"I didn't think of it," he said. "We was busy, and besides, how would I know how to get him in touch with them? Don't have no phone number or nothin'."

"My husband and sister have to be worried sick." My voice was quiet now. I'd given in. There was nothing I could do.

He set down his knife. "Then they'll be damn glad when they find out you're okay, Miss Maya," he said. "Won't that be a happy homecomin' for y'all."

I got to my feet. My shin stung a little. I'd barely noticed until now. I turned and walked toward the house. I'd never know the truth. The only thing I did know for certain was that I'd be the one delivering Simmee's baby. And that, I hoped and prayed, would be a good thing.

37

Rebecca

THE CONTEMPORARY CHURCH WAS HUGE, YET THERE WASN'T enough room for all the people who were trying to crowd into the interfaith memorial service. Every major television network had crews and equipment along the aisles on either side of the sanctuary, and in Rebecca's opinion, they were taking up more than their share of space, keeping out people who truly needed to be there. Only one of the major roads leading to the church was open. It was filled with broken asphalt and potholes, and buses and vans were backed up for miles. Many people had to get out of their vehicles and walk the rest of the way to the church, and the service began more than an hour late.

Rebecca, Adam and Dorothea sat in one of the reserved front pews. Janette's parents and brother sat near them, along with the families of a police officer, two firefighters and several other prominent area residents who had been lost to the storms.

Despite the decongestant she'd taken, Rebecca's head felt twice its normal size, and the voices of the minister, priest and rabbi came to her as if through layers of flannel. Yet she didn't care. She wouldn't have cared if her head fell clean off her shoulders. The numbness she'd felt when Maya had first disappeared was back, and she was glad. She tried to pay attention to the speakers, but they couldn't break through the wall she'd built around herself, and she was barely aware of the weeping and sniffling coming from the pews behind her.

Adam suddenly touched her arm as he rose to his feet, and for a moment, she felt confused, forgetting that he was to speak. She watched him walk up the two broad marble steps to the altar. Behind the pulpit, he looked pale as he cleared his throat. He was clean shaven now and freshly showered, but like her, he still wore his DIDA uniform, since they had no other clothing with them. Besides, when the service was over, they planned to go directly back to work. They were working the same shift again, and she was glad.

Adam began speaking, and for the first time since the service began, Rebecca was able to absorb what was being said. He talked about Janette and the helicopter pilot. He had no notes, but he spoke about them easily, and she knew he'd found time to speak to their families to learn about those two lost lives.

Then he began talking about Maya, telling the people filling the pews about his wife. What a skillful, committed doctor she was. How much she loved children. She'd longed for children herself, he said, but maybe there was a reason she hadn't been given any. Maybe she needed to spend her short time on earth helping as many children as possible. His voice grew stronger instead of weaker as he spoke, and Rebecca watched the color slowly return to his cheeks. With each word, each thread that connected him to her in their shared love of Maya, he grew more beautiful to her.

"She was afraid to come to Wilmington," Adam said. "She preferred working in the safety of her office and the hospital.

Working at a disaster site was far outside her comfort zone. But she overcame her fear to come down here. She showed us a courage we never knew she had, and her disappearance brought out in us a courage we never thought we'd need."

Rebecca swallowed past the lump in her throat. For the first time in two weeks, she felt her heart expand. Emptiness was replaced by something close to acceptance. After Louisa's death, Dorothea had delivered the eulogy to a church filled with the couple's many friends, and she'd quoted a proverb: "Grief shared is half the grief." Rebecca remembered those words now as she listened to her brother-in-law. Her *family*. She shut her eyes. *Thank you, God, for Adam.*

She opened her eyes as Adam continued speaking, but her thoughts had slipped to Brent. He'd called her again the night before, expressing sympathy over the termination of the search and asking her one more time to marry him. "Life is too *short*, Rebecca," he'd pleaded. She tried to imagine Brent's reaction if *she* had been the one in the helicopter crash. She tried to picture him in the pulpit where Adam now stood, but it was impossible. He never would have volunteered to speak. He hated speaking even in professional venues, yet it wasn't fair to judge him on his prowess as a speaker. She knew he loved her. Not the way Adam loved Maya, though. Had *once* loved Maya. Their problems had run deep, but that didn't change Adam's respect for her or the admiration that was coming through so clearly and tenderly in his words.

She didn't want Brent. Not as her husband. Not even as her lover.

Adam left the pulpit and walked down the two marble steps. His gaze was on hers as he approached their pew. He gave her a smile both tired and resigned, and she saw that his cheeks were wet.

She reached toward him, one arm outstretched as he took his seat next to her. She wrapped her hands around his arm and leaned close to him.

"Thank you," she whispered, and in her heart, grief dueled with hope, sorrow with possibility.

38

Maya

FOR THE FIRST TIME, I WAS GATHERING EGGS FROM THE CHICKEN coop with Simmee. During my time at Last Run Shelter, I'd allowed her to gather the eggs and tend to the chickens each morning, while I remained in bed, acting as though our breakfast food came from the supermarket. From the beginning, when I was needy and hurt, she'd taken care of me. Waited on me. In the last few days, though, I realized that I needed to reverse our roles. Simmee was tired, anxious and, I was quite certain, depressed. There was something leaden about her, and it worried me. I didn't tell her about Larry showing up at Lady Alice's or my confusion over why I was still there when everyone knew I was desperate to leave. I didn't want Simmee caught in the middle of that mess. It was the last thing she needed.

So, bright and early that morning, right after Tully left the house with his fishing gear, I'd asked her to show me how to take care of the chickens.

"Ain't no big science to it," she'd said. We started gathering the eggs from the nesting boxes, and she told me how much feed to give the chickens and how often to fill their water dish. Neither of us said it, but we both knew what we were thinking: this would be my job for at least a couple of days after Simmee had the baby.

"I'll cook," I said, as we carried the eggs toward the house. I'd lit the coals in the grill before starting our work in the coop, so I knew they would be hot enough by now. Adam and I had a six-burner gas grill, and until the day before, I'd never cooked anything over charcoal in my life. Yesterday, though, I'd lit the fire and made it hot enough to boil a pot of water, into which I placed Simmee's sewing scissors, a couple of lengths of twine and small squares of cloth I'd cut and planned to use as gauze. I wanted to be ready for the baby's birth. When I looked in the bassinet to see what Simmee had in the way of bedding, I was surprised to find a large Easter basket. It was cheaply made of pink and purple plastic wicker, and it contained a small, green flannel blanket, a few neatly folded cloth diapers and a box of sanitary pads. When I questioned Simmee about the basket, she said she planned to use it to "cart the baby around." I thought about the wearable baby carriers I'd researched for my own babies. When I got home, I would find a way to send her one of them.

There was an old mattress in the bassinet itself. It had been inserted into a pillowcase, but it was too soft to be safe for the baby, and I lay awake the night before, trying to think of things I could stuff into it to make it firmer. Lady Alice had cut one of her old quilts into swaddling blankets, and I thought a couple of them would do the trick.

I expected Simmee to start washing the eggs herself once we were in the kitchen, but she didn't put up a fight when I told her to sit down and let me do it. She sank into one of the kitchen chairs, awkwardly, left hip first, then right, as if she were trying to sit on a few eggs herself without cracking them.

"I'll come out with you when you're ready to cook," she said. I smiled at her. "I can do it," I said. "I'm not totally inept."

"What's inept?"

I couldn't think of a single definition that wouldn't involve even more complex words. "Useless," I said. Close enough. "I'm not totally useless."

Simmee sighed. "That's how I feel these days," she said. "Useless."

"You're saving your energy. That's a good thing."

I was cracking the fifth egg into the bowl when I heard her draw in a long breath. I turned to look at her. "Are you all right?"

She pressed her lips together, and at first I thought she was in pain. My hand held the empty egg shell above the bowl. "Simmee?"

"It was my fault my mama died," she said.

I dropped the shell into the garbage pail. "Simmee," I said, in the voice I might use to soothe a child who thought she'd seen a ghost, "how could it possibly be your fault?"

"I was all turned funny," she said. "Lady Alice had trouble gettin' me out at first, and I guess somethin' tore open in my mama and she bled to death."

I didn't pick up the sixth egg. "Has anyone ever said it was your fault?" I asked.

"You ain't got to be no genius to figure it out." She pulled the sugar bowl close to her on the table and started toying with the spoon.

"The word 'fault' implies that a person actually did something to cause harm to someone else," I said.

"What's 'implies' mean?"

"I mean…you were a baby just trying to be born, Simmee." I felt the knot in my chest. "You didn't do anything intentional to hurt your mother."

"Gran said Daddy was crazy in love with Mama." She moved the spoon back and forth a few times in the sugar bowl. "He said he didn't want nothin' to do with the child that kilt her. That's why he left."

"Maybe he was so racked with grief that he wasn't thinking straight," I said charitably, working hard to keep the anger out of my voice. "Whatever his excuse for leaving, it wasn't your fault."

"He never got over it." Simmee tilted her head up a little to look out the window. I followed her gaze, expecting to see Tully returning home early, but there was no one there. "He never come to see me or nothin'. Gran didn't even know his whole name. He and Mama weren't married."

I couldn't get a handle on the *real* fear behind her words. She and Tully weren't married, either. Was she afraid she would die and Tully would blame the baby and desert him or her the way she'd been deserted?

"Tully would never do anything like that. And besides," I added quickly, "you are *not* going to die."

"You don't know what it's like comin' up without a mama," she said.

I didn't understand the flood of emotion that washed over me. All I knew was that I was going to tell her. I knew it the moment she said those words. Maybe the moment she said it was her fault her mother had died. I'd never told a soul the truth about that night, and why I was going to tell Simmee, I couldn't have said. A shared vulnerability, perhaps. An intimacy I couldn't quite name.

I wiped the egg white off my fingers with the rag that hung from the drawer handle. Then I sat down kitty-corner from her at the table.

"My mother's dead, too," I said. "And my father. And it really *is* my fault that they died."

Her eyes widened. "What do you mean?" she whispered as though someone might hear us.

"Do you remember the day we were at Lady Alice's and we heard Tully shoot something in the distance? Remember how I freaked out?"

She nodded.

"That sound." I shuddered, remembering the *crack* of gunfire as it echoed through the forest. "It made me remember things I don't like remembering."

"What kind of things?"

I folded my arms across my chest, hugging myself. Holding on tight.

"My sister—"

"Rebecca."

"Yes. Rebecca." I pictured Becca, not as she looked now, but as she had then. Her hair long and brown. Her body slender, but curvy. Her clothes, a little too tight. "When she was eighteen, she had a boyfriend named Zed. He was…not a nice guy." I hugged myself even tighter. "I was jealous of Rebecca. She was pretty and seemed so much more mature than me. I was…awkward, and I was only fourteen."

"Same as me when I met Tully."

I hadn't thought of that. I tried to imagine Simmee as young and gullible as I had been. Thank God Tully had turned out to truly care about her. "Rebecca was so in love with Zed." His name tasted like acid in my mouth. "You know how sometimes you can be drawn to the bad boys."

Simmee looked at me blankly, and I realized she didn't understand that attraction at all.

"Our parents said she couldn't see him anymore. Becca fought with them…it was a big mess. I knew she was sneaking out to see him, but after a while, she stopped."

"Were your parents mean?"

"No. No, not at all." I suddenly pictured my parents. I so rarely allowed myself to think of them, but every once in a while they'd slink into my mind unbidden, frozen in time, only a few years older than I was now. I let go of my arms and rested my hands on the table, but they were shaking so hard that I curled them into fists and dropped them to my lap instead.

"One day, I was walking home from school and Zed pulled over and offered me a ride and I got in. He was so…" I shivered. My memory of him from that day—his dark hair, his smiling blue eyes—morphed suddenly into Zed wearing the ski mask. Nausea teased me. I pressed my hand to my forehead, resting my elbow on the table.

"You shouldn't of got in." Simmee was whispering again.

"You're right. I shouldn't have," I whispered back, then found my voice to go on. "But I thought he was so…cute, and he told me I looked pretty. That was all it took. He said Rebecca was a coward for not going out with him any longer. That she let our parents say who she could or couldn't see. Then he asked *me* out."

Simmee sucked in her breath.

"Not on a date, exactly." It seemed extremely important that I get this right. If I was finally going to tell the story, I wanted it to be the truth. "He asked me to meet him that night at a park by my house. I was so excited." I hugged myself again. "I felt like…he made me feel older, like I could *finally* have something Rebecca couldn't have. You never had a brother or sister, so it's probably hard for you to understand."

"I understand," she said. "I seen it with Jackson and Larry all the time. Jackson and all his brothers."

"So you get it," I said. "Boys never even looked at me. I was gawky. I was very easily seduced." I hunted for a simpler word. "Easily—"

"I know what you mean," she interrupted.

"I started sneaking out to meet him at the park nearly every night." I hated this memory. I wanted it to belong to someone else. Not me. "We'd go riding around in his car. I couldn't believe how lucky I was to be with him."

"Did he try to do it with you?" Simmee asked.

I shook my head. "He was too smart for that," I said. "He kissed me a couple of times, but he wanted to reel me in slowly." The thought of the kisses that had thrilled me then sickened me now. "We'd just drive around. He'd give me beer or a joint—"

"Weed."

"Right. I hated it, but pretended I loved it so he'd like me. I thought I was having grown-up kind of fun for a change."

Simmee smiled uncertainly, and I looked away.

"Becca was miserable, and I…I felt a little guilty, but I was too happy to really care." I remembered how Zed talked about my parents. What assholes they were for not letting Rebecca see him. How much braver I was than my sister for sneaking around behind their backs. I always squirmed when he put down my parents.

"Finally, one night, he forced himself on me."

"Oh, no," Simmee said.

I wrapped my hands around the sugar bowl. What had I expected to happen? That Zed would be content to drive around with me night after night with nothing more than a kiss before dropping me off at the park again? In my fourteen-year-old fantasy world, I'd imagined us getting married one day. I saw myself as a virgin on our wedding night. I'd been incredibly stupid.

I couldn't tell Simmee the details. It was bad enough to remember them myself. My skin still crawled at the thought of him running his hand up my bare thigh, pushing the leg of my shorts to one side. I still couldn't wear shorts without feeling exposed and vulnerable. *You wore the right thing tonight, Maya,* he'd laughed, unzipping his jeans. *You won't even have to take these off.*

I fought him, but he was so much stronger than I was. *You wanted to be like Rebecca, didn't you?* he'd said.

Why didn't I scream? I was so scared someone would come and I'd get in trouble, and that seemed even worse than what was happening to me. Still, when he rolled his body between my legs and I felt his penis tear into me, I would have howled if he hadn't slapped his hand across my mouth. I cried instead, my body shaking as he ripped the innocent child right out of me.

"He raped you," Simmee said.

"I thought I deserved it because I was sneaking out with a boy my parents hated." How did this sound to Simmee? Fourteen probably didn't seem too young to have sex for the first time. "Did you and Tully…? You were just fourteen when you met him."

Simmee's eyes widened. "Oh, no. We didn't do nothin' like that, and he sure never would of raped me." She nearly smiled. "I probly would of done it with him, but he treated me like a kid sister in the beginning. I was fifteen the first time, an' he used condoms till we decided to have a baby."

"Really?" I hadn't expected that level of sophistication from Tully, or that her baby had actually been planned.

"Did you tell anybody he raped you?" Simmee asked.

"No." I rubbed my neck. *"And* I kept on seeing him. He told me if I didn't, he'd tell Rebecca what was going on, and I didn't know what to do. How to…*save* myself." I stared out the window, my gut roiling. "I was a wreck. I stopped hanging out with my friends because I couldn't talk to them any longer. They were talking about the fourteen-year-old boys in our school, and I…I was so screwed up."

"What's it have to do with your parents getting kilt, though?" Simmee asked.

"I got pregnant," I said.

She sucked in her breath. "You *did?* You had a baby?"

"No. No." That baby would be twenty now. In my weakest moments, I pictured him or her. Imagined the love between us.

"You had one of them miscarriages," Simmee said softly.

"No." I folded my hands beneath my chin. "My father...he noticed I was getting sick in the mornings, because he drove me to school every day."

"He figured it out?"

I nodded. *My good, gentle Daddy.* "Instead of taking me to school one day, he took me to the park—the same one where Zed and I hung out at night. He said he knew something was wrong. He was really, really kind." My voice broke, and I wasn't sure I'd be able to go on.

Simmee reached over to smooth her hand over mine on the table. Back and forth. Back and forth.

"I started crying and told him everything," I was finally able to say.

"I'm sorry, Miss Maya," Simmee said.

"I expected him to get angry with me, but he held me. He rocked me in his arms like I was a little girl. He said he'd help me. I didn't understand much about abortion—" I looked up at her. "Do you know what an abortion is?"

"'Course," she said.

"He said he wouldn't put me through having a baby. He was going to arrange an abortion for me without telling my mother, and he was going to make sure Zed never came near me again. I felt terrible that I was going to have an abortion," I said, "because my mother had taught me it was wrong. But

I also couldn't imagine myself pregnant. I *especially* couldn't imagine giving birth. I viewed the whole thing through a child's eyes."

"You *was* a child," Simmee said. "I think I was older when I was fourteen than you were."

"I think you're right," I agreed.

"So what happened?"

"I told Zed that my father knew everything and that I was pregnant and was going to have an abortion. He was furious. He said it was his baby, too, and I had no right to get rid of it. He wanted to know where I would have the abortion so he could go there and blow the place up, and he said if my father thought taking a life was no big deal maybe he deserved to have *his* life taken. I think that's when I realized he was crazy, and I was so glad my father was going to make him stay away from me." It wasn't until years later that I learned my father had retained a lawyer and planned to have Zed locked up for statutory rape. Another father might have tracked him down and beaten him to a pulp, but Daddy was far too civilized for that. "So Daddy took me to the clinic and I had the abortion," I said. "When we got home, though…" I looked at Simmee. "This is so hard to remember."

"Tell me." She tightened her hand around mine, just a little.

"We were in the driveway, and my mother ran out of the house and I thought she'd figured out where we'd been. I was terrified of what she'd say. I was mostly terrified of her…her *disappointment* in me. She opened the car door and I expected her to…I don't know. To yell, I guess. But she got in and slammed the door shut and screamed at my father to drive."

"Why?" Simmee frowned.

"Because Zed was there. In the driveway. I didn't realize it right away, because he was wearing a ski mask…a mask that covered his whole face. Except for his eyes." I swallowed hard once. Twice. "That's how I knew it was him. His eyes…he was holding a gun." The old terror swelled inside me, and I heard my mother's screams. "I ducked behind the driver's seat, and then he started shooting. Blood was…it was everywhere, and the gun was so loud." I pulled my hand from Simmee's to cover my ears, as though I could block out the sound of gunfire and breaking glass that still filled my nightmares.

"Maya," Simmee said softly, and somewhere I registered the fact that she had never simply called me *Maya* before, omitting the *Miss,* as though we were suddenly equals in age. In social status. In *heartbreak.* She reached for my hand where it covered my ear, and drew it back to the table, cradled it in both of hers. Her eyes were red. "Poor little girl," she said.

"My sister." My voice broke. "Rebecca came out of the house and threw something at him. This boot cleaner we had." I pictured the boot cleaner on Lady Alice's porch. "She threw it at Zed. And he ran away. I didn't see any of what happened, because I was hiding behind the seats."

"Did the sheriff ever catch him?"

"The police did, yes. Rebecca told them he was one of my father's students who was angry over something. That was true. He was one of Daddy's students. She didn't say anything about him being her ex-boyfriend, and I didn't say anything about my connection to him either, because then Rebecca would have known that it was my fault our parents were…gone. The cops went to the place he was living and there was a shootout and Zed was killed."

"Good," Simmee said. "He deserved it."

"Becca and I never talked about it," I said. "I know she probably blamed herself, just like I did. Like I still do. I was always afraid she'd somehow figure out it was all my fault."

"It *wasn't* your fault," Simmee said. "Not even a little bit.

You said yourself, you was just a kid. You wasn't the one that shot the gun."

"It still feels like it was my fault. That's how it's always going to feel."

"Just how I feel like my mama dyin' was my fault, but you were right. It wasn't. I was a baby, and you was a kid. Ain't neither of our faults."

I looked at the table, where she had locked her fingers with mine. "The abortion left scars," I said. "They think that's why I keep losing my babies."

Simmee unlaced our fingers and turned my hand over, peering at my palm. "What you told me explains somethin' I seen here," she said, her fingertip lightly touching my palm. "Here on your lifeline. This little square? It's s'posed to mean you been in prison sometime, but I knew you wasn't the type that ever was in prison. Now I get it though." She looked at me. Bit her lower lip. "You made a prison right inside your own head."

39

Rebecca

REBECCA'S PATIENT, A MIDDLE-AGED WOMAN WITH A MIGRAINE, leaned toward her, "Oh, good Lord," she whispered, pointing to the corner of the busy clinic, "look at that."

Rebecca turned her head. In the corner, Adam was bandaging a shoulder wound on a guy whose entire back was covered by a tattoo. A bald eagle sailed across a blue sky, the American flag waving in a breeze behind the bird's wing.

Rebecca swiveled back to her patient, giving her a look of mock horror. "Yikes," she said quietly as she handed the woman a bottle of pills. Her own head was still a bit achy, though her cold was nearly gone.

"Why would anyone do that to his body?" the woman asked.

"No way!" The man suddenly shouted so loudly that everyone in the room turned to look. Rebecca saw him leap to his feet, his hand over the bandage on his shoulder. He couldn't have been more than eighteen.

Adam, syringe in hand, looked up at him in surprise. "You really need a tetanus shot," he said. "You said the hinge was rusty and—"

"Uh-uh!" The guy grabbed his T-shirt from the gurney. "I'm scared of needles, man!" he shouted, heading for the classroom door.

Adam looked over at Rebecca and burst out laughing, and half of the people in the clinic, patients and staff alike, joined in.

"Oh, good Lord," Rebecca's patient said again as she stood to go. "Do you believe it?"

Rebecca smiled. It felt so strange to smile. So very strange.

That morning, she'd told Adam that she'd broken up with Brent—although she didn't tell him Brent's response. Brent had hesitated a moment after she told him, then asked, "So who are you fucking there?" His assumption—and the way he delivered it—irritated the hell out of her. It was only his hurt and disappointment coming through, she knew, but it still irked her. Breaking up with him had been the right decision. The relief she felt in every cell of her body told her so.

She was cleaning her examining table, readying it for her next patient, when a teenage boy suddenly burst into the room. His blond hair was so long that, at first glance, she thought he was a girl,

"My mother passed out in the hallway!" he shouted.

Rebecca glanced at Adam. He was shaking hands with a woman who held a squirming little boy in her arms. "I've got it," she said, and started to follow the boy out of the clinic. Fainting in the airless hallway while waiting to see the clinic staff was nothing new. Fainting *anywhere* in the school was nothing new.

In the hall, she saw people huddled around the woman on the floor.

"Let me through!" she said, and when they parted, she caught her breath. *Maya?* The woman was Maya's height and weight and her blonde hair was cut in Maya's chin-length style. Rebecca rushed forward, filled with irrational hope. She dropped to the floor next to the pale, unconscious woman, knowing she was not her sister, yet still wishing there was some miraculous way to turn her *into* Maya.

She rested her fingers on the woman's neck, searching un-successfully for a pulse.

"Run back to the clinic," she told the boy. "Tell Dr. Pollard we need the crash cart. Hurry!"

Rebecca raised the woman's polo shirt and began chest com-pressions, ignoring the sickening feeling in her own chest as she crunched down on her patient's rib cage. In less than a minute, she heard Adam pushing the crash cart toward her in the hallway.

"Ambu bag!" she called. Glancing toward him, she saw the startled look on his face as he took in the woman's features. He sank to the floor opposite Rebecca. Attaching the moni-tor leads to the woman's chest, he whispered, "For a minute I thought—"

"I know," Rebecca said.

Adam pressed the bag to the woman's mouth and began squeezing it. "EMS driver's getting the backboard," he said.

Rebecca glanced at the monitor. Nothing. She took the paddles from the defibrillator and Adam leaned back as she de-livered the shock. *Come on, honey,* she whispered.

The monitor registered an irregular series of beats that eased into a thready, sluggish rhythm. Good enough for now, she thought.

The EMS driver appeared carrying a yellow backboard. "The medics are at the hospital," he said. "I'll drive, but you two'll have to come with her."

"Great," Adam said under his breath.

He wouldn't be familiar with the back of an ambulance,

Rebecca thought, but disaster work had made her a Jill of all trades. She'd be able to find what they needed. If she did one thing today, it was going to be to save the life of this woman who looked so much like Maya.

Inside the ambulance, Adam quickly intubated the woman with the ease of an anesthesiologist, despite his grumbling about the equipment, while Rebecca started a second IV. *Like we've been working together all our lives,* she thought. The driver turned on the siren, but the roads were filled with potholes and the going was slow. They'd all be deaf by the time they reached the hospital, but she didn't care as long as they could keep their patient's heart pumping and oxygen flowing. That was all that mattered.

When they finally arrived in the E.R., the woman was quickly whisked into one of the treatment rooms. Rebecca watched the doors close behind the gurney, and bit her lip, folding her hands together almost as if she was praying. She glanced at Adam.

"Wow," he said. "That was spooky."

"I'm just glad we got her back," Rebecca said, then winced at her words. "You know what I mean." She nodded toward the door. "This patient."

He nodded, giving her an empathetic smile. "I know exactly what you mean." He tossed an arm across her shoulders. "We're a team, you and me," he whispered, as if no one should hear. As if it was a secret.

A few minutes later, she and Adam were in the ambulance once again, heading back to the school. This time, though, Adam drove and Rebecca sat in the passenger seat. The EMS driver had bumped into his elderly aunt in the waiting area of the E.R., and he wanted to stay with her. He'd handed Adam the keys. "I'll find a ride back later," he'd said.

There was far less traffic on the road leading away from the hospital than there had been leading to it, and they were quiet in the ambulance. Rebecca was tired, both from the tail end of her cold as well as from the frantic effort to save their patient. But she felt exhilarated, nevertheless. High from saving a life. She leaned against the door as they bounced along the road, her gaze on Adam. He was smiling, and she guessed he felt the same euphoria that she was feeling. *We're a team, you and me.* His perfectly shaped fingers tapped the steering wheel to music only he could hear, and he nodded his head to a soundless rhythm. His hair was too long, curling over the collar of his uniform vest. She felt an unexpected joy at being with him, and then an ache that stretched across her chest and rose high into her throat.

She loved him.

He glanced at her and she wondered if the emotion, so raw and exposed and *wrong,* was written all over her face. If he were not her brother-in-law, she might have said something provocative. Suggestive. Instead, she felt her throat grow red and hot, and quickly looked away. Uncomfortable, she reached toward the cluster of knobs and buttons on the dashboard. "Is this the radio?" she pointed to one of the buttons.

"Looks like it," he said.

She started to push the button just as they hit a pothole. Losing her balance, she leaned hard on the console and its array of toggle switches between their seats. Suddenly, the siren began to blare.

She jumped. "What did I hit?"

"Turn it off!" Adam shouted.

She tried to read the lettering above each toggle switch, but the ambulance was bouncing from pothole to pothole and she couldn't make out the words.

"I have no idea which one to press!" she said.

Adam glanced at the console, but quickly jerked his eyes back to the road as they dove into another hole in the pavement. The siren squawked above their heads, and the cars and trucks in front of them drove onto the shoulder of the road to let them pass.

Rebecca toggled the switches on the console, feeling as if she were in a comedy sketch, and before she knew it she was laughing. By the time she found the right switch and the interior of the ambulance filled with a welcome silence, they were both laughing so hard they could no longer see the road.

Adam called the hospital to check on the Maya look-alike as they walked back to their trailer after their shift that evening.

"Fantastic!" he said into the phone.

"She's doing okay?" she asked as he flipped his phone closed.

"No major damage," he said. "Now we've got a good excuse to celebrate."

They'd picked up a six-pack of beer, a bag of tortilla chips and a jar of salsa after the siren fiasco, and she'd been looking forward to indulging in them all afternoon. Now, though, she was not so sure.

"We should invite Dot over," she said, knowing perfectly well why she was making the suggestion: she didn't want to be alone with Adam, especially not with a couple of beers in her. She'd do something stupid. Something they'd both end up regretting. This was not some guy she could quickly bed and forget, nor did she want to. *Family*. That's what he wanted and what they both needed. Her feelings for him felt both right and wrong. Until she could sort them out, she wouldn't play with fire.

"She'll drink on duty?" he asked.

"Hell, yes," Rebecca said. "As long as she's not working in the clinic. She'll drink us under the table."

Adam looked reluctant as he dialed Dorothea's number and issued the invitation. He got off the phone with a shrug. "She'll be over in a little while," he said, as they stepped into the trailer. "She asked why we didn't buy a six-pack for each of us."

Rebecca poured the salsa into a bowl, while Adam pulled two beers from the refrigerator. They climbed onto the double bed and sat opposite one another, their backs against the trailer walls. Rebecca crossed her legs and took a sip from the bottle. She would talk about Maya. Safe subject. She'd keep Maya foremost in her mind.

"Okay," she said, "did that woman today look like Maya's twin or what?"

"Totally freakish," Adam agreed.

Thank God it wasn't Maya.

The thought slipped into her mind so quickly she couldn't stop it. She lowered her eyes to her beer bottle, her face hot again, as though she'd said the words out loud. She started peeling the label from the bottle, unable to look Adam in the eye.

She was ready to let Maya go. She *had* to let her go. She could no longer tolerate the uncertainty.

"I keep feeling she's not dead," Adam said suddenly.

She couldn't quite read his tone. She glanced up from the bottle. "Intellectually, though, you know she's gone, right?" she asked.

He looked thoughtful as he leaned forward to dip a chip in the salsa. "Well, I guess if I didn't think that, I'd still be out there looking for her." He chewed the chip. Took a swallow of beer. "Where do you think she is?" he asked.

She raised her eyebrows. "Do you mean…her body? Or her…"

"Her soul." He looked suddenly shy, and so, so vulnerable. The open, trusting beauty in his face made her throat ache again, as it had in the ambulance. *You are so beautiful,* she wanted to say. *So beautiful, I don't know what to do.*

"I can't think about it." She tore the label clear off the bottle. "When my parents died, I tried to convince myself that they were in heaven together. That's what I was brought up to believe—by my mother, anyway. My father was totally…faithless, I guess you'd say. But it all seems like magical thinking to me."

"Well, I choose to believe that's where she is," Adam said. "I choose to believe she's an angel, singing karaoke with a good voice."

"What?" Rebecca laughed. "She didn't have a good voice."

"No kidding." Adam smiled. She loved the way his overgrown hair curled over the tops of his ears. "Maybe in heaven, though, she could have one."

Rebecca remembered Maya and their father singing along with the tape deck in the car. Their father had a good voice and Maya did not, though that didn't seem to matter to him. They sang stuffy old show tunes. To this day, any rendition of "Oklahoma" or "Edelweiss" could make her toes curl.

"Didn't she tell you about the wedding we went to where she sang karaoke?" Adam crunched down on a tortilla chip.

"No way. She'd never…I can't picture it. And she really couldn't sing."

"This is true," he said. "But you know how funny she could be when she had too much to drink?"

"Actually, no." One more thing she hadn't known about her sister.

"She was a little tipsy at the reception, and we egged her on and she finally got up and did it." He laughed. "God, she was terrible, but she got points for being a good sport."

"What did she sing?"

"'Dancing Queen.'"

"No!" Rebecca said. She already had the beginning of a buzz, and it felt good. Excellent, actually. It was a relief to shut down her thinking for a while. "Tell me you're joking," she said.

"I'm not." Adam held the bottle in front of his mouth and started singing, waving his free arm dramatically through the air. "Dancin' queen, la la la la, dancin' queen!"

"Oh my God, I wish I'd seen that!" Rebecca laughed. "Although, seeing this impersonation is nearly as good."

Adam chuckled as he leaned back against the wall, and Rebecca watched him take a long pull on his beer. "How 'bout that siren?" he asked, and they both cracked up again. She was laughing so hard she didn't even hear the trailer door open. Adam must have, though, because he lifted his head toward the trailer's interior, where Dorothea stood in the dim kitchen light, hands on her hips.

"I see you two have reached the hysterical laughing stage of grief," she said.

She was smiling, but Rebecca felt a stab of guilt, and she sat up straight. "What are you talking about?" she asked.

"You know," Dorothea said. She walked straight to the refrigerator and took out a beer. "Elizabeth Kübler-Ross's five stages of grieving?" She kicked off her shoes and joined them on the bed, sitting cross-legged on Rebecca's side of the wall. Aging hippie, Rebecca thought. Except for the beer she was swigging, Dorothea looked like a yoga instructor for seniors.

Adam began ticking the stages of grief off on his fingers. "Denial—check. Anger—check. Bargaining." He looked at Rebecca. "Did we do that one?"

"Definitely," Rebecca said. "Remember? If we got her back, I was going to talk to her every single day."

"Right. What's the next one?"

"Depression," Rebecca said soberly. "We're still there."

"Right. And acceptance?" He shook his head. "We're never going to get to that one."

I'm nearly there, Rebecca thought. Was it wrong to reach acceptance so quickly?

"Well, Kübler-Ross, brilliant though she was, left out the hysterical laughing stage," Dorothea said. "That's where the two of you are. I could hear you out in the parking lot."

"You should have heard us in the ambulance today." Adam's legs were stretched out in front of him, and he tapped Rebecca's knee with his toes.

"Did you go through that stage after Louisa died?" she asked Dorothea.

"Hell, yes. I'm still in it," she said. "Every time I look at the damn purple cabinets in my kitchen, I get hysterical."

Rebecca laughed.

"If I didn't laugh," Dorothea said, "I'd cry."

"Exactly," Adam said. He passed the bowl of chips to her, and she took one and dipped it in the salsa.

"Getting serious for a moment," Adam said, his gaze on Dorothea, "I'd like to join DIDA full-time."

"What?" Rebecca asked.

Dorothea cocked her head at him. "Now's not the time to make that decision," she said. "You're tired. You're living in a situation that feels a thousand times removed from the real world. You just lost your wife. *And* you're drinking. Not the time." Then she added, "And there's no money working for DIDA."

"I don't care about the money," Adam scoffed. "It might not be forever. It might only be for a year or two. But right now, this is what I want to do."

"'Cause you can fill up the empty place with this work," Dorothea said.

He hesitated. "I suppose that's part of it."

Rebecca wondered if that's why *she* liked working with DIDA herself. She'd always said she loved the challenge. Loved being able to help where help was so desperately needed. The physical risks. The excitement. Was she trying to fill an empty place inside her? She remembered Dorothea telling her she was like a well that was impossible to fill.

"I hope you *do* decide to stick with DIDA, Adam," she said, with none of the emotion she was feeling, "but Dot's right. Now's a bad time to make the decision."

"Call your office," Dorothea said to him. "Tell them you're not coming back for a while. Piss them off. Then stay here and see how you feel in a few more weeks."

"I will," he said, "but I don't think I'm going to change my mind."

Rebecca smiled at him across the bed. She rested her hand on the top of his foot, giving it a squeeze, and for the second time that day, felt an unabashed sense of joy.

40

Maya

I WAS ALONE IN THE CHICKEN COOP, TENDING THE CHICKENS on my own for the first time. I'd risen in the near dark of early dawn, surprised to find I was first to be up, and I went about the business of gathering the eggs and feeding the chickens, only a little worried that something was wrong. Simmee was always up long before me.

I heard the squeak of the screen door and looked up to see Tully walking toward the coop, his rifle slung over his shoulder.

"Morning," I said coolly. I hadn't forgiven him for not telling Larry about me.

"You turnin' into an ol' hand at this stuff, ain't you?" He motioned toward the chicken coop.

"I wouldn't say that," I said. "Where's Simmee?"

"Got a bellyache." He looked toward the path. "She's sendin' me over to take care of Lady Alice's roof. Givin' me a hard time about it. I'll try to get us somethin' for supper, so we can save what I smoked yesterday. But you check on her for me, will you?"

"All right," I said, wondering if Simmee's bellyache could

be the start of labor. It would be like her not to put two and two together.

I'd fed the chickens and put six eggs in the basket by the time the screen door squeaked open again. I waited for Simmee to appear around the corner of the house, but she didn't. I was about to call her name when she called mine.

"Maya?" Her voice was little more than a hoarse whisper. Quickly, I left the coop and walked toward the house. She stood on the stoop in a sleeveless blue dress that ballooned over her belly, and she leaned heavily against the doorjamb. Her cheeks were florid, made even more so by the pallor in the rest of her face.

"Are you all right?" I asked.

"Is Tully gone?"

"Yes," I said, hurrying toward her. "Do you want me to go after him?"

She shook her head, then screwed up her face as though she might cry. "Oh, *Maya,*" she moaned. "Them pains started in the middle of the night. I think the baby's comin'."

In the middle of the night? "Tully just said you had a stomachache." Could Tully be that dense?

"That's what I told him," she said. "I been tryin' to hide the pain from him."

I stepped closer to her, confused. "Why, honey?" I asked. "Why do you want to hide it from him?"

She gave a quick shake of her head, and I knew I wasn't going to get the answer now. For the first time, I noticed she had the ball of twine in her hands, the one I'd cut lengths from to tie off the umbilical cord. Why was she carrying it around with her?

"Has your water broken?" I asked. "Did a whole lot of water come—"

"In the bed." She suddenly cringed, nearly doubling over. "Oh!" she said.

I glanced at my bare wrist to begin timing her contractions, forgetting that my watch had died in the floodwaters. "Do you know how often the pains are coming?" I stepped past her to open the door. "Let's go back to the bedroom, all right?"

"No." She stood woodenly on the stoop. "Not now. We got to—"

"Then let me get Tully," I said. "He should be here with—"

"No!" she said. "I sent him to Lady Alice's on purpose, 'cause I had a feelin' the baby was comin'."

Was she embarrassed at having Tully with her during labor and delivery? I had to remind myself that we were not in Raleigh. This was a different culture. Nearly a different *era*. "It's okay," I said. "Come on. Let me check you and see what's happening." I tugged a little at her arm, but she squirmed away from me, nearly toppling off the stoop.

"Maya!" The word exploded from her lips on a puff of air. "I'm so scared."

"I know," I said. "But you don't need to be. I'm sure you're fine. If you'll let me examine you, I'll be able to see the baby's position. Then I can reassure you that what happened to your mother won't happen to you." I prayed that was the truth and that I would find absolutely nothing amiss.

"I don't…" Simmee shook her hands in front of her like a kid who was excited or anxious, the loose end of the ball of twine flapping in the air, and again I thought she was embarrassed. She'd probably never had a gynecological exam before. Most likely she'd never seen a doctor in her life. "I figgered wrong." She pressed her hand to her mouth. "I'm so sorry. I should of told you things before now, but—"

"Told me what?" I wondered if she knew something about her condition that I needed to know.

"I was too scared," she said.

"What, honey?" I said. "Tell me now. It's okay."

Her gaze darted toward the woods. Toward the path to Lady Alice's. "We need to go someplace."

I nearly laughed. "Not today, we don't," I said. "You're going inside and we're going to figure out how soon this baby will be born."

She shook her head. "I need to show you somethin'." She stepped off the stoop and waved toward me to follow her. "C'mon."

"No, Simmee!" I said firmly. She was acting so childish and strange that I thought the only approach to take with her was parental. "Nothing you need to show me can be that important. I want you to get in the house now!"

She turned and smacked me on the arm with her fist. Not hard, but hard enough to let me know she meant business.

"You gotta come with me!" she said. "I'm sorry! You're gonna be so mad at me."

I grabbed her shoulders. "Simmee, listen to me." Beneath my hands, I felt her body tremble. "I don't know what you're talking about, but I'm not going to be mad at you, okay? I care about you. I care a lot. You're a wonderful girl. A wonderful *woman*. You nursed me back to health. Now you need to let me take care of *you*. Please. Let me check the baby's position. Then we can—"

"No!" She nearly shouted as she pulled away from my grasp. "Come with me!" She marched down the path toward Lady Alice's, disappearing around the first bend, and I saw no choice but to follow her.

She was moving quickly and I hurried to catch up. It suddenly occurred to me it was Lady Alice she wanted. Not me. That was why she thought I'd be angry at her. Why she was apologizing. When I reached her, she suddenly stopped on the path, clearly in the throes of another contraction, and I lightly touched her back. "I understand you want Lady Alice with you, Simmee. And that's just fine. You go back to the house and I'll get—"

"No!" she growled. "Shut up!" Her face was red, streaming with perspiration and knotted with pain.

"Breathe slowly," I said. "Take long deep breaths. It will help with the pain." I'd lost track of the contractions. Were they about seven minutes apart? Five? I had no idea. All I knew was that they were too close together for comfort.

She ignored my suggestion to breathe deeply, letting the contraction play itself out, and then continued walking, hugging the ball of twine to her chest as if it were an infant. I followed, confused and helpless. Walking would hurry her labor, and I didn't want to go too far from the house, but Simmee showed no sign of stopping. She plowed ahead, suddenly turning off the path into the undergrowth.

"Where are you going?" I stopped on the path. In the distance, I could hear the tapping sound of a hammer: Tully at work on Lady Alice's roof.

She didn't answer, and I had to follow her into the brush or I'd lose her.

"We shouldn't go this far from the house!" I quickly raised my arm to prevent a branch from smacking me in the face.

"Hush!" She turned to glare at me and, as if remembering her manners, added, "Please."

"I don't want you to end up giving birth in the woods," I argued, but she ignored me.

I followed her deeper into the brambles and ankle-grabbing vines, slapping mosquitoes Simmee didn't seem to notice. Was she having a psychotic break? That was the only explanation I could think of. All I knew was that she seemed to be picking up speed while I lagged behind, uncertain of where in the morass of weeds and vines I should place my next step. I tripped once. Twice. She turned only long enough to tell me to hurry, and I tried my best, but this was her turf, not mine. I was lost, in more ways than one. I should have tried harder to take control when I still stood a chance of doing so. I was so turned around in the woods, that even if I decided it would be best to make my way to Lady Alice's to get her and Tully—and I was now certain that *would* be best—I wouldn't have known which way to go. One tree trunk looked like another. Each long, twisted vine was just like the next. I thought of calling for Tully, but we had moved far from Lady Alice's house by now. I was certain of it, and I knew my shout would be swallowed by the trees.

Every few minutes, Simmee let out a groan and I wasn't sure if the sound was due to pain or anxiety—or insanity. She only stopped once or twice more, gasping for breath before she charged forward again. I pleaded with her to turn around, but she was completely ignoring me now.

We walked for at least ten minutes, though to my aching legs it seemed much longer. The undergrowth grew tighter around my shoulders, stealing oxygen and whipping against my cheeks. Ahead of me, Simmee's hair was a wild gossamer cloud around her head and down her back, and I could see scratches on her bare legs from the brush.

When I felt as though I couldn't take one more step, I spotted the glimmer of water through the trees.

Oh my God. Had we walked all the way to the opposite side of Last Run? Simmee kept walking, parting the brush with her arms, and I had a sudden, horrible thought. Was she going to walk straight into the water? Drown herself? Was this mad dash across Last Run her attempt to end her life before labor became too excruciating? Did she see a quick death by drowning as preferable to the fate her mother had suffered? The thoughts spun quickly through my mind, but I knew my imagination was getting the best of me. There was deep water far closer to the house. If drowning was her goal, she didn't need to cross the island to do it.

"Where *are* we?" I asked as we neared the bank. "Why are we here?"

Simmee only let out a sob and turned left, walking parallel to the water's edge, though still deep in the undergrowth. All at once, she stopped and began flailing at the brush with her arms. If she had not already lost hold of her sanity, I knew she was losing it now. I rushed forward and tried to grab her hands.

"Simmee! Simmee! Look at me! Look at—" I stopped, suddenly aware of what lay buried beneath the thicket of vines and branches in front of us: a boat. It was in the water, tucked beneath an outcropping of sandy earth and a network of tree roots and tied at bow and stern to saplings that arched over the water. I stared at it in shock.

"I don't understand," I said.

"I hid it." Simmee leaned against the trunk of a spindly pine tree, winded. "Tully thought it washed away, but it didn't. When he brung you to us, he said you was a doctor, and I thought, 'I got to keep her here.' Wasn't so much 'cause you was a doctor. I just wanted an outsider. I *needed* an outsider. But I told Lady Alice I wanted *you* to birth the baby. Not to tell Larry you was here. I knew you could help me."

"Why?" I frowned. "Help you how?"

"I brung the boat around this here side of the island and tucked it up here like this. Tully never comes this way and I covered her up good. You can't even see her from the water."

"The boat has been here all along?" I felt a flash of fury.

She didn't answer. Instead she squeezed her eyes closed and opened her mouth wide as though she wanted to let out a scream, but she made no sound at all.

"Take a deep breath," I said again, and this time she did.

"Okay." I tried to sound calm. My flash of anger was only that—a flash. There was no time for more than that. All at once, I understood what was going on: this was the only way she could get to the mainland to have her baby. Tully wouldn't take her. She needed *me*. The outsider. "Okay," I said again. "I'll…" I studied the boat, trying to figure out how to free it from its camouflage of vines and brush. "Should you get in first, or—"

"What?" She looked at me as though I was the one who'd lost her mind.

"You want to go to the hospital, right?"

"No!" she wailed, slapping her hand on the side of the tree. "No, no, no!"

"*What*, then?"

"I just need to *show* you." She turned and quickly tied the end of the ball of twine around the trunk of the tree. "We got to get back to the house," she said. "Then you got to make this baby come *fast*. Fast, before Tully comes home."

She was already walking through the brush again, back the way we'd come, trailing the twine behind her. I stared after her for a moment, too stunned to move.

"Come on!" she shouted, stringing the twine over a branch as she walked. "You need to be able to git back here on your own."

She *was* crazy. How had I lived with her for nearly two weeks and not picked up on it?

"I don't understand!" I hurried after her, shouting at her back, my frustration finally coming to a head.

"You need to find your way back here with the baby," she

said. "I told you how to go once you're out on the water, remember? Up the creek and then you just keep going left. Left at the fork and left into the river by the old shed. Remember? I told you!"

"I'm *not* taking your baby!"

"Yes, yes, yes, yes, yes!" She hunched over with another contraction. They were coming faster now. She pulled in long, gasping breaths while I looked on helplessly. "You have to," she said through the pain. "Please, Maya. Please, please."

I thought I saw a brief moment of sanity in her eyes as she pleaded with me. Either way, I wouldn't argue with her now.

"Okay," I said, thinking *whatever.* "Let's just get back."

She ran out of the twine long before we reached the path.

"Break the branches!" she said, one hand braced under her belly now as she walked. With the other hand, she grabbed the branches of saplings, yanking at them, grunting with the effort. "You need to leave a trail for yourself."

I did it. I snapped branches. Trailed vines from one tree to the next. Anything to humor her. To hurry our way home.

By the time we reached the house, she was clearly in agony. I didn't have to tell her to go to her bedroom. From the bassinet in my room, I grabbed the Easter basket, where I'd stored the sterilized scissors and other supplies. By the time I'd scrubbed my hands and put on a pair of gloves from my backpack, I found Simmee already lying on her bed, underwear stripped off, legs bent and spread above a layer of towels.

"Make it come fast!" she said.

"It'll come when it's ready, honey." I spoke quietly to try to calm her down. I gently felt the baby through her belly. "Head down. Bottom up," I said, hoping to reassure her. "Perfect."

She started to push. I wished I had some idea what was going on inside her, but I didn't want to do an internal exam and increase the risk of infection. With her water broken, her wild trek through the woods and the less than pristine environment the baby would be born into, the fewer risks I took, the better. All I knew was that there was virtually no time at all between her contractions now.

"Swear to me you'll take the baby," she moaned.

"We can talk about it later," I said. Simmee would be saner later, when the pain and fear had worn off.

"Now!" she said, and it came out like a howl.

I saw the baby's head crowning. "Don't push!" I said. "Pant." I demonstrated. I didn't know if she obeyed me or not, I was so intent on carefully delivering the baby's head without tearing her. Simmee started to scream, the first truly violent sound she'd made, and she turned her head into her pillow to catch it. Within moments, the baby's head was cradled in my hands, and the little body still inside its mother rotated a quarter turn as though it had been born a thousand times before. After one more ferocious contraction, the baby slipped into my hands. He was big and loud, already crying, and suddenly every-thing—*everything*—made sense. Wiping the infant's face clean with the damp cloth at my side, I took in his full, perfect lips, his broad nose and black, curly hair and understood all too well the source of Simmee's desperation.

Simmee reached for him, and I laid the baby on her belly. Crying quietly, she held him close—so close that for a second, I was afraid she was hurting him.

I tied off the cord, feeling the warmth of the infant's skin against the back of my fingers. The warmth of Simmee's skin. *I love this baby with my complete heart,* she'd told me.

"Let him nurse if he will," I said to her after I cut the cord. She wept as I helped her raise her dress above her breasts. She wore no bra, and I watched in awe as instinct took over and the baby latched on with ease. Simmee gasped, then leaned forward to press her lips to his head. The familiar surge of envy I always felt when witnessing intimacy between a mother and her child swept through me.

She looked at me. "I didn't think he'd be so…this color," she said.

"He'll get darker," I said. "It's hard to say how much."

She ran her hand over his hair. "Tully'll kill me," she said softly. "He'll kill the baby."

"No, Simmee, I'm sure you're wrong." But I wasn't sure at all.

She lifted her head from the baby, but looked down at him as he nursed. "Sweetheart," she whispered, "you look just like your daddy, an' I love you. You gonna have to forgive me." Abruptly, she pulled him from her breast and held him toward me. "Take him now," she said, as the baby whimpered. "Put him in the basket. You gotta take him now before Tully comes back."

I hesitated, absolutely frozen, as she held the baby toward me.

"You need to deliver the placenta," I said finally, gently pushing the baby toward her breast again. "The afterbirth. The nursing will help it come out." I didn't know what Tully would do, but I knew what Simmee needed from a medical perspective—and that felt like the *only* thing I knew at the moment. I would focus on that and that alone. Otherwise, I would go crazy myself.

Simmee hugged the baby to her breast again with a sob. "You don't understand, Maya," she said. "Tully kilt Jackson!"

"What?"

"He made up that lie about it bein' an accident. He knew Jackson was sweet on me and he kilt him."

"No," I protested.

"He told me exactly how he done it. And the reason he won't go to no hospital? The reason I'm the one who goes to the store with Larry? The reason Tully come out here in the first place, livin' in that tent and all? The reason he don't never leave Last Run? It's 'cause the police want him, 'cause Jackson ain't the first person he kilt." She leaned over again to press her lips to her baby's curly dark hair. "He done this to me, too." She touched the scar on her eyebrow. "He said I was too beautiful and he just took the butt of his rifle and whacked me."

"Oh, Simmee." I leaned back, horrified.

"He saw me kiss Jackson. I said it was just a friendly kiss, on account of us knowin' each other all our lives, but that was a lie and he knew it. He already 'spects this baby is Jackson's even though I told him no way that could happen. That we never done it. We done it a zillion times, though. I loved him so much, but it was all wrong." She let out a whimper so soft that at first I thought it had come from the baby. "He said he'd kill it if it come out black," she said.

Fear overwhelmed me, a fear so old it felt ancient. It was the fear from that horrible night in my childhood driveway and from the restaurant in Durham. For a moment, I thought of myself instead of the woman and baby in front of me. By now, surely everyone thought I was dead. No one would miss me if I were to simply disappear.

"He'll kill *me*, Maya. Please." Simmee hugged the baby, rocking him back and forth. "I'll tell him the baby was sick, and the boat washed back up and you took him to the hospital."

"I...he won't believe that," I said. "And I can't leave you here if there's a chance he might hurt you."

"He won't hurt me if you go now. Go *now!*" She started to pull the baby from her breast again, but I held him in place with both hands and she didn't fight me. I saw the war inside her. The desire to hold her baby close as long as she could, and the longing to protect both him and herself from danger.

"How would you explain the boat coming back?" I asked.

"I'll think of something." She stroked her baby's skin, trying to squeeze a lifetime of touches into a few brief minutes. "He probly already left Lady Alice's by now and is out huntin'. Don't make too much noise. He can hear a rabbit munchin' weeds a mile away."

If I hadn't already been caught up in her panic, I was now. *Don't think about it,* I told myself. *Don't think about Tully.*

"The pains are comin' again," she said.

"Good," I said. "That's the afterbirth. Go ahead and push."

"Please, Maya." She groaned with the effort of pushing. "Just go. I'm all right."

"I need to be sure the placenta—" Even as I spoke, I saw her belly contract. *"Push,"* I said.

She did, and the placenta slipped onto the towel. I scooped it and the towel up and carried it out into the yard. Into the trees. I placed it on the ground, and my gloved hands shook as I checked to be sure the placenta was whole. Then I left it and the towel to the animals and rushed back inside.

When I returned to the bedroom, she was again holding the baby out to me. *"Go! Go!"* she shouted.

I stared at the baby. Her perfect, beautiful son. "I'll get him back to you," I said. "I promise. Somehow."

"No! Don't ever try. He'll kill him. I planned this perfect. You got to *leave!*" She held the baby in the air between us, and after two seconds' hesitation, I reached for him. Even so, she didn't let go at first. She clung to him, her face drenched with tears. "Love him for me," she said.

"I'll keep him safe," I whispered, and she released him gently into my arms.

41

Rebecca

THE BATHROOM IN THE TRAILER WAS INSANELY SMALL, THE shower nearly claustrophobic, but she wished she had the time—and a large enough water supply—to stand under the spray for the rest of the day. She was on her lunch break and she'd dropped off a list of supplies to Dorothea, then taken a much needed run. The clinic had been crazy all morning and even though she'd only had two beers the night before, she'd been battling a minor hangover. Or maybe it was just that she and Adam and Dorothea had stayed up too late talking the night before. They'd talked about DIDA and Maya and Louisa and nothing and everything, the conversation often bittersweet, and Rebecca had been glad for Dorothea's presence. It wouldn't have been a good night to be alone with Adam. She'd felt too close to him and entirely too vulnerable. Although they'd switched to iced tea and bottled water once the beer had run out, she'd felt as buzzed as if she'd been drinking tequila, and this morning had passed by her in a fog.

She stepped out of the shower and was toweling off when

the bathroom door suddenly burst open and Adam took one step into the room.

"Whoops!" He backed out quickly, and she heard him chuckle on the other side of the door. "Didn't know you were here," he said. "Sorry."

Rebecca stood in the tiny bathroom, the towel clutched in her hands. He'd seen her for two seconds, maybe less, but that had been long enough for her to feel the quick sweep of his gaze over her body. She leaned back against the wall, holding the wadded-up towel to her chest, her mind spinning back to the conversation she'd had with Dorothea less than an hour ago. She'd found Dot in the kitchenette of her trailer, up to her elbows in paperwork, and Rebecca felt as though she was looking at her future. It was not a pretty sight. Maybe she and Brent *should* direct DIDA together, she'd thought as she surveyed the mess on the table. She would give him all the paperwork. She'd go out of her mind if she had to shuffle papers all day.

"Brent told me you turned him down," Dorothea had said when Rebecca handed her the list of supplies.

"Oh," she said. "How'd he sound?"

Dorothea shrugged. "He'll live." She glanced at the list of supplies, then set it aside. "It was the right call on your part."

"I know." She reached for the doorknob. "I'm going for a run and then head back to the school."

"Did you feel this way about Adam even when Maya was alive?" Dorothea asked.

Rebecca's hand froze on the doorknob. She turned back with a frown. Dorothea was innocently pushing papers around on the table.

"*What* way?"

Dorothea raised her head, giving her a look that said it all. *Busted.*

Rebecca had sighed. She'd walked the two steps to the table and sank onto the settee. "No," she admitted. "Not like this. I was always crazy about him—you know, as Maya's husband. Who wouldn't be? But I—"

"It's not a crime, babe."

Rebecca had lifted one of the papers from the table and looked at the text without reading it. "Well, it feels like one. Maya's body hasn't even been found," she said, then added quickly, "And we have *not* slept together, so don't even go there."

"Who was going there?" Dorothea tried and failed to look guileless.

Rebecca dropped the paper to the table and let out a breath. "It's way too soon and it's one-sided, anyhow," she said. "I think I'm just—"

"What makes you think it's one-sided?"

"Well, for starters, he's grieving for his wife."

Dorothea had shaken her head. She'd folded her arms and leaned hard on the table. "You're so busy looking at him," she'd said, "that you haven't noticed how he's looking at you."

Well, now she *had* noticed. She'd felt his eyes sweep over her. He may as well have been touching her. She *wanted* him to touch her. It still felt wrong, though. Whether it *was* wrong or not, she couldn't get past the way it felt.

Stop thinking, then. She wrapped the towel around her body, tucked it in above her breasts and left the bathroom.

He was closing the refrigerator door, a bottle of juice in his hand. "Sorry 'bout that." He gave her an apologetic smile. The window spilled a sliver of light down his forehead, his cheek, his chin. It pooled in his left eye like honey. Turned his brown hair gold on the left side of his head. He was her family and he'd quickly become her closest friend. Now she wanted more than that.

She walked toward the refrigerator and stood in front of him.

"Adam?" she asked, and she hoped he understood the question she was posing without her having to explain.

He did. He set down the bottle of juice and rested his hands on her sides, his thumbs close to her breasts through the towel. He leaned his head down and she felt his lips on her neck. She drew her head back so that his lips would meet hers, and when they did, she felt the rush of heat between her legs. The point of no return. His fingers lightly grazed the tops of her breasts as he freed the towel, and it slipped down her body to the floor.

Two weeks, she thought. *Maya's only been gone two weeks.*

She caught his hands in hers and pulled away, shaking her head in apology.

"I'm sorry," she said. "This is so wrong, and it's totally my fault. And I just...I can't."

He was slow to nod. He bent over, his hair brushing her thigh as he picked up the towel. "I know," he said, as he wrapped it around her. "It's okay."

She tucked the loose ends of the towel above her breasts again, her fingers shaking. "I'm so..." She looked to the left. The right. Anywhere but into his eyes.

Images filled her mind: Cradling phantom babies. Kneeling next to the Maya look-alike lying in the school hallway. Spotting her parents on the bleachers. Squeezing her hands around Tristan's delicate rib cage while she lost herself in Adam's dark eyes. Recoiling from the stack of paperwork on Dorothea's table.

"Bec?" Adam ran his hands down her arms. "You all right?"

She lifted her hands to her face and began to cry. "I'm so screwed up," she said.

"Hey." He pulled her close. "No you're not."

She pressed her fingers against her eyes. "I am," she said. "I'm a mess."

"Come on." He led her over to the couch and she sat down, lowering her hand from her face to hold the towel tightly against her breasts. "You have a right to be a mess," he said. "We both do."

He didn't understand. He couldn't.

"It's not just Maya," she said.

"Tell me what it is then." He took one of her hands from where it clutched the towel and held it on his knee. "Tell me," he said again.

"I don't know who I *am* anymore."

He frowned. "What do you mean?"

"Remember what you said about my family story?" she asked. "Maya's and mine?"

"Yes."

"How I'm…I don't remember exactly what you said. Tough and wild. I sleep around. I—"

"I never said that."

"You know that's part of the story, though," she said. "How I don't want kids. How I'll be the director of DIDA someday. Right? That's all part of the story, isn't it?"

He nodded.

"Well, lately, I feel…" She didn't know how to put it into words. "Sometimes I feel like I'm anything but tough. Like I'm a total wimp. More like Maya than myself."

"I don't see that." He looked solemn. "You are seriously the strongest woman I know."

"Everyone has all these expectations of me, Adam! I have to jump out of planes. I have to fly off to God knows where at a moment's notice. I have to take over DIDA. I—"

"You love all that stuff," he interrupted.

"I do! But I feel locked into it all. It doesn't feel like my choice anymore. I'm living the life everyone else expects me to live, when what I might really want…" She shook her head. "Maybe I *do* want kids. How would I know? I've never even allowed myself to think about it because kids don't fit into the life I'm supposed to live. But ever since Maya's miscarriage, all I can think about are babies and kids, and lately all I can think about is…I keep thinking about *you*." She looked down at her bare knees. "I feel close to you, and that feels good and it's terrible for something to feel good when Maya is gone."

He rubbed his thumb over the back of her hand. "I know," he said, and she could tell that this was one thing he *did* understand.

"I feel fragile right now, Adam. Where did the tough woman go? She's gone. I'm like an eggshell, cracking into a million pieces."

He smiled. "I like that image," he said.

She pulled her hand away. "Well, I don't!"

"I do." He put his arm around her. "Come here and I'll tell you why." He reached for her, and she let him pull her closer to him on the couch.

"Why would you say that? Why do you like that image?" she asked.

"Because sometimes cracks in an eggshell just mean that a new chick is trying to be born."

"Oh." She went still in his arms, touched. He rubbed her back and she pressed her face to his shoulder. Then she smiled to herself, giving him a mock slap on his thigh. "Did you just call me a *chick?*"

He laughed. Leaning away, he smoothed his hand over her damp hair. Her cheeks. Her throat. He kissed her again and everything inside her began to melt. But she *was* stronger than she'd given herself credit for. She didn't want to regret this moment.

She drew away from his arms and stood up. Taking his hand in hers, she leaned over to kiss his cheek.

"Thank you," she said, and she walked toward the bathroom, knowing she'd made the right choice. This was not the time. Not today. Not yet.

Someday soon, though, it would be.

42

Maya

THERE WAS NO TIME TO THINK.

I held the basket close to my body on the narrow path that led to Lady Alice's, Simmee's words playing in my brain: *He probly already left Lady Alice's by now and is out huntin'*. What would I do if I ran into him on this trail? *What would I do?* I walked as quickly and quietly as I could, listening for the sound of Tully's hammer on Lady Alice's roof, but that steady, reassuring tapping had ceased. I heard nothing other than my heart beating in my ears. The day was hot, but it had grown overcast and the forest was dark. The mosquitoes were out in force, and I worried about them feasting on the baby. He was so silent that I had to stop to be sure he was still breathing.

In the gloom, I was afraid I'd miss the first torn branch that would lead me off the path, but I finally spotted it. The long white scar on a slender tree trunk was almost impossible to miss. I only hoped that *Tully* would miss it as he approached it from the opposite direction.

It was a relief to be off the main path, where'd I'd been afraid of coming face-to-face with him, but the thick undergrowth offered me new fears. I saw, or at least I hoped I was seeing, where Simmee and I had clawed our way through the brambles. I scoured the forest for the next torn branch and found it as well, but after that, I felt turned around. Had I lost our trail? How long had we walked through the forest after the twine ran out? *He kilt Jackson.* My lungs burned. My breathing was so rapid and the air so thick, that I felt dizzy.

The crack of a rifle suddenly echoed through the woods and I dropped to my knees with a yelp as if I'd been shot. I wasn't totally sure I *hadn't* been. I stayed rooted to the ground for a moment, my fingers on the handle of the basket and my heart pounding hard against my ribs. How far away was he? The sound of the rifle could have been three yards from me or three miles. Either way, he was too close. I got to my feet and saw, almost directly in front of me, the end of the twine tied around a branch. I let out my breath in relief.

I untied the twine, not wanting Tully to stumble across it. Then I followed the trail Simmee had marked with it, gathering the twine in my left hand, and carrying the basket in my right. I nearly tiptoed through the brush, yet every step I took seemed to snap a twig or rustle a leaf. I listened hard as I walked, but the only other sound I heard was my own rasping breathing.

Then the thing I'd been hoping would not happen, happened: the baby began to cry.

"Shh," I whispered, moving on. Moving faster. "Shh, sweetie. Please." But he continued to cry, louder and louder, oblivious to my mounting panic.

I stopped walking. Setting down the basket, I leaned over and swaddled the baby more tightly in the green blanket. I touched one of the many creases in his tiny neck, where he still bore traces of blood and vernix. His eyes, a beautiful slate-gray, opened, and he looked at me as if he could truly see me. For a moment, his crying stopped and I felt the connection between us, the thread that ran from his eyes to my heart.

"It'll be okay," I whispered. I lifted the basket, grabbed the wadded end of the twine and began fighting my way through the brush once again.

"Hey!"

I jerked at the sound of Tully's voice. It seemed to swim around me, coming from all directions at once.

"Who's there?" he shouted.

Oh, God. I pictured him somewhere behind me, raising his rifle, getting me in his sights. The baby started crying again, and I whimpered as I ran, knowing that the cries would allow Tully to zero in on our location with ease. *He can hear a rabbit munchin' weeds a mile away.*

I finally saw the dull sheen of the water through the trees ahead of me. I followed the twine, and the dingy white bow of the johnboat came into view, more exposed than I remembered it from only a few hours earlier. I looked at the secure knot Simmee had used to tie the bow of the boat to the sapling. I should have brought a knife, but it was too late for that now. I tore at the knot until my trembling fingertips bled, finally freeing the rope. I started in on the knot securing the stern, but then realized it would be safer to free the boat once the baby and I were in it.

Behind me, I heard a ripping, tearing sound. Branches breaking. Vines stripped from the ground by their roots. I pictured Tully's long legs cutting easily through the undergrowth, his rifle slung over his shoulder as he followed the baby's cries. It may as well have been a monster coming after me rather than a human being, for the panic I felt. A monster would be less frightening at that moment. I imagined Tully's arms raising the rifle, taking aim.

Leaning over the bank, I set the basket on the floor of the boat, then climbed in next to it, trying to keep my balance. The rope extending from the stern was easier to unknot. Once I'd freed the boat, I expected it to slip into the open water where I could let the motor down, but the boat stayed rooted under the cantilevered ledge of earth and roots. *God, please, please.*

"Hey!" He was closer now, maybe close enough to see me. Certainly close enough to hear the baby's cries.

Adrenaline filled every cell in my body. I pushed against the ledge with strength I didn't know I had, and with a sudden jerk and a sickening tilt to the left, the boat broke free. I lowered the motor into place and yanked on the cord. Once, twice. It sputtered and sputtered again, but on the third try, it coughed to life. I quickly steered the boat away from shore just as Tully burst from the forest onto the bank.

"Hey!" he called. "What the hell do you think you're doing?"

"The baby's very sick!" I shouted over the sound of the engine. "I'm taking him to the hospital. Get Lady Alice to check on Simmee!"

"Come back here!" he called, and I wondered if he'd heard what I said. "I want to see the baby! You have no fuckin' right!" I waited for him to raise the rifle. I was ready to duck down in the boat. "Maya!" he shouted again. "Get your butt back here!"

I was terrified, but I also knew that I was the one with the boat. The one with the power. I opened the throttle all the way, anxious to get out of the range of his rifle. Anxious to get *away*. I could taste my freedom. *Finally.* I had a mess on my hands: a baby that wasn't mine, a young woman who needed help. But at that moment, all I wanted was to find a way home to my husband and my sister and my life—although I knew it would not be the same life I'd left behind. Nothing would ever be the same.

I tore my gaze from Tully to the water in front of me. I knew the creek, still swollen and wide and rough, circled the island. Once I saw the dock, I would turn left to get to Ruskin. The nearest town, she'd told me. *Just keep going left*. Behind me, Tully still shouted, but I could no longer hear his words. Soon the bend of the creek put him and his rifle out of sight, and my breathing settled down. Even the baby picked up on the calm, lulled nearly to sleep by the raspy hum of the motor. "We're safe," I said, and I wasn't sure if I was talking to the baby or myself. *We're safe,* I thought, *but is Simmee?*

The boat. Tully had to wonder about the sudden appearance of his beloved johnboat. How could Simmee possibly explain its reappearance, on the *other* side of the island, and so coincidental to the birth of the baby? She was resourceful, I thought. She would find a way. She probably had it figured out already.

I steered the boat away from Last Run and within minutes, spotted the fork Simmee had told me about that day on the dock. *Are you listening? It's rude not to listen.* I nearly smiled. She'd thought of everything. It hurt, though, to think of her alone in her house right now, her body a wounded mess from the birth, her spirit crushed by the loss of her baby. I couldn't afford to think about it. There would be time later. Now, I only needed to follow the creek to the river and civilization. I felt like shouting with the joy of being free.

All of a sudden, I remembered the rope. I'd left it tied to the tree on the bank. Tully would see it. He would know. He might not figure out every single detail, but at the very least, he would know he'd been played for a fool. By Simmee. By me.

He kilt Jackson. He'll kill me.

I pictured Tully studying the rope in his hand. Putting two and two together. I saw him, brimming over with a lethal mix of fury and humiliation, racing back to the house. Ahead of me, the scrubby trees that formed the fork in the creek came into view. I stared at the left fork, the water that would carry me home. A voice in my head cried out, *You're safe! Just go!* But the voice was no match against the image in my mind of a defenseless girl and an enraged man. I looked away from the fork, away from escape, even before I turned the boat around.

Could I beat him to the house? I knew his anger would spur him quickly through the woods. I spotted the dock and steered toward it. Drawing the boat close to it, I shut off the engine. I tied the boat to a metal loop jutting from the dock, set the basket on the wooden platform and tried to climb out, my haste making me clumsy. I finally managed to boost myself onto the dock and, grabbing the basket, I ran up the path toward the house.

Simmee was curled in a fetal position on the three-legged chair in the living room, and she looked up, startled, when I raced into the room with the basket.

"No!" she wailed.

"You need to come with me!" I said. "Don't speak. Trust me, Simmee. Hurry. The boat's at the dock."

She looked at me blankly, her mouth open. Then, as though drawn by a magnet, she reached for the basket.

I caught her hand, pulling her to her feet. "Tully's on his way," I said. "He saw me leave. He knows the boat was tied there."

She darted a quick look toward the kitchen, her eyes wide with fear.

"Your baby needs you," I said. "Come on."

She came with me without a fight then. She was clearly in discomfort from the birth, but she moved quickly and word- lessly. I ran into the bedroom and grabbed one of the pillows for her to sit on and a couple of sanitary pads from the open box on the bed, and in a moment we were out the door. In another few minutes, we were on the dock. In the wood beneath my feet, I was certain I could feel Tully pounding the earth as he ran toward the house. I helped Simmee into the boat, handed her the basket and climbed in myself. Trembling from head to toe, I pushed the boat away from the dock.

Simmee reached into the basket and lifted her baby to her chest again. She held him close, her eyes shut in quiet rapture, and I was the only one who saw Tully raise his rifle to his shoulder. I was the only one who heard the *ping* of the bullet against the side of the johnboat. With a ferocity I never knew I possessed, I opened the throttle wide and we shot above the surface of the water like a meteor across the sky.

43

Rebecca

CROUCHING BY THE SHELF OF ANTIBIOTICS IN THE PHARMACY, Rebecca searched for tetracycline to give the teenager she was treating. She was smiling to herself. She'd been smiling ever since leaving Adam and the trailer an hour earlier. She wasn't sure exactly what the future held for them, but it seemed full of promise and that was all that mattered.

She found the bottle and was getting to her feet when her phone rang. She glanced at the caller ID. A hospital in Fayetteville? She wondered if one of the patients she'd sent to the hospital that morning could have been taken all the way to Fayetteville. Setting down the bottle of antibiotics, she flipped her phone open.

"Dr. Ward," she said.

"Becca!"

The phone fell from her fingers to the floor, landing with a horrific splintering sound. The National Guardsman who was stationed in the room to keep an eye on their drugs reached down to pick it up, but Rebecca had already dropped to the floor and was scrambling for the phone, praying it still worked.

"Are you all right?" the National Guardsman asked, but she barely heard him. Sitting on the floor, she lifted the phone to her ear. "Who is this?" she asked hesitantly. She didn't know what to hope for.

"It's Maya, Becca! I'm all right. Where are you?"

She couldn't breathe. She felt as if a bull had rammed into her solar plexus. "Where am *I?*" she managed to say. She wrapped her arms around her legs, nearly curling into a ball on the floor as she clutched the phone to her ear.

The National Guardsman crouched next to her. "Doc?" he asked. "Are you okay?"

"Yes," she said quickly. "Go get Adam. Hurry!" Then into the phone, "Oh, my God, Maya!" she said. "We thought you were dead! Where *are* you?" She remembered the hospital name on the caller ID. "Are you hurt? Have you been in the hospital all this time?"

"It's much too hard to explain right now," Maya said. She sounded so good. So *alive.* "I just need to let you know I'm okay. I'm at the Cape Fear Valley Hospital…or Health Center. I'm not sure exactly what it's called. In the birth center."

"The *birth* center?"

Maya laughed. She actually *laughed!* Rebecca pressed her fist to her mouth, knowing that she was winning and losing something precious, all at the same time.

"I told you," Maya said, "it's too long to explain. Are you still at the airport?"

"No, we're at a school and…Maya, I'm coming there. I'm coming right—"

She looked up as Adam rushed into the room. *"Bec!"* he said when he saw her crumpled in a ball next to the pharmacy shelves. Like the Guardsman had done a moment earlier, he dropped to the floor next to her. "What happened?" He touched her shoulder gently. Gingerly. "Are you hurt?

Smiling, not bothering to check the tears that coursed down her cheeks, she shook her head. "She's alive," she said, holding the phone toward him. "Maya's *alive!*"

44

Maya

IT HAD TAKEN A WHILE, AS THINGS ALWAYS DID IN THE E.R., BUT Simmee was now in a room at the hospital's birth center, and she was frightened. We had not seen her roommate, whose bed was curtained off, and Simmee kept glancing at the curtain as if she was afraid someone was spying on us.

"Are you sure they'll bring him back?" she asked me. The baby, who Simmee was calling Baby Jack, was in the nursery being examined by a pediatrician and getting a good bath.

"One hundred percent sure," I said from my seat next to her bed. While the nurse had been helping Simmee in the shower, I'd spoken with the hospital social worker, telling her I wanted to take responsibility for Simmee and the baby. I knew the social worker was now on the phone with Child Protective Services, trying to see how that could be arranged. My plan, which had taken shape in my mind during our wild boat trip up the river, was that I would take Simmee in as my foster child until she was eighteen—and beyond. I would do whatever was necessary to get her on her feet in the world outside Last Run Shelter, and I would not allow her to spend a single night in a group home. Not one night without me. Already in my mind, I'd turned the guest room in our house into Simmee's room and had the mural painted on the wall of the would-be nursery for Jack.

I knew it was going to take more energy and stamina and legal maneuvering than I could imagine at that moment, but I didn't care. I would take it one step at a time. My first step would be getting Adam to accept the idea. That, I worried, would be the steepest step of all.

Losing her baby had been Simmee's greatest fear as we'd traveled up the Cape Fear toward Fayetteville. A close second, was her fear that Tully would be able to track her down. That's why we'd put a good distance between us and Last Run Shelter before I was able to persuade her to let me dock the boat in what looked like a well-to-do neighborhood. I left Simmee and the baby in the boat while I ran up the bank to a sprawling contemporary house. The woman who answered my knock agreed to call an ambulance, and although she was curious, she honored my plea not to come down to her dock. Simmee was skittish enough as it was. Besides, we'd had little time to talk in the boat, and I had plenty of questions for her.

The river was flat and calm by the woman's house, though still extremely swollen. Simmee and I sat in the boat next to the dock, surrounded by the earthy smell of the water and the leafy branches that hung over our heads.

Sitting there, I thought of how close she and Tully had seemed. I still remembered Tully standing next to her in the kitchen, contentedly inhaling the scent of her hair.

"I never would have guessed that things weren't…right between the two of you," I said, as we waited in the boat.

"I was pretendin'," she said. "I been pretendin' for a long time."

"You didn't love him?"

She hesitated. "I used to like him, early on. Everybody else loved him, though," she said. "He was so good to Gran and Lady Alice. Jackson liked him, too. Gran said God sent him, and I should stick with him. But I had a yen for Jackson from the time I was little."

Another johnboat motored past us on the water, and Simmee lowered the baby to the basket so he couldn't be seen. I turned to look at the two old men in the boat, their fishing tackle sticking up from the bow. One of them waved to us, but I didn't wave back, and Simmee and I breathed a sigh of relief when the boat disappeared from sight. As if knowing the coast was clear, the baby started crying. I moved closer to Simmee, helping her lower her dress over her shoulder and breast so he could nurse.

"This poor child needs a diaper." Simmee winced momentarily as the baby latched on.

I moved back to my seat in the stern. "I know." I was a little worried about him. The green blanket was soaked beneath his tiny bottom. "He'll be cleaned up very soon," I said.

She smiled down at her baby, and I could hardly believe it had only been a few hours earlier that I'd watched her nurse him for the first time in her own bed. It seemed like a lifetime ago.

She touched the baby's cheek, then looked up at me. "Jackson was so good, Miss Maya," she said. "I wish you could of met him. But Gran said me and Jackson bein' together just wouldn't work out, on account of him bein' black, and that I should snap up Tully. She said if I pretended to love him long enough, I'd start feelin' it for real. So I tried, but it didn't work."

"It must have been really hard for you," I said. I hadn't noticed the dark circles beneath her eyes, the chalk-white of her face, until that moment. I hoped she wasn't losing too much blood.

"I never saw no bad in Tully, though," she said. "The only bad thing was when me and Jackson would laugh about somethin' from when we was kids. Tully said it wasn't polite, since he was left out, kind of. So me and Jackson would talk by ourselves sometime." She shook her head. "But bein' alone with Jackson…I just kept lovin' him more and more, and same with him." She looked down at her baby, and I guessed she was seeing Jackson in the little boy's face.

"He's beautiful, Simmee," I said.

"He is." She smiled, but her face quickly clouded over.

"Somehow, Tully figured out our feelin's, 'cause he said it wasn't right for me to ever be alone with Jackson. That was the first time we fought, me and Tully. The first time he hit me, I was so shook up. Mixed up, too. I still liked him, 'cause of all he done for us, but I hated him, too. I couldn't get away from him, though. Where would I go?"

How trapped she must have felt. Even then, sitting in the boat miles from Last Run, I knew she didn't understand that she was free. She was too afraid that I was leading her into a different kind of trap, one with police and social workers, and I guessed that I was. It would be worth it, though. In time, she would understand all that the world outside Last Run Shelter could offer her.

"One day Jackson saw some bruises on my arm and my chin." She touched her jawline. "He asked me a mess of questions, an' I finally told him about Tully hittin' me. I said maybe I deserved bein' hit for talkin' back to him, but Jackson said nobody should hit a girl, no matter what. He told me to keep pretendin' like I loved Tully, and that he'd get me away from him, but he couldn't leave till he talked Lady Alice into goin' with us. I was really scared 'bout leavin'. Last Run was all I knew." She looked at me. "It's *still* all I know."

"It's going to be all right," I reassured her.

A larger boat passed by us, closer to the opposite bank, and Simmee crouched over, trying to hide both herself and the baby.

"They can't see anything from where they are," I said, but Simmee stayed hunched over until the boat was well out of sight. Our own little craft rose and fell over its wake.

"I got so scared when I figured out I was pregnant," she said as she straightened her back again. "Me and Tully always used them condoms. Me and Jackson, not so much. So I quick told Tully I wanted a baby with him and he was real happy and we stopped usin' condoms, so he thought it was *him* got me pregnant. Jackson said we'd leave before the baby come, whether Lady Alice would go with us or not. We'd go someplace Tully couldn't find us. He said maybe Wilmington. He said we wouldn't stand out so much in a city and he'd have a easier time gettin' a job."

"Simmee." I frowned. "I'm confused, though. What would you have done if I hadn't shown up?"

She shook her head. "I don't know. I couldn't sleep trying to come up with what to do. I thought maybe I could get Lady Alice to sneak the baby away once she figgered out it was Jackson's, or…I just didn't know. I was gettin' scareder and scareder. Then you showed up and everything got real clear to me."

We heard the ambulance siren in the distance, and the closer it came, the closer she hugged the baby to her.

"I don't want to go back to Last Run," she said, her eyes pleading.

"You don't have to."

"Where will I go, though?"

"We'll work it out," I said, afraid of making promises I might not be able to keep, but I already knew what I wanted to do. What I wanted to happen.

"I'm sorry I lied to you 'bout things, Miss Maya," she said. "I just...I didn't know you was gonna end up matterin' so much to me. I didn't know I was gonna end up lovin' you."

"It's okay," I whispered past the lump in my throat, and if I hadn't already known I loved her as well, I knew it then.

The nurse poked her head in the room, and I turned in my seat to look at her. "The police are on their way up," she said. I nodded.

"Can I git my baby back now?" Simmee asked her.

"Very soon, sweetie," the nurse said. "The pediatrician was a little late getting to him."

Simmee looked at me anxiously after the nurse left.

"Promise me they'll bring him back?" she asked.

"I promise."

She knotted her hands together on the covers, looking toward the door, then back at me.

"They won't tell Tully where I am, will they?" she asked, for at least the third time.

"No." She'd been upset when I told her I'd called the police.

"Police sometimes take people's kids away from them," she said now.

"I won't let that happen." The words sounded familiar to me. They were the same words Rebecca had said so long ago, after our parents were killed and the authorities wanted to put me in foster care.

Simmee glanced toward the door again. "What do I tell them?"

"The truth," I said. "Just stick to the truth." I leaned forward, gently tapping her arm. "*You* are not in trouble," I said.

She looked over my head toward the doorway, and I turned as two police officers, a man and a woman, walked into the room. I stood to greet them, resting my hand on Simmee's foot through the blanket, and I felt the current of anxiety running through her.

The male officer introduced himself and his partner as they stood at the foot of Simmee's bed.

"I didn't do nothin' wrong," Simmee said the second the man closed his mouth, and I could see her mind at work. She didn't know if leaving Tully had been wrong. If living with him when she wasn't married to him was wrong. If having a baby with Jackson was wrong. If fleeing Last Run was wrong. She was scared and covering all her bases.

I smiled at her as I sat down again. "They know that, Simmee." I leaned toward her. "Listen to me. *Everyone* is on your side," I said, as much for the benefit of the cops as for her. "Everyone just wants you and the baby—Jack—to be safe and healthy."

"That's right, ma'am," the female officer said to her. I'd already forgotten her name and couldn't read her badge from where I sat. She nodded to me. "Dr. Ward told us about your boyfriend, though, and that he allegedly killed two people, so we need to ask you some questions about him."

Simmee looked at me, and I nodded. "Tell them everything you told me," I said. "Tell them the truth and you'll be fine."

So she did, her voice softer and more tentative than I'd heard it before. She told them information she hadn't yet revealed to me. Tully's last name was Thompson, she said, and only then did I realize I didn't even know *her* last name. It was Blake. The other person Tully had killed had been his old girlfriend. Her name was Kelly, and he'd lived with her in Myrtle Beach.

"He told me he choked her to death in the parkin' lot of a Wal-Mart," she said, "and he said he kilt Jackson with a…" Her voice broke, her pale face caving in on itself. Her grief was unbearable to see. Irrationally, I suddenly wished that I *hadn't* called the police.

"With what, miss?" the female officer asked.

"With a hoe." Simmee pressed her hand to her mouth.

"When did these alleged murders take place?" the man asked.

"What's 'alleged' mean?"

"Did Tully tell you when he killed his old girlfriend?" I asked. I was afraid that if one of the officers defined *alleged,* Simmee would be afraid they didn't believe she was telling the truth.

"Sometime before I knew him, so more'n three years ago," she said. "An' Jackson was just two, three months ago."

"Did Tully have motivation to kill Mr. Harnett?" the man asked.

Simmee looked at me, and I started to define motivation, but I could tell she understood the meaning of the word. She was afraid of the answer. She pulled in a breath and let it out in a determined puff. "Me," she said. "I was the motivation. I loved Jackson, and him and me was makin' plans to leave Last Run together, 'cause Tully was mean to me. But we made a big mistake."

She shut her eyes and a crease formed between her eyebrows at whatever she was remembering. None of us pushed her. We waited, and when she opened her eyes again, they were dry but full of anger.

"Jackson come over early one mornin' to go fishin' with Tully. Tully was out doin'…I don't know what-all, somethin' with the chickens, I guess. Me and Jackson was in the kitchen and he kissed me. Just light, like. Tully was at the door and seen it. He started shoutin' and goin' crazy. Me and Jackson said it was just a friendly kiss, and finally Tully settled down, like he believed us." She looked at me again. "I thought he *did* believe us," she said. "They left to go fishin' then, but a few minutes later, Tully come back. Said he told Jackson he forgot somethin'. What he forgot was to smack me with his rifle." She touched her eyebrow. "Then he went out and kilt Jackson with the hoe."

"How do you know that?" the male officer asked.

"He told me. He pretended to Jackson's mama like Jackson had an accident, but he told me the truth and said if I didn't behave, he was gonna kill me, too." She'd sped up now, hurrying through the story. "That's when he told me about the girl. Kelly. That he'd kilt her 'cause she cheated on him, and y'all was lookin' for him—" she nodded to the officers "—but you'd never catch him. I didn't know what to do. I thought of gettin' to Larry's and tellin' him the whole thing—"

"Larry is Jackson's brother in Ruskin," I said.

"But Larry don't like me," Simmee said. "He likes Tully, and I knew he'd tell Tully and then Tully'd find me and kill me. Then he started bein' nice to me again, like nothin' happened. He kept talkin' 'bout how much he loved me and I was scared, so I just pretended I loved him back."

"Is Jackson Harnett your baby's father?" the female officer asked her, point-blank.

Simmee hesitated, and I could tell she was afraid that the wrong answer could somehow cost her her child.

"It's okay," I said, although the question annoyed me. I didn't see how it was relevant.

A nurse picked that moment to wheel the baby into the room. He was crying in that rhythmic mewing way that always made my breasts ache with longing.

"Oh," the nurse said, when she saw the police. "Do you want me to bring him back later?"

"No, now!" Simmee was already reaching toward the clear

plastic bassinet, and I had to smile. She didn't care that Baby Jack's paternity was written on his face. She only wanted him back in her arms.

"Let's give them privacy," I said to the police officers, and they followed me into the hallway.

The female officer—Sgt. Rice, her name badge read—and I walked into the waiting area, while the male officer stayed behind in the hallway to make a call. A few minutes later, he joined us where we sat in a corner of the room, away from the prying eyes of the other visitors.

He nodded at his partner.

"Her story checks out," he said.

"What does that mean?" I asked.

He looked at the notepad he held on his knee. "Kelly Angelman was strangled in a Wal-Mart parking lot in Myrtle Beach three and a half years ago. Guy she was seeing said her ex-boyfriend was the most likely culprit, and he matches the description you gave of Tully. Tully's name is off, but only by a bit. It's Braden Thomas Tullman and he went by Braden back then. We've got an amphibious unit heading to Last Run Shelter right now."

I thought of where Tully might hide at Last Run, and suddenly feared for Lady Alice. "Jackson Harnett's mother is there," I said. "She's the only other person on the island. Please make sure she's not harmed." Lady Alice would be so confused. "And can someone explain to her what happened? Why Simmee and I disappeared?" I thought of adding, *And someone needs to tell her what happened to her son,* but didn't. She would learn the truth soon enough.

"I think we have enough information from Miss Blake for now," Sergeant Rice said. She gave me her card, and I gave her Rebecca's number as well as my own.

"I don't have a cell phone right now," I said. "I'll get one as soon as I can."

I knew as I walked back to Simmee's room, though, that replacing my BlackBerry would be one of the last items on my very long list of things I needed to do.

45

Rebecca

"SHE DIDN'T SOUND AFRAID," REBECCA SAID AS THEY BOUNCED over the potholes on Route 17.

"She knows she's safe now," Adam said, "and she knows we're on our way."

They were still shell-shocked. There'd been the mad scramble to find a car. Dorothea'd made a few phone calls and finally discovered that the old Honda parked next to the school belonged to one of the volunteers, a seventy-year-old widower moved to tears when he heard the news. "Keep it as long as you like," he'd said, pressing the keys into Adam's hand.

Adam's duffel bag was in the backseat, and it contained all he'd brought to Wilmington with him. Rebecca knew he wouldn't be returning to the school. Everything was going to change yet again.

"How will you get home from Fayetteville?" she asked. Her throat was so tight, it was hard to speak.

"I'm going to call a limo company," he said, and she could tell he'd been thinking about it. Planning it. "I don't know what she's been through, but I'm sure she'll need some creature comforts."

"Right," she said. She watched the countryside open up on either side of the road and thought about how, only a few hours earlier, she'd nearly made love to him. They'd come so close. She looked over at him now, letting out her breath. "Thank God we didn't—"

"No kidding," he said, before she could finish the sentence. Then he glanced at her, reaching over to touch her hand. "You mean so much to me, Bec."

She couldn't speak, but she managed a nod.

"Are you okay?" he asked.

"I'm all right."

Adam returned his hand to the steering wheel. "What a roller coaster, these last couple of weeks, huh?"

They fell quiet again, Adam going over the speed limit now that they were traveling on a well-paved highway. Rebecca pictured Maya's blond hair. The cornflower-blue of her eyes. The way she'd tilt her head a bit to one side as she listened intently to what someone had to say. Rebecca wanted to leave Wilmington, too. She wanted to spend time with her sister, but she needed to stay at the school until both she and Adam could be replaced. Besides, she wanted some time to herself. She had to clear the past few weeks, with their fantasies and longings and *craziness,* from her mind.

As she had in the ambulance a couple of days earlier, she watched Adam's face as he drove. He was lost in his own thoughts, and she saw the smile raising the corners of his lips. She felt an unwelcome ache in her heart.

It was possible to feel two wildly conflicting emotions at the same time, she realized. Remembering Maya's phone call and the life in her voice filled her with joy. Watching Adam, though, with that smile on his face as he thought about reuniting with his wife, hurt her to the core. The closeness they'd shared. The hope she'd allowed herself to feel for a future with him. She would have to pretend it had never existed.

There were joys and sorrows that couldn't be measured. She would savor the joy and brush the sorrow aside, she thought, as she wiped away the tear that burned the corner of her eye. Adam had never been hers to begin with.

Maya, though. Maya would be her sister, always.

46

Maya

"THAT POLICE LADY WAS NICE." SIMMEE WAS SMILING NOW, HER relief palpable in the air of the hospital room. She'd nursed the baby, but was still holding him. She couldn't get enough of him, and it was as though she was afraid that if she put him in the bassinet at the side of her bed, someone might wheel him away for good.

"They're on your side," I said.

"Yeah," she agreed.

Her roommate had visitors and, from behind the curtain, we could hear voices chattering happily in Spanish.

"Is that real Spanish?" Simmee whispered to me, and it occurred to me that she'd probably never met a Spanish-speaking person in her life.

"Uh-huh," I said.

"I heard people speak Spanish on TV," she said. "Some of 'em could speak Spanish *and* English. They must be real smart."

I smiled. "You can learn Spanish some day, if you like," I said.

"Me?" Her face was a mixture of disbelief and hope. I

needed to be careful not to allow my own hope for her raise impossible expectations. She had a way to go before she'd master *English*. But she had potential. I had no idea where it would lead her. All I knew was that I wanted it to lead her someplace wonderful.

"Maya!"

Rebecca and Adam burst into the room, and I got to my feet, grinning and holding out my arms. Rebecca reached me first, pulling me into a bear hug. She sobbed against my neck. I couldn't ever remember seeing her cry like that before. Adam's embrace, when Rebecca finally let go of me, was quieter, tighter, more intense. I felt his arms around me like bands of steel. He couldn't seem to speak.

"I'm all right," I reassured him. "I'm fine."

He finally drew away from me, his eyes wet, his hand still on my arm as if he wasn't about to risk losing me again. I smiled at him. At my sister.

Then I turned to Simmee, who still had not put Jack back in the bassinet. "Adam and Rebecca, I'd like you to meet Simmee Blake. She's been taking care of me for the past couple of weeks."

"We been takin' care of each other," Simmee corrected me.

Rebecca walked to the side of Simmee's bed and held out her hand. "Thank you, Simmee," she said. "I understand you've had quite an adventure today." She nodded toward Jack. On the phone, I'd told her and Adam the bare facts: I'd helped Simmee give birth and then we escaped from her abusive husband via boat. There'd been no time to tell them anything more.

"Yes, ma'am," Simmee said. "You could say that."

Adam acknowledged her with a nod, his hand still on my arm. "Let's go to the cafeteria and catch up," he said.

"All right," I agreed, but I saw the alarm in Simmee's eyes.

"I'll be back," I said. "Let me put Jack in the bassinet for you and you get some sleep. I know you're exhausted."

She looked down at her baby, then nodded reluctantly. I lifted him from her arms and set him carefully in the bassinet, pushing it close to her so that she could touch him. I knew she was afraid to close her eyes. Afraid he would disappear if she didn't guard him.

"Sleep, honey," I said. "I'll be back soon."

In the cafeteria, Adam bought coffee for Rebecca and himself and, after I mentioned that I hadn't eaten all day, a tuna salad sandwich for me. I told them everything: My vague memory of the crash. Tully's account of how he rescued me. My injuries. Lady Alice. Simmee nursing me those first few days. The hidden boat and our escape.

Adam moved his chair right next to me as I talked, holding my free hand. From across the table, Rebecca kept reaching over to touch me, too, as if assuring herself that I was not an apparition. I tried to lighten the horror of my ordeal because I could see that they had suffered at least as much as I had, if not more. They'd thought I was dead. I tried, but I couldn't quite grasp what the days had been like for them.

"I'm sorry you had to go through all this," Adam said. "I'm sorry I guilted you into coming. I'll never forgive myself for that."

"Adam," I said, both touched and shaken by his melodramatic tone. "I promise you, I'm okay."

"Rebecca and I talked on the way here," he said. "She needs to go back to Wilmington, but I'm calling a limo to take you and me home to Raleigh." He smiled. "How does that sound?"

"Oh," I said. He was way ahead of me, moving in a direction I hadn't even considered. I hadn't thought of going home yet, much as I longed to be there. "They're keeping Simmee overnight, so I thought I'd get a hotel room close by." Then I added, almost as an afterthought, "Will you stay with me?"

"Don't you want to go home ASAP?" Adam looked surprised.

"What will happen to her?" Rebecca asked. "The girl? Simmee? She's only seventeen, right? Will CPS take over?"

I drew in a long breath. What was so clear in my mind wasn't going to be clear in either of theirs.

"I've gotten very close to her," I said. "I'd like her to come home with me." I looked at Adam. "With us. I've spoken with CPS about it. I can't let her and the baby go into foster care."

Neither of them spoke. I had the distinct feeling they wanted to look at each other, but instead they kept their eyes on mine.

"They have special homes for teen moms and their babies," Rebecca said finally. She sounded as though she was talking to a ten-year-old. "That would really be best for her."

"I don't want her to go into any sort of home." I faced my husband. "I know this is asking a lot of you, Adam," I said. "You wanted your *wife* back, not your wife, a teenager and a baby." I actually laughed. "But this is very important to me."

"You've only known her two weeks." Adam frowned.

"A lot can happen in two weeks," I said. The cells in your body could rearrange themselves in two weeks, I thought. They could change you from weak to strong. I remembered Tully raising his rifle as Simmee and I sped across the water earlier that day. I hadn't even ducked. All I'd thought about was getting Simmee and the baby away from him. "I know it's hard for you to understand how important she's become to me," I said, "but she has."

"Yes, but it's ridiculous to have her move in with you." Rebecca was shaking her head as though I'd lost my mind. "I don't think you get what this has been like for Adam," she said. "I know it's been no picnic for you, either, but he thought you were *dead*, Maya, and I think this is…I think you're really being selfish."

Adam put his hand on Rebecca's arm. "It's okay, it's okay," he said to her, almost in a whisper, and I had a glimpse into their world from the past two weeks. They'd been there for each other, sharing their worry and their grief. They had always been close; now they were closer. Sitting with them, I suddenly felt a bit like an outsider, but that was all right. I was glad they'd had each other. That neither of them had had to go through it alone.

"Look," Adam said to me. "I'll talk to Protective Services, all right? I'll make sure she's safe and that she's placed some-place where she gets the care she needs and where she can learn how to take care of a baby and—"

"Adam," I interrupted him. "I need to do this. And not just for a day, or a couple of days. I'm going to help her. She has no one." Maybe Rebecca was right. Maybe I *was* being selfish. But I knew what I wanted: No more fertility treatments. No more pregnancies. I wanted to explore adoption. And I wanted to take care of Simmee for as long as she needed me. So was that being selfish? It felt more like I was finally being honest. With them. With myself.

Adam let out his breath in frustration. "I just want us to be together right now, Maya. *Home* together. The last thing I want is to share you with a stranger."

"Maya." Rebecca leaned toward me, her voice softer now. "You've been through so much. I get that you're overwhelmed. I think you need a break from everything you've been through." She shook her head. "God knows how much of that accident you witnessed and the impact it had on you. Then being trapped on an island with a madman. Trust me, honey. This isn't the time to make a big decision. You need some downtime just to focus on recovery."

Adam nodded. "You're like…I know this isn't exactly the

same, but you know when someone is kidnapped and after they're found, they need to be deprogrammed, and—"

"She doesn't need to be *deprogrammed,*" Rebecca said. "It's just that she—"

"I know it's the wrong word," Adam interrupted her. "She needs time, that's all. Time to settle back into her life."

"She shouldn't go back to work right away, either," Rebecca said.

"Don't even think of it," Adam added.

"She needs a vacation," Rebecca said.

"No, not a vacation," Adam said. "But not work, either. Just time at home with me and Chauncey until she feels safe and secure again."

I listened to them scrambling all over each other, talking about me as if I weren't sitting in front of them, trying to fix me. Trying to make me who they were most comfortable with me being. *Now* I felt trapped—maybe more trapped than I had at Last Run Shelter. They were pushing me into my old role. My protective sister. My take-charge husband. The guy who wanted his own child at all costs. Good people, both of them, but in two weeks' time, I'd left that old role behind. The realization made me smile.

"Hey, you two!" I said so loudly a couple of people at the next table turned to stare. "Cut it with the third person. I'm alive and I'm right here."

They looked at me as if suddenly realizing that fact.

"I know you both love me," I said, "but *listen* to yourselves. Right now, I think I'm the only one of the three of us who *is* thinking straight. I'm the only one who knows what she really needs."

"But you *don't* know," Adam said. "If you think bringing that girl home with—"

"Listen to me!"

Two pairs of brown eyes widened in my direction.

"I'm *doing* this. I'm taking care of Simmee. I'd love your support, but I'm taking care of her with it or without it." I looked at Rebecca. "You of all people should understand. You wouldn't let *me* go into foster care."

"You were my sister. That was totally different."

I thought of Simmee. I pictured her exhausted in her bed in the maternity unit, one hand on the baby's bassinet, afraid to let go of him for even an instant.

"She's...she's my sister. My daughter. My friend." I looked at Rebecca. "I know you're trying to take care of me," I said. "But I'm thirty-four years old. I'm not your needy little sister anymore. I don't need your protection. But that girl in the maternity unit? She needs mine."

Rebecca reached across the table to take my hand. "I love you," she said.

"And I love both of you so much." I squeezed her hand, then let go. "But we've been living a lie. All of us." I looked at my husband. "I've been so afraid of losing you that I've tried to be someone I'm not. I wanted a baby, too, Adam. So much. But I would have given my body and my...my *heart* a rest from that struggle long ago if I weren't trying so hard to hold on to you."

He frowned again. *"Maya..."*

"And Becca." I started to say that I'd never told her the truth about the night of our parents' murders. About my relationship with Zed. The abortion. But now was not the time. Now was the time for me to go back to Simmee's room, because while my husband and sister were nursing their own fears, Simmee was the one whose fear was most grounded in reality. And I realized, with no small surprise, that I was the one who felt no fear at all.

Epilogue

Maya
One Year Later

FROM THE NURSERY, WHERE I'VE COME TO RETRIEVE JACK'S stuffed elephant, Lucky, I can see our backyard. The green, leafy wall of trees surrounds the grassy ellipse, where we've set the picnic table with paper plates and plastic cups. Lawn chairs dot the yard, and there's baby gear everywhere. Simmee invited three of her friends and their toddlers over to celebrate Jack's first birthday with us, and I smile as I watch one of them shoo Chauncey away from her diaper bag. Chauncey gives up and saunters over to the grill, where Rebecca is in charge of the burgers and hot dogs. I see her say something to the dog. I imagine she's telling him he doesn't stand a chance at getting a tidbit tossed his way, but I know Chauncey's big brown eyes will get to her sooner or later.

Adam is bent over slightly, holding Jack's hands as the little boy walks along the edge of the yard, exploring the garden. Jack tips his head back to look up at him, and Adam lets go of one of his hands to point at a daylily. Jack will be walking by himself in a week or two, I predict. He's the sort of baby people can't help but coo over. His skin is the color of my cream-laced morning coffee and his eyes are a pale amber, but it's his smile that captivates strangers on the street. There's a bit of the devil in that smile, and as tough as this year has been for all of us, I think Simmee has some tougher years ahead of her with her rambunctious little son.

Simmee's kneeling next to one of her friends, playing with the friend's baby, but she has her eye on Jack. She's an overprotective mother, but who can blame her? She's in a program with other teen moms, including the three here at Jack's party, learning how to be a good parent. She's way ahead of most of those girls in the parenting department, but she still has plenty to learn about living in the twenty-first century. She's a quick study, though. Adam bought her a computer to help with her schoolwork as she studies for her GED, and she figured out Facebook faster than Adam, Rebecca and me put together. She started with her little circle of friends from the teen moms group, and yesterday she told me she has over one hundred, which would scare me if I weren't so proud of her. Adam gave her the "be careful on the Internet" lecture, and I know she was listening, because she said she doesn't want her real name out there. Period. I think she still has nightmares about Tully, but I don't. Tully is locked up forever.

No one lives at Last Run Shelter now, at least not that anyone knows of. Larry finally persuaded Lady Alice to move in with him and his family. I don't know how he did it; I only know that I'm glad he did. We've visited her twice at Larry's. Lady Alice, Larry, his wife, Emma Lorraine, and their two teenage sons are Jack's family, and they accept Simmee and the baby to varying degrees. Lady Alice, of course, dotes on her grandson.

I hear Rebecca call to Simmee and her friends, and the girls begin to stand, gathering up their kids as they head toward the grill. I guess the burgers are done. I reach into Jack's crib for Lucky and head for the stairs.

Shortly after my return from Last Run Shelter, Rebecca and I shared the truth about the night of our parents' murders with each other, twenty years too late to save ourselves from the guilt of our separate secrets. I'd been afraid she would blame me if she knew the role I'd played, and she'd been afraid I'd blame her for the same reason.

"We were *both* to blame," she said, when we'd each revealed the truth.

I'd shaken my head, remembering Simmee's words to me when I'd told her the story. "Neither of us was to blame," I said. "We weren't the ones who pulled the trigger."

Last week, Rebecca and Adam told me they're expecting a baby in May. I know they were nervous about telling me, just as they were nervous in February, when they told me how close they'd become while I was missing, and just as they were nervous in April, when they told me they were getting married. By the time they'd told me about their relationship, Adam and I had been separated for two months, a parting that had been as amicable as that sort of thing can be. Simmee had worried that she was the cause of our breakup, but I assured her it would have happened whether she'd been living with us or not. Adam and I wanted different things. It was both that simple and that complex. I'm glad for him and Rebecca, and now that I've started the process to adopt a little girl from Ethiopia on my own, I think they finally believe me. For the first time since my parents died, I feel as though I'm part of a real family.

So, for a short time, there had been a triangle between the three of us, of which I'd been completely unaware. My sister, my husband and me. Now the triangle has become a circle, and a circle can encompass so much more. It can hold not only the three of us, but a young woman and her baby, as well, and it will expand to take in whatever children will follow, and whatever men might wander into our midst. Whatever friends.

Every family has a story, and I love that those stories are etched in sand rather than granite. That way we can change them. We can bury the lies and embrace the truth.

And we can move forward.

★ ★ ★ ★ ★

Read all about it...

MORE ABOUT THIS BOOK

2 Questions for your reading group

MORE ABOUT THE AUTHOR

6 Why I write

7 Q&A on writing

10 A writer's life

11 A day in the life

12 Top ten books

WE RECOMMEND

13 _Breaking the Silence_

14 An extract from _Breaking the Silence_

MIRA

QUESTIONS FOR YOUR READING GROUP

1. What do you think originally attracted Maya and Adam to each other? When the book opens, Maya hopes that the baby she's expecting will change her marriage for the better. Do you think she really believes that? Do you think Adam feels the same way?

2. How do you feel about Maya keeping her abortion a secret from Adam? Is there room for secrets in a marriage? Where do you draw the line?

3. Why do you think Maya was slow to reveal her marital problems to Rebecca?

4. If Rebecca had never been in the picture, do you think Maya and Adam's marriage could have worked out? Why or why not?

5. What role did Maya and Rebecca's relationships with their parents play in their adult lives?

6. Discuss Rebecca's love/hate feelings towards Maya. What were the roots of Rebecca's resentment? What hints did you have into the true nature of Rebecca's feelings for Maya? How do you think she felt when she learned Maya was alive? Which emotion was stronger?

7. Relationships between sisters—indeed, between siblings—are often complex. Could you relate to the relationship between Maya and Rebecca?

8. Maya is described at one point as having been a happy-go-lucky child who changed dramatically after the murder of her parents. Do you think it's possible for one event to have such a strong influence on the rest of someone's life?

9. Rebecca is drawn as an athlete, while Maya is the brain in the family. Yet Rebecca was first to enter medical school. What do you think prompted her to become a doctor? Rebecca begins to question her motivation for joining DIDA, wondering if it was altruism, a need for excitement, or something else. What do you think was her motivation?

10. At one point in the story, Rebecca thinks that Maya is a better person than she is despite Rebecca's work with DIDA. Why do you think she feels that way and what sort of impact does that belief have on her?

11. One of the strongest themes in the book is that of self-forgiveness. What does each sister have to forgive herself for in order to move on? Do you think either of them is able to do that successfully?

12. A yearning for a child is another central theme in the story. Adam, the last in his family line, longs for a biological child. Maya longs for any child to nurture. And Rebecca, who never wanted a child to begin with, suddenly finds herself experiencing a baby hunger of her own.

    i) Can you understand Adam's longing for a biological child and the extent he's willing to go to have one? Do you think he's being fair to Maya in his quest?

    ii) Discuss Maya's decision to end her fight for a biological child. What is the push/pull that went into that decision? How did her time at Last Run Shelter help her make that decision?

    iii) Rebecca's baby hunger is perhaps most striking, since her true feelings seemed to creep up on her. She is a classic example of having made a decision about something important when she was younger and not acknowledging the change in herself over the years until it suddenly hits her in the face. Can you relate to that? How and why do people hide their true yearnings from themselves?

13. Few things are as horrific as not knowing what has become of someone you love. Rebecca wonders if Maya is dead or alive, if her death came quickly, if she's wandering in the woods alone. What impact does this not knowing have on her? Does it change the core of who she is and, if so, in what way?

4

Read all about it...

14. Families can get comfortable with the status quo, with each person carrying out the role they have played since they were young. When one person changes, it can throw the entire family into turmoil and the family may subconsciously try to keep that person from changing. This is sometimes true, for example, in families in which one parent is an alcoholic. It's the devil the family knows and members of the family may subconsciously sabotage the alcoholic's recovery. How does this concept come into play with Rebecca and Maya? Do you think Rebecca wanted Maya to succeed in her DIDA work at the airport? What did Rebecca have to gain by Maya remaining fearful? Does this also hold true for Maya? If Rebecca changes, how might that change impact Maya?

15. Were you hoping Maya and Adam would end up back together? Discuss any tension you felt as you read about Rebecca and Adam's growing closeness. In chapter 41, Rebecca and Adam come close to making love. Would your feelings about either or both of them have changed if they'd given in to that desire?

16. Simmee came to represent certain things for Maya. Maya talks about Simmee as sister, daughter and friend. Describe the evolution of their relationship from Maya's perspective.

17 Why do you think neither Tully nor Lady Alice told Larry that Maya needed to leave Last Run Shelter? Did they have the same motivation or were they each operating from a different need to keep her there? What do you believe were Tully's true feelings for Simmee?

18. The sisters ultimately reverse their roles, in sometimes subtle, sometimes dramatic ways, with Rebecca becoming weaker and Maya becoming stronger. Where do you see this happening? What is the cause of this change in each of them and what impact does it have on them?

19. The word "lies" in the title is used both literally and figuratively. Discuss all the lies referred to in the title.

20. In the opening of the book, Maya says that every family has a story. The author implies that not only does every family have a story, but each individual in that family does as well. How does this fit for you and your family? Do you think a person can ever truly change his or her family story?

WHY I WRITE...

I always wanted to be a writer and wrote many small, terrible books as a pre-teen. But I also had a strong desire to be a social worker, having read a book as a teenager about the different ways social workers could help people. By the time was ready for college, becoming a successful writer seemed li a pipe dream, so I received both my bachelor's and master's degrees in social work. Then a funny thing happened. I was at a doctor's appointment and the receptionist told me the doctor was running very late. There were no magazines in th office, but I had a pen and a pad...and I had an idea that ha been rolling around in my head for more than a decade. I began writing and couldn't stop. At first, I thought of my writing as a hobby, but after about four years I had a completed novel. A year later I had my first contract. I continued working as both a social worker and a writer for several more years until I decided to write full time. I love writing. It's hard to imagine a better career and I have plenty more storie to tell.

AUTHOR BIOGRAPHY

Once a medical social worker, Diane Chamberlain is the award-winning author of twelve novels that explore the complexities of human relationships—between men and women, brothers and sisters, parents and children. Diane lives in northern Virginia.

Q&A ON WRITING

What do you love the most about being a writer?

It's so rewarding to be able to touch thousands of people with my stories. I love hearing that a reader lost a night of sleep because she couldn't put down one of my books! That's the best compliment I can receive.

Where do you go for inspiration?

When I begin to think about writing a new book, I see story possibilities everywhere. My mind and imagination are suddenly open to all the universe has to offer. I devour newspapers and magazines, watch movies, go to art museums, talk to people and even listen in on conversations in restaurants (not intentionally—I just can't help myself when I'm in story-gathering mode!). The story that ultimately arises from all of this is a composite of so many different ideas that I can rarely recall the initial inspiration.

What one piece of advice would you give to a writer wanting to start a career?

First, study the craft of writing. I have read many manuscripts in which the idea is brilliant, but the writing is so poor that I know it stands no chance of ever being published, which is heartbreaking. Read as much as you can so that you understand how stories are told. What draws you in? What keeps you interested? Take a class and share your writing with others to get feedback. Finally, get out and live your life so you have experiences to write about. Writers often tend to be introverts who like to closet themselves away, but we really do need the stimulation of being part of the world in order to understand people and the situations they get themselves into.

You have a master's degree in social work and worked as a youth counsellor and in the field of medical social work, as well as having a private psychotherapy practice. How does this background inform and influence your work?

My background helps me understand how people "tick." It also gives me a deep appreciation of the struggle people face as they try to cope with tragedy. I loved being a social worker and love being a writer. I feel lucky to have had two careers that let me touch people in a positive way.

8

Read all about it...

How did you feel when your first book was signed?

It's impossible to explain the joy I felt that day! It had been a long time coming and the realisation that my story would finally reach readers was simply amazing and very rewarding. I called my family and my writer friends. It was exciting... However, the book wasn't actually published for a very long two and a half years!

Where do your characters come from and do they ever surprise you as you write?

They surprise me all the time! I love creating characters and breathing life into them. I want them to be both believable and memorable to my readers and I spend much of my writing time getting to know them. When I was a clinical social worker, I took a seminar on hypnotherapy. During that training, I not only thought about how useful the techniques I was learning would be for my psychotherapy clients, but how they could help me understand my characters as well. In the beginning, I approached using this new tool in a very formal way. I'd sit in a comfortable chair with a pad and pen, put myself in a light trance and imagine I was the character. Then I'd start writing about "my" life, in the first person, from the character's point of view. I didn't censor myself, but simply let the words flow. As my subconscious took over, I learned things about my character I never would have come up with consciously. It's an astonishing experience and often full of surprises. If *I'm* surprised by what happens, I'm quite sure my readers will be as well. Our subconscious minds are amazing things if we just tap into them. Now that the technique is second nature to me, I often use it when I'm feeling perplexed by, or simply out of touch with, a character. I close my eyes and ask her to tell me what's going on with her or perhaps how she's feeling about another character in the story. Sometimes the answers I receive are pure gold.

Which book do you wish you had written?

E.B. White's *Charlotte's Web*, and not only because I would now be very wealthy! I have always loved that children's book and it was an early inspiration in my longing to write. It's a beautifully crafted book and a lovingly told story.

"...I love creating characters and breathing life into them..."

Read all about it...

Do you have a favourite character that you've created and what is it you like about that character?

I have many favourites, but CeeCee from *The Lost Daughter* is definitely one of them. I like that she's a blend of vulnerability and strength. I think many readers can relate to those qualities in her. I also like that, despite the fact that she's done something very *wrong*, she's still a person with high moral standards. It's that conflict that forces her to make a devastating choice at the end of the book and it's that conflict that truly humanises her.

...I'm
...ed by
...ppens,
...ite sure
...aders
...be as
...."

A WRITER'S LIFE

Paper and pen or straight on to the computer?

Both. I often start with paper and pen and then hit a certain point when ideas are coming too quickly for me to keep up. That's when I move to the computer.

PC or laptop?

Both. I am more comfortable working on my PC because I love my big monitor and ergonomic keyboard. But I also love working in coffee shops, so my laptop is a must.

Music or silence?

Music, but without lyrics. I listen to particular soundtracks when I write. I like soundtracks with high drama, such as *Braveheart, Blood Diamond* and *Dances with Wolves*. They make me feel very emotional and that is reflected in what I'm writing

Morning or night?

I'm a night owl, definitely.

Coffee or tea?

Coffee. Half caffeine, half decaf, with a little milk.

Your guilty reading pleasure?

Hmm...I don't think I have one. I really must work on that.

The first book you loved?

Charlotte's Web by E.B. White.

A DAY IN THE LIFE

This depends on where I am in the writing process. If it's early on, you might find me lolling around the house with a faraway look in my eyes as the story begins to take shape in my imagination. If I'm outlining, you'll find me hunched over my dining-room table, surrounded by note cards, each one containing a scene from the book, as I move them around to form a cohesive story. If I'm in the middle of the book, I'll often start my day at a local coffee shop, going over what I wrote the day before. Then I'll come home and get to work at the computer. If it's the last few months before deadline, you'll find me at the computer bright and early, then all day long, then late into the night. And I'll have a crazed, frantic look in my eyes!

Read all about it...

TOP TEN BOOKS

Poisonwood Bible by Barbara Kingsolver, which was not only a great read, but an eye-opener for me into the twentieth-century history of the Congo.

Gift from the Sea by Anne Morrow Lindbergh, because of its connection to the sea and beach and because of its exploration of a very real marriage.

White Horses by Alice Hoffman, because it was the first book of hers that I read and it inspired my early writing. When I reread my first novel, *Private Relations*, I can recognise the passages that were written during my "Alice Hoffman phase."

Prince of Tides by Pat Conroy, because it's beautifully told and fantastic, gripping story about a wildly dysfunctional family—my favourite kind.

The Time Traveller's Wife by Audrey Niffenegger, because it's so inventive and so very touching.

The Colour Purple by Alice Walker, because I started sobbing on page one.

The Miracle of Mindfulness by Thich Nhat Hanh, because it keeps me centred.

I Know this Much is True by Wally Lamb, because it's an amazing story, wonderfully told. I reread it when I want to write from a male character's point of view. It helps me understand how a man thinks and feels.

Beloved by Toni Morrison. I didn't love it until I had to reread it for a book club. Then it suddenly came together for me and I've reread it several times since.

Eat, Pray, Love by Elizabeth Gilbert, because it's about three of my favourite things: food, spirituality and relationships

A child trapped in a silent world

Laura's promise to her dying father was simple: visit an elderly woman she'd never even heard of before. How could such a generous act result in Laura's husband's death?

Her five-year-old daughter, Emma, was witness to her daddy's suicide and refuses to talk about it…or to talk at all. Frantic and guilt-ridden, Laura contacts the only person who may be able to help, a man she's met only once before—a man who doesn't know he's Emma's real father. Together, guided only by a child's silence and an old woman's fading memories, the two unravel a tale of love and despair, bravery and unspeakable evil. A tale that unbelievably links them all.

For fans of JODI PICOULT, this is a must read.

Available now from all good booksellers

Read all about it...

BREAKING THE SILENCE
by Diane Chamberlain

Read on for an exclusive preview

Coming soon from MIRA Books

Something was wrong. Laura knew it the moment she stepped out
her car in the town-house garage, although she couldn't have said
at triggered her sense of dread. As she neared the door, she could hear
child crying inside the house. Was it Emma or some other child?
e sound was unfamiliar. A wail. A keening.

Panicked, Laura struggled to fit her key in the lock, finally managing to
sh the door open. Stepping into the foyer, she found Emma sitting on the
ttom step of the stairs, hunched over as though her stomach hurt. Her wai-
g turned to screams and she leapt from the step into Laura's arms.

"Sweetheart!" Laura tried to keep her own voice calm. "What is it?
hat's wrong?" Maybe Emma had bugged Ray to read to her and, in his
ur mood, he'd yelled at her, but this seemed an extreme reaction. Emma
s usually more resilient than this. Emma didn't answer her. She clung to
ura, standing now, but pressing her head against Laura's hip.

Laura looked through the living room towards Ray's office, a patch of
ld forming at the base of her neck. Emma's screams could not mask the
llness in the rest of the house.

"Where's Daddy?" she asked, as she walked towards the office, Emma
nging to her more tightly with each step. "Ray?"

The office was empty, the pages of Ray's manuscript still piled on his desk.
ay?" she called, as she walked back towards the foyer and the stairs.

"Stay here," she told Emma, gently pulling the little girl's arms
om around her hips. "I'll be right back."

She climbed the stairs, the cold patch at the back of her neck spreading
wn her spine. She walked through the doorway of the bedroom she shared
th Ray. It was empty. Ray must have gone out. He'd left Emma alone.
at's why she was so upset. That would not be enough to undo Emma,
ough, and Laura remembered seeing Ray's car in the garage. She was
out to leave the bedroom when she noticed a stain on the wallpaper on

the other side of the bed—a red stain in the shape of a butterfly. Biti
her lip, she walked slowly around the foot of the bed. Ray lay on the flo
next to the window, his head in a pool of blood, a gun in his hand.

Staggering backwards, Laura crashed into the dresser, knocking h
jewellery box to the floor. She scattered the jewellery with her feet
she fled from the room and down the stairs.

Emma's wails had turned to a whimper and she sat huddled
the floor of the foyer, her eyes on Laura. Laura grabbed her by the ar
and led her into the kitchen, where she used the phone to call 911.

"Is this an emergency?" the dispatcher asked.

Laura's brain felt foggy. Ray was dead. There was nothing anyo
could do to change that fact, no matter how quickly they got to the hous

"Is this an emergency?" the dispatcher repeated.

"My husband shot himself," Laura said. "He's dead." She had a sudde
desperate need to get out of the house. Ignoring the dispatcher's questions, s
dropped the receiver to the kitchen floor, grabbed Emma once again and r
with her outside to the small front porch.

Sitting down on the old wooden bench Ray'd picked up at a garage sal
she pulled Emma onto her lap. *I'm in shock.* The thought was clinical ar
detached. She was nauseated and a little dizzy and, although she knew t
air was cold, she couldn't actually feel it. This is what shock feels like. H
eyes couldn't focus, even as the police cars, the ambulance and the fire truc
pulled in front of her town house, sirens blaring. Neighbours came out to the
yards or peered through their windows to see what was happening, but Lau
simply stared at the snow covering the front lawn. All she could see, thoug
was the butterfly-shaped stain on the wallpaper in the bedroom.

"He's upstairs," she said to the first police officer who approached he
She pressed her chin to the top of Emma's head as the army of EMTs marche
past them and into the house, and she closed her eyes against the image of wh
they would find in the upstairs bedroom.

Emma had stopped crying, but her head remained buried in the croc
of Laura's shoulder. She was really too big to sit on anyone's lap, but she ha
made herself fit and Laura did not want to let go of her. The little girl shivere
in her light sweater and Laura rubbed her arms. What had Emma seen? Ha
she heard the gunshot and gone into the bedroom to investigate? Might sl
have actually been in the room when Ray did it? Laura should not have le
her with him. She should not have been gone more than an hour.

It seemed like a long time before one of the police officers returned to th
porch, carrying jackets for her and Emma. He'd brought Ray's down jack
for Laura and she put it on, pressing the collar close to her nose to breathe i
her husband's scent.

Who was in the house when it happened?" the officer asked, pulling a notepad from his pocket. He stood on the walkway, one foot resting on the step.

"Emma." Laura nodded towards her daughter, who had once again folded herself to fit in Laura's lap.

The police officer studied Emma for a moment and seemed to decide against questioning her.

"And you were out?" he asked.

"Yes."

"Do you know why the jewellery box and its contents were on the floor?"

"I knocked into it after I found him," she said. The image of the jewellery spilled across the floor seemed like something she'd seen days ago, not mere minutes.

"There was a note in the bedroom," the officer said. "Did you see it?"

"A note?"

"Yes. Taped to the dresser mirror. It read, 'I asked you not to go.' Does that mean anything to you?"

Laura squeezed her eyes shut. "I had to visit someone this morning and he didn't want me to go."

"Ah," he said, as though he'd found the missing piece to the puzzle. "There was a big age difference between you and your husband, huh?"

The question seemed rude, but she didn't have the strength to protest. "Yes," she said.

"So, was this 'someone' you had to visit another man?"

Laura looked at the policeman in confusion. "Another...? No. No. It was a woman. An old woman. But he asked me not to go and I went anyway. I was always leaving him. Always working. I left him alone too much. It's my fault."

"Now, don't jump to conclusions, ma'am. Did your husband suffer from depression?"

She nodded. "Terribly. I should have realised how bad it had got, but—"

"He has an old scar obviously made from a bullet in his left shoulder," the officer said. "Was that from some previous botched suicide attempt?"

"No. He got that fighting in Korea." He had survived Korea. He had not survived his marriage to her. Guilt rested like a boulder in her chest.

The police officer nodded at Emma. "Do you think I could ask her a couple of questions?"

Laura leaned back to shift Emma's head from her shoulder. "Honey," she said, "can you tell the policeman what happened? Can you tell me?"

Emma looked at them both in silence, her eyes glazed. And that's when Laura realised that her daughter had not spoken a single word since she'd got home.

From the bestselling author of
The Lost Daughter

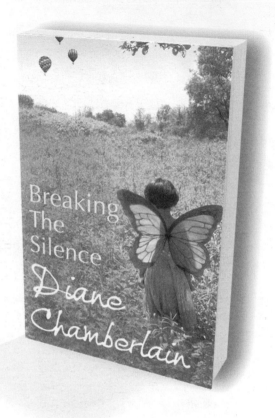

Laura's promise to her dying father was to visit an elderly woman she'd never heard of before. But the consequences led to her husband's suicide.

Tragically, their five-year-old daughter Emma witnessed it and now refuses to talk. Laura contacts one person who can help—a man who doesn't know he's Emma's real father. Guided by an old woman's fading memories, the two unravel a tale of love, despair and unspeakable evil that links them all.

What if your child was accused of mass murder?

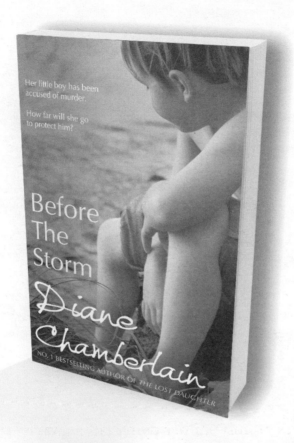

Born with Foetal Alcohol Spectrum Disorder, fifteen-year-old Andy Lockwood is now a hero after helping dozens of children escape a burning church.

Laurel lost Andy once through neglect and is determined to make amends. Yet when Andy is suspected of arson, Laurel must ask herself how well she really knows her son – and how far she'll go to protect him.

Would you live a lie to keep your child?

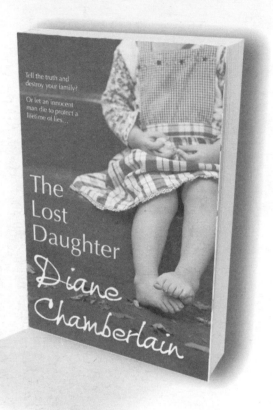

Twenty years after pregnant Genevieve Russell disappeared, her remains are discovered and Timothy Gleason is charged with murder. But there is no sign of the unborn child.

CeeCee Wilkes knows how Genevieve Russell died—and what happened to the missing infant. Now she must decide whether to tell the truth and destroy her family. Or let an innocent man die to protect a lifetime of lies.

www.mirabooks.co.uk

MIR

Her family's cottage was a place of innocence for twelve-year-old Julie Bauer – until her sister was murdered.

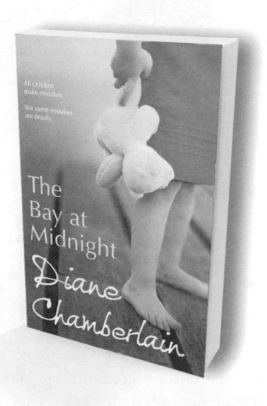

It's been many years since that August night. Now someone from her past is asking questions about what really happened. About the person who went to prison for Izzy's murder—and the person who didn't.

Now Julie must revisit her past and untangle the complex emotions that led to one unspeakable act of violence on the bay at midnight.

www.mirabooks.co.uk

"Two little girls are missing. Both ar seven years old and have been missin for at least sixteen hours."

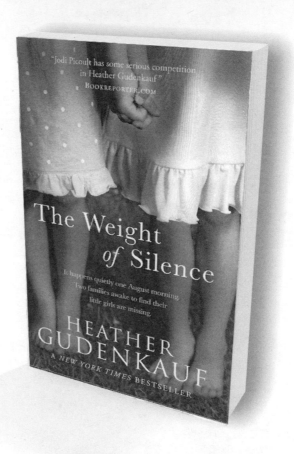

Sweet, gentle Callie suffers from selective mutism. Petra Gregory is Calli's best friend and her voice. And both have disappeared.

Now Calli and Petra's families are bound by the question of what has happened to their children. As support turns to suspicion, it seems the answers lie in the silence of unspoken secrets.

www.mirabooks.co.uk